THE
CHECK
DOWN

THE CHECK DOWN

BRANDY PELLETIER

Developmental editor: Melanie Yu at Made Me Blush Books

Copy/line editor: Beth Lawton at VB Edits

Cover design: Sarah Hansen, Okay Creations

To anyone searching for a little magic:
Griffin Lacey has entered the chat.

And to football pants, for enhancing tight ends everywhere.
Thank you for your service.

Also by Brandy Pelletier

Between the Lines
Keeping the Score

AUTHOR'S NOTE

The Check Down is intended for adult readers, ages 18 and up. It contains adult language and explicit sexual scenes. There are also some content warnings I'd like you to be aware of before you start reading. This book contains mentions of situational depression and cheating (but not by either MC), and a brief mention of a loved one's passing. If these are sensitive topics for you, please put your mental health first.

The Check Down Playlist

"Hoodies On, Hats Low" | FreeSol
"Will I Ever Make It Home" | Ingram Hill
"Break Up With Him" | Old Dominion
"Fresh Out the Slammer" | Taylor Swift
"Crush" | Tessa Violet
"Starving" | Hailey Steinfeld, Grey, Zedd
"Look After You" | The Fray
"Maybe It Was Memphis" | Pam Tillis
"End Game" | Taylor Swift feat. Ed Sheeran & Future
"Velvet Elvis" | Kacey Musgraves
"Walk in a Room" | Muscadine Bloodline
"Fallin' All in You" | Shawn Mendes
"Let Me Touch Your Fire" | A R I Z O N A
"Nervous" | Maren Morris
"Kinfolks" | Sam Hunt
"Sunday Kind of Love" | Reba McEntire
"Jackson" | Johnny Cash & June Carter Cash
"this is how you fall in love" | Jeremy Zucker & Chelsea Cutler
"Memphis; The Blues" | Zach Bryan & John Moreland
"The Alchemy" | Taylor Swift

Chapter One

Griffin

The drive from Holly Holler, Arkansas, to the outskirts of Memphis takes an hour and twelve minutes. But that's *if* the traffic cooperates.

I thought I'd left my hometown in plenty of time to make it to the stadium before the Blues' home game this afternoon, but the brake lights stretched as far as the eye can see in front of me on I-55 indicate that my guesstimation might have been off. I huff an impatient breath and drum my fingers on the steering wheel. It only takes about thirty seconds to give in to the urge to check the *Waze* app on my phone. Again.

As soon as I swipe it open, my phone vibrates.

My assistant's name flashes on the dashboard screen, and I release a sigh from deep in my chest.

"Seth," I say as I inch forward another five feet and then brake. "Please tell me you have some traffic miracle up your sleeve, my man."

His chuckle crackles over the line. "I feel like I'm in one of those action movies where I'm the expert hacker directing the superhero's moves so he can outrun the bad guys and save the damsel in distress."

"The only damsel that will need saving is my ass if I'm late for my first game with my new fucking team." I scrub a hand down my face. "Just get me there. Please."

"I'll do my best, considering I'm 220 miles away at the moment." For several seconds, he's silent, the only sound his keys clacking. "Okay," he finally says as I roll forward a few more feet. "We're gonna side street and back alley you to the stadium from here."

When I texted Seth fifteen minutes ago with an SOS, I sent him my location so he could see three steps ahead of me while I attempt to maneuver my SUV through the madness. The exit he wants me to take is as bumper-to-bumper as the highway, but maybe I'll catch a break somewhere up ahead.

I'm afraid to check the time. It's been a few miles since I was brave enough to let my eyes wander to those neon green numbers. Had a moment of panic then, so I refuse to look until I'm parked outside the players' entrance. Generally, the team arrives at least three hours before the pregame warm-ups, but since this is my first game with my new team, I was hoping to be the first to show up.

Another sweep of cars gets through the red light at the end of the exit ramp, but I'm not one of them. A twinge of tightness has me rolling my right shoulder a few times to limber up. I've been sitting still for too long.

I'm so goddamn ready to get back to what I do best: playing fucking football.

And hopefully winning some fucking games while we're at it.

With a deep breath in, I close my eyes. This sport, the sport I love—that I live, eat, sleep, and breathe—was almost ripped away from me a couple of months ago, when the team I'd spent my career with let me go after surgery to repair my torn labrum. I never want to experience the despair I suffered during those dark days after I got the news, when getting out of bed and eating became

Herculean tasks. I never want that heavy boulder of anguish in my gut again.

This chance with the Blues? It's my last shot to leave football on *my* terms. I can't let anything distract me or take my focus.

Seth clears his throat. "You should get there in time, Griff. It might cut short the face time you wanted to have with your teammates before warm-ups, but you'll make it."

He's right, but I don't tell him that. He doesn't need to know just how much I rely on him. But the truth is that I'd be an absolute shit show without him. Seth's been my personal assistant for the past four years. Never thought I'd love having a dude for a PA, but after my last female assistant ended up in my bed, my agent, Kevin, insisted that I only have male assistants until I retire.

Kevin can be a douche, but he was right. Vanessa was the third assistant I fucked.

Never said I was a choirboy.

I haven't earned the nickname Racy Lacey for nothing.

The light turns green, and I follow the line of cars turning left, only to hit the brakes for what feels like the hundredth time since I hit that exit ramp. This street is as backed up as the highway. I can't hold back a groan.

When Seth snickers through my speakers, I blurt, "Have you asked Daniel to move yet?" He's been nervous to ask his boyfriend of eight months to make the move from Nashville to Memphis with him.

"No. And thanks for the reminder."

I bite back a chuckle at his salty response. "Anytime."

It's been a whirlwind of a few weeks for Team Lacey. After I'd spent a month hanging with an old teammate, despondent after getting dumped by the Tors and defeated by the lack of offers after my injury, Kevin called with an offer from the Blues. During the season opener, their starting tight end took a brutal hit that tore up his knee and ended his season. The other tight ends on the Blues' roster are newbies, so the team wanted a veteran to round out the offense.

Enter Griffin Lacey.

Ten-year NFL veteran with two Super Bowls and seven Pro Bowls on my résumé.

My world has revolved around that brown pigskin since the day I first strapped on a helmet at the age of six. My brothers and I played peewee, and the three of us remained devoted to the sport through middle and high school. Tucker and I went on to have successful college years on the gridiron. Before my junior year at Oklahoma, my coach approached me about making the switch from quarterback to tight end, and since I'd do anything to keep playing, I agreed. Ended up thriving in that position and was drafted by the Tennessee Tors in the third round.

It's been a week since Kevin's call with the Blues' offer, and I'm still in disbelief. I drove up from Georgia over the weekend and met with the team on Monday morning. That afternoon, I signed a one-year contract with the Memphis Blues. Started practicing with the team Wednesday and have been doing it every day since. Practice and team meetings and film-watching and play-memorizing. Learning schemes. Trying to find moments to bond with my new teammates and trusting Seth to handle the rest of my business. Answering my mom's teary phone calls about playing for my hometown team.

Back in Holly Holler, there's a framed photo on my parents' mantel of the three of us Lacey boys at the team's very first home game. In it, Shaw and I are almost the same height—we're only seventeen months apart, so we've been neck and neck on the growth charts all our lives. He's got one arm slung around my shoulder and the other straining to hold up a chunky baby Tucker. I swear, that kid's been solid muscle since birth. We're all sporting Memphis Blues T-shirts on our rounded kid bellies and huge grins on our faces. Shaw's shows off a gap where he'd pulled a top tooth the night before. He brought those two crumpled dollar bills from the tooth fairy that day and spent them on ice cream at halftime.

A car horn blares somewhere ahead and pulls me from memory lane. As I make the turn Seth has instructed, there's a sickening crunch, and a sudden jolt propels me forward. My car stops inches from the back bumper of the truck idling in the traffic ahead.

"Fuck." I glare at the indistinguishable offender in the rearview.

"That did not sound good."

"Seth," I grunt. "I gotta call you back. Some asshole just rear-ended me."

I don't wait for his response before disconnecting the call and stepping out. The heat rising from the concrete matches the heat rising in my chest as I straighten. I'm about to lay into this dickwad and use the most imaginative curses in my repertoire when a girly sandal slips out of the red sedan. A girly sandal on the end of a shapely leg. I follow that leg up until I find the hem of a ruffly dress. When my brain registers the tiny flowers on the material, my gaze shoots to her face, where big brown Bambi eyes shine with terror.

I wasn't rear-ended by some pretentious blowhard in a shiny red BMW. No, it was a cute-as-fuck brunette in a sundress. All those curses waiting on deck retract like measuring tape.

"Oh God, oh God, oh God." As she scurries to the front of the car to check out the damage, I check *her* out.

She's on the tall side, but she's still several inches shorter than my six-five. Her thick, dark brown hair is slicked back into a neat ponytail. Shit, I can't let my thoughts delve where they'd like to about *that*. Her flawless ivory skin lacks the golden tan so many Southern girls sport, like she spends most of her time indoors. A quick check of her left hand reveals an empty ring finger. As she bends over to check her bumper, the hem of her dress inches up and exposes more of her perfect legs. And I'm a red-blooded American male who hasn't been laid in several months, so when she straightens, there's no way I can't check out her rack.

Her breasts are full and round and...heaving. Heaving because she looks like she's seconds away from a panic attack.

"Oh, God, sir, I'm so very sorry." She turns to me, knees shaking. I can't even catalog the details of her face because all my attention is drawn to her full bottom lip as it wobbles.

Shit. Hysterical females and I don't mix.

I raise my hands in an attempt to calm her, but it's futile.

She lets out a squeak and takes a single step closer. "Look at you. You must be heading somewhere important, dressed like that." She waves at my light-blue dress shirt and bespoke navy pants. Pants that cling to my skin the longer we stand out in this oppressive heat.

She's pacing when her last statement registers. She doesn't know who I am. I'm not an egomaniac. I don't expect every human I meet to recognize me, but it's rare when one doesn't. Rare and refreshing.

An angry honk blares from several cars behind us, and the brunette jerks to a stop. Her wide gaze slowly meets mine, and when her Bambi eyes fill with tears again and that bottom lip really starts to tremble, I'm hit with an overpowering need to pull her into my arms.

What the actual fuck? I choke that sensation down. I should be stressed. Frustrated. Pretty sure Trixie and Mom are the only females I've ever had the urge to comfort like that.

I clench my fists before sliding them into my pockets and finally finding my voice. "Are you hurt?"

"Me?" A wrinkle forms between her dark brows, and she looks over one shoulder, then the other, like she expects to find another soul with us on this sidewalk. With a sniffle, she turns back to face me. "No, I'm fine. Oh God, are *you* hurt?" More tears line her eyes as she scans me from head to toe.

Her perusal gives me another chance to study her. Thick dark lashes frame her soulful brown eyes. A straight nose with a slight upturn at its tip. Full rosy-pink lips. Her oval-shaped face is mostly free of makeup. She's a natural beauty.

Exactly the kind of distraction I don't need.

A quick check of my watch has my stomach sinking. "Uh, listen. I know it's against standard fender-bender protocol, but I really have to head out."

"W-wait. No. The police have to file a report." Brunette beauty wrings her hands and resumes pacing. "Oh God, I need to sit down."

She stops and smooths the back of her dress, eyes on the ground beneath her, like she's going to plop herself down on the scorching concrete. Before she lowers herself all the way, I grasp her elbow and haul her up. Pull her closer to me.

Catch a whiff of something floral and sweet.

"You're shaking. Are you sure you aren't hurt?" I try not to fixate on the sensation of her skin in my rough palm. I lead her to my SUV, open the back door, and move the suit jacket draped across the seat.

"Here. Sit." She obeys my soft command and sits sideways on the leather bench.

"You-you're being so nice to me. I hit your car, and you're being so kind. I feel terrible. I'm so, so sorry. And you're going to be late for whatever has you dressed up like this, and oh, God, I'm so sorry." Her chest is heaving again as the words tumble out of her.

My own chest tightens in concern. "Hey, take a breath."

She looks up at me, and I can't fight the urge any longer. Taking her hands in mine, I use my thumbs to rub soothing circles on the inside of her wrists.

I'll worry about where the fuck this urge to comfort her came from later. Right now, I focus on calming her, evening out her breathing.

Brows furrowed, she studies the way our hands are joined. "What's your name?"

"Griffin."

"Griffin," she repeats, and goddamn, do I like the way it flows from her lips like honey.

"And you are…"

She locks eyes with me and swallows thickly. "Brynn."

Brynn.

"It means hill."

Confused, I tilt my head and frown.

"My name," she explains. "Welsh origin. It's derived from the Welsh word for *hill*." She pulls her hands from mine and twists the ruffles on her dress absentmindedly. "My parents are nature enthusiasts, of a sort. Not that you need to know that." One side of her mouth lifts, along with one shoulder.

Damn, I'd pay top dollar to turn that half smile into a full one.

I clear my throat. As much as I'd love to spend more time with the beautiful distraction in front of me, duty calls.

I'm pulling my phone from my pocket, ready to hand it over to get her number when she face-palms and mumbles, "The car. Jack is going to be livid about his damn car."

Hold up. There's a *Jack*?

She's once again twisting the ruffles of her dress. "Jack. My boyfriend. It's his car." She rolls her eyes. "He loves that damn car. I'm never going to hear the end of this."

My chest tightens at this new information. Well, shit. There's a Jack.

Lucky bastard.

That's it, then. She's taken.

It's just as well. Must be the universe's way of keeping me focused on what's most important right now: getting back on the turf.

One more glance at my watch spurs me into action. I need to get her number, but I'll send it on to Seth so he can handle all the insurance and repair shit. Once I do that, I'll delete her contact information from my phone and be done with Brynn the brunette beauty.

"Brynn."

She bites the inside of her cheek and looks up at me.

"I really do have somewhere to be. It looks like your car took the brunt of the damage."

She rolls her lips and blinks like she's fighting more tears.

"Hey," I say, unable to resist trying to soothe her. "That's what insurance is for." Phone held out, I nod at it. "Put your contact in here, and my assistant will handle all the details."

She takes in a deep breath and scrutinizes me, her brow pinched, like she wants to argue with me. But after a deep sigh that makes her shoulders slump, she takes the device and starts typing.

While she frowns down at it, I step back from my vehicle and survey the street around us. Traffic has eased up a bit, but we're still getting angry honks and raised middle fingers from drivers who are forced to swerve around us.

When she hands my phone to me, I read her full name: Brynn Nelson.

I swipe open my camera app and snap a few pictures of the damage to both vehicles. There's a scratch and a small dent on the bumper of my new Cayenne. Correction: Seth's new Cayenne. I promised it would be his when he made the move to Memphis. Both of my vehicles are at the farm.

Jack's car isn't so lucky. The plastic cover of one headlight is splintered, and the hood is slightly crunched in. Still, it's drivable.

I return to Brynn, who is still sitting in my back seat. She's hunched over, rubbing her sleeveless arms like she's warding off a chill, even as a heat haze rises from the ground around us.

"I'll forward these pictures to you. For your insurance."

She sits up and eyes the hand I've extended to help her out of the car. "W-wait, we can't leave until the police make a report. Insurance might deny coverage if we do."

Without a word, I wriggle my fingers.

Her eyes dart from my hand to my eyes and back again. After a beat, she huffs a breath and accepts my silent offer.

The moment her hand is in mine, I swear an electric jolt races through me. It's so unexpected and potent, my knees almost buckle.

But she's Jack's, whoever the hell he is. So I shake off the sensation. As I walk her to her car, I resist the urge to guide her with a hand to the small of her back. "If insurance has an issue with it," I tell her, "I'll take care of it."

She jerks to a stop, her hand slipping from mine, and she rounds on me. "You'll take care of it? What does that mean?" That little wrinkle forms between her brows again as she stares me down. It's so fucking adorable, I twist my lips to quell a smile.

"It means I'll handle it. Pay for the damages or whatever." I wave a hand.

She tracks the gesture, her frown deepening. "But it wasn't your fault. *I* did this. I'm to blame. How can you be so flippant about it? Why would you offer to pay for something you didn't do?"

I lift a shoulder and let it fall lazily. "Because I can."

Eyes narrowed, she crosses her arms, and it takes every ounce of self-control I possess to keep myself from admiring the way this position pushes her tits up.

"Because you can? What kind of answer is that? I can't have a random stranger, whose car I *hit*, by the way, paying to fix Jack's car."

"Sure you can." I mimic her stance, crossing my arms. The movement causes my shirt to pull tight over my shoulders, and the stretch of cotton across my sweaty back reminds me it's time to wrap up this encounter. As she scans the street around us, like the hustle and bustle of Memphis can provide her with answers, I lose the battle I've been waging for the past few moments.

I take a peek. And I am not disappointed.

They're high and perfect, and she's showing the barest hint of cleavage. The view is so tantalizing, my mouth fucking waters.

See, definitely *not* a choirboy.

When I wrest my gaze back to hers, my face flames. She's caught me. Her eyes are wide and locked on me, and a pink hue flushes her ivory skin. Still, I own that shit and give her a sheepish smile in return.

The same smile that has gotten me out of countless scrapes with Donna Lacey.

What the fuck, right? I'll never see this woman again.

Loosening her arms, she straightens and juts her chin, her brown ponytail swinging with the movement. "Who *are* you exactly?"

A niggle of dread seeps through me at the question. She might not recognize my face, but will she know my name? So far, I've reveled in her ignorance of my celebrity. But I'm shocked that a passerby hasn't screeched to a halt in the middle of the street and really fucked up traffic to demand a selfie or an autograph. Though I suppose Memphis is pretty different from Nashville. Maybe while I'm here, I won't be subjected to the scrutiny and pressure and hero-worship I've suffered my whole career.

God, the thought almost knocks the breath right out of me.

This last chance I've been given means my sole focus must be football. Not endorsements or appearances or parties. Or women.

With that in mind, I quash the sliver of disappointment that's nicked me at the idea that I'll never see her again. Hand extended for a shake, I answer her question. "Griffin Lacey. It's nice to meet you, Brynn Nelson."

She takes my hand before my words register. I watch her beautiful face as she works out my identity. Her eyes widen when it hits her, and I give her a wide grin before striding back to my SUV.

As I pull back into the crowded Memphis traffic, I allow myself one final glance in the rearview.

Brynn stands motionless on the blistering concrete, mouth agape and one hand over her heart like she's willing it to slow.

I know the feeling well. My heart was galloping like a thoroughbred the entire time I was in her proximity.

But she's Jack's. And I have a comeback to make.

CHAPTER TWO

GRIFFIN

"Tough game, Lacey."

I lift my heavy head and regard the young player who gives me a sympathetic smile. I've got a good ten years on Devon Greenway, but I sure as hell didn't provide him with a stellar example of our shared position out there on that field today.

My first game with my new team was absolute shit. I dropped three passes and fumbled on third and goal in the fourth quarter. The media is going to have a field day. I can see the headline now: *Rusty Lacey fumbles in Blues debut.*

I muster a brisk nod for Devon. That's all I've got left in me. But he takes the bench next to me and carries on as if we didn't lose an important conference game minutes ago.

"What'd you think of their coverage adjustments after the half?" He swivels wide, curious eyes my way as he hunches over to unlace his cleats. He's smart to ask; we'll face this opponent again later in the season. Though I've been a piss-poor mentor for the kid today, he's eager to learn all he can, and he soaks up every tidbit I share like a sponge. His hunger for game knowledge is apparent in everything I've witnessed of him this past week.

I like him immensely. Have since the moment I met him, and I hope I can teach him a thing or two.

Despite his chill demeanor, the mood in the Blues locker room is somber. Coach Mundy gave us the old "keep your chins up, boys" speech a few minutes ago, and now we're dragging our feet, going through the motions of getting showered and dressed.

The media awaits.

Instead of offering Devon insight into our opponent's defensive strategies, I give him a compliment. "That catch you made in the third on second down was fire." I'm not blowing smoke. The kid has skills.

He beams, his smile wide. "I played wide receiver all through high school and college. I can be light on my feet when I need to be."

I chuckle. Tight ends are not known for being light-footed.

"Wouldn't have had to go all ballerina tippy-toes if I had your height, though." He stands and tugs his jersey over his head, then gets to work on the rest of his gear.

"Ballerina tippy-toes, huh? Think my little sister had that doll when she was younger."

Devon and I twist at the voice. Quarterback Beau Dempsey grins at us as he dodges guys in every state of undress on his way to his locker.

"Sister? She single?" Devon jokes.

Beau gives him a good-natured eye roll. "She'd eat your lunch, Greenway."

Devon wraps a towel around his naked lower half. He turns on the charm as he says, "I'd love to be on her menu."

Beau snaps a rolled towel at him on his way to the showers, but he dodges it and cackles, the sound rising above the locker room din.

Confusion swirls in my gut. These guys are surprisingly upbeat after a tough loss.

I open my mouth, ready to share that thought with Beau, but he speaks first.

"Don't beat yourself up too much about today," he says as he rubs a tanned hand through his sweat-soaked hair, the dampness making it appear darker than its usual sandy-brown shade. "You've been in the league long enough to know that bad days are inevitable. It's how you handle the bad days that matters."

I've only spent a handful of hours around Beau Dempsey this week, but I could tell immediately that he embodies the *C* patched on his jersey. The four gold stars beneath the white letter are further evidence of his grit and dedication. The guy's only four years into his career, and he's been captain since the beginning.

He jerks his jersey up over his head and joins me on the bench. "We'll find our rhythm, old man," he jokes. He busies himself with removing his pads and the athletic tape on various body parts, but his tone turns serious as he asks, "How's the shoulder?"

"Feels good. My mistakes today were mental; the shoulder had nothing to do with it," I assure him.

With a nod, he stands and wraps a towel around his waist. "I'm glad you're here, Lacey. Let's hang out sometime. Outside of all this." He lifts his chin, gesturing to the now almost-empty locker room. "And don't let that room," he tilts his head to the exit, "get to you today, either. Give 'em that Racy Lacey charm, and they'll forget all about the drops."

There's no way those vultures won't mention the drops. But I give Mr. All-American QB a confident nod that belies the heaviness in my limbs.

After my turn in the media room, which is somehow as brutal and not as bad as I expected, I step into the hall, ready to get out of here, and discover my new head coach leaning against the wall, hands in the pockets of his khaki pants.

Bobby Mundy has been the Blues' head coach for the past ten seasons. He's well-respected in the league, and from what I've heard over the years—as well as what I've witnessed this past week—he runs a fair and positive ship. Reminds me a lot of the former teammate I stayed with in Georgia. He builds up the boys on his team at the local high school rather than pointing out every damn mistake.

Night and day from my previous head coach.

Coach Mundy extends his hand as I approach. He's gotta be close to my parents' age, but the man doesn't look a day over fifty.

"Just met your family." He gives me a warm smile that stretches his silvery-blond mustache wide. "Good folks. Mighty proud of you."

There's a pinch in my chest at the thought of my family. He's right. They're my biggest supporters. "Yes, sir."

"Tried to recruit your brother. The fighter. That kid's built."

I shake my head, but there's no stopping the smile that spreads across my face at the mention of Tucker. "He's pretty busy these days. Just opened up his own gym, and he's training a few kids who want to follow in his footsteps."

"Yeah, he mentioned that." He straightens and rubs the back of his neck. "Listen. Lacey." He huffs a breath. "You're a hell of a talent, and all the talk about you being too old and washed up is hogwash."

I roll my lips to hide the smile that threatens to escape. *Hogwash* is one of Fred Lacey's favorite words. Fixating on this similarity with my dad is damn helpful with keeping me from dwelling on the rest of his words for too long.

Old and washed up.

If Coach notices, he doesn't let on. "I know days like today won't become a habit for you. Shake it off, and we'll see you bright and early tomorrow."

Shoulders heavy, despite all the pep talks, I dip my chin. "Yes, sir."

He narrows his eyes, considers me for a beat, then slaps my bicep and starts back toward the coaches' offices.

I make it five steps in the opposite direction before he calls my name. "We do things kinda different round here," Coach Mundy says, hands on hips, his voice echoing in the stark hallway. "They tell you about the event on Tuesday night?"

"My assistant mentioned something about it."

"Season-ticket holders have been integral to keeping our team in this city. Memphis is a small market, and there's been talk here and there for a long time about relocating to a more populated city."

I nod. The rumors pop up every few years, especially after sub-five-hundred seasons.

"The organization holds this event every year. It gives some of those diehard fans a chance to rub elbows with the team. Gives us the opportunity to thank them for their dedication." He heaves a breath. "It's asking a lot of you guys to give up one of your off nights, but it's tradition."

"I'll be there, sir."

His whiskers twitch as he smiles. "Good man. I'll let you get to your folks, then."

I pass a few team personnel and players on my way to the family zone, and before I even round the corner, I hear them.

Stopping in the corridor, I give myself a moment to breathe before I approach them. Strains of my mom and dad's amiable bickering fill the air of the quiet hallway, with Aunt Dottie's opinions sprinkled in. I swallow the lump in my throat and blink back the rogue tears that threaten to spill.

My family is *here*, and they got to see our last name on a Blues uniform today.

What a fucking privilege.

That thought strengthens my resolve to give all I've got to this season. It might be my last year to play, and if that's the case, then I want to go out on top.

Coach is right. I'm leagues better than today's performance.

I don't want to let him down, or the team. But what really paralyzes me, makes my gut feel like granite, is the thought of letting down the people waiting around the corner.

After another deep breath, I steel myself, push my shoulders back, and round the cinder block wall.

It takes them a second to notice me, but when they do, Mom's voice shrills above the rest.

"*There's* my baby boy."

"Mom, he's thirty-four years old," Shaw grunts.

"Oh, pooh," she waves him off. "He's still my baby. You're all still my babies."

I step up close and wrap her in my arms. "Hey, Mom."

After a tight squeeze, she pulls back, eyes shining with tears, and palms my scruff. "So proud of you, Griff." The rest of my people circle up and form a cocoon around me, like they can protect me from the shit show of the game they witnessed.

Always a man of few words, Dad gives my head an affectionate rub. "Tough game, son," he murmurs. Then he steps back to let Tucker close in.

He's my little brother in age and height only. Though he stands a couple of inches shorter than me, he almost lifts my feet off the concrete when he hugs me, the ferocity of it forcing an *oof* from my lungs.

"Damn, seeing you in those blues today made me fucking emotional, bro."

"He wept like a damn baby." Shaw's deep voice cuts in.

Tucker and I turn in unison to face our older brother. With a smirk, he shoos Tucker out of my arms, then leans in to give me a perfunctory bro hug—the pull-in with one hand and a smack on my shoulder blade is a Shaw specialty.

He's the least emotional of us Lacey boys. Since we were kids, I've only witnessed him lose his shit once.

Hope I never see it again. It was brutal.

No, these days, Shaw operates at a low simmer that makes most folks steer clear.

"You catch a case of the dropsy down in Georgia?" He regards me with narrowed eyes. They're bluer than the gunmetal hue Tucker and I share with Mom. He's got Dad's eyes, a piercing, clear blue the color of the Caribbean.

"Shaw, don't be a dick." Trixie shoves him with one arm while wrapping the other around my back. "You'll get 'em next week, Griff."

I hug her back and tweak one of her ginger pigtails as her mom sweeps in for a hug of her own.

"Uncle Roo would've been so dang proud today," Aunt Dottie whispers in my ear, her voice quivering with emotion. Her husband, Trixie's father, passed away ten years ago, but the thought of him never fails to stir emotion.

"Thanks, Dot," I choke out past an unexpected knot in my throat. Fuck, I miss that red-headed, larger-than-life force of nature. My Uncle Rooster was one of my favorite people on the planet.

I catch Trixie's watery eyes over my aunt's shoulder but huff a laugh when they roll to the ceiling the second a heavy arm slings across my shoulders.

"Griff, gotta say, having our own suite softened the blow of the game's outcome."

I smack Camden Little's abdomen with the back of my hand. He and Tucker have been joined at the hip since kindergarten. The guy might as well be a Lacey, too.

"Yeah, it was good?" I look at Mom for confirmation. My one nonnegotiable request when the Blues made their offer was that my family have a reserved suite for every home game.

"It was perfect." She nods her affirmation, her bleach blond bob bouncing.

We stand in silence for a moment. Their expectant, hopeful gazes settle on me and weigh down my shoulders like sacks of feed.

"Well, best be gettin' back." Dad rubs the Blues logo covering his belly with one hand and jingles his keys in the other.

I swallow hard. "Yeah. Thanks for coming, guys."

"We wouldn't have missed it, Griff." Aunt Dottie clasps Trixie's hand, and they both beam at me.

"Fuck, why am I about to cry again?" Tucker tilts his head back and massages his eyes. "We'll see him at home in a couple hours."

Laughs echo off the concrete wall.

"Stop being a goddamn wuss." Shaw's tone is gruff, but he grips the back of Tuck's neck in a fond hold.

"Shaw Morgan, watch your mouth," our mother scolds. Like most southern mamas, she hates when we curse. We Lacey boys swallowed enough soap in our teen years to clean a pigsty.

After my aunt reminds us all to drive safely, we say our final goodbyes, and my family starts up the ramp toward the parking lot.

"You wanna ride with us, Silly Rabbit?" Camden asks Trixie, bumping her shoulder with his. My five-three cousin rears back and gives him a swift punch in the bicep that makes him howl with laughter. He's been goading her with that nickname since they were kids.

The rest of the group starts in on the two of them or on each other, all the while moving toward the exit.

I watch until they disappear from view, my hand gripping the strap of my leather bag.

Knuckleheads. The Lacey clan is loud and boisterous, but I wouldn't trade them for the fucking world.

———◦○◦———

"Man, I hate wearing a suit."

I bring the flute of champagne I swiped off a passing tray to my lips and eye the three-hundred-pound lineman sulking against the bar next to me. D'Angelo Sweeney tugs at his collar, then swipes his hand across his brow.

With a swat to my arm, Beau leans in. "Big D here dresses in business casual on game days."

I snicker at the nickname. "Yeah, I saw that T-shirt and gym shorts combo on Sunday."

"It's impossible for some of us to compete with your swagger, Lacey." D'Angelo turns and grins at our QB. "Besides, you know I can't keep all *this* contained, Cap." He smooths a hand down his thick frame like he's outlining the sensual curves of a woman's body. "Gotta keep myself comfy on game day. Helps me keep your ass off the turf."

"This *Cap* nickname strictly because of your captain status?" I ask Beau.

With a roll of his eyes, he opens his mouth to answer, but wide receiver Tyrell Jefferson, who's standing to my right, pipes up. "Look at this mug." He squeezes Beau's cheeks, which have gone pink, then gives one a pat. "This is freaking Captain America right here."

The offensive guys launch into a thorough ribbing of Beau's boyish good looks, but it's layered with a deep respect and appreciation for their leader.

"Now we got ourselves another pretty boy to compete for the ladies," D'Angelo says with a nod in my direction.

I smirk and finish off my champagne. Pointing at the group with the empty glass, I say, "They're all yours, gentlemen."

The guys' answering whistles and catcalls draw several looks our way.

"Aw, hell. You telling me I'll never know what it's like to have Racy Lacey as my wingman?" Devon lowers his head and pouts like a kid who's been told Santa isn't real.

"I'll be your wingman, Greenway. Name the time and place."

I might be determined to keep distractions to a minimum, but that doesn't mean I'm not down for a good time. In fact, good times of the one-night variety, if I can find willing participants who'll accept a zero-strings offer, are exactly what I'm looking for.

"You taken, Lacey? Back together with that smoke show you were with a while back?" Tyrell asks, referring to my most recent ex, Kate.

I roll my shoulders, trying to knock loose my immediate discomfort. We've been split up for over a year now, but she's the last woman I was seen with. There's no way in hell I'd consider rekindling any kind of relationship with her, given how we ended, but I keep that to myself. Instead, I keep my response simple. "Nope. Not taken. Not looking, either. Gotta focus on the game. I'll worry about the rest when I'm ready to walk away for good."

Like my mind has been taken over by an external force, an image of a floral sundress hits me. Fuck. I give my head a quick shake to dislodge it.

"Respect." As Tyrell tips his beer in my direction, he's pulled away for a photo op with a group of fans.

We've been hit up for pictures and autographs pretty regularly since arriving an hour ago, but there's been a welcome lull for the last few minutes. This group is the first since I snagged that glass of champagne.

I lean closer to Beau. "There's no way this is all the season-ticket holders, right?" This hotel ballroom is crowded, but it's nowhere near the number I was expecting.

"No way," he says with a *pssh*. "Our season tickets number is somewhere in the twenty-thousand range. This event is for the top-tier. The people who donate a significant amount to the team's community outreach programs and charities."

"So these are the richest of the rich folks?"

He closes his green eyes and barks out a laugh. "Pretty much."

Beau pulls out his phone, his face lighting up. "Hey, my fiancée is planning a barbeque at our new place in a couple weeks. She wants to invite the entire O-squad and a few others. You in?"

Maybe it's pathetic how good it feels to receive a simple invite like that. But to be so easily accepted after coming in at the last minute like I did, then having a shit first game, is, frankly, a little shocking. "Hell yeah, man, I'm always down for barbeque. Where's your new place?"

"Out on Mud Island. Moved in right before the season started. You got a place in town yet?"

With a hand stuck in my trousers pocket, I dip my chin. "Close on it next Tuesday."

"Cool. Where?"

I chuckle. "It's actually a whole damn building. On South Main."

Beau's brows raise, and he lets out a puff of air.

"Yeah, three-story building. First floor houses a tattoo shop. My brother's buddy rents the space from this old oil-and-gas tycoon, but Mr. Moneybags wants to sell off some of his real estate. Tuck's friend was going to have to move his shop unless the new owner agreed to keep him as a tenant. I wanted a place in the city, so much to Donna's dismay, Tuck suggested I check it out."

"Wow. Donna's your mom?"

"Yep. She's been convinced I'd stay out at the family farm since I signed the contract. But I'm not making a two-hour round trip to work every day."

"Don't blame you," Beau says, handing his empty glass to a passing server. "You won't mind living in the city like that?"

I follow suit and hand off my glass, taking a moment to consider my answer before responding. "It's very different from where I've been living for the past several months, but in Nashville, I had a condo downtown, and I liked it fine. Plus, the setup at this place is sweet. It's two stories, with a gated lot out back for parking. It's as private as you can get in the middle of a city."

"Sounds sweet," Beau confirms. "What are you thinking about—"

Tyrell hustles over, cutting off Beau's words. He's been off schmoozing, but now his dark eyes glow like they're full of secrets.

"Guys," he starts, his tone hushed but excited. "Cockburn is here."

I gather from the guys' eye rolls and disgusted faces that the person he's referring to is not a favorite. "Excuse me, did you say this person's name is *Cock*burn?"

Chuckling, D'Angelo explains, "Naw, we just call him that. His real name is Cogburn."

"And I take it we're not a fan of this Cogburn?"

"Ugh, no." Devon's top lip curls, his usual happy-go-lucky demeanor gone. "He's front office, and a real douche. Works under Phillips."

Shane Phillips is the GM for the Blues, and he's a big reason I'm here. I've only met him a handful of times, but he, like Coach Mundy, has a solid rep. So the guys' dislike of this Cogburn guy is telling.

Beau, ever the diplomat, chimes in. "He's kind of a blowhard. He's worked for Shane for the past few years. Fortunately, we don't deal with him much, but he's shown his butt enough to earn that nickname."

"He's a dick," Tyrell states, his voice a little too loud. "But," he says, quieter now, "he's a dick who showed up tonight with a looker on his arm. Please tell me how Cockburn can pull a woman like *that*."

He swings his arm wide, and when I follow his line of vision across the ballroom, my heart lurches in my chest.

Fuck.

Because the woman on the weaselly-looking frat boy's arm is brunette beauty Brynn, wearing the hell out of a dark-green dress.

CHAPTER THREE

BRYNN

The tap of Jack's wingtips on the ceramic tile pulls my attention from the window. I've been staring outside, lost in my thoughts, for close to thirty minutes. He was adamant that we leave at seven, so I was sure to be ready early, lest he have another thing to gripe at me about.

Seems I can't do anything right these days.

Like I knew he would, Jack complains about his car every chance he gets. I haven't told him who the victim of my distracted driving was. It'll come up soon, I'm sure. Though I don't know whether it will help or hurt my case when he discovers that I rammed into *that* particular rear end.

Nope. Not letting my mind wander *there*.

Griffin Lacey.

I'd never admit this out loud, but for the past fifty-six hours, he's popped into my mind far too many times, and at the most random moments.

Of course, I felt like an utter moron when he told me his name. I should have recognized him. Jack's been talking about him non-stop for weeks. But in my defense, I'm not even one iota interested in football (American or European), so my brain had no visual to connect to.

And what a visual I've been missing out on.

I blink to clear the memory of him from my mind, and like every other time I've thought of his tall, powerful frame and his charming smile, my insides clench. That sensation, like always, is quickly followed by a wave of nausea.

No woman with a live-in boyfriend should be having such thoughts about another man. One she crashed said boyfriend's car into, at that.

Jack pauses in the middle of the kitchen to check his smart-watch. A text. I know because his lips lift in the smallest of smiles. Then he whips out his phone to text the person back.

He's shared that same smile with his phone or watch many times over the past month. A couple of times, I've dared to ask him who he's texting. His reply? *It's just work stuff.*

"You're wearing green?" He gives me a once-over, scrutinizing the hunter-green cocktail dress with lace bodice and cap sleeves I bought especially for tonight.

"What's wrong with green?"

Jaw going rigid, he looks down at his navy tie. When his icy stare returns to my face, he huffs an impatient breath. "The team is called the Blues, for Christ's sake. How is it going to look if my date shows up wearing the color of one of our biggest division rivals? The rivals who beat our asses two days ago, no less."

His *date*. Not his girlfriend. I add it to the mental list of griev-ances I've been keeping lately. The list that makes me feel like a crappy partner.

"I'm sorry." And I am. But I can't hold back the snark that laces my next statement. "I didn't know I'd be expected to wear blue to *all* the things."

"Brynn…" He pinches the bridge of his nose and shakes his head. "I don't want to fight with you tonight. Let's just go."

I don't have the energy to fight either. And isn't that telling? Couples who are *in it* together fight, right? Then the passionate making up follows.

Both the fighting and the passion are missing from this situation Jack and I have settled into. It's relatively comfortable most of the time, but it's like we've painted ourselves into a corner, and the only way out is to make an absolute mess.

Shoulders back, I snag the matching clutch that cost way too much from the island and stand. "You look nice," I tell him as I stride his way in my velvet flats.

I reach Jack's side, ready for him to lead the way, but he's engrossed in his phone.

Distracted. Like he's been for the past few weeks.

After a moment, he looks up, eyes wide like he's surprised to see me here. "Oh, uh, thanks. Let's head out. Downtown traffic is going to be a bitch."

Somewhere inside me, another petal wilts and falls away.

I pause on the front porch of the bungalow Jack and I share, weighed down by the sultry September air, as he locks the front door. I wiggle my toes in the stuffy velvet shoes and grimace. I'm regretting them already, but I don't own any open-toe flat shoes fancy enough to wear with this dress, so here we are.

Heaven forbid I wear the strappy heels that would make me taller than my *date*.

"We'll have to take yours." Jack holds out his hand without looking at me, his tone flat.

He leaves it at that, but as I fish my key ring out of the clutch, the words he isn't saying ring loud and clear: *Because you wrecked mine.*

Once we're inside my Forester, he adjusts the driver's seat position with an annoyed huff. He's only an inch taller than me, so the need for dramatic seat adjusting is unnecessary. I keep *that* thought to myself.

As he fiddles with the buttons to get the settings right, I study the man I've shared a bed with for the past four years. He's classically handsome, with light brown hair styled to perfection and clean-shaven cheeks that frame a straight, symmetrical nose. Nice lips. Crystalline eyes that match the sky reflected on a frosty winter lake.

Eyes a similar color, but so very different from the blue ones I stared into a couple of days ago.

Those eyes were warm and captivating, a soft bluish gray that twinkled with mischief and mirth. That sharpened with concern when their owner comforted me. That made me feel *seen* for the first time in a long time.

I graze my fingertips over the spot where Griffin soothed my wrist, like I can conjure the sensation by recreating the movement. Recreate the way his strong hands held me so gently, but with a firmness that made it clear he wouldn't let go until I was steady.

If I close my eyes tight enough, I swear I catch a whiff of his fresh air and cedar scent.

No. I force my eyes open. I shouldn't be having such thoughts about a man who isn't Jack.

With a pinch to my wrist to clear my mind—a distraction from the knowledge that *he* will most likely be there tonight—I turn to focus on the man beside me.

"Is Shane bringing a date tonight?" I ask, extending an olive branch by segueing into Jack's favorite topic: his job. His boss, the general manager of the Memphis Blues football organization, is a notorious love-'em-and-leave-'em type. Better known as a *rake* in my line of work.

He blows a raspberry, but a corner of his mouth lifts as he answers. "Who knows with him? I thought he was still seeing that blues singer, but he mentioned a Tiffany on Sunday, and I'm pretty certain that other chick's name is Londa or Linda or something like that." Jack speaks of Shane's exploits with pride, the way a besotted mother might brag about a wayward son with a resigned *boys-will-be-boys* tone.

"I really liked the one before the singer. The dental hygienist. Cathy, I believe."

I fiddle with the lace skirt of my dress as Jack sets his phone to play a sports podcast through the speakers. We listen to strangers ranting or waxing poetic about sports every time we're in a car together. I used to complain about it, beg him to allow me a turn to choose how to fill the silence on drives, but after his one-thousandth explanation about how it's important to his job, I gave up trying to compromise.

Jack snorts, the sound derisive. "Cathy was more like three women before the singer, bun."

I cut my eyes to him, heat simmering inside me at the dig in his statement, even though he softened the blow with his pet name for me.

His silent message is that I'd know that if I attended more of his work functions. He's frustrated that I'm not a football fanatic who joins him in the owners' suite for every home game.

I don't hate sports. But in my home growing up, they were not a focal point. Apart from being a stressed-out member of the high school swim team for two years, I didn't participate in any in my youth. Whereas Jack's lived and breathed athletics his whole life.

Where Jack has aspired to be a GM since puberty and spent many, many mornings and evenings on well-maintained sports fields, my childhood Saturdays were spent on overgrown hiking trails or warm, sandy beaches.

We're silent for the rest of the ride downtown. At the valet stand, we have to practically swim through the muggy evening air before we're ushered into the cool hotel lobby.

Jack takes my hand and plants a kiss on the back of it before twining his fingers between mine, shocking me so acutely I jolt. I blink rapidly, surveying him, as I attempt to interpret his rare PDA.

Sex. He only touches me like this when he's anticipating intimacy.

And I can count on one hand the number of times we've been intimate in the last few months.

We're both young professionals dedicated to advancing in our careers. The excuses are typical: too tired, too depleted, too stressed, too busy.

Too unsatisfying.

There's that, too. At least for me anyway. He gets off every time.

Before we enter the ballroom, he leans in, his warm breath feathering over my cheek. "Try to make some friends tonight, dear." After a quick squeeze, he releases my hand, freeing him up to greet the important individuals that surround us as soon as we step over the threshold.

His comment hits its mark like a sucker punch to my gut. I let out a shaky breath and fist my hands—an attempt to keep from curling up in the fetal position right here on this lovely ornate carpet? Possibly. Or to prevent myself from decking my boyfriend with a strong right hook that would make my pacifist parents cheer?

Too soon to tell.

My lack of friends here in Memphis is an unhealed scab Jack loves to pick at, and it's been the source of just about every argument we've had since I moved here. It's not that I don't *want* friends. How could I not? The problem is that I don't quite fit in here. I can't relate to the team WAGs or the significant others of the front office staff. And at my job, I'm the lone Millennial slice of cheese in a Boomer and Gen Z sandwich.

Plus, making friends in adulthood can be freaking hard.

Pulling a calming breath deep into my lungs, I unclench my hands and paste on the friendliest smile I can muster as I step closer to Jack, who's now talking to Shane. He must feel guilty for the jab because he lifts his elbow and offers his arm with a small smile.

I take it and anchor myself to him, much like I've done with my whole existence in this city. Jack's the strong oak, rooted and unmoving, while I'm hanging on to a branch waiting to find earth of my own to plant in.

Conversation and laughter fill the grand ballroom as super fans and members of the Blues organization mingle and pose for selfies. I scan the room, trying in vain not to look too long at the clusters of muscly, athletic guys who stand head and shoulders above everyone else.

Doing my best not to search for a specific tall, muscly guy like I'm in a real-life version of *Where's Waldo.*

It's no use. It was ridiculous to even try.

Shane's voice pulls me from my quest. "Good to see you here with this guy tonight, Brynn." He tips his Bud Lite my way.

"Thanks, Shane." I bob my head and peer around him, looking for a Tiffany or a Linda or a Londa, but it appears that he's flying solo tonight.

An older gentleman sporting a thick mustache steps up to Shane's side. "Geneva requests your presence for a group picture," he says with a friendly smile.

As he shakes Jack's hand, his name and importance snap into place in my mind. Bobby Mundy, Blues' head coach. And the Geneva he referred to is the team's owner. She's the matriarch of the Russells, the family who's owned the team since its inception in the mid-nineties.

"Jack, good to see you and your lovely companion again." Coach Mundy takes my hand but keeps his focus on my boyfriend. "Geneva will want you in one of these pictures, so you might as well tag along." He pops a shoulder and turns my way, his smile affable. "My Tamara's around here somewhere, Brynn. I'm sure she'd love your company." A soothing warmth flows through me as I return his smile. He and I have only met a handful of times, and he must be introduced to hundreds of people each year, yet he remembers my name. It's impressive and surprising.

Before I can sputter out a thank you, Coach Mundy grips Shane's shoulder, and the three men stride away, leaving me alone in a sea of strangers. I shuffle through mental images of people who work for the Blues, hoping to land on one of Tamara Mundy that will aid me in finding her in all this chaos, but I come up empty.

Oh well. Maybe I'll save *making friends* for a different night.

Determined to find a server with a tray of Prosecco or water or anything to coat my parched throat, I spin on my heel, only to crash into a massive warm frame covered in...fur?

Oversized brown paws grip my upper arms to steady me, and a muffled "sorry" comes from somewhere near the giant hound dog's throat.

King. The Blues' mascot.

"So sorry, ma'am." A lanky young man appears beside King, holding a heavy camera. "Care for a picture?"

I give my head a quick shake, cheeks heating. "That's all right."

There's a couple standing nearby, clearly waiting for their turn with the beloved mascot. But whoever's in the giant furry suit is determined to stick with me. He wraps me up in a hug, then maneuvers to my side and rests a heavy paw across my shoulders.

"Big smile," the photographer prompts, and I acquiesce, ready to end this whole encounter and hunt down a damn drink.

As I sidestep away, the waiting couple swoops in for their photo op, and King blows me an exaggerated kiss. With a parting expression that's half smile, half grimace, I hustle away. My target? One of the two bars on opposite sides of the ballroom.

Weaving through the people crowding the ballroom makes me even more desperate for liquid relief, but it doesn't detract from my not-so-subtle examination of every tall, dark-haired man I squeeze by. Disappointment snakes its way through me when I make it to the bar without laying eyes on him. I blow a wisp of hair out of my eye and place my order.

Guzzling a hearty swallow of the Prosecco, I turn my back to the bar to survey the room. This time, searching for Jack. When that task proves to be futile as well, I decide to wait here until I get a "where are you?" text from him.

I stake a spot at the side of the bar, resting an elbow on the corner. As I do, the crowd parts in the middle of the ballroom, making space for King and some of the Blues players to gather together for a picture. This break in the throng affords me the perfect view of my boyfriend across the room.

He's tucked against the far wall. With another woman.

All the voices and noise filling the giant space fade into silence. He's so close to her, he can probably determine whether she's a dedicated flosser. His arm is propped on the wall above her head, and she's smiling and laughing at him like he's her effing moon and stars. When she grabs his lapel affectionately and pulls him even closer, my stomach knots, and I bite my cheek so hard, I'm sure it'll leave a mark.

The intimacy between the two of them is not new. Or professional. As I assess them, all those smiles aimed at his smartwatch or phone snap into focus.

My stomach has untwisted and is free-falling when a looming presence appears from my right. I glance that way long enough to notice a crisp white shirt under a light-blue jacket, but before I can register any other details, my attention zooms back to Jack.

The woman tucks a strand of ash blond hair behind an ear and bats her lashes at the man I uprooted my whole life for. The man I followed to a city I still feel like an outsider in, even though I've lived here for years.

Jack tilts his head toward the crowded room—a reminder, perhaps—and she releases her hold on his suit jacket. Each takes half a step back, putting them at an appropriate distance. The whole intimate exchange lasted less than a minute, but every second has been branded into my memory.

Certainly didn't have *Brynn's entire world implodes in forty-five seconds* on my bingo card for tonight.

Beside me, a throat clears, like the death knell of my relationship. Finally, I focus on the person beside me, and the blood drains from my face when recognition hits.

He's not looking at me, thank God. His glare is fixed on the individuals who've caused my heart rate to short circuit. His jaw tenses and his eyes narrow, movements that act as defibrillators to my heart, causing me to press a palm to my chest to reassure myself that the organ is functioning.

Griffin Lacey turns to me, his blue-gray eyes softening. "If it'll make you feel better, I'll let you ram his car into mine again."

I can't help the laugh that breaks free, and the smile he gives me in response makes my tummy flip-flop.

He lowers his head, moving in so close I catch a hint of his scent. "*Or* I'll stand lookout while you go all Carrie Underwood on his ass."

The man is tall and solid, and he's dressed in a light-blue linen suit that makes his eyes appear more blue than gray. The look fits his stature perfectly.

The brief distraction of his charm fizzles out at the trace of pity there, and mortification swoops in. Unable to look at him, or at anyone, I study my hands to hide my embarrassment and devastation. A tingling sensation starts in my fingertips and creeps up my body while warmth saturates my face and chest.

"Hey." His deep voice is full of a concern that makes my cheeks heat even more. "Brynn."

My name from his lips sends tingles of a different sort through my core. But I shake them off and force my eyes to his. "How'd you even know..." I can't finish my question. Can't give voice to what we just witnessed.

Griffin doesn't need me to. "Saw you on his arm earlier." He shrugs and takes a step closer. "Figured he was the owner of the Beamer."

Instantly, the memory of the nervous call I made to my boyfriend right after the fender-bender bubbles up.

"Jack? I'm so, so sorry, but I've been in an accident, and—"

"An accident? Like a car accident? Is the Beamer okay?"

The man seriously asked about his car before he checked on my well-being. One of many red flags I've chosen to ignore over the years. Perhaps the reddest of them all.

Until tonight.

"Brynn," Griffin says again.

I have to crane my neck to make eye contact when he's standing this close. For a moment, I study him. Warm blue-gray eyes, hooded under thick, dark brows. A straight, aquiline nose. His ears stick out a tiny bit, like the universe tried to tamp down his perfection with a slight overcorrection. Rather than lessen his rugged attractiveness, it only adds a cuteness that's rare for a man who's got to be in his thirties. Cute *and* rugged? Who could resist that combo? His hair, a brown so dark it's almost black, is cropped close to his head.

Does he keep it this length all the time? Does he have a standing appointment with a barber? Do NFL superstars even *go* to barbershops, or do they hire professionals to make house calls?

I give my head a small shake. Why the hell am I thinking about barbershops right now?

He rubs a hand over his short, dark beard and regards me with a frown. "Do you wanna get out of here?"

Do you wanna get out of here?

The question clangs through me, the multiple implications for *here* lining up like an organized list.

Do I want to get out of this *room* full of strangers where I just witnessed my boyfriend more than flirt with another woman? Yes.

Do I want to get out of this *city*, a place so vibrant and quirky and rowdy it makes me feel like a beige impostor? Also yes.

But I can't leave this event with the man watching me with a challenging gleam in his eyes. Can I?

The people pleaser in me says absolutely not. But something about Griffin Lacey makes me want to be impulsive.

I glance around, searching for someone who might save me from this decision, but then I remember that I don't know anyone here.

Except Jack. And this man. Sort of. The man who's wearing a smile that makes me want to say yes.

I buy some time by asking, "Don't you need to stay?"

He peers around the bustling ballroom. "I've posed for plenty of selfies and signed enough jerseys." His lips twist to one side. "I can get you one."

"I don't wear sports jerseys," I blurt before I can think my response through. *Damn it.* I close my eyes and hope that when I open them, I'll discover tonight was all a terrible nightmare.

No such luck. When I lift my lids, I'm still standing in a crowded ballroom with a hot football player staring at me like I'm a puzzle he can't quite figure out.

His dark brows—drawn together from my bluntness, no doubt—smooth out. "No worries. And my invitation for an escape is still on the table, even if you did just reject my jersey." He slips his hands into his pockets and rocks back on his heels.

"Oh my gosh, I'm so sorry." I give him a weak smile.

"No worries, Brynn."

Holy hell. The way his gravelly voice forms the phonemes of my name makes goose bumps blanket my body.

"What do you say?" he asks, ducking closer and meeting my eye. "Wanna blow this popsicle stand?"

When he rolls his lips, waiting for my answer, I want nothing more than to say yes. I don't care where we'll go or what we'll do, but I want to go on an adventure. With him.

Maybe it's reckless, but I bite my lower lip and nod. Once.

The smile that overtakes his face is enough to convince me to follow him anywhere. I have no doubt it's worked its magic on countless women before me. But I won't let myself think about that tonight.

Griffin rubs his palms together, a mischievous glint in his eye. "If you trust me, I've got a way out of here that—"

"I trust you." The ease with which those three words escape surprises me, but that makes them no less true. I trust this personable, brawny jock even though we've been acquainted for a collection of mere moments.

His charming smile melts and is replaced with a solemn nod. Like he somehow understands what a rarity it is for me to offer myself so freely. "Follow me."

He strides off, and I follow, doing my best to keep enough distance between us so that it's not obvious that we're leaving together while trying not to lose him in the heavy crowd. Instead of exiting through the mezzanine and main elevators, he heads to a mostly hidden door beside the stage on one end of the ballroom. He sneaks a glance around and then opens it while ushering me through. After we step into the small space, his warmth is a wall at my back as he secures the door. Then, he silently leads me through a series of smaller rooms and corridors until we reach a door marked with a stairwell symbol.

Our footsteps echo loudly against the cinderblock walls as we descend, but still, we don't speak. Once we're on the main floor, he turns away from the main entrances, from the lobby that has to be teeming with fans and hotel guests. After a few more labyrinthine twists and turns, we exit via a service door into the muggy Memphis night.

I'm out of breath after our quick escape, but I wheeze out, "Where to now?"

"Now," he says, that charming smile plastered on his face, "Let's get some *real* food. I'm starving." He absently rubs his stomach.

My eyes track the movement as I wonder what kind of pack that fabric hides—six or eight?

He bobs his head to the right, in the direction of Memphis's crowded tourist spots, and starts down the sidewalk, his gait purposeful. Three steps into our trek, he slips his hand behind his back and wiggles his fingers.

The same gesture he made when he helped me from his back seat after our collision. Without glancing back or slowing his movement down the street, he keeps his hand there, his long fingers dancing above his football-honed ass.

Jack's words from earlier tonight spring into my mind: *Try to make some friends tonight, dear.*

I reach forward and take Griffin's waiting hand.

I think I'll do just that.

Chapter Four

Griffin

We keep our fingers linked all the way down 2nd Street.

The sun has tucked in for the night, the twilight sky deep shades of blue and purple above the brick buildings of downtown. The street grows more crowded the closer we get to Beale, but I keep my head down and lead Brynn to one of my favorite restaurants, hoping like hell no one stops us. On our trek, I allow myself one look back. She's doing her best to keep up with my brisk pace. Her head is down, focused on her steps, but her brow is furrowed.

She's probably thinking about that asswipe Jack.

I kept my eyes peeled for those brunette waves from the minute Tyrell pointed her out, but still. What were the odds that I'd approach her at the exact moment she discovered her boyfriend cozying up to another woman? I hadn't seen them when I stepped beside her, ready with a line that was sure to get a laugh. But the devastation on her face made it vital that I find the issue that put it there.

The guys call him *Cockburn*. What an apt moniker.

The second she flashed those big brown eyes my way, I knew I'd do anything to remove her from that situation, even if only for a short time.

Throughout our entire jaunt down the sidewalk, one thought cycles through my head: *Griffin, you will not hit on this gorgeous woman tonight.*

Because that's my default when a beauty like Brynn crosses my path. Sure, I could probably charm her into my bed for one night; she's vulnerable and might be down for a revenge fuck. But in the harsh light of day, she'd regret it. And for some ridiculous reason, I don't want to be a regret for this woman.

No, I want to be a safe shelter for her. For now, at least. Which fucking boggles my mind.

I've never experienced this. This pull to provide comfort to a woman who isn't related to me. It's the same urge that hit me after our traffic mishap, but it's magnified tonight. Like some force out of my control is drawing me to her. Like my body has been taken over by a well-adjusted, mature male zombie. But without the appetite for brains and the oozing guts.

Shit, I spent too much time this summer playing *Resident Evil* with Tuck.

Am I attracted to Brynn? Fuck, yeah. Is my desire to be a listening ear for her winning out over my dick's desires? Yep, for the first time in my life.

Damn. Maybe Racy Lacey is losing his mojo.

The foot traffic picks up as we near the corner of Beale Street. Our steps slow to accommodate, and our bodies instinctively draw closer.

Still holding my hand, Brynn tips her head back and considers the sign above our destination. "I've never been here before."

I can't stop my mouth from dropping. "You're for real?"

Nodding, she bites her bottom lip.

That's all it takes for my head to have a serious discussion with his downstairs counterpart. "How long have you lived in Memphis?"

I hold the door open for her, and her fingers fall from my grasp.

She steps past me, peering at me sheepishly through her lashes. "Four years."

I sigh. "We're tabling this travesty until we get a table."

She smirks at my bad joke but steps closer as she takes in the diner. It isn't too crowded, thank fuck. We're in the sweet spot between the dinnertime rush and the late-night crowds who gather after they leave the bars, so we get a table right away.

A waitress takes our drink orders as soon as we slide into the booth, and I point to Brynn to confirm. "Sausage and cheese plate?"

"I'm sorry?" Her dark brows knit together. "That's a thing?"

Head tilted, I study her, and she mimics me, even narrowing her eyes like mine. But she twists her lips to keep a smile at bay.

Gah, she's fucking adorable.

She's also another man's woman, the little goody-two-shoes voice I usually ignore reminds me. I'd like to throat punch that guy.

"That's a thing," I turn to our patient waitress. "A thing we'd like to order."

"Sure *thing*." She smirks. "And I'll try to keep the vultures away the best I can."

I don't need to sneak a glance, because I feel them. All the eyeballs pointed in our direction.

I'm used to it. But Brynn is not. So I'd give this gruff waitress the keys to Seth's new car if it meant keeping this dining experience from becoming a fan frenzy.

In Nashville, I rarely attempted a sit-down restaurant without taking several preliminary steps—calls to management, rooms blocked off, renting out private spaces, bodyguards. That our table hasn't been swarmed confirms that Memphis is exactly where I need to be. In my periphery, I spy a lone cell phone lift to snap a picture, but other than that, the diners gawk for a moment, then return to their plates.

"Trish," I say, reading the name tag pinned on the woman's shirt, "we might be in the clear. But thank you for looking out."

Once Trish whisks off to get our drinks, I lay my palms on the table. "Now," I say to Brynn. "Please tell me how you've lived here for four years and have never eaten at Blues City Cafe. This is a Memphis institution."

Brynn shrugs and fiddles with the napkin-wrapped silverware. "There are lots of Memphis institutions I've never been to."

"Graceland?"

Her eyes dart to mine. "Check."

"The Pyramid?"

"It's a Bass Pro Shop," she hedges.

"It's an adventure," I argue, though I'm smiling. Can't help it when she studies me with those serious brown eyes.

Her lips twist to the side again. She wants to give in, but she's not quite allowing herself. Is this a common theme in her life? If so, then I'm hella surprised she accepted my invitation to leave the Peabody.

"What's with the sausage and cheese thing?"

Now it's my turn to shrug. "A sausage and cheese plate."

She crosses her arms and cants her head, waiting.

I deserve a fucking gold medal in restraint for not checking out her tits right now.

"It's a staple in Memphis. When you eat at a barbecue joint, you gotta start with a sausage and cheese plate."

"Like a charcuterie board?" She arches her brow.

"Like a sausage and cheese plate," I laugh, my chest expanding at our banter. "You'll see."

She doesn't question me further. Damn, maybe she meant it when she said she trusts me. Yet another reason to keep this strictly platonic. My gut, along with the wariness swimming in her eyes, tells me she doesn't bestow that gift upon many people in her life.

And tonight the one person she should trust the most let her down in a big way.

"You have siblings?" I ask as Trish sets a platter in the middle of the table.

Brynn studies the tray, then gives her head a shake. "None," she confirms. "What about you?"

"Two brothers. One older, one younger."

"Ah, middle child. That explains a lot." Before I can question that statement, she tips her chin to the plate of deliciousness between us. "So. Literally sausage and cheese on a plate. With a pickle bonus I wasn't expecting."

I bite back a chuckle. "Those pickles are fucking tasty. You don't like 'em?"

She shakes her head. "Not a gherkin fan."

"Noted." Before I dig into the savory smoked sausage that's making my mouth water, I pull up the notes app on my phone. I title a new note with her first and last name, then list *only child* and *hates pickles* underneath.

She squints, curious, but doesn't question me.

Don't ask me why I'm compelled to do this. Just feels fucking important to keep track of this shit in case I need it later.

We eat in silence for a few minutes. Every now and then, I study her, the way her eyes close when she first bites into the hickory-smoked sausage or how her tongue darts out to lick barbecue sauce off her lips. How she kind of smiles right before she pulls another cube of cheese off the toothpick with her perfect white teeth. When she catches me, my hand freezes over the tray. Her cheeks pinken, and she gives me a shy smile.

That look sends heat rolling through me. Fuck, I'm in trouble.

It's doused quickly, though, when an image of her devastated expression from earlier hits me.

You can't go there, Lacey.

I close my eyes for a beat, hoping like hell that when I open them, I'll see her through different lenses. Lenses that frame the woman across from me as a friend, not a potential lover.

It's a struggle, but I force my brain to come up with get-to-know-her-as-a-friend questions. Not get-into-her-pants questions.

"So, Brynn Nelson, not a gherkin fan, what do you do with your days?"

She swallows before she answers. "I teach English lit at Townes."

I'm impressed and intimidated. Townes is a small, private university here in Memphis. Very prestigious. This woman is an academic, and no doubt a helluva lot smarter than me. "Whoa." I lean in closer, elbows on the table. "So can I call you *professor*?"

One corner of her mouth inches up. "No. I don't have my PhD. Yet."

"Yet? So you're working on it?"

She presses a napkin to her lips and nods. "I've been working on it since I moved here. Started working on my dissertation this semester."

Pushing back against the booth, I whistle. "I'm guessing it's not about sports."

The laugh that leaves her is a pleasing tinkling of notes that makes my smile grow wider. "No sports involved. More like nineteenth-century female novelists." She waves a hand like it's no big deal.

"Damn it," I grouse, wearing a mock frown. "Guess that means you won't need my expertise after all."

She barks out one single "ha" but quickly sobers. "You never know."

I pop another piece of sausage into my mouth and chew as I assess her. "Where'd you grow up?"

"Florida. Cocoa Beach. My dad worked for NASA."

Fuck. This woman is going to bowl me over by the end of the night. "No shit?"

"No shit. He was an electrical engineer there. Retired about five years ago. My mom..." She sighs, then clears her throat. "She's a small-business owner."

That sigh piques my interest. "What kind of business?"

"Uh, it's a little beach shop." She picks up her water glass, takes a swig. Stalling. Her cheeks flush again, and she won't meet my eye.

My imagination runs rampant. What kind of "little beach shop" would embarrass her?

"Brynn?"

Her gaze finally settles back on me. "Yes?"

Fighting a smile, I straighten. "Does your mom own a sex shop on the beach?"

"What? *No*," she sputters so loudly that when she snaps her mouth shut, she peeks around to see if she caught the attention of anyone nearby. "No," she repeats, softer, her chin lowered. "It's nothing like that. It's..."

I splay my hands on the table in front of me and tilt closer. "I'm dying here, professor."

"Not a professor." Her eye roll and bossy tone only make me want to call her that more. "It's just that my parents are a little...unconventional."

"Nature enthusiasts," I recall. "That's what you said, right?"

Her thick, dark lashes fly open. "Yes." Shoulders bunched, she studies her water glass as if she's never seen one before. "They definitely love nature. They're—they're wonderful. I love them dearly. But..." She sucks in a deep breath, fixes her gaze back on me, and whispers, "They're hippies."

Head tilted back, I laugh, the sound bursting from deep inside my chest. This woman is so goddamn captivating. When I manage to contain my amusement, I lower my chin and find her gaping at me, a mixture of fascination and disbelief on her face.

"You're hilarious."

Her responding scowl is so damn cute. "I'm not."

"Here I was worried you were going to confess that your parents are wanted criminals or doomsday preppers, but then you hit me with the truth: they're a couple of free-spirited beach hippies. Please tell me they have a Volkswagen bus."

She shakes her head. "Sorry to disappoint. They drive hybrids."

Fuck. I haven't laughed this much in months. "Damn. What a wasted opportunity."

That earns me another eye roll.

"I want to meet these beach hippies one day."

She snort-laughs. "If that ever happens, prepare for my mom to ask for details about your sex life." The instant the words leave her lips, her face turns a shade of pink that would rival the hue of my mom's beloved azaleas. She slaps a palm over her mouth, her eyes as round as the now-empty plate between us.

I know it's a bad idea, but I say it anyway: "I'm an open book in that department. She can ask away."

In response, her lips part, and I swear her eyes darken.

Shit. I shouldn't say things like that to a woman I have no intention of being more than friends with. Shouldn't be wishing she'd ask me about my sex life herself so I could describe in detail all the ways I'd love to make her—

Nope. *Keep it in the fucking friend zone, Lacey.*

Chest heaving slightly, Brynn takes a drink of water. Sets her glass on the table only to snatch it up again for a second swallow. With one hand, she gathers her wavy hair at her nape and drapes it over her shoulder. I'm attuned to reading the nuances of a defenseman's body language, so it's second nature to collect a list of Brynn's physical tells and catalog them for later.

She's nervous. That's clear. So I steer the conversation back on track. "You never did tell me what kind of shop your mom has."

She exhales a sigh, and her skin returns to its natural ivory shade. "I didn't. It's a hippie beach shop called Celestial. Seashells, incense, postcards, hemp jewelry, all-natural soaps. But the big draw is the crystals."

I take a sip of my own water, reveling in the sound of her voice. "Crystals?"

"Yep." She nods tentatively. "Crystals for healing. For prosperity. For your chakras."

With a smile, I set my glass down. "That's cool."

She bites the inside of her cheek. Another tell.

"But you don't believe in all that." I'm not asking; her skepticism is clear as day.

"I don't." She hunches close to the table, shoulders rolled in, a flash of remorse on her face. "It baffles me that my dad, who spent his whole career immersed in math and science, also believes in the healing power of crystals. But he swears by them. They both do. And I just...can't."

"Does that upset them?"

"Not much upsets them. They're the most laid-back people on the planet, and their only daughter is so type-A, it hurts." She lowers her head, fiddles with her napkin. "They've learned to embrace my rule-following tendencies. But we experienced plenty of growing pains to get where we are today, especially when I was a teenager. Most adolescents are embarrassed by their parents, of course, but imagine if your parents rode a tandem bike to your school to attend your academic assemblies or asked your teacher if they could make her pot brownies to celebrate the start of summer."

I run a hand over my mouth to hide a grin. "Please tell me your teacher took them up on that."

A breath escapes her, and she deflates. "She did not, thank goodness."

"I'm not buying all that type-A bullshit, by the way," I tell her.

Her brows raise.

"Nah. There's a free spirit lurking in there, Brynn Nelson. You should give yourself permission to set it loose."

She wrinkles her nose, but before she can dispute my claim, Trish returns to take our order.

I can't decide between the ribs and the fried catfish, so I ask for the combination platter, even though I'll regret it during tomorrow's practice. During the season, I do my best to stick to eating healthy, but I can't deny the call of this place's best dishes. Brynn orders the skillet shrimp after Trish and I assure her it's an excellent choice.

As Trish steps away from the table, a grizzled older gentleman wearing a Blues hat sidles up. "I knew that was you, Racy." His smile stretches wide and he extends his hand, then pumps mine in a vigorous shake. "Told Pearlene it was you. She said not to bother you and your lady friend. But how can I pass up the chance to meet the man who's gonna help the Blues reach the big show?"

A few tables over, a woman gives him the evil eye.

He waves at her and points back at me. "It's him, Pearl," he bellows across the restaurant.

As a few diners watch our interaction with piqued interest, I glance at my *lady friend* and brace for the annoyed look I'm used to seeing on my dates' faces when this happens. Instead, I find her smiling at this exchange.

Not that she's my *date*. Definitely a friend. Who happens to be a lady.

"Would you like a picture?" Brynn asks. She gestures to the phone in the man's hand.

With an excited string of words that are hard to make out, he swipes it open and passes it over. I put my hands on the table, ready to stand, but before I can get my legs under me, the gentleman makes himself at home in the booth beside me and slings an arm over my shoulders.

Brynn takes our picture, and with a smile, she gives the man his phone.

Instead of returning to his table, which good fan etiquette requires, he waxes on about how I'm going to make a difference for the Blues this season. As much as I love his confidence in me, every proclamation makes my collar feel a little tighter. Makes a drop of sweat trail down my back.

Because what if I can't perform this season? What if Sunday's game wasn't a fluke, but a new normal? This could be my last season in the league. The thought of going out with a whimper makes my gut twist into a hard knot.

I can't let this town—this team—down.

I sign a napkin for him, and, finally, the man thanks both of us profusely before returning to his table.

I sip my water, ready to apologize to Brynn, but she pipes up before I can speak.

"What's it like?" she asks, her eyes bright but filled with moisture. "To be a source of joy for so many people?"

Her excitement pulls the most honest answer from my chest. "It's humbling. And terrifying. And fun. Disturbing at times. Intense. Unrelenting. Exhilarating." I huff a laugh. It still blows me away that *this* is my life, even after ten seasons. "Like a mash-up of all those things, really." I shrug and clear my throat of the thickness that's gathered there.

She nods slowly, understandingly, with a soft smile. "That's a lot of emotions to experience at once. Most of us live with the burden of keeping a small number of people happy. Family, friends. But to feel like you're responsible for carrying a whole city's happiness? That has to be daunting."

I marvel at her. How is it that, though she's just met me, she can discern what I haven't found words for in a decade? With a few succinct sentences, she's not only summed up the fear nipping at my heels, but she's also given me peace and assurance that my feelings are valid. I roll my shoulders back, and I swear the pressure glides off them like a marble down a chute.

Peace and validation. Fuck, I need more of those in my life.

Our dinners arrive, and we dig in. Conversation is limited as we chow down, revolving mostly around inquiries about how delicious our choices are.

When she asks me how my fish is, I go full dumbass again, without a thought. I scoop up a forkful of the deep-fried flakiness and hold it over the table for her to sample. She blushes, but she grips my hand and pulls it toward her mouth, never breaking eye contact. And as her lips close around my fork, my pulse goes haywire.

Friends don't feed each other bites of food, you idiot. I imagine my conscience as a tiny cartoon replica of myself that sits on my shoulder and shakes a fist every time I cross the line. That little dude is pissed as hell at me right now.

I clear my throat and open my mouth, only to stick my foot in it again. "What are you going to do about Cock—" *Fuck.* "Uh, um, about your boyfriend?"

Awful save, fuckwad. Eyes closed, I berate myself, wishing I could rewind the last few moments. But when I swallow down my mistake and force myself to look at Brynn, she's got her arms crossed and her eyes narrowed.

Shit. She's going to ask me about that slip-up. Do I tell her that the guys on the team have given her boyfriend a crass nickname? Will she tell him about it? If so, will he confront my teammates?

I'm still running through scenarios when, like a punctured balloon, Brynn deflates. Her shoulders droop, and she drops her hands to her lap, her chin trembling. "I don't know what to do about him."

"He doesn't deserve you." I startle myself with the admission. Where the fuck has my filter gone?

"You don't know me well enough to say that." It's a statement, but there's no authority in her tone. Only sadness.

I rub a hand over my buzz cut and blow out a breath. "I don't need to know more than I already do. Any man who doesn't worship the ground you walk on isn't worthy of you."

Her eyes shine with unshed tears, but I forge ahead. Strangely, tiny cartoon Griffin isn't waving any flags.

"Any man who would act like *that* with someone else when he's in a relationship doesn't deserve the devotion of an amazing woman like you. Being with you is a privilege. He's gotta earn that shit, and let me tell you, Brynn, he sure as hell didn't earn it tonight."

"I moved here for him, you know." Her voice is so hushed, I have to lean forward to make out the words. "We met in grad school at Vanderbilt. We had mutual friends. My roommate was dating one of his, so we hung out in the same group all the time. We were friends for a while, but eventually, he started making sure that we sat next to each other when we'd go out. That we were on the same team on game nights. One night, he walked me back to my apartment after a trivia night at the bar down the block, and he kissed me. It was easy to slip into a relationship with him." She shrugs and swipes at an escaped tear. "We did the long-distance thing for a year when he got the job with the team. He begged me to move here. So I applied for the position at Townes and got it. And here we are."

Her sadness makes my chest ache with an unfamiliar tightness. She's revealed so much, and what I'm hung up on is the fact that our time in Nashville coincided.

This woman and I have shared the same city twice. That's gotta mean something, right?

"Can I tell you a secret?" She angles her body closer and peers around the dining area, ensuring no one else is near. "I don't like living in Memphis." With a grimace, she straightens against the back of the booth.

Huh. That has my heart sinking a little. I fight the urge to argue, to try and convince her she's wrong about the city I've loved for most of my life, but my words alone won't change her mind. "Why don't you like it here?"

She tilts her head one way, then the other, as she contemplates. "It's more of a me issue, really. I feel like a jerk for telling you that. You obviously have a huge stake here."

"It's not just because I play for the Blues, though. My hometown is an hour from here. This place was my childhood ideal of a big, exciting city. It was such a thrill for my brothers and me to come here when we were kids."

"I just...gosh, Griffin, I don't fit in here. I'm an anomaly. I hardly venture out of our neighborhood or the university campus. We've been to the obvious places, like Graceland. Jack and I toured that right after I moved here."

My heart lifts a little. Not all is lost. "That's it, then. You haven't experienced the true Memphis magic yet."

"I've seen some of—"

I cut her off. "No. It's more than the buildings or landmarks. True Memphis magic comes from the people, too. They're the soul of this place. You, Brynn Nelson, not a gherkin fan, haven't experienced this city with the right tour guide."

She shakes her head, but the ghost of a smile flickers on her lovely face.

Tiny cartoon Griffin waves his arms over his head like he's signaling a plane on a deserted island. He knows I'm about to be a dumbass again.

"Let me show you *my* Memphis."

Her breath catches the tiniest bit as she fiddles with an earring. She's interested. "What do you mean?"

"What do your Tuesdays look like?"

She frowns. "Tuesdays?"

"My day off."

"Oh." Her skin flushes pink again, but she clears her throat. "I have two morning classes. And then an office hour from ten to eleven."

Hands laced on the table, I smirk. "So you're free after eleven on Tuesdays?"

"I—yes."

"Cool. I can show you what you've been missing."

"The Memphis magic?"

"The Memphis magic."

She pulls her lower lip between her teeth. "I don't know..." she hedges. "I mean, Jack..." Her voice trails off, and her eyes dart here and there, avoiding my face.

Her hesitancy is about Cockburn. I can handle this.

"Brynn," I start, ignoring the way my heart double-times when I say her name.

She drags her attention back to me, blinking, still gnawing on that lip.

I give her the hard sell. "Regardless of what you decide about your boyfriend—whether you kick his ass to the curb or you give him another chance—we can still be friends. We'd be doing cool stuff together on Tuesdays as *friends*."

"Just as friends?"

I nod. "Just as friends."

She gives me a soft smile, but I swear there's a flash of something in her dark eyes. Disappointment, maybe? Or maybe I imagined it, because in a blink of her lashes, it's gone.

"He'd be cool with you having a guy as a friend, right?"

She hums, then in a muted tone, says, "I don't think he'd notice, honestly."

Not wanting her to sink farther into sadness about that asswipe, I clap my hands so loud, she flinches. I'm not letting her say no to this. "It's settled then. Tuesdays after eleven. You and me and Memphis magic. Friendship and good vibes. You can call it *Tuesdays with Griffie.*"

That earns me another eye roll, but there's a smile, too. One so bright, it's like she's been plugged into the sun.

One so brilliantly beautiful, I wonder if I might be the biggest dumbass in the history of dumbasses.

In fact, little cartoon Griffin's holding up a sparkling trophy that reads *World's Biggest Dumbass.*

I brush an imaginary piece of lint off my shoulder, visualizing the motion sending the tiny dude flying off into oblivion.

Fuck him. What does he know?

Friends. I can absolutely be *just friends* with this woman. She's still in a relationship, for one thing. But even if she gets rid of his ass, I've got to keep my focus on the game. This team, this season. I promised myself from the start that I wouldn't let any outside forces distract me from giving this season my damn all.

If this is the end of my career, I'm determined to go out on top.

Brynn and I will be friends, and I'll show her why Memphis is a great place to live, all while I'm kicking ass as the starting tight end for the Blues.

My new friend sizes me up as I conduct these mental gymnastics. But when I extend my hand over the table and say, "We're gonna come up with a bestie secret handshake," she slips her hand into mine without hesitation. Then she does her best to copy my attempt at an elaborate bro shake.

She laughs at the awkwardness that comes with neither of us knowing the next move in the made-up-on-the-spot choreography, but the triumphant grin that shines on me when we both end the shake with a fist bump?

Fuck, I'm in *so* much trouble.

CHAPTER FIVE

BRYNN

*"L*et me show you *my Memphis."*

Griffin's invitation clangs through my mind like a brass bell as we leave the restaurant. He refused to let me split the check, arguing that "friends buy sausage and cheese plates for one another all the time in Memphis, professor." Once it was paid, he led me out the door with a hand on the small of my back.

We aren't five steps from the restaurant when a fan recognizes Griffin and asks for a selfie. As he obliges and steps in close to the guy, my phone buzzes in my clutch, so I pull it out to find a lone text from Jack.

Where are you?

I left the event an hour ago, and he's only now texting me?

I'm debating whether to respond when Griffin returns to my side.

"Ready?" he asks, a brow raised.

I nod, and we're off again. This time, he doesn't wiggle his fingers. Disappointment slashes through me before I can stop it.

Just as friends. I chastise myself as we turn the corner and head back to the hotel. I'm still giving myself a lecture when he touches my arm and gently crosses behind me so he can walk on the left, closest to the street. And, damn it, those warm tingles that have surged through my body frequently since we escaped the ballroom return.

We're silent for the first part of our stroll, but then Griffin clears his throat. "I've been thinking about our first excursion."

I glance at him sidelong. He's well over six feet tall and built of solid muscle. His posture is relaxed: hands in pockets, head tipped back like he's searching the heavens for an idea. I allow myself a glimpse of the way his linen suit jacket encases his broad shoulders, of the way his pants in the same light-blue strain across his quads when he walks. The clothing fits like it was made for him. Surely, it was.

Does he venture out to a custom tailor? Or does one come to his home to measure and pin and present fabric samples?

Maybe, eventually, during one of our tours of Memphis, I'll work up the nerve to ask him about house calls from barbers and tailors.

"Our first outing should highlight what Memphis is best known for."

"Sausage and cheese plates?"

His lips quirk to the side, the expression spotlighted by the streetlamp we pass.

"No, smart-ass." He spreads his arms wide, like the answer is right here.

For a moment, I'm distracted by the sheer length of them. How would it feel to be wrapped in their embrace?

The sound of his voice brings me back to the moment. "Memphis is the home of the blues. Rock and roll. You like music, right?"

I certainly don't listen to Jack's damn sports podcasts when I'm alone in my car or when I force myself to walk on the treadmill in the guest room. No, I fill those moments of solitude with the most random playlists imaginable. Everything from Bruce Springsteen to Johnny Cash to the Spice Girls to Queen to One Direction. Broadway musical soundtracks. Nineties grunge. Motown's biggest hits. Eighties one-hit wonders.

Yeah, I love music.

And this city does claim the birthrights to musical genres that have become the soundtracks to our lives. One might think that would endear this place to me, right? It hasn't.

You haven't experienced this city with the right tour guide.

With a small shake of my head, I say, "I love music."

His responding wide grin triggers a torrent of nerves to flood my insides.

"Me, too." He bobs his head. "I've got a pretty sweet vinyl collection." Our steps slow as we near the valet station at the hotel, where well-dressed Blues fans stand in clumps.

Griffin stops several feet away from the clusters of people, and with a gentle grip on my elbow, he pulls me into the shadow of the building. "Do you need a ride? Or do you want me to help you find your, uh—Jack?"

I slip my phone from my clutch, navigate to the ride-share app, and flash the screen at him so he can see the request I made before we left the cafe. "Jorge is driving me home. In fact..." I scan the street until I find a black Camry with the service's neon sign on its dash parked along the curb. "Ah, I think that's him."

"Let's make sure." Confidence marks every step he takes as he approaches the now open passenger window and bends to peer inside. "Who are you here for?" he questions in his deep baritone.

The driver gapes at first, but then he checks his phone and sputters, "B-Brynn."

My new friend straightens to his full height and shines his dazzling smile on me. "All right, Brynn not-a-gherkin-fan. I still have your number. I'll text details for our excursion Tuesday."

"Memphis magic and music."

"That's right." His smile softens as he studies my features.

My chest aches with reluctance. Talking and spending time with someone new—a friend—has been such a balm to my soul. I wish the night wasn't over.

"Until Tuesday." I bridge the distance between us by extending my hand. He clasps it, engulfing it with his own massive hand.

We fumble through the sequence of grips, slides, and slaps we attempted earlier, both of us laughing as we make mistake after mistake. But we wrap it up with a fist bump again, and after a nod, Griffin opens the back door of the car.

As I secure the seat belt, he sticks his head inside and turns to the driver. "Hey, Jorge," he says with a lift of his chin. "My friend here is precious cargo. No grand prix shit."

Jorge, still stunned that an NFL superstar has escorted his latest fare to his car, only blinks back.

"Bye, Brynn. See you soon." With a wink, Griffin closes the door and taps twice on the roof.

We've gone two blocks before Jorge snaps out of his stupor. "That was Griffin. Lacey." He gasps. "Racy Lacey touched my car. Wait until I tell my boys about this. They're gonna lose it." He finds me in the rearview mirror, eyes wide. "You know him?"

"He's a...friend." A comforting warmth floods my body, but it dissipates quickly when I remember Jack's waiting text.

Where are you?

What I want to respond with: *Not where I want to be.*

What I actually text back as Jorge zips through the streets of downtown Memphis:

> Sorry, I wasn't feeling good. Ordered a ride and I'm on my way home.

Those three little dots bounce at the bottom of my screen, and my stomach knots as I anticipate his reaction. Will I get an *Ok, bun. See you at home*? Or a *You couldn't tough it out a little longer?*

Neither, it turns out. Instead, the dots disappear altogether.

In the five years we've been together, I've never told Jack more than a little white lie. As I go through the motions of my bedtime routine, the guilt of keeping the truth of where I went tonight already sits heavy on my shoulders. Before I turn off the lamp and snuggle Barnaby to my chest under the covers, I check my phone one last time. Jack still hasn't messaged me back.

I toss and turn, my mind filled with nothing but images of Griffin. The way his smile lights up his entire face. The chameleon color of his eyes, shifting from slate gray to cornflower blue, like the sky. His strong hands, and the way his touch makes my skin tingle.

I'm on the verge of drifting off when the front door opens and closes again. My body locks up in dread. Do I leave the comfort of our bed to confront him about the blonde? Or do I put it off until tomorrow, or the next day, or the next day, or *never*?

Will the two of us stay stuck in this holding pattern, more roommates than romantic partners? For how long?

In the end, Jack makes the decision for me. He's not quiet as he moves about our cozy home, dropping my keys on the table by the front door, filling a glass with ice and water, opening our bedroom door. He pauses in the doorway, sees that I'm still awake, and then starts undressing with brisk efficiency.

"I'm getting a shower" is all he says as he emerges from our shared closet wearing only his boxers. Showers before bed aren't unheard of for him, but I can't help but wonder if the reason for tonight's is because he smells like her.

I curl into a ball, my back to his side of the bed, and clutch Barnaby tighter. The white noise of the shower lulls me, blessedly, and the last thing I remember before sleep takes me under is the mattress dipping under Jack's weight.

When my alarm wakes me Wednesday morning, I'm alone in bed, and the scent of fresh-brewed coffee wafts from the kitchen, so I shower and dress as quickly as I can, determined to have this out before Jack leaves for work.

He doesn't look up from his phone when I enter the kitchen, nor when I place my steaming mug of coffee on the counter across from him. I study the planes of his downturned freshly shaved face. How the hell has *this* become my life? I'm stuck—in a relationship, in a city, in a doctoral program—I'm not even sure I want to be in anymore. Do all thirty-year-olds feel this way? Mired in purgatory? On the cusp of true adulthood, yet feeling unequipped to make the transition?

I'm terrified about confronting my boyfriend, but Griffin's words from last night give me the courage to do it anyway.

Being with you is a privilege. He's gotta earn that shit.

"Who's the blond I saw you with last night, Jack?"

My voice startles him. With a palm on his chest, he regards me with wide eyes. "Shit, bun. Give me a heart attack, why don't you?" He blows out a slow exhale, squares his shoulders, and gives me his full attention. "I talked to a lot of people last night. You'll have to be more specific." He blinks a few times, all innocent and curious.

My pulse accelerates, but I fight to maintain my cool, keeping all emotion from my tone. "The one you looked super cozy with, up against the wall. The two of you were mighty close to each other." Maintaining eye contact is a struggle, but I succeed. "Didn't look too professional to me." I cross my arms so he won't notice my shaking hands.

Jack's composure doesn't slip, but color creeps above the collar of his pale yellow button-down. He fixes an indulgent smile on his face. "You're cute when you're jealous, bun."

"Who is she, Jack?"

His smile slips a fraction. "I guess it could've been Andi—er, Andrea. Vernon. She covers the Blues and the Bears for SNN." Nonchalant, he lifts one shoulder. "She tries to flirt exclusive insider info out of anyone who'll talk to her." He brings his Blues mug to his lips and takes a sip. As he sets it down again, he says, "You know how the media is. We've gotta play their game. So if it appeared like I was flirting back, I assure you it was for the sake of the team and nothing more."

I assess him, unconvinced of his innocence, but at the same time doubting myself. Maybe the closeness and the flirty smiles *were* for the sake of the team. Jack's job is priority number one for him. I accepted this before we moved in together. For a long time, that's what I thought I wanted, too—to be with someone who was fine with coming in second place. We've maintained this relationship with the understanding that our careers come first for years.

But maybe that's not good enough for me anymore.

Maybe I want to be someone's first place.

And maybe I'm ready to make someone *my* first place, too.

Jack slides off his stool and comes around the bar. "Bun…" He grasps my upper arms and twists me so that we face each other. I steel myself for more excuses. Instead, he simply says, "I've got to get to the office. It's my turn to cook dinner, so I'll pick up steaks on my way home." He gives me a gentle shake to force my attention from the buttons on his shirt. "Have a good day." With a quick peck on my cheek, he heads to the front door, leaving behind the sharp menthol scent of his aftershave.

I stand frozen until a honk outside startles me. While his car is being repaired, he's been getting a ride with one of his work buddies. I hold my breath for a moment, then I bask in the silence as I finish my coffee and start my day. I'm still as unsure about my relationship with Jack as I was last night, but it's a relief to be alone for now.

⸺◈⸺

Jack and I maintain the holding pattern for the next couple of days. I don't bring up the blond again, and he carries on as if I never mentioned her to begin with. He pecks my cheek each morning before he dashes off to work. On the weekend, he travels with the team to their away game in Houston.

I teach, hold office hours, and conduct research for my dissertation, all the while peeking at my phone to see whether Griffin's texted details about Tuesday.

As I leave the library on campus on Monday afternoon, my phone buzzes in my back pocket.

Griffin

Tomorrow. Meet me at 1927 Madison Ave at noon.

A ribbon of giddiness twirls through me, only to be tempered by reality. *Slow your roll, Brynn. He's a friend. And you still have Jack.*

I try hard not to take special care in choosing my outfit on Tuesday morning, but the discarded clothes I pile on the end of the bed before I leave for work are evidence of my failure. Since it's still warm, I opt for a short-sleeved chambray shirtdress. I pair it with my rose-pink Vans, not knowing whether we'll be walking a bit.

Time ticks by at a painfully slow pace, and I panic when a student sticks her head in my door five minutes before my designated office time is up. Luckily, she only has a few clarifying questions about a recent assignment. Once we're both confident that she's on the right track to complete it, I force myself to take my time packing up my laptop and locking up my office, even though every molecule of my body screams at me to hurry.

Preferring to be surprised, I've refused to look up the address that Griffin sent. All I know before I arrive is that it's located in Midtown. I find a place to park behind the building, and when I round the structure, Mr. Tall, Dark, and Handsome is waiting for me.

If we weren't *just friends*, I might swoon at the sight of him.

He's dressed more casually than I've seen him before, in jeans, Adidas sneakers, and a faded, worn Oklahoma football T-shirt that looks soft stretched across his broad chest. Covering his dark hair is a tattered khaki ball cap with a round logo that says *Lacey Farms* under a cluster of bean pods.

"Hey, not-a-professor." He breaks into that full-wattage smile that makes me the good kind of nervous. "Ready?" he asks, holding a hand out. "Let's get it right this time."

We attempt the elaborate handshake, but our fingers get twisted up halfway through.

I toss my head back and laugh. "It's two slaps before the fist stack, remember?"

"Yep." He nods, biting back a smile. "Go again."

This time I describe each step as we do them. "Regular shake. Slide into bro grip. Finger slide. Two snaps. Two slaps. Fist stack. Pinkie promise. Pull apart. High five. Fist bump."

"Again," he commands, giving me a glimpse of the intense singular focus he must possess when he's on the field.

We attempt it once more, this time without my step-by-step commentary.

"*Yes*," he growls when we execute it without a single mistake.

"So, where's this music I was promised?"

"Patience, grasshopper. I thought we'd grab a bite first. Tuesdays are now officially my cheat days." He pats his flat stomach, then points to the sign above the green- and white-striped awning. "This place has amazing burgers. I'm guessing you've never been?"

I shake my head, surveying the front windows and the patrons at tables inside.

"When our parents brought us to the city as kids, we'd take turns picking where we'd eat. This was Tucker's choice, every damn time."

"Tucker's your brother?"

"Yeah, he's the baby." Griffin pulls the door open and waves me inside.

Once we're seated, I ask, "What was your pick, when you were a kid?"

He barks a laugh. "I had a few favorites. They're on the Tuesday agendas, don't you worry."

That he's thought about our future Tuesday plans sends that giddy thrill coursing through me again. I bask in the warmth of his company. *Finally.* I'm finally building a real friendship here.

We spend the rest of lunch discussing our favorite musical artists and songs. He lists his favorite records in his collection, and I rank the top five best concerts I've attended. (Coldplay takes the top spot.)

He insists that we ride together to the next location, so I follow him to the lot. When he stops next to a vintage convertible, I gape at him. "This is yours?"

"My dad's." He smooths a reverent hand along the jewel-blue hood. "The three of us pitched in and gave it to him last Christmas."

"It's a Corvette, right?"

He nods and gives me an impressed smile. That simple move sends pride flooding my body.

"What year?"

"It's a 1961. It doesn't quite correspond with the era we're about to experience, but it's close."

Griffin barely fits in the car. Nonetheless, he looks right at home driving it. With his ball cap and sunglasses, he's an American icon behind the wheel. And when he grins as my hair whips around my face during the cruise to our next destination, despite my attempts to tame it, I laugh. Uninhibited. It's freedom in my lungs. In my soul.

I can't remember the last time I allowed myself the liberty to simply *enjoy*.

"You ready to tour the birthplace of rock and roll?" he asks after we exit the Corvette.

I'm too busy wrangling the rat's nest that my hair has become to answer, and I'm batting it from my eyes when the warmth of him seeps into me, stealing my breath.

"Here," he murmurs. "Let me help." A soft chuckle stutters out of him as we both smooth and finger-comb the errant strands.

His touch sends a heady shiver down my spine.

"I'll make sure to have a hair tie next time."

"I kinda like this look for you, professor." The low rumble of his voice does funny things to my insides. "Wild and unleashed."

The twinkle in his eyes is infectious, and I make a vow to myself: Tuesdays will be a day of yeses. I'll enjoy every new experience, every bite of food, every moment of friendship with this man. I'll let myself *live*, damn it. And I'll push away my worries about Jack and my dissertation and not fitting in, along with the myriad stressors that plague the rest of my week.

"Sun Studio is where Elvis recorded his first song." He shares other tidbits as we step into the unassuming brick building.

The cool air that greets us as he ushers me across the black-and-white tile floor to buy tickets is refreshing. When I pull out my wallet to pay for mine, Griffin shoves it right back into my purse.

"Not-a-professors don't buy their own tour tickets in Memphis."

Lips pursed, I huff. "I'm going to be faster than you one day, Lacey."

"We'll see about that, Nelson. Speed is part of my job description."

"Right. That whole *Racy* thing. How silly of me to forget."

"That's one interpretation of the nickname. There are one or two more out there. Depends on who you ask."

"I'm asking you, sir. Where'd it come from?"

Griffin takes his card from the cashier and slips it into his wallet. "That is a tale for another time, I'm afraid."

We stake a spot off to the side of a bar to wait for our tour time. When a lady vacates the stool at the end, he gestures for me to take it. As I'm propping a hip on the black vinyl, someone behind us whisper-shouts, "That's Griffin Lacey!"

He stiffens next to me, his eyes apologetic under the brim of his hat. "I'm sorry," he mutters before he turns to the small crowd that's now circling us.

Despite his initial reaction, he remains good-natured and professional while the throng clamors for an autograph or a photo.

One stocky man even has the gall to lean in and nudge Griffin with an elbow. "That your girl, Lacey?"

My cheeks flame, and my stomach bottoms out, but Griffin takes the invasive question in stride. With an arm thrown over my shoulders, he lifts his chin and addresses the crowd. "This is my friend and personal gherkin taster, Brynn. Her name actually translates to 'lover of gherkins' in Welsh. Did y'all know that?"

Various heads shake and murmurs of *no* sound out around us.

"She thinks Coldplay is way overrated, but we won't hold that against her, will we?"

More *no*s ring out from the crowd, and a few dubious looks are cast my way, but the crowd eats up his every word.

My stomach dips as I watch him work. Gah, the ridiculousness of this man makes me like him even more.

A cute young guy with dreadlocks sporting a crop top appears in a doorway and calls for the group's attention. He introduces himself as Josh, a local musician, and explains that he'll be our guide as we tour the historic studio. As the group follows him upstairs, Griffin and I drift to the back of the pack.

I bump his arm with my shoulder. "Personal gherkin taster, huh? I need to add that to my CV when I get home."

"I hear they're in high demand these days." He huffs a laugh, but then his smile slips. "I'm sorry if you were uncomfortable back there. The last thing I want is for your picture to be splashed all over social media. And for rumors to fly about who you are to me."

Right. Because we're *just friends*.

He must see the glimmer of hurt I thought I'd masked, because he rushes to say, "I couldn't care less what people think about me. But I would never want you or your relationship to suffer because of our friendship." He pauses at the top of the stairs, so I do, too. "I'm assuming you're still in a relationship…"

I force a swallow and nod. "I am."

Lips pressed together, he studies me, taking in my expression like he can find a different answer there. "Listen, I'm the last person who should give anyone relationship advice, but…" He heaves a drawn-out sigh. "But I do know that settling for crumbs doesn't fill you up. It keeps you starving."

With a sympathetic smile, he shuffles toward the group, leaving me on the top step to process his words. The truth in them causes gooseflesh to ripple across my skin. But Josh has launched into the tale of Sam Phillips, and I don't want to miss a second of this tour with my friend, so I shove his words and my reaction to them into a tidy compartment in my brain, to be unpacked later.

But those goose bumps remain for the rest of the tour. Not because of the icy blast from the AC. No, it's the step back to a bygone era and the stories surrounding some of the most beloved musicians and songs in history that have chills peppering my limbs.

And when I stand in the same spot Elvis stood so long ago, when he auditioned for Phillips, and my gorgeous NFL friend poses me for a picture holding the icon's microphone? Well, *those* goose bumps appear for a wholly different reason.

Chapter Six

Brynn

A quiet campus library is the last place most thirty-year-olds would choose to be on a Friday evening, right?

Yet here I am, tucked into a mahogany carrel at the back of Bingham library, knee deep into research on nineteenth-century gender roles. I rub the fatigue from my eyes and close down the document I've been working in for the past few hours. After one surreptitious glance around, I open up the folder in my drive labeled *Old Syllabi* and navigate to the Google doc titled *Draig 1.0*.

This 72,000-word document has been a bright spot for me over the past year. I'd even go so far as to say that it's the main source of joy in my life these days.

Until my Tuesday afternoons were booked for the foreseeable future, that is.

I scan the paragraphs I added last week to refresh my memory, then bring my fingers to the keys and start typing. The words flow from me like the current of the mighty river a few miles west of here. I get lost in my imaginary world of knights and faeries and witches and magic. This fictional story of my heart is a retelling of the Arthurian legend, one where the character of Arthur is a fearless young witch named Eleri rather than a king. She discovers her magic when she encounters a mysterious knight named Gethin and his warrior dragon, Aethon.

Just as I get to a long-awaited first kiss scene, my phone buzzes on the table, pulling me back to reality. A quick glimpse out the library's windows tells me I've been in my fantasy land for longer than I intended.

"Shoot."

Jack

When will you be home? I'm ordering dinner.

I tap out a quick reply and pack up my things.

Twenty-five minutes later, I barrel into the house juggling my purse, laptop satchel, keys, and emotional support tumbler. "Sorry, sorry. Time totally got away from me."

Jack pauses mid-bite to watch my entrance, but he doesn't say a word. A paper sack and wrappings from my favorite sandwich spot litter the kitchen table. The scent of the food causes my stomach to churn with hunger.

"Thanks for getting dinner," I say as I slide into the chair across from him.

His response is a curt nod. Then he's back to scrolling on his phone.

With a sigh of relief, I unwrap my sandwich, so ready to sink my teeth into the soft bread and turkey and cheese and...*pickles*?

Pickles. On my sandwich.

I open the sub on the paper wrapping and stare at the slimy green disks that cling to the top half of the bread.

There are six of them.

My whole body tenses.

Across from me, oblivious, Jack crunches on a kettle chip.

For a moment, I consider what I should do from here. Do I yell at him, demand he tell me why, after five years of dating and four under the same roof, our relationship feels more like that of roommates than lovers? Or should I rage at him about Andi-Andrea-whatever-her-name-is until he confesses that she's the mystery texter who's been stealing his smiles lately? Should I break down in tears about the *fucking pickles* on my sandwich? Maybe hit him with the trifecta, all three at once?

It really doesn't matter. If I'm being honest with myself, I know none of those reactions will change the reality.

This relationship has run its course. I'm not going to grow old with the man across the table. And I'm tired of pretending.

It's been a week and a half since I witnessed possible evidence of cheating, and I should've confronted him days ago, but I've talked myself out of it countless times. Am I willing to throw away a five-year relationship because of a perceived affair? One I don't have indisputable proof of? Part of me has been convinced that this man—this man I moved to a new city for, whom I've shared my life with—would never do *that* to me.

Then there's all the uncoupling logistics. The emotional upheaval of breaking apart a five-year relationship is daunting.

But I can't put it off any longer.

I wish one of Mom's crystals was tucked into my pocket. One for summoning courage. Which one would she suggest? Bloodstone, perhaps. No—aquamarine. Even though I don't believe a pretty rock is that powerful, I'd give anything to have a piece of my parents with me right now.

Instead, I put on my proverbial big girl panties, clear my throat, and take a deep breath. "Jack, I think we should break up."

His eyes snap to mine, his mouth turned down in confusion. As he processes my words, his brows pull tight, then even out, and his lips roll together, then spread into a thin line. He looks from my face to the table and back again, where his focus falls to my sandwich.

His eyes widen in understanding. "Sorry about the pickles, bun. I think they come on the sandwich."

I resist the urge to remind him that I'm aware. That I've been ordering this sandwich on the app for years. That the *customize* button is there for a reason. That he himself has correctly ordered this for me dozens of times.

He huffs an impatient breath at my silence. "Just take them off." He reaches for the sandwich, but I yank it away.

"Taking them off is not enough. The bread is soggy and soaked with pickle juice. Now the whole sandwich will taste like them."

"Brynn." He pinches the bridge of his nose, sighs. "Do you want me to reorder the damn sandwich? Do you want me to order something different? For fuck's sake, what's with the dramatics? I forgot to leave the pickles off your sandwich, and you tell me we should *break up*?" He coughs a bitter laugh. "Please. Be serious."

"I am being serious." My voice is soft, but steady. I lift my chin and force myself to look him in the eye. "We need to end this. Neither of us is happy."

"Who told you I'm not happy?" Nostrils flaring, he sits back in his chair and crosses his arms. "Are you seriously breaking up with me over goddamn *pickles*?"

Am I ending a five-year relationship because of six pickle slices? Of course not. The pickles were the last straw in an already stuffed-to-the-brim basket of straws on a geriatric camel's back. They're the last line squeezed onto an already filled-top-to-bottom page of scribbled, handwritten reasons.

We've been careening toward this breakup for a while now. But neither of us has been brave or determined enough to jump off the speeding train. Until now.

We've let complacency become a third wheel in our relationship. Only, recently, I've discovered that it's no longer enough. We both deserve better.

"It's not about the pickles." I grip the edge of the table so hard my knuckles whiten. "We're not a good fit anymore. Maybe we used to be, but we've both changed over the years, and we've become too comfortable."

"What's wrong with comfortable?" he sneers, chin lifted.

I close my eyes for a beat, wishing like hell I could fast-forward to the acceptance phase of this. "It's not good enough for me. For either of us." I sigh, forcing my shoulders from where they've risen practically to my ears. "Are you telling me that you see us getting married, growing old together? Maybe that vision existed in the past, but right now, in this moment, can you honestly look at me and tell me that I'm your forever?"

He opens his mouth, but the words don't come. And isn't that telling? He can't even find the words to fight for this. For *me*.

Instead, he straightens and squares his shoulders. "Is there someone else?"

A quick slice of anger flashes in his eyes, but I fight a reaction. I keep my features neutral, even though my heart rate kicks up. A six-five football hunk flickers through my thoughts, but I blink his image away. No, I'm not ending things with Jack because of Griffin. We're friends, and even though I'm attracted to him, I can't let myself go there. I won't be a woman who dumps her boyfriend one day only to leap into a new man's arms the next. I won't judge women who do, but that's not the path for me. And in my heart-of-hearts, I know that even if I'd never met Griffin, ending things with Jack would be the right decision.

Griffin isn't even interested in me in that way.

"No," I say, my tone even. "There's no one."

His jaw ticks, but he nods. "Nothing I say will change your mind, will it?"

With my hands clasped in my lap, I shake my head. "No. I'm sorry."

That night, I sleep in our guest bedroom. I snuggle Barnaby close and ready myself for an onslaught of sadness. But the tears don't come. I know then, without a doubt, that I've done the right thing. The brave thing.

And I sleep better than I have in years.

The sounds of tittering female voices followed by a deep, captivating male one rouse me from my research. Snapping my laptop shut, I peer into the short hallway that leads to the main English department office. It's empty, but from the sound of things, there's a group gathered in the main office. More laughs and giggles capture my curiosity.

As I'm rolling my chair away from my desk, ready to investigate, that male voice, closer this time, playfully scolds, "Y'all be good now."

And then Griffin Lacey's tall frame fills my open doorway.

"You-you're here." That last word squeaks out of me, and I forget to breathe.

"I'm here." With his hands in his pockets, he props one shoulder against the doorjamb. He's wearing a navy Hawaiian-style button-down covered in tiny pink flamingos. His chinos match the exact light pink shade of the birds.

Griffin Lacey is standing at my door. Wearing pink pants. Looking as effortlessly cool as ever.

"But...what, er, how did—" A glance at the clock allows me a moment to collect myself. "It's eleven-fifteen. Your text said we'd meet at noon. How'd you find me?" I blabber on. "And did a tailor make those pink pants specifically for you?"

"Whoa, not-a-professor." He straightens and steps into my tiny office, his bulk filling it almost completely. This space is only big enough to hold my desk, two chairs, and one overstuffed bookshelf. It wasn't built to house NFL superstars with supersized charisma.

Griffin ticks his answers off, one finger at a time. "My text did say noon, but there's been a change of plans. More on that in a moment. Google is very helpful in supplying campus maps when one needs to find the English building. And my new friends Helen and Trinity were happy to point me in the right direction."

"I bet they were," I smirk. The feminine giggles that echoed down the hallway moments ago made that obvious.

His grin widens. "And as for the pants, that's classified." He folds himself into the ancient wooden chair across from me, trying and failing to hide when he attempts to get comfortable.

"Sorry. Those chairs were made for timid college freshmen. Not strapping tight ends."

"No worries, professor." He rests his laced hands on his abs and leans back as far as he can. Another grimace, followed by a flirty raise of his brow. "Strapping, huh?"

I ignore the look and straighten a stack of papers on my desk. When he grimaces again, I have to ask. "What's wrong?"

He waves a dismissive hand. "Eh, it's fine. Just took a hard helmet hit to the ribs last night. Pads can only do so much."

The Blues had the first of this season's two Monday-night games last night. It was refreshing to have a few nighttime hours to myself, not having to tiptoe around Jack's foul mood.

Nevertheless, I'm concerned about his pain. I angle forward, resting my forearms on my desk and clasping my hands. "We can save today's outing for next week."

"Nope." He straightens. "No way I'm gonna let a little bruised rib ruin our day."

An embarrassingly fierce wave of relief hits me, outweighing my concern for his comfort. It probably makes me a crappy friend. But I've been holding on to these Tuesday plans like a lifeline, especially since Friday night.

"What's on the agenda for today, sir?" The text that lit up my phone Sunday afternoon only mentioned a meeting spot and time.

His eyes twinkle in that merry way that makes it impossible for me to resist any suggestion. "Did you know that fall is my favorite time of year? And not just because of football," he says before I can answer his question. "There's a hint of fall in the air today, so we're going to take advantage of it."

He's right. That slight nip of coolness encouraged me to quicken my pace as I walked to the English building this morning. It's unseasonably cool for the end of September, so if we're going to be outside, I'm grateful I chose a shirt with longer sleeves.

"What do you have in mind, Mr. Lacey?"

He tips his chin, gesturing to the door. "Let's find out."

He waits in the hall while I pack my laptop and class notes. When we reach the main office, Helen, the head secretary for the English department, waggles her silver brows at me and eyes my companion. She's a grandmotherly comfort to me here, and probably the person I'm closest to. Our unlikely connection began during my second semester at Townes, when she discovered me steeping a mug of tea in the department breakroom one winter afternoon. She asked if I had an Earl Grey in my tea tin and joined me at the table with her own mug of hot water. It's become a ritual for us on the days I'm on campus until dark. We gift each other new flavors every Christmas.

"Have fun," she calls as we breeze through the office, her tone making it clear she'll want a detailed explanation about how *this* happened.

"No convertible today?" I ask when Griffin leads me to the passenger door of a huge silver Ram pickup.

"Nah. Dad only loans her out a couple days at a time."

"So this is yours." I climb up into the behemoth, and as I settle in the seat, I resist the urge to caress the supple leather. It's the most luxurious truck I've ever been in.

"This is one of mine, yes." He winks and shuts my door.

I study the dials and controls and large touchscreen on the fancy dashboard as he rounds the front of the truck. "How many cars do you own, Mr. Lacey?"

I'm expecting him to admit to an exorbitant amount, but as he clicks his seat belt into place, he laughs and says, "Two."

"Hmm, disappointing," I joke. "I thought for sure you'd tell me seven."

"Why seven?" He grabs my headrest and twists his upper body, then backs out of the parking spot.

My mouth goes dry at his proximity, but I manage a swallow and stutter out, "One—one for each day of the week."

"Ahh." He comes to a stop and straightens. "Nope. Just the two. One to carry each of my Super Bowl rings."

"*Wow*." I drag out the word.

Head tipped back, he hoots out a laugh. "If it makes you feel any better," he says, "I did buy a whole-ass building last week."

For the rest of the drive, he tells me about the historic building and his apartment. And about the tattoo shop a friend of his brother owns below it. By the time we pull into a lot next to Mud Island Park, I'm drunk on Griffin Lacey—on his scent, on his laugh, on his charm, on *him*. He's intoxicating.

"Here's what's on the syllabus for today, professor." We exit the truck, and side by side, we make our way to a concrete path. "We're gonna take a little walk down the mighty *Mississipp*. Then some friends of mine are hosting a barbeque, so I thought we'd stop by."

I jerk to a stop. "Football friends?" I try to keep my tone neutral, hiding my anxiety. But like a switch has been flipped, my skin heats.

I push my sleeves up, searching for relief, and work to contain the tension in my body. Do I tell him the truth? Admit that I've never felt welcome at the football events Jack has dragged me to? That the one time I tried to befriend a group of the team's WAGs, they gave me the cold shoulder the entire night?

Griffin gives me a patient smile. "They're friends. Some of them do play football, but they're harmless, I promise. Beau and his fiancée moved into their new place a few months ago, so they're having some of the offense over to celebrate and team-build."

"Oh, okay." My voice is small, and fear still grips me. I hate it. I hate it so much I can't even look at him.

"Hey. Brynn." He says my name gently, the word floating on the air between us.

Still, I keep my focus averted. I study my sensible sandals until two gleaming white sneakers that probably cost more than my entire outfit slide into view.

"Hey," he tries again, and this time I acquiesce. When I finally tilt my chin up, I find genuine concern in his blue eyes. "I promised them I'd swing by, and I'd like you to meet them. They're great. Meeting new people is a part of that Memphis magic I've been telling you about. But if you feel uncomfortable in any way, we'll leave immediately. Okay?"

"Okay."

"Good." He tilts his head. "Let's stroll."

He leads me to a sign marked *Cairo, IL* next to a concrete canal filled with gently flowing water. "You've never been here?"

"No, but I know what it is—a replica of the Mississippi River."

"Correct, professor. Let's walk through a few states since it's such a beautiful day. Every step we take is roughly one mile of the river."

As we amble along the replica, a breeze off the actual river to our right stirs tendrils of my hair, chilling me and compelling me to lower my sleeves. Since it's lunchtime on a weekday, the park is relatively empty, though we meet a few moms with littles and a handful of couples as we make our way down the path.

"We've established that you don't like pickles." That stupid word—*pickles*—almost causes me to miss a step, but I recover, and he doesn't notice my blunder. "What, then, is your favorite food?"

"Soft pretzels," I answer, without hesitation.

Brows raised, he assesses me. "Really?"

"What?"

"Nothing." He shrugs. "It's just...unexpected, I guess."

"What's your favorite?"

"Cereal."

"Cereal?"

"Yep. The more sugary, the better. Cap'n Crunch, Froot Loops, Frosted Flakes, Lucky Charms, Cinnamon Toast Crunch."

"Cap'n Crunch always tore up the roof of my mouth when I was a kid. Not that I talked my parents into buying it for me more than a couple of times. They usually bought Grape Nuts or Mueslix."

"Then you didn't have a chance to build up the mouth-roof immunity. I swear mine has calluses from the stuff. My brothers', too."

We walk in companionable silence for a few minutes, and I lift my face, enjoying the juxtaposition of heat from the sun and cool, crisp air.

"With cheese, right?" Griffin asks.

I assess him as I work to decode his words. "Pardon?"

"Soft pretzels. You dip 'em in cheese, right?"

"Actually, no. I like them plain. With all the salt, of course."

"No cheese?" He splays a hand over his chest. "You're breaking my heart, not-a-professor."

We both laugh. God, it's easy to be in his company. It's comforting to know he's aware of my quirks but likes me anyway.

As we cross over a small footbridge, he pulls out his phone and taps it a few times before slipping it into his back pocket. The back pocket of his pink pants. That are doing incredible things for his tight, round bu—

Nope. That is not friend territory. It's no use berating myself. Now I'm thinking of how badly I want his tailor information to be de-classified. I'd like to send that person a cookie bouquet. With a card that says, *You're out here doing the Lord's work. Thank you for highlighting one of His greatest creations—Griffin Lacey's tight end.*

"You know where you can get a killer soft pretzel?"

Griffin's voice sends my inappropriate thoughts scattering like dandelion seeds in the wind.

I'm too stupefied to answer, but he doesn't wait for a response. "At the stadium."

"Oh."

"Those concession stands are legit. My brothers and I would save our allowance for weeks so we could buy snacks at the games we went to. One time, Tucker ate so much cotton candy that Dad had to pull over twice on the way home so he could puke."

He's quiet for a moment, thoughtful, and like I can read his mind, I know exactly what he's going to ask next, so I brace for it.

"You ever, uh," he stammers. "You ever go to any games with your, er, Jack?"

Without permission, a response that has nothing to do with football escapes me, as if I have zero control over my vocal cords and mouth. "Jack and I broke up."

He halts, causing his body to jerk back, as if he's slammed on the brakes, so I stop as well. The second my body stills, it's wrapped in a solid, warm embrace.

Holy hell. Being hugged by Griffin Lacey is like being cocooned in a delicious-smelling weighted blanket. I bury my nose in those tiny pink flamingos and let it happen. I've been starved for affection for the past few months, so I take the opportunity given and find comfort in a friend's arms.

"I'm so sorry," he murmurs against my crown. The words are followed by a slight pressure—his chin, resting on top of my head.

We stand that way a few moments longer. I ache to squeeze him back, but I refrain, because that way lies danger. I'm in too deep as it is, my overwrought brain rushing to document every nanosecond of this: Griffin's cedar and fresh air scent. The softness of his shirt against my nose and cheeks. The weight of his chin on my head. The perfect amount of pressure and warmth he exerts on each cell of my body.

I pull away first, but Griffin keeps a firm grip on my shoulders.

"Are you okay?" Right now, his irises are the color of the cloudless sky overhead.

"I'm okay." It's the truth. And I take comfort in it.

"When?"

"Friday night."

"What—" He shakes his head once, then says, "And you're really okay?"

We cross over a narrow portion of the miniature Mississippi and head back to the trailhead.

"I'm really okay." I give him a smile that turns into a grimace. "Other than the about-to-be-homeless part."

"Homeless?"

"The house is Jack's. He moved here a year before I did. He isn't kicking me out tomorrow or anything, but we can't keep living together. I applied for faculty housing on campus yesterday, but they're full until the end of the semester. I need to find a place to stay for three months, but most apartments want you to sign a lease for a minimum of six months." This predicament is compounded by my lack of friends in Memphis. I considered asking Helen if she has a spare bedroom I could rent, but I couldn't work up the nerve.

"You could move in with me."

Now it's my turn to slam on the brakes.

With my heart in my throat and my jaw on the ground, I stare at him. There's no mistaking the pink that's creeping into his cheeks. Or the sincerity in his gaze.

"Griffin, I didn't tell you that so—"

"I know." He clears his throat, which reminds me to take a freaking breath. "You weren't hinting. I see that. But I own a whole damn building. My apartment is two stories. You'd have the top floor to yourself. I only go up there to get things from my office.

And let's be honest, I'm not an office kind of guy. I'm more a studies-plays-on-an-iPad-while-lounging-on-the-couch kind of guy. So I'm never up there."

The rapid-fire heartbeats in my chest don't slow as I consider his offer. Is this insane? Moving in with a guy I've only known for a couple of weeks? *Of course it is.* So why, then, am I about to agree to be his roommate?

He continues his hard sell. "I'm not there much during the day, and the weekends we're out of town, of course. You'd have the place to yourself. Except weeknights. And you said it's only for three months?"

I nod absently. Three months. That'll pass in a blink, right?

My football star friend stands resolute, hands on hips. But his damn eyes twinkle. "C'mon, you know you wanna say yes."

God, I do. This man could convince me to rob a bank. Or graffiti a building.

Or move in with him...

"Okay. I accept."

Planned or not, the words shock the air out of my lungs. Like the free-fall at the crest of a roller coaster. Should I raise both hands in the air or cling to the safety bar for dear life?

His response? An undiluted, full-fledged Griffin Lacey smile. The kind that makes me feel weightless.

"Awesome, roomie." He holds his hand out, ready to seal the deal. "We forgot this earlier."

So we complete our intricate handshake, then, in a daze, I follow him back to his truck.

My chest goes tight as we park behind several luxury cars and SUVs that line the curb in front of a charming, two-story home. The tan siding of the home and the tall, white columns and trim showcase the slender floor-to-ceiling windows on each floor perfectly. And the welcoming front porch and second-story balcony lend a hint of quaintness to the whole package. The lots on this street are narrow, so homes sit close together in a way that resembles the historic double gallery houses I saw in New Orleans when Jack and I visited a couple of years ago.

On our way up the front walk, Griffin ducks and tilts closer. "Remember: we can leave whenever you want."

I nod as we step up onto the porch and give him my best reassuring smile.

The interior of the house is modern yet cozy. Rich walnut floors, smooth eggshell walls decorated with bold, framed prints, and a mix of leather and upholstered furniture in shades of espresso and taupe. The space is crowded with bodies: tall, broad football players and their significant others. For a fleeting moment, I worry that they'll think I'm Griffin's date.

But after the players in the living room greet him with bone-jarring bro hugs and handshakes, he gets ahead of the assumptions.

"Yo!" he shouts, silencing the entire room. "This is my friend Brynn. Make her feel welcome, please."

Cheeks burning, I plaster on a smile and give the crowd an awkward wave. Griffin remains a steady presence at my side as curious eyes scrutinize me. When I realize those inquisitive stares are paired with friendly smiles, I lower my shoulders.

A cute younger guy with smooth brown skin and a flirty smile pulls his beer from his lips and tilts his head, thoughtful. "Hey, Lacey, isn't she—"

The Blues' quarterback smacks the back of his head affectionately, cutting him off. Without missing a beat, Beau Dempsey closes the distance and extends his hand. "Hi, Brynn. I'm Beau. Nice to meet you."

His slow-as-molasses southern drawl is a balm to my insecurities. With a smile, I slip my hand into his. He stands a couple of inches shorter than Griffin, his body a little less bulky, too. But the man is gorgeous. He's the only Blues player besides Griffin that

I could pick out of a lineup, and that's only because the city has plastered his handsome boy-next-door face everywhere.

"Thanks for having me. Your home is beau—"

"Oh, hello! Welcome!" An enthusiastic blond sidles up to Beau and happily allows him to pull her into his side. She's beautiful. Perfect sun-kissed skin, thick blond waves that hit just below her shoulders. Eyes a blue so dark they're almost violet. A beauty pageant smile that showcases straight, white teeth.

She and Beau are a perfect match.

"I'm Paige Keller," she says, her voice light, bubbly.

"Brynn." I hold out a hand.

Rather than shake it, she swoops in for a hug. "Oh, gosh," she warbles as she squeezes me, the last word sounding more like *gawsh* with her accent. "I'm a hugger. I hope that's okay." I've literally just met her, but strangely, her fresh scent is comforting, so I let myself bask in a hug for the second time today.

"Now." She takes both of my hands in hers and backs away from the group. "Come hang out with the girls in the kitchen. I'll introduce you to everyone."

My blood pressure spikes, but I allow her to pull me away from the safety of Griffin's side. Before I can panic, though, a large, reassuring hand presses into the small of my back. "I'll go with you ladies, grab myself a drink."

He doesn't let go until after all the introductions have been made, and, feeling more at ease than I could have imagined, I give him a tiny nod. With a secret wink, he returns to his teammates. And I spend the next half hour getting to know some of the nicest, funniest women I've met in Memphis. These ladies are nothing like the group I tried to befriend shortly after moving here.

When Paige announces it's time to eat, I excuse myself to find a bathroom. I make a wrong turn as I'm headed back to the kitchen and end up near the butler's pantry, where Paige fetched my beer earlier. At the sound of deep voices in the walk-in space, I freeze.

One voice belongs to Griffin. I recognize the next voice, too—it's the young guy Beau smacked when Griffin and I arrived. "She dumped Cockburn's ass, and now she's gonna be your roommate?" I slap a palm over my mouth to keep from laughing at the butchering of Jack's last name. Do they really call him that? Griffin almost slipped up a couple of weeks ago, so that's likely.

Holy hell, they call my ex-boyfriend Cockburn.

"And you can handle that—having her as a roommate?" That voice, full of concern, but also authority, belongs to Beau. He asks the question confidently, like the team captain he is.

"Yeah, it's cool." My future roommate's tone is nonchalant. "I told y'all—this season is my one priority. I won't let anything stand in the way of finishing strong. No distractions, right? Besides, it's not like that with her. We're just friends."

Scuffs of footsteps in the pantry send my heart racing. Without a second of hesitation, I rush back to the bathroom. By some miracle, I make it without being discovered eavesdropping. My stomach twists with guilt for listening to their conversation, but more so because of Griffin's words.

We're. Just. Friends.

I've been telling myself the same thing since he offered his friendship. And our time together has been so good for me.

So why does hearing that phrase from his mouth hurt so damn bad?

I rewash my hands, stalling so I don't meet them in the hallway, and assess myself in the mirror. My cheeks and nose are tinged pink from our river walk, but the dark half-moons under my eyes are less prominent than they've been in years. Must be all that peaceful sleep I've been getting lately. That's something to celebrate, I suppose.

I take a deep breath, focus on my mirror image, and whisper the reminder once more: "You're just friends. And that will have to be good enough."

But the sheen in my eyes proves that neither of us—real Brynn nor her reflection—believes the lie.

CHAPTER SEVEN

GRIFFIN

*I**t's not like that with her. We're just friends.*

Those words have played on a mental loop all damn week. And every repeat brings with it a heavy knot that settles under my rib cage. One that makes it hard to breathe as we run through these two-minute drills. At least we don't wear pads on our Friday run-throughs.

To add to the tightness of that restricting knot, now Brynn's going to be my fucking roommate for three months?

Tiny cartoon conscience Griff turned in his two-week notice when that offer passed my lips.

At least she dumped Jackwad Cockburn.

That's why I was compelled to offer her a spare bedroom. I'd made not-so-subtle suggestions for her to dump his ass every time he came up, so I felt somewhat responsible for her change in living situation.

Beau's snap count hits me, bringing my focus to the play. Despite the way my brain's taken off more than once today, I run my route flawlessly and catch his pass at the back left corner of the end zone. When the whistle blows, we collect on the sideline, where the coaches go over last-minute adjustments.

Offensive coordinator Rasheed Dobbins adjusts his cap and waves Beau and me over. Dobbins is one of the youngest OCs in the league; he's been praised for his inventive and sometimes risky play-calling, but what most don't see is how methodical and deliberate he really is. He reviews a couple of pass-plays for this week's game against Chicago before we join our teammates and head to the locker room.

After that loss in the second week, the Blues have won both on the road and at home, giving us a three-and-one record. More importantly, my own gameplay has improved drastically since that day. I'm settling into the rhythm of the team dynamics and coaching styles. And Beau and I have connected, both on the field and off, in the past few weeks. A ride-or-die friendship with my QB is something I haven't had for the past few seasons, and I've missed it.

Football is full throttle these days, and I'm fucking stoked.

So why the hell do I rush through my shower, anxious to hurry home and greet my new roommate?

After ensuring a TA could cover her classes this morning, Brynn moved her things in. She insisted that she didn't have much to haul over and it would only take her a couple of trips in her SUV. Even so, I had a moving company waiting at Jack's Cooper-Young address at eight a.m. I also arranged for Lux, Tucker's buddy who's renting the first floor, to let her into the back gate and building.

"Hey, Lacey. Jefferson and I are hitting up Beale Street tonight. You in?" Devon Greenway peers at me from the locker room doorway, expression hopeful.

Greenway's been begging me to be his wingman since I got here. In years past, I would've jumped at the prospect of a wild Friday night out with my teammates, even with an early Saturday practice looming. Today, though, all I want to do is get home and check on Brynn.

"Man, raincheck?"

The way Devon's shoulders drop has a niggle of guilt working its way through me.

I sigh. "Brynn moved her stuff in today, and I feel like I should be there. In case she needs help."

He perks up at the mention of her name. "Oh, that pretty young thing you brought to Beau's?"

"She's older than you." I try—and fail—to keep annoyance from leaching into my voice. The last thing I need is for one of my teammates to make a move on her.

"But she's younger than *you*. And I love older women." He wags his brows, his broad smile proving that he doesn't need me to be his wingman. The kid's got charisma for days.

Beau chuckles from his locker a few spots down. "Greenway, pretty sure that one's off the market, even if she *is* single." He gives me a knowing look.

With a frown, I shove the rest of my gear into my bag with more force than necessary. "I told you—"

"You're right, Cap." Devon interrupts from the door. "Let's see how long Racy keeps his head in the sand before he chokes on it." With that, he salutes us and saunters into the hall.

"Best behavior, Greenway!" Beau hollers after him.

"No pro-mis-ses!" Devon singsongs.

"That one's trouble." Beau says, his tone affectionate. His easy expression vanishes quickly when he turns to me, and suddenly, he's leveling me with a look that would give Donna Lacey a run for her money. "Know what else is trouble?"

Frustration courses through me as I square up with him. "It's not like that."

"Mm-hmm. So when some dude comes over to pick her up for a date—"

"A date?" I scoff, hands on my hips. "She just ended a five-year relationship. I highly doubt she's ready to date."

"You sound pretty sure about that." His lips twitch. He's baiting me, but damn him, it's working.

The thought of some rando showing up at the apartment to take her out has my heart racing. And not in the way it was half an hour ago.

But Beau keeps at it. "Interesting that you know how long her relationship lasted."

"We. Hang. Out. We talk about our lives. Like friends are known to do."

With one brow cocked, he snags his duffel off the bench, then he's heading for the door. "If you say so, Lacey." At the threshold, he turns. "Paige and I are getting dinner and drinks near your place tonight. Wanna join us? It'll be way more low-key than painting the town with Jefferson and Greenway."

"Cool. Text me the details." I shoulder my bag and make my way toward him.

"Feel free to bring your *friend* along. Paige likes her."

Once my engine is running and I'm buckled in, I take a few moments to enjoy the quiet. As the cab cools, I check my phone for the first time since this morning. Two missed calls from my mom. Of course. She has a typed copy of my weekly schedule on their refrigerator, but she calls during every Friday practice, without fail. I also have several missed texts. One name in particular catches my eye and sends a heady thrill bubbling through my bloodstream.

She sent three in a row this morning:

Brynn

Why is there a Mighty Movers truck in the driveway right now?

Griffin.

You didn't have to do this, but thank you.

It's a little after four when I pull up to the gated parking area behind my building. Brynn's gray Forester is parked beside Lux's motorcycle under the carport next to the back door. Seth's newly dent-free Cayenne is here, too, in one of the visitor spots along the nine-foot privacy fence.

He exits the building just as I tap the lock button on my key fob.

"Just met your new roommate," Seth says as he approaches.

"Were you nice?"

He opens his mouth to protest but breaks into a smile instead. "I'm always nice."

Now I'm the one preparing for a comeback, but he beats me to it.

"*With* one exception."

Correct. He and my ex, Kate, butted heads on the regular. The guy tried his damnedest to throw a celebration when we ended things.

He slips his hands into the pockets of his well-pressed khakis and rocks back on his heels. "So..." he drags out. "What's the deal with you and Gorgeous up there?"

I groan. Not him, too. "We're fucking friends, Seth."

He smirks. "Are you fucking friends or *fucking* friends?"

I smirk back, though the expression is probably more menacing than anything. "Have you talked to Daniel today?"

"Low blow, Lacey." Seth squares his shoulders and straightens. He's several inches shorter than me, but the effort is admirable. "He's on his way here for the weekend, if you must know."

Seth's boyfriend opted not to move to Memphis for the time being, so the two are attempting a long-distance thing. I gave Seth the choice to stay in Nashville and do his job remotely, but he balked at that idea. Can't say that I don't appreciate his dedication, I guess.

"How's the apartment?" He found a nice one-bedroom in a development about twenty minutes from my place.

"Empty. I've been kinda busy."

That's an understatement. He's been in town for a little over a week, and he's spent the bulk of that time organizing my move and getting my place set up. He purchased all of the furniture sitting upstairs (after sending me pictures via text for approval), and he coordinated with the movers who brought my things from my parents' house and the townhouse in Nashville. The guy deserves a major bonus for ensuring that I haven't wanted for a thing since I moved to town.

He's really good at his job. I'm about to tell him so, but he doesn't give me the opportunity.

"So," he blurts, "you've only known this woman for a couple weeks, right? Are you sure she's legit? Like, she's not some undercover jersey chaser or a low-key psycho lying in wait?" His forehead wrinkles as concern shapes his features. "I didn't get those vibes from her, but I just..."

"She's legit," I assure him.

It's wild, but I've trusted her from the moment she stepped out of that red BMW. I've never questioned whether she had ulterior motives for befriending me. Hell, I can't say *she* befriended *me*. It was definitely the other way around. She's genuine and kind, and living with her, even if it's temporary, feels *right*.

"Cool. Had to check, you know?" His pale, freckled skin flushes pink, and he gives me a sheepish smile.

"Appreciate you looking out."

We endure the heat for a few minutes while we run through my schedule for the next few days and part ways. Then my duffel and I head up to my new home.

The stairs lead directly into the open-concept living room, dining area, and kitchen. I pause when I reach the hardwood of the space and take a long look around, imagining the apartment through Brynn's eyes. Does she like it? Or does she think it's too masculine?

The wall across from me is exposed brick, save for the cased opening that frames the stairwell to the top floor, and the modern built-out surround that showcases the glass-front gas fireplace. A large gray leather sectional defines the living area, flanked by two cadet-blue upholstered armchairs. Tucked into the corner next to the four plantation-shuttered windows that overlook South Main are two of my prized possessions: vintage *Pac-Man* and *Ms. Pac-Man* arcade machines.

When that first paycheck from the Tors came in a decade ago, I purchased them. Shaw, Tucker, and I grew up vying for the top score on the lone arcade game that sat next to the cash register at the diner in my hometown. Shaw and I were neck and neck for years, taking turns entering our initials next to the number one spot, until one Saturday when Tuck raided our grandmother's piggy bank for quarters and spent the entire day trying to best us. He kept the top spot for eight months and has never let us forget it.

I toss my bag into the laundry room off the hallway past the kitchen, then head upstairs to check on my new roommate.

"Brynn?"

"I'm here," she calls from behind the partially closed door. The third floor houses what is now her room, a spacious bathroom, another spare bedroom currently stuffed full of unpacked boxes and football paraphernalia, and my office.

When I nudge open the door, I find her standing next to the bed, surrounded by boxes and a couple of large storage tubs. There's an open suitcase on the nondescript navy comforter Seth picked out before he knew it would be occupied by a long-term guest.

"Sorry about the mess." Her words flit in and out of my consciousness as I take her in. Her thick dark hair is haphazardly twisted up into a messy bun on the top of her head. Fuck. I have to fist my hands at my sides at the thought of setting those locks free and running my fingers through them. With a thick swallow, I force my eyes to her face. She's not wearing a stitch of makeup. Those big brown eyes are framed by darker lashes. The faint freckles splashed across her nose and cheeks are like tiny droplets of leftover sunshine. Her rosy-pink lips stretch into a smile and then constrict to form a word. When they repeat the motion, my brain finally goes online—she's said my name twice.

"Uh, sorry, I—" A fluffy sage-colored heap next to the suitcase catches my eye. Without thinking, I grab it and hold it up for further inspection.

It's a stuffed dragon, well-loved and a little threadbare in patches.

"What's this?"

She snatches it out of my grip and hugs it to her chest, her shoulders curling around it protectively. "Uh, nothing." Her face flames the brightest I've seen it as she steps back like she's considering crawling under the bed.

The need to comfort her rears up so fast it takes my breath away.

Deciding she'll probably recover quicker if I ignore her reaction, I reach for the nearest tub and pull off the top right as Brynn shouts, "You don't have to—"

The tub is labeled *fragile*, and it's filled to the brim with an assortment of dragons—figurines, snow globes, statues, and smaller plush reptiles—are dragons considered reptiles? There are fierce creatures ready to take flight or scorch an enemy. Cute pastel-colored critters nestled among clouds and flowers. Iridescent dragons. Clear glass dragons. Some painted an array of colors, and some whose scaly details are etched into a single shade of gray or black or green. They range in size, too. Some are no bigger than my palm and some look like they could be used as a weapon to knock someone out.

"You collect dragons."

With an audible swallow, she nods. "Yeah."

It's clear she's mortified. She shouldn't be. I'm desperate to know all facets of Brynn. This is another piece of who she is, and it's adorable as fuck.

I pull one of the black dragon figurines from the pile. "This guy is badass."

Her shoulders relax a fraction. "My parents brought him home from Poland a few summers ago."

"No shit?" I hold him up higher and run my finger down the intricate scales and spikes along his tail.

"No shit." She loosens her tight grip on the stuffed dragon she's clutching to her chest. Her brown eyes search mine for a second, and when they soften a fraction, I know she's going to let me in. "This is Barnaby. My dad brought him home when I was eleven. I had the flu. He told me I needed a dragon protector to fight off sickness and loneliness. I've slept with him almost every night since."

Fuck. A strange, uncomfortable sensation climbs up my spine. *Am I jealous of a stuffed dragon?*

"Who named him Barnaby?"

"I did."

"And was Barnaby the start to your dragon collection?"

"Hmm, pretty much." She perches on the edge of the mattress and tucks one leg beneath her.

The expanse of bare skin I'm only now noticing instantly causes my mouth to water. In a pair of navy gym shorts with the Townes logo stamped on one thigh, she swings the leg still hanging off the bed in a lazy arc that is doing its damnedest to hypnotize me. As she launches into her story, all I can think about is wrapping those creamy, bare thighs around my hips.

"While I was sick in bed, I read this book about a boy who finds a mysterious rock in the mountains. It turns out to be a dragon's egg. I devoured the story, basically made it my whole personality, as a bookish kid tends to do. I sketched dragons in an old notebook. They were terrible. I am *not* an artist. But my parents nurtured my interest. They gave me figurines and whatnot for holidays and birthdays and just because. When they traveled, they brought new ones for my collection. Still do. Rather than posters of cute boys, the walls of my bedroom were covered with mystical dragon posters through middle school and high school."

I set the badass black dragon on the chest of drawers next to the door. "Feel free to hang cool dragon posters up in here."

She loosens a sweet laugh.

"Really," I say. "I want you to make this place feel like your home while you're here."

"Thank you." Her eyes shine, but she blinks back the emotion. "And thank you for the moving truck, even though it was totally unnecessary." She places Barnaby between her pillows. "I met Seth earlier, by the way."

I grin. "He's intense, right?"

"He certainly takes his job seriously. I've been thoroughly briefed on the inner workings of Team Lacey. Game day and practice schedules, housekeeper schedules, food delivery schedules, haircut schedules." The corner of her mouth kicks up. "But alas, no tailor schedules were shared."

I'm grinning so wide my cheeks hurt. "I told you, professor. That's classified." My tailor, who lives and works in Nashville, is not a secret, but I like that she's so curious. If I'm not careful, though, this woman will have me sharing all of my secrets with her.

Like how I'm pretty sure I'm gonna have to bolt out of here and jerk off in the shower if her shorts ride up any higher.

Fuck.

Fuckity fucking fuck.

I can't have thoughts like that about my temporary roommate. About my *friend*.

One about-face coming right up. "Do you still have that dragon book? I like to read or do puzzles when we travel."

"Puzzles?" She tilts her head, the move causing her bun to flop a little to the left.

I prop myself up against the wall, arms crossed, and take in a cleansing breath. Perfect. This line of conversation is exactly what I need to slow the blood flow to my dick. "Crossword puzzles. My mom buys the magazine ones for me at the grocery store back home."

"That's precious," she says, her eyes dancing. "And yes, I still have the dragon book, but it's at my parents' place in Florida. It's actually a series. The fifth one came out a couple of years ago, but I haven't had the time to read it. If you like fantasy stories like that..." Lowering her head, she drags Barnaby back into her lap. She toys with his wings and stammers, "I-I started writing a dragon story a while back." As soon as the words leave her lips, she squeezes her eyes shut.

My heart stumbles in my chest. My professor is an aspiring writer?

"Yeah?"

She nods shyly, her eyes still downcast.

Chest tightening, I straighten and take a step closer. "Tell me about it."

"You're the first person I've even mentioned it to."

Warmth spreads like syrup from my chest into my limbs at her admission.

She fixes her dark, expressive gaze back on my face. "It started as a lark, an idea I've had kicking around in my brain for years. But the second I sat down to get some words on the page, they poured out of me. An endless stream, like I was in a trance. When I finally came to, I had written over five thousand words."

I whistle. "Not too shabby, not-a-professor."

"It's not a big deal," she shrugs, attention fixed on the dragon again, back to fiddling with his wings.

"Don't do that."

Brows pinched, she snaps her head up.

I take another step closer and shove my hands into my pockets. "Don't hide your shine, Brynn."

God, I love saying her name. Sure, I get a kick out of calling her *professor*. But the way that single syllable rolls off my tongue?

It's like a fucking hit of dopamine.

"I don't know what to say to that," she confesses, her mouth turned down.

"Here's what you say." I clear my throat. "*Hey, friend-slash-roomie, I did this amazing thing—I started writing a kick-ass dragon book, and I was wondering if you'd like to read what I've written so far. And I'll say I abso-fucking-lutely want to read it. Hit up my private email.*"

She tips her head back, laughing. "Sadly, your private email was one detail Seth neglected to share with me. That and your tailor's secret identity."

"Oh, he's fired, then."

Her giggles cement the grin on my face; I couldn't wipe it away if I tried. "For now, how do you feel about a burger and a beer at one of Memphis's best dive bars?"

She perks up, shoulders back and chin high again. "That sounds amazing. Do I have time to shower?"

Goddamn it, Lacey, don't think of her in the fucking shower.

I almost choke on my own saliva. "Uh, yeah. Plenty of time. And full disclosure: Beau and Paige invited us."

Her eyes brighten. "Did they?" But in a blink, her hopeful expression shutters. "Wait. They're okay with me tagging along, right?"

I want to take a damn sledgehammer to this woman's insecurities. I don't know if Cockburn is the reason she doubts herself or if there's some untold trauma from her past, but I'm fucking determined to rid her of them. Forever.

"Paige specifically told Beau to make sure you were invited, professor."

"Okay." The deep breath of relief she exhales makes my chest ache. "I'll be down in a few."

While she's in the shower, I text her the email address that only my immediate family and Seth have. If she doesn't send me that dragon story, I'll bug her about it until she relents.

Forty minutes later, I'm waiting by the stairs, shooting off a message to Beau, when Brynn appears, looking like an absolute smoke show. Tight ripped jeans, a loose black silk blouse with the sleeves rolled up and an extra button undone at the top, and red strappy wedges. Her brown hair is styled in waves and her makeup is minimal, as usual.

As she descends the stairs, I work to convince myself that my words to Beau were the truth. Surely she's not looking to date so soon after her breakup. She needs time and space before she's ready to get back on the horse. Right?

Though I seem to remember getting back on the horse pretty quickly, and frequently, after my breakup with Kate.

Shit.

On our walk to the bar, my gut churns. Because it hits me: as her roommate, I actually *might* have to stand witness to her getting back out there. Going on dates. I'll have to suck it up and smile and be supportive, because that's what a *friend* would do. Because my comeback has to remain my number one focus.

When we step inside the bar down the street from the apartment, Beau and Paige have already found a table. And a small crowd has found them. They're surrounded by four fans, asking Beau for autographs or selfies. When Paige sees Brynn at my side, her face lights up.

"Yay, you're here!" She clasps Brynn's wrist and pulls her into an empty seat.

Once the fans recognize me, there's another round of napkin-and-ball-cap signing and I have to break out my celebrity smile for photos. But after that initial wave, the patrons return to their drinks and let us be.

We spend the next two hours laughing, drinking, and eating the bar's famous soul burgers.

"You know this place is rumored to be haunted?" Paige asks between bites of her burger.

"Really?" Brynn wipes her mouth and takes a swig of her beer.

When her tongue darts out to catch a stray droplet, I'm mesmerized. But when Beau catches me looking and smiles like a smug son of a bitch, I tuck into my burger like it's my last meal.

Paige, it appears, is oblivious to her fiancé's presumption. "Your new place is in a historic building like this, right?"

"Yeah." I wipe my hands on my napkin and set it beside my plate. "Built in 1920."

"You think it's haunted?"

Brynn snaps her head up, her brows shooting up into her hairline, making Paige cackle. "I hope not," Brynn says. "You haven't experienced any paranormal activity, have you, Griff?" Shit. Her affectionate use of the nickname does funny things to me. Warm, fuzzy things that I like too damn much.

"Uh, can't say that I have. I'll ask Lux if he's had any ghosts show up asking for tattoos."

"Oh, I met him today, too. He was so nice."

"Who's this?" Paige asks, dropping a forearm to the table and leaning in.

"Lux. He's a friend of Tucker's. My younger brother. He's renting the downstairs space from me."

"He's hot. *And* he has an accent." Brynn fans herself and leans closer to Paige, sharing a moment of levity with her new girlfriend.

Paige *oohs* and wags her brows.

But me? I see fucking red and grind my teeth so hard it makes my jaw ache. Not to mention that my grip on my beer bottle is concerning. I take a deep breath to calm my racing pulse, then roll my shoulders back once. Twice.

The girls gab on about how hot tattoos and British accents are; thank fuck they didn't notice my almost-Hulk moment.

But it didn't go totally unnoticed.

Beau Dempsey's smug grin is back, and it's reached epic proportions. When he gives me a told-you-so dip of his chin, I want to punch my friend in his perfect Captain America face.

I ignore my QB and affect an easy expression. I can act as though the way Brynn is describing the single man who shares our building as *hot* doesn't bother me.

Because it shouldn't bother me. Right?

Halfway through another round of beers, Paige invites Brynn to meet her and some of the WAGs at some hair place. The happiness evident in Brynn's demeanor is almost enough to quell the jealousy from before. Almost.

After Beau and I pay our tabs, the bartender sidles up to the table. "Hey guys, uh, seems a slight crowd's gathered outside. A few photographers. Guess word got out that you're here." He gives an apologetic shrug and collects our receipts.

My QB and I exchange a look. This is the first time I've had to deal with this since moving to Memphis, but it comes with the privilege of playing the sport we love on the biggest stage. It's a necessary evil I've been accustomed to for a long time.

Paige has been a part of Beau's life long enough to understand it, but Brynn's never had to deal with nosy photographers following her home or shouting rude questions at her.

At the thought, a fierce protectiveness rises in my chest. I'd do just about anything to shield her from all of it.

But we can't stay here all night.

"We'll take the lead," Beau offers. "We parked around the corner, so some will follow us. That'll leave fewer for y'all to deal with."

Brynn and I follow them to the door, though we stay hidden as they step out into the fray. The six paps hovering on the sidewalk break into a snapping frenzy, bright lights flashing and questions hurling like mad.

"Whoa," Brynn breathes beside me. "It's like feeding time for the sharks at an aquarium."

"Yeah. I'm sorry about all this."

She smiles up at me and says, "Lead the way, Lacey."

Beau's gamble about splitting them up proves fruitful. When I open the door to the cool night breeze, only three photographers remain. Still, they crowd the space outside the bar like they're making a goal-line stand. The best way to handle them has always been to maintain a brisk pace all the way down the street, so I rest my hand on my lower back and signal for Brynn to take it with a finger wiggle.

Within seconds, her delicate fingers interlock with mine. Then I cut a path through the photographers and a few rubberneckers who've been drawn to the camera flashes.

All the way down South Main, all I can think is how fucking perfect her hand feels in mine.

CHAPTER EIGHT

GRIFFIN

I type *allergic to kiwi* onto the ever-growing Brynn Nelson note in my phone, then scroll through the entries I've added since she moved in: *Dragon collector. Morning person. Swims on campus M, W, F. Likes tea before bed some nights—black tea only on weekends. Loves candles. Terrible at* Mario Kart. *Scared of spiders.*

I thumb back to the bottom and add *loves french toast.* As I slide my phone into the back pocket of my jeans, I make a mental note to ask Mom how to make fucking french toast. Because the pure joy on Brynn's face when our waitress slid that plate in front of her? Fucking breathtaking. And I'm desperate to see it again.

To be the cause of it.

"Mmm," she moans around a forkful of her breakfast.

The sound causes me to drop my fork onto the table with a clatter. Before I can catch it, it falls to the floor.

I signal to our waitress for a clean one, and once I have it, I duck my head and dig into my omelet, hoping like hell I can ignore any more sounds like *that* from the woman across from me.

We've lived together for five days now, and I've taken myself in hand in the shower every morning for the past four days. Wishing it was her hand instead.

This is a fucking problem.

"French toast might be a close second to soft pretzels, by the way." She takes another bite that leaves a dusting of powdered sugar on the corner of her mouth.

I resist the urge to swipe it away with my thumb, instead dipping my chin to silently signal its presence.

"Oh." Warmth suffuses her cheeks as she wipes it away. "My dad made it for breakfast every Sunday."

"Our Sunday morning breakfast tradition was biscuits and gravy. Donna Lacey makes a sausage gravy that puts all others to shame." Memories of the piles of fluffy buttermilk biscuits overflowing from the bread basket in the middle of our kitchen table make my mouth water. "We'd race to the table, hoping to be the first to slather on the fresh-churned butter while Mom finished up the gravy at the stove. Most weekends, she baked canned biscuits. Homemade ones take so long, and the gravy is plenty time-consuming. But my granny moved in with us after Gramps passed, and from then on, we got her homemade biscuits and Mom's gravy, and we Lacey boys lived like kings."

"You're close with your family." Her statement is punctuated with a serene smile. "I wish I lived closer to my parents. I miss them."

"Have them come up. Take them to a game." I've invited Brynn to attend the past two games, but she declined. I'll wear her down, though. I'm not above recruiting Paige to help.

She doesn't watch sports, but I think maybe she'd come to support me and even Beau if not for the risk of running into Cockburn. As far as I know, he's still clueless about his ex-girlfriend living with a player of the team he works for. When she moved out, Brynn told him she was staying with someone from work until faculty housing opened up.

"Hmm. Maybe."

I leave it at that, and we finish our brunch in companionable silence. Afterward, as I pull up to our next destination, Brynn angles forward in the passenger seat and peers out the windshield.

"It's an arcade?"

"What better way to follow up eating at Arcade than to spend time in an *actual* arcade?" I put the truck in park and shift so I'm facing her. "It's not a Memphis institution like the restaurant, but I promise you a good time."

She swivels my way, her lips parted and her brow furrowed. "But it looks closed."

She's not wrong. There's only one other car in the lot. Even on a Tuesday afternoon during the school year, this place is typically busier.

"It's not closed to us," I tell her as I push my door open.

Catching my meaning, she gasps. Then she scrambles out of the truck. "Wait," she says as I head for the entrance. "You rented it out?"

"Yep."

"Griffin." Her tone is firm, but her voice is farther away than it has been.

I grasp the door handle and look back, finding her feet planted on the asphalt of the parking lot, hands locked on her jean-clad hips. She's paired them with a soft blush-colored sweater that's both cozy as fuck and tight enough to tantalize.

"Why?"

I lift a shoulder. "I didn't want you to have to deal with a repeat of Friday night."

She steps closer but doesn't cross the threshold. "You didn't have to do this, you know. But since you did, I'm ready to kick your ass in some Skee-Ball."

"Pfft. We'll see about that." I trail behind her as she steps into the neon glow, doing my best not to stare at her ass. "I majored in Skee-Ball."

Her sweet laughter fills the space as we step up to the counter to collect our tokens from the lone employee, a bored, college-age girl who doesn't even look up from her phone as she hands us the buckets.

"Where to first?" I ask as we survey the place. The room is dark, the only sources of light coming from the machines. Every arcade game imaginable winks at us with bright, come-hither lights.

"How about we put that degree to the test? Skee-Ball." She darts around a couple of head-to-head game tables and makes her way to the lanes on the opposite wall.

"You're on, professor. Prepare to be schooled."

Eyeing one another, we drop our tokens, and when the heavy balls are released, we begin. My aim suffers because I can't help but keep my eye on Brynn's score. We're neck and neck until she sinks her last ball into the 10,000 hole near the top of the bull's-eye.

"Yes!" With a pump of her fist, she spins my way. "Rematch?" The competitive gleam in her eye is so fucking hot. I fight the urge to haul her body into mine and kiss that gloating smirk off her lips.

Holy shit, Lacey, cool your jets.

I swallow back the desire that's threatening to take over and grin. "You're on."

We play three more rounds and end up tied, two-two. Next, we take on the basketball shoot-out. Though I'm certain my height will make this an easy victory, I barely eke out a win.

"Are you a ringer?" I growl after she sinks another basket during the second round.

"Ha! Definitely not." This she says as her next ball teeters on the rim and drops into the net.

"For someone who isn't into sports, you sure are good at this." I miss my next shot and push up the sleeves of my Henley.

When the timer buzzes, Brynn is in the lead.

"I think it's time we up the stakes."

"What do you have in mind?" Her tone is pure flirtation. I pivot, finding her watching me, her lips parted and those gorgeous dark eyes so damn hopeful. I'm drawn closer, like we have fucking magnets in our chests, my gaze lingering on her lips a moment too long. All it would take is a single step to close the small distance, and I'd change our whole dynamic.

The flashing lights reflecting in her irises snap me back to the present. She's as fixated on me as I am on her. But the distance between us now may as well be miles. Because I made a commitment to myself when I signed with the Blues. I can't get wrapped up in her more than I already am. So I step back. And when her face falls and her posture sags, I mentally cuss myself out.

I clear my throat, desperate to make her smile or laugh again—anything to get that wounded expression off her beautiful face. "Uh, how about this? We'll pick another game, and whoever wins gets to ask the loser a question. And *you* must answer truthfully."

Her face brightens, and she straightens her spine. "Even though you said that like *I'm* the one who's going to lose, I accept your terms."

Without missing a beat, we seal the deal with our secret handshake.

After a heated air hockey battle, Brynn emerges victorious. With a brow cocked, she tilts her head and asks, "Tell me the true origin of the *Racy Lacey* nickname."

I groan and blow out a breath. This isn't a secret. If she'd done a Google search, she'd already know. But if she's asking, she hasn't. Like she wants to hear it from me, and that makes my chest ache.

I brace against the air hockey table, crossing one ankle over the other, and gesture to a metal bench across from me. Brynn obliges and pulls her feet up to sit crisscross like she's a kid gearing up for story time at the library.

"That nickname is the media's doing. My teammates didn't call me that until well after the press started."

She nods, brows raised, patiently waiting for the rest.

"I can't say it originates from one incident or trait, really. But I'm fucking fast for a big guy. Was even faster when I started playing. I ran a four-five-five in the forty at the combine before I was drafted, which is almost unheard of for a tight end." I pause, twist my lips, duck my head. "And there are a couple other factors to blame for the nickname..."

"Other factors?"

With a sigh, I peer up at her. "I tend to be a little foul-mouthed."

She gasps and covers her heart. "You don't say."

I pop a shoulder and smirk. "Been fined a time or two for my colorful vocabulary."

"What else?"

Now my cheeks heat, because damn, I enjoyed the hell out of my twenties. I've never regretted it. Not until this exact moment. Though I have no interest in analyzing the contrition creeping through me right now. The thought that this woman might see me in a less positive light after I confess this makes my gut sour with shame. But I can't change my past. And it's all online anyway.

"For the first several years I played, I, uh, frequently enjoyed the company of women." I expect her to blush or grimace, but her expression doesn't waver, so I force myself to elaborate. "I was photographed with a different girl almost every time I partied."

"And now?" She visibly swallows, her slender throat working.

"Do I party now? Sometimes. Do I sleep with multiple women?" My voice is pure gravel. "No."

No, I don't have multiple sexual partners, professor, because there's only one woman I want to fuck, and I can't have her.

She gathers her hair at her nape and pulls it over one shoulder, her nervous tell, and keeps her focus fixed on me. The intense eye contact makes me sweat. This moment between us is heavy—heavier than the almost-kiss from earlier—and I like it too damn much to disrupt it.

Brynn's the first to cave. She clears her throat and drops her feet to the floor. "Okay, *Racy*. Now I challenge you to that *racing* game." She points at the side-by-side leather seats situated behind a pair of steering wheels.

"You're challenging me to a driving game? Do you remember how we met?"

Her mouth drops open when my words register, but then her lips twist to one side in an effort not to smile.

"I might need to give you a head start," I tease.

That remark earns me a swat to my arm, and I clench my hands into fists to keep from tugging her to me.

When I win the race by a landslide, Brynn shifts in her seat, ready for my question.

Going easy on her, I ask the first thing that springs to mind. "What's your middle name?"

"That's your question?" Her eyes flash, like there's a story here. It's confirmed when the color of her face rivals the red sports car on the screen in front of us.

"Yep, that's what I'm going with."

She fidgets with the hem of her sweater for a moment, then pops up from her seat. "I'm sure you can come up with a better one than that."

Her evasiveness turns me into a dog with a bone. I press my lips together, pretending to mull it over, but then shake my head. "Nope. I'm happy with my original question."

She wrings her hands and chews on the inside of her cheek, but she keeps her attention averted.

"Remember the terms of this game that you shook on, professor. You must answer truthfully."

"Fine." She crosses her arms, and this time, I let myself peek at the perfect breasts this defensive position accentuates. God, what I'd give to get my hands on those—

"It's Amethyst."

I blink to keep myself from blurting out something that'll clue her into my thoughts. "What's amethyst?"

She huffs, her expression going flat. "My middle name."

"Is Amethyst?"

"Yes."

I hold back a chuckle. "No way."

With a grunt, she scans the empty arcade. "Way. I told you my parents love crystals. My birthday is February first, and the birthstone for February is—"

"Amethyst," I finish for her.

"Yes."

"Brynn Amethyst Nelson?"

"That's me." She gives me a weak smile.

"I need proof."

Dubious, she studies me for a silent moment. Then she rummages through her purse. Side-eyeing me while she continues her search, she asks, "You really didn't know?"

"How would I know?"

"You didn't run a background check on me?" To most, her laugh might suggest she's joking, but the tension in the sound is clear to me, and her eyes tell a different story. "Here you are, Mr. Multimillionaire," she says, yanking her wallet from her purse, "letting a poor college instructor nobody move into your home after only knowing her a couple weeks." She's embarrassed and lashing out.

She holds her license out, but I don't take it. Instead, I make a colossal dumbass mistake and step closer. Her sweet floral scent—the one I've caught whiffs of around the apartment for the past few days—fills my nose. Fuck, this close, it's hard not to want to trace the smooth skin of her jaw around to her nape and pull her in. But I settle for a gentle chin grip.

"Hey." When she zeroes in on me, I continue. "You remember that night at the Peabody? When you told me that you trusted me?"

She nods as much as my hold allows.

"That's a two-way street, professor. I trust you. Implicitly."

"That's—that's good," she whispers.

"It is. And we're done playing for answers. You want to know something, just ask me. I'm an open book."

She swallows thickly, composes herself. "What's *your* middle name?"

"Michael."

"When's your birthday?"

"Tomorrow." I grin.

She jerks back, and my hand falls away. "What?"

"It's tomorrow. October eighth."

Blinking, she shakes her head. "Griffin. Your birthday is *tomorrow*? Why didn't I know this?"

"You've really never googled me?" I can't help but puff out my chest.

"Your ego knows no bounds," she scoffs. "And no, I don't google my friends. Though apparently, I should so I'll know when their damn birthdays are."

Her dramatics make me grin. God, I love when sassy Brynn comes out to play.

"Wasn't keeping it a secret, professor." I cross my arms and look down my nose at her, holding back a smirk. "I can get Seth to type up a personal stats memo just for you, if you'd like."

"Not necessary." She turns on her heel and starts for the Whac-a-mole. "I'll consult Google from now on." She lifts her chin, haughty as fuck, and my pulse picks up. "So, any big birthday plans?" she asks as she hefts the mallet.

I wait to answer until she's finished whacking the hell out of the elusive moles. Or trying to. She's terrible at it, but she puts her all into it anyway.

"Some of the guys are taking me out tonight."

She hands me the mallet and presses a token into the slot for my turn. Not one mole escapes my pounding.

"Ugh, show-off." Her smirk melts into a smile. "So tonight is boys' night, but what about tomorrow?"

"I've got practice." I shrug. "Just another Wednesday."

"What about your family?"

"They took me to dinner after the game on Sunday."

"Hmm." Her brows lower in concern. "We can't let your real birthday pass without some kind of celebration."

Warmth washes through me at the regard in her tone. "Why not?"

"*Because*," she emphasizes. "Birthdays are a big deal. The day you were born is a big deal."

"Your family goes big for birthdays, huh?"

She nods. "Yeah, they do." The wistfulness in her voice makes my chest ache. That tone, though, is quickly replaced by one full of determination, and she wears an expression to match. "Can I cook dinner for you tomorrow?"

I jerk my chin up. "You cook?" We've only lived together for a handful of days, but I haven't seen any evidence of Brynn being a closet amateur chef.

"I'm a terrible cook." She winces. "Like, really awful."

"But you want to cook dinner for me?"

Another nod. "Yes. I promise I won't burn down your building."

"All right, not-a-chef, make a birthday dinner to remember."

Her answering smile hits me in the solar plexus. I'd probably let her burn down the fucking building if she'd promise me one of those smiles every day. Being with Brynn only makes me crave more time with her. I've never in my life experienced a connection this deep with anyone in such a short time.

It's fucking terrifying. An out-of-control sensation that I both hate and want.

She pulls her phone out of her pocket to check the time. "I have time for one more. What's it gonna be, Lacey?"

"Oh? Big plans tonight?" I swallow down the panic threatening to choke me. If she tells me she has a goddamn date—

"Big plans at the library. I've kind of neglected my research lately." She wrinkles her nose and heaves a deep sigh.

Relief floods my lungs with my next inhale, but I do my best to ignore the reaction.

Brynn, oblivious to my relief, struts up to the Dance Dance Revolution game. "Ready to show off your moves, big guy?"

"This?" I rub a hand over my buzzed hair. "I might break the damn thing."

She considers me, starting at my head and working her way down to my shoes before sweeping back up.

Shit, her assessment brings me way too much pleasure.

Phone still in her hand, she swipes it open and gives the screen a few taps. Then she holds it up to my face. "That sign says max capacity is 450. And according to Google, my friend weighs 248 pounds." She waves the device, where my stats are pulled up. "Maybe you're scared you don't have the right moves."

I wag my brows. "Oh, I've got the right moves, professor."

Even in the dim lighting of the arcade, there's no mistaking the pink hue that stains her cheeks.

"But my style," I say, ducking in closer, "leans more toward the two-step and line dancing."

She steps up on the platform, and I do the same, my shoes spanning more than a single square that surrounds the blue arrows.

"Racy Lacey knows how to two-step?" she asks, brows arched like maybe she's impressed.

I chuckle. "All the Lacey boys know how to two-step. It's a requirement."

Her brows furrow, so I explain.

"My aunt owns a honky-tonk in our hometown. Aunt Dottie made sure the three of us—four, counting Tuck's buddy, Camden—learned how to two-step before we graduated from high school. She said any nephew of hers would know how to properly spin a lady around the dance floor."

"Hmm," she muses. "Can't say that I've ever two-stepped before."

Before the last word has left her mouth, my own commits the bad habit it's developed when Brynn's around—blurting without consulting my brain first. "I'll take you for a spin soon."

Her eyes light up, and her gorgeous face, wide with hope, makes me a little dizzy.

But I'll ignore that for now, too.

⸺◈⸺

"Cheers to thirty-five." My QB clinks his beer bottle against mine, then settles back against the leather seat in the round booth where we're holding court. This VIP corner of the club is roped off, but that doesn't stop bold, tipsy fans from trying to sneak past the two beefy bouncers stationed at either end. This place is dark and loud and strobe-y enough to cause seizures, but the younger guys insisted we come here after we ate our weight in ribs at Rendezvous.

"Thanks, Cap." With a pull of my beer, I relax into the creaky leather seat. "He's going to be feeling that tomorrow."

I tip my head, gesturing to Devon Greenway. He's slurping a frozen concoction from a neon pink yard glass while he boogies on the dance floor with a couple of our teammates and a gaggle of scantily dressed women. It's a Tuesday, so the dance floor is empty save for the group circling the Blues' players like bees to a hive. I would've been content to call it a night after dinner, but Greenway and Jefferson wore the rest of us down.

Jefferson, who's broken away from the cluster on the dance floor, flops into the booth next to Beau. "Lacey, you're missing out. It's your birthday, dude, and you can have your pick." He throws an arm out, gestures to the women tossing their hair and laughing at Greenway's sloppy attempt at a moonwalk. "Or, hey, I bet they'd let you guest DJ."

"You know we have practice at seven a.m., right?"

With a shake of his head, he looks at Beau. "Please don't let me get this old."

"You show up to practice hungover tomorrow, and Coach'll take care of that for you, I'm sure." Beau lifts his chin.

"Aw, man. Not Cap, too," Jefferson wails. "Greenway," he shouts across the club. "Save me from these old geezers." He snatches up a leftover shot, downs it, and throws himself out of the booth. Then he's hurdling over the velvet rope and hitting the dance floor again.

"Gah, to be that young again," I lament.

"You'd want to go back to those days?" Beau points his beer at the crowd as a techno version of "Dancing Queen" thumps through the speakers.

"You're nowhere near my old geezer status." The guy's only twenty-seven. "It's too soon for you to be sitting on the sidelines."

"This game ages you." He finishes off his beer and signals the waitress to close his tab. "Plus, this was never my scene, even in college. And Paigey would kick my ass if I came home wasted on a weeknight."

"Ah, the old ball and chain." My tone is lighthearted, at odds with the heaviness settling in my limbs. I'm fucking jealous that I don't have someone soft and warm waiting for me at home like my friend does. Though I'd never admit that out loud, even after a couple of beers.

You could *have someone like that waiting for you at home, you dumbass*. I wash the thought away with another swig of the brew.

Beau studies me a moment, thoughtful. "Where's your roommate tonight?" This fucker. He's been tenacious about this lately.

"I'm not her keeper, you ass."

He rewards me with a cocky smirk.

"But if you must know, she's working at the campus library."

He crosses his arms, his lips tipping higher, the expression growing more obnoxious by the second. I don't tell him it was on the tip of my tongue to invite her, even though our group text said "boyz night only," and I certainly don't tell him that the thought of her wanting to cook a special dinner for my birthday makes my insides gooey.

"You'd be her keeper in a heartbeat if you thought she wanted that."

The smugness in his tone makes me blurt, "Who says she doesn't want that?"

Beau's brows reach for his perfectly styled hairline, but he doesn't respond.

"I mean," I stammer. "I think she might be..." The words dissolve before I can finish the thought. A deep-seated loyalty to Brynn won't let me admit the truth to the guy who's quickly become a confidant.

"Getting too attached?" he guesses. His smug expression has morphed into a concerned frown.

"Maybe." I sigh. "We had a moment, earlier today, and I..." A vision of those big brown eyes and soft pink lips assaults me. God, I wanted to kiss her so fucking bad. "I'm worried I'm sending her mixed signals."

Every one of these conflicting feelings bubbling under the surface is a huge-ass red flag, warning me to step back, put some distance between Brynn and me.

"Look, I'm Team Lacey all the way." Beau uncrosses his arms and tilts forward and rests his clasped hands on the table. "But if she's into you, and you're into her, would it be so bad to pursue this, see if it could be something real?"

Something real? Some days, Brynn is the most real thing in my life. Football can be a fickle mistress—the highest of highs and the lowest of lows. It's a lesson we all learn the hard way. But when I was escorted to the locker room at the end of last season, in so much pain I could hardly think straight, I vowed that I wouldn't let the game end me that way. I would fight tooth and nail to come back swinging. Then, after I'd gone under the knife to repair my shoulder, my team let me go, and depression descended like a suffocating blanket. My mother and Tucker had to coax me out of bed while I rehabbed at home. The chance the football gods have given me here? I can't fuck it up.

No matter how tempting it is to give in to my desire for Brynn.

Beau's silent as I work through my thoughts. I clear my throat and lock eyes with him. "It *could* be something real," I say, practically shouting over the heavy beats of the music. "But football needs to be my number one right now. Maybe after the season—"

"If she's still available."

With an impatient huff, I push away the panic that hits me. "If she's still available."

"You know the best way to clear up those mixed signals?" Beau lifts his chin toward the dance floor, where two girls grind on one of my teammates. "Take another woman home tonight. That'll drive home that 'just friends' message loud and clear." He actually air quotes *just friends*—smug Beau has returned.

"Maybe I will." The lie makes me nauseous. There's no way in hell I'm bringing another woman into my bed when the one I want is sleeping one floor above me.

An hour later, after making sure Greenway and Jefferson get into the correct Uber, I wave good night to my QB and head home—alone.

Chapter Nine

Brynn

"I'm telling y'all, if Carlos proposes, I'm keeping my maiden name." The table erupts with laughter.

I smile at the women seated around the table, though the joke is lost on me.

Paige, clearly reading my confusion, tips closer. "She's dating Carlos, on the O-line."

Smile still planted, I give a little shake of my head.

"Carlos Butts. He's number sixty-four."

"No way am I gonna be Gina Butts," the woman across from us wails.

More giggles and chuckles ring through the air. This time, I join in, letting a small laugh escape.

The quiet raven-haired woman next to the potential future Mrs. Butts consoles her with a pat on her shoulder, then looks my way. "I love what he and Griffin are doing on the sidelines."

Paige introduced this woman as D'Angelo Sweeney's longtime girlfriend, Charmaine. The group turns curious eyes my way, but again, I'm clueless.

"She doesn't watch the games, y'all." Paige waves it off like it's no big deal, but there's an intake of breath from somewhere at the table.

My cheeks heat in embarrassment as the group assesses me.

Charmaine angles forward. "Carlos and Griffin make it a point to stand next to each other on the sidelines as often as they can. When they do, their jerseys read—"

"Lacey Butts!" Gina cackles, sending the rest of the table into another bout of laughter.

Our food arrives, and the women go quiet. We're all occupied with our salads or BLTs or fancy grilled cheeses for a few moments.

I swallow down a bite of my sandwich and peer around at the charming restaurant's glass-bricked booths and the tables set among vintage hair dryers. "This place is so cute. It really used to be a beauty shop?"

"Mm-hmm." Gina sets down her BLT. "Ms. Priscilla had her hair done here back in the day."

"You should come to a game, Brynn. You can always sit with us." This from Shannon, the center's very pregnant wife.

"I've been before, I just…" I flush again, under the scrutiny of so many curious eyes. "Y'all are so different from the WAGs I met then." Instantly, I cringe, regretting my bluntness, but they all smile or laugh.

"When did you hang with Blues' WAGs?" Shannon asks, holding her fork in midair.

"I told y'all—she used to date Shane's assistant." Paige's firm tone sends the message that I will *not* be elaborating on my ex.

I'm so thankful I could cry. I convey my appreciation with a nod, and she winks back.

With a *harrumph*, Gina points her fork at one woman at a time. "I guaran-damn-tee you she's talking about Blair Barkley and her crew."

Elise, the stunning redhead at the end of the table, pipes up. "Oh, honey, that bitch has been gone for a minute. Her husband was traded to Denver two seasons ago. With the HBIC gone, most of her minions have scattered. Though there are still a couple of hangers-on." She eyes the rest of the women with a knowing glint.

There are head bobs and *mm-hmms* to confirm.

"Yeah, we're way nicer than those heifers." Charmaine's smile shows off her adorable dimples.

Despite my best efforts, I can't resist giving in to the kindness of these women. "Okay, okay," I say with a sigh. "I'll come to a game."

The whole table breaks out in cheers, once again causing a blush to work its way up my neck and into my cheeks.

"The Laceys have a suite. You could sit with them if you don't want to hang with the WAGs." Shannon gives Paige a quick glance but focuses on me again. "What's the deal with you and him, anyway?"

The group freezes, and Gina's utensils clang against her plate like a gunshot. Paige shoots daggers at Shannon, who simply gives an abashed shrug and rearranges her salad with her fork.

The heat I felt a moment ago is nothing like the inferno that engulfs me from head to toe as they scrutinize me. With a thick swallow, I consider how to answer. Do I tell these virtual strangers that I have a huge crush on my friend and temporary roommate? A swarm-of-butterflies, can't-breathe-when-he's-near, makes-me-feel-sixteen-again crush that's grown to epic proportions in the two weeks we've shared an address? Do I tell them that my life flashed before my eyes—in a good way—last week when he almost kissed me at that arcade? That he made my whole year when he scarfed down every bite of the pasta dish I spent hours on for his birthday? That when he asked for seconds, I almost wept with pride?

Do I tell them how terrified I am that my crush is turning into something *more*? Something powerful and irrevocable?

Paige opens her mouth to come to my defense, but I place a hand on her forearm and swallow down my discomfort. "We're friends. Friends who happen to be rooming together for the next few months. I've got a place lined up in the faculty townhomes, but it won't be available until the semester is over."

By the pursed lips and raised brows, it's obvious some of these women want to probe deeper, but they're either too polite to try or scared of Paige's mama bear vibes. I don't blame them for being curious. How often do we hear that men and women can't ever be *just friends*?

Though I'd gladly leap if Griffin ever indicated that he'd jump with me, he's made it clear that our relationship will remain firmly in the friend zone. But our newfound friendship is precious to me, and the last thing I want is to jeopardize it. It's revived me, bringing me back to life like a wilting flower after a spring shower, and I'm soaking up every drop of companionship he offers.

Even if that almost-kiss haunts my dreams. And my waking hours. Because if he's so intent on remaining friends, why the hell did he study my mouth like he was dying for a taste of it?

The rest of the meal passes without invasive questions. Mostly, the women regale me with tales of what it's like to have a famous athlete for a partner. Several safe questions about my life are lobbed my way, as well, so I'm included in the conversation far more than I expected when I arrived.

"See? That wasn't so bad." Paige waves goodbye to the rest of the group from the sidewalk, then she links her arm through mine and leads me to our parking spot down the street. "Sorry about Shannon. Her filter's wonky sometimes, but I promise she's harmless."

"Thank you for including me. It really means a lot. And everyone was super friendly." A lump forms in my throat, but I blink back the emotion before it has a chance to dig in. For the first time since I moved here, I have a handful of *real* friends.

"Of course, girlie." She bumps her shoulder into mine as we amble to her SUV. "When we met, I knew you'd be special to me. I had that meant-to-be feeling, you know?"

I nod, too choked up to respond. I suppose maybe I sensed it, too, though it's been so long since I've connected with anyone that I didn't trust it.

"When you meet someone, but you could swear you've known them your whole life? I have a knack for these things." She sighs, a smile tipping her lips. "I knew I was going to marry Beau within five minutes of meeting him. Gah." Her expression instantly dulls. "I hate away-game weekends," she pouts. "And two in a row is the worst."

The Blues eked out a win in New York last weekend, and today, Griffin and his teammates are flying to Washington after their morning walk-throughs and meetings. I imagine two weekends away from one's significant other would be hard. Funny how it never bothered me when Jack traveled with the team.

We're a few feet from the car when she says, "Beau said that Griff is nervous about this Washington game."

Heart fluttering—its default when a certain tight end is mentioned or in my proximity—I draw to a stop and twist to face her. "Why is he nervous?"

"He was injured on their field last season. When that late hit dislocated his shoulder and tore his labrum?"

My heart sinks. "I knew he was injured last season and needed surgery, but I didn't know this game was weighing on him." I roll my lips together and study the grass separating the street from the sidewalk, making a mental note to text Griffin some words of encouragement when I get home.

"Hey…Brynn." Paige's soft voice shifts my focus back to her. "He'll be all right. It's what they do—they get back on the horse." She nods to reassure me, and I copy her head bobs with my own. "And you know how I said I have a knack for knowing things immediately when I meet people?"

"Yeah?"

She purses her raspberry-glossed lips. "You and Mr. Racy Lacey?" she says, a brow arched. "I'm not sure which one of y'all is in denial, or if it's both of you. But there is nothing *just friends* about this whole situationship."

I open my mouth to protest, but Paige grabs my hand and squeezes.

"Don't worry, though," she insists. "Your secret's safe with me. But if you ever want to talk about it, I'm here for you. And I promise not to tell Beau. The man is a bigger gossip than his Great-Aunt Clara."

Paige spends the drive back to Griffin's trying to convince me to travel with her to the away game in two weeks.

I find myself wanting to say yes; it's in Charlotte, which is a short flight from Memphis. And it's in the same time zone as my parents. It may seem silly, but it would make me feel closer to them.

After Paige drops me off, I slip off my shoes, light my favorite candle, and cozy up on the huge sectional sofa. As my body melts into the soft leather, I regard my phone. What should I say to Griffin? *You got this*? *Break a leg, but not a shoulder*?

My phone buzzes in my hand, making me flinch, but when I see who the message is from, my heart double-times.

Griffin

> This is me. On the plane. With nothing to read.

A selfie comes through next. He's propped his chin on a fist, and he's gazing out the plane window with a bored expression on his handsome face. I take a moment to appreciate the way his broad shoulders fill the frame. Then I zoom in. An immediate warmth flushes through me as I admire the shape of his lips and how blue his eyes are in this shot. Like a kid worried about being caught with her hand in a candy jar, I zoom out and glance around the empty apartment.

Crossword puzzles for the win!

Griffin

I finished the last book. Mom's supposed to bring me more next weekend.

I hear mobile games are all the rage these days.

C'mon, professor. I'm in the mood to get lost in an epic story.

Paige did mention his concerns about this game. A distraction would probably help. Before I have a chance to second-guess myself, I navigate to my drive and share *Draig 1.0* with Griffin's personal email address. Then I squeeze my eyes tight and hold my breath until another message buzzes through.

It's another selfie, and this time, he's sporting a goofy, open-mouthed grin. I laugh at his youthful expression. Until, that is, the reality of what I've done crashes down, making my stomach drop.

Please don't tell me if you hate it. Or if it's bad.

I've never let anyone read it, so I'm not even sure if it's readable.

It's probably total garbage. Hope it gives you a good laugh.

[crying laughing emoji x 3]

Those three little response bubbles tease me for an interminable length of time, then disappear.

A wave of dread washes through me, and I flop over on the couch, burying my face in the plush softness. It's only a moment before another buzz makes me bolt upright.

Griffin

> Professor. Chill. If it's from your brain, it's guaranteed to be amazing.

I read the words several times, willing them to sink deep into my soul, where I can keep them forever.

It's moments like this that add fuel to the fire of my crush. He's gorgeous, a perfect physical specimen, of course. But he's also hilarious and kind, and he has the canny ability to say just what I need to hear at just the right time. He does the most thoughtful things—like scheduling movers and ensuring I'm comfortable at a gathering before walking away. On the surface, those gestures might seem ordinary or insignificant, but they're more than meaningful to me.

Griffin's little acts of service remind me so much of the small ways my dad shows his big love for my mom. Like bringing her coffee in bed every morning and starting her car for her on cold days so it can warm up before she leaves.

The giddiness building inside me deflates, though, when those words I overhead that afternoon filter into my thoughts.

It's not like that with her.

Maybe all his little gestures are nothing more than friendly, charitable acts. Simply one friend helping another when she's down on her luck.

Paige was right—one of us *is* in denial. And it's not my hunky NFL superstar roommate.

I spend the rest of the afternoon catching up on research and trying not to be obsessive about checking my phone for Griffin's reactions to my story. I even update my résumé and LinkedIn profile before I deep dive into a search of small, liberal arts colleges in Florida.

Now that Jack and I are no longer together, I don't know that I even want to stay in Memphis. Sure, I've made a few friends, but are they enough to keep me here?

It's best that I have a backup plan.

Since I had a big lunch, I make myself a bowl of cereal for dinner, being sure to snap a picture of the colorful, sugary pieces floating in the pristine milk and send it to Griffin.

> You're a terrible influence. Cereal for dinner.

My phone chimes a few bites later.

Griffin

> Niiiiice. Dinner of champions.

Still nothing about my book. I'm dying to know what he thinks. Maybe he started reading it and gave up after only a few paragraphs. Ugh.

I'm left to stew in my insecurities until bedtime. It isn't until I'm brushing my teeth that my phone buzzes on the bedside table. I force myself to finish the rest of my nighttime routine and get comfortable in bed, Barnaby tucked to my chest, before I let myself reach for it.

His first text is a selfie. In it, he's shirtless, leaning against the headboard in his hotel room. The picture doesn't show anything below his collarbone, but the glimpse of dark hair and chiseled pecs sends heat creeping through me, forcing me to shove the thick comforter down to my waist. His blue-gray eyes are narrowed, his dark brows drawn close, and short stubble highlights the smirk playing on his lips.

The next text is a single word.

Griffin

> Professor.

A thrill zips down my spine.

Griffin

> This Gethin character. He's my favorite.

I huff a laugh. Of course he's a fan of the brooding, mysterious knight.

Griffin

> Need I point out that Gethin and Griffin are VERY similar names? The similarities don't stop there either. We're both dark-haired and devastatingly handsome.

> The name literally translates to 'dark and swarthy' [eye roll emoji]

> You and your name translations. What does Griffin mean, I wonder?

> Pain in the ass.

> You wound me, Hill. I've already looked it up. Feel free to call me Lord or Prince anytime.

That one pulls a snort-laugh from me. Sitting up, I type my response.

> Hill, huh? I think I'll stick with Racy for you.

Griffin

If you must, not-a-hill. Don't worry, I won't tell anyone that I'm the inspiration for your hot, charming, badass warrior knight.

I started writing that before I met you, so…

Feel free to reveal my contributions in the acknowledgments. You know, when this becomes a real book. Because it's really fucking good, Brynn.

My heart pangs, and the phone screen blurs in front of me. I have to blink several times to make out his next message.

Griffin

I mean it. It's so damn fun and exciting. It's got high-stakes adventure, cool-ass dragons, and a touch of romance. I couldn't put it down. Beau had to drag me from my seat on the plane when we landed. I had just gotten to the part where Eleri makes the deal with Aethon for the sword, and I didn't want to stop. I love it. Please keep going.

Really?!?! I'm so happy you like it! [smiling face emoji]

For real. I made it to their first kiss scene after dinner, but stopped because my head is killing me. I'll get back into it tomorrow on the ride home.

Griff! Why are you texting me if you feel bad? Go to sleep. Hope you feel better when you wake up.

No worries. I sometimes get stress headaches the night before big games. I'll rally.

You're going to kick ass, Lord and Prince of Football. Sweet dreams.

Putting Lord and Prince of Football on all my social media. Be good, professor. See you tomorrow night.

I return my phone to the charging pad on the table and snuggle into my pillow. With a smile and Barnaby's soft, worn wings between my fingers, soothing me, I drift off.

Turns out, denial is a powerful sedative.

Chapter Ten

Brynn

The following morning, I let myself luxuriate in bed longer than usual. Enjoying the quiet, I sink deeper into the warmth of the bedcovers and think back to the discovery I made last Sunday when Griff was in New York:

Mug in hand, I opened the fridge to grab the coffee creamer. Instead, I froze at the sight of a tiny orange dragon perched on the shelf next to the bottle. Plastic and no taller than my pinkie. Another one, blue this time, was waiting for me on top of the spoons in the silverware drawer.

I've found twenty more hidden around the apartment in the last week—nestled on my candle, by my toothbrush holder, on top of the TV remote. He even hid one inside one of the tennis shoes I leave by the back door in case of dash-to-the-car emergencies.

When I brought them up, he shrugged and said, "Huh. Dragon invasion. Weird."

My prankster roommate and I have settled into a routine over the past couple of weeks. On Mondays, Wednesdays, and Fridays, he's out the door before my alarm goes off. Those are my late days on campus. I have classes until five, and then I usually swim a few laps at the natatorium before I return home. After I shower away the chlorine, we chat in the kitchen. His dinner is always grilled chicken or fish with broccoli and a protein shake from some super healthy delivery service. Since I have early classes on Tuesdays and Thursdays, we meet up over breakfast, where he downs a massive bowl of cereal while I inhale my coffee.

Tuesday afternoons, of course, are still reserved for our Memphis Magic meet-ups.

Since Griffin is out of town this weekend, I shower and get dressed, then stroll to the nearest coffee shop, enjoying the brisk mid-October morning. My stomach does a little flip when I notice the Blues jerseys in line ahead of me. But when I overhear their conversation, my heart clambers up my throat.

"That's what SNN reported this morning. Lacey is questionable for today's game. Mundy said it would be a game-time decision."

Dread hits me so violently I have to suck in a breath. Is this because of the headache? Has it gotten that much worse? Knowing Griffin, it would take something awful to force him to sit out a game. He talks about football like it's a cherished family member. He's hinted to me about how low he sank when the Tors released him and he thought his career was over.

"Ma'am, do you know what you want?" The barista's squeaky voice pulls me from my fretting. So lost in my worries for my friend, I didn't even realize the men in front of me had placed their orders. I consider forgoing an order altogether so I can rush home and switch on a sports channel, but the purple-haired teenager's put-out expression keeps me on course.

"A latte and a muffin, please."

She asks me so many questions about my drink order, I'm not even sure what I'll get at the pickup counter. But as soon as I've got the hot cup and crinkly bag in hand, I dash back to the apartment.

Television tuned to the Sports Now Network, I pace in front of it, clutching my latte. The anchors discuss every other team playing today in excruciating detail, breaking away to on-field reporters in every city in America *except* the one I'm invested in.

Finally—*finally*—the anchors highlight the Memphis-Washington game. They cut away to a blonde in a fitted navy blazer who's standing on the sidelines of an empty field. I pull up short and narrow my eyes at the screen.

It's Andrea/Andi, the woman Jack was *professionally* flirting with last month.

"Lacey's status remains a game-time decision. The seven-time Pro Bowler is suffering from a flu-like illness, and team sources report that if he does take the field, he will receive IV fluids to prevent dehydration. Lacey has been an integral component of the Blues' offense this season, scoring three touchdowns in the last four games. He's become one of Dempsey's favorite targets. It'll be interesting to see how Coach Mundy and offensive coordinator Rasheed Dobbins adjust their schemes if Lacey is unable to play."

Flu-like illness. Okay, that's better than an injury. But it's going to kill Griff if he can't play today.

The Blues' game is scheduled for the afternoon, so I distract myself with laundry and essay grading until kickoff.

At exactly three-thirty, I switch to the channel airing the game and freeze when the camera pans the Blues' sideline and I catch a glimpse of number 89.

He's hunched over on the bench, head in hands, and from what I can see of him, he's pale as a ghost. But he's toughing it out for his team. I fall a little bit in love with him for being so resilient.

One of the commentators, not Andrea/Andi, to my delight, gives an update. "As for the Blues' veteran tight end, it's been reported that Lacey has been suffering from flu-like symptoms since early this morning. Let's get an update from Candace, who's on the Blues' sideline."

"That's right, Tom," the woman who must be Candace says. Her dark hair is pulled back, and she's dressed in a blue professional-looking wrap dress. "It's been reported that Lacey turned in early last night, complaining of a headache, and woke sometime before dawn with a fever, chills, and nausea. As a precaution, the team isolated him at the hotel, and he was driven separately to the stadium rather than arriving on the team bus. Coach Mundy told us before kickoff that he left the decision to sit out or play up to the two-time Super Bowl champ, and when asked about Lacey's answer, he laughed and said, quote, 'That kid's got no quit. He demanded he be allowed to suit up and claimed that if Jordan could do it in the '97 NBA finals, he could darn well be there for his team today.' Now let's send it over to Steve, who has the latest about Washington's game plan for today."

Watching the game is pure agony, not because I'm not a sports girlie, but because my friend is suffering through it. Even though he remains on the sideline for most of the plays, it's evident that football is in Griffin's blood. Every time he steps on the turf, he gives everything he can. The few times the camera zooms in on him, his blanched face reflects true grit and determination. He makes a few key catches, and as soon as the whistle signals a play is dead, he jogs over to the bench and collapses. Most of the team steers clear and gives him space, but Beau and the other tight end, Devon, check on him once or twice and smack his pads when they walk away.

Me? I'm a ball of emotion the entire three hours. Proud one moment, frustrated the next—with Griffin, for insisting on putting his body through this, and with the coaching staff for allowing him to.

Paige sends me a two-word text at halftime that makes my eyes leak:

> You okay?

I want to ask her how she does it, how she watches Beau put himself in harm's way week after week, knowing there's a chance one play-gone-wrong could change their lives. Before I can, misery scorches my stomach. Because Griffin isn't mine to worry about in the way Paige worries for her fiancé.

Rather than spill my secret fears and longings to my friend via text, I send her the most succinct, honest response I can:

> I'll be okay when I know he's okay.

After the game, I spring into preparation mode. Griffin's fridge is already stocked with electrolyte-dense sports drinks, but I make a quick grocery run to pick up saltine crackers and applesauce. Then I do a Google search for the best chicken noodle soup in the city and place online orders at the top three results. Lord knows, if I attempt to make it myself, it would probably make him sicker. Back at the apartment, I change the sheets on his bed—and find a tiny purple dragon snuggled between the clean towels in the linen closet—even though his housekeeper changes them every Thursday. Fresh sheets never fail to help me feel like a new person when I'm sick.

I'm in the middle of attempting to write a battle scene in my dragon story when my phone lights up. My pulse takes off at the sight of Griffin's name. It's after ten, so the team's plane must've landed.

"Hello?" I press a hand on my chest and will my heart to settle.

"Brynn? This is Beau." The quarterback's slow drawl does nothing to calm my frazzled nerves. "Listen," he says, "we just landed, but he's wiped. I'm gonna drive him home. We'll worry about getting his truck tomorrow. Just wanted to confirm you were home so he's not alone."

"Yes." My voice is frantic, so I force a calming breath into my lungs. "Yeah, I'm here. Thank you so much for giving him a ride."

"Sure thing. He got more fluids on the way back, but the team docs want him to go heavy on liquids for the next day or so. And Coach has insisted that he not show up for practice tomorrow."

"Oh, that's good. I'll keep him home."

"Good luck with that." He chuckles. "We'll see you in a few. I'll text when I get there."

"Okay. Thanks, Beau."

I'm in danger of wearing a path in the plush rug by the time his text comes through. I rush downstairs and slip into my old sneakers—no dragon this time—and step out into the chilly darkness to meet the guys.

When Griffin opens the passenger door, Beau leans across the center console and eyes me. "He hasn't puked for a couple hours, so that's a good sign."

"Thanks, Cap," my roommate grumbles. He makes slow movements as he exits the SUV.

Once he has his legs under him, I swoop in to offer as much support as I can. With one arm wrapped around his waist, I shoulder his leather duffel bag with my free hand and give Beau a quick wave.

"Professor, I'm gonna crush you." His voice is raspier than usual.

"I'm tougher than I look."

"Mmm." He leans into me a fraction more, but he's still keeping most of his weight off me. "Never doubted it."

We make our way into the building and begin a slow trudge up the stairs. "You're burning up, mister." The heat radiating from his body scorches my arm through his damp T-shirt. "When was the last time you took something for the fever?"

His response is incoherent. Rather than try to decipher it, I decide that if he's still this warm, it won't hurt him to have another dose.

We make our way into his bedroom, where he plops down on the side of the bed and rests his elbows on his knees so he can brace his head with his hands. "Head hurts so damn bad."

"Let me get you something for that. Be right back."

I sprint into the kitchen, where I've left a new bottle of Motrin on the counter. When I return to his bedroom, I fumble the huge tumbler of ice water, almost spilling the entire thing.

Because Griffin Lacey is standing before me *shirtless*.

My mouth goes so dry, I consider taking a huge swallow of the water that's still left in the cup.

Oh my God. He's glorious. Even better than my wildest fantasies have imagined for the last month. And believe me, they've been vivid.

This reality—in living color, close enough to touch—is magnificent. I soak up every detail—every dip, curve, and muscle—until I'm sure I could sketch him from memory if I had even one ounce of drawing talent. The way his back muscles bunch and stretch as he twists to throw his shirt across the room. The smattering of dark hair on his chest, those hard pectorals that beg me to rake my nails over them. His abs, so precise in their arrangement, as if they were stacked by the most meticulous bricklayer. And the dark trail of hair beneath his navel.

Holy hell.

When Griffin reaches for the waistband of his joggers, I waver between letting this play out or having the self-control to stop it. He hooks a thumb in the elastic, and when he drags it downward, I realize he's got a hold of both joggers *and* underwear.

"Griff!"

He startles when I shout his name. It's clear that, in his fevered haze, he didn't realize I was standing here.

"Wh-what are you doing?"

Geez, what a dumb question, Brynn.

"Sorry. I'm so goddamn hot." He thumbs his waistband again, and this time he pushes only the joggers down his thick, sturdy thighs. He toes them off both ankles and sinks back down on the side of the bed.

All the while, his colorful boxer briefs do little to hide his assets—including an impressive bulge—from my hungry eyes.

"Is that Tony the Tiger underwear?"

He glances down and nods. "They're *grrreat*." He gives me a cheeky wink.

This man. Flirting even while he's sick as a dog.

My skin heats until it's as warm as his. "You did not just say that."

"I did. And if you like these," he mutters with a sloppy wave of his hand, "there are a variety of equally enticing pairs in one of those drawers."

"Okay, I'll bite."

He wags his brows, the move making me desperately wish I could pause this scene and reverse it like some cheesy nineties sitcom.

"I *mean*," I emphasize, "that I'll *ask* you about them. Are you a closet wacky-underwear collector?"

"Sorta." He lowers to the mattress with his eyes closed. "My brothers and I put them in each other's Christmas stockings. Been doing it since we got our first summer jobs and had all that minimum-wage cash burning holes in our pockets."

He swings his strong legs up onto the mattress, and as his weight sinks into it, he lets out a long sigh. With effort, I wrestle the ridiculously high thread count sheets and thick hunter-green comforter out from under him and then over his prone body. He pats the side of the bed in invitation, but his eyes remain closed, so I fiddle with the remote to dim the pendant light that hangs over the table.

"Here." I perch on the edge of the mattress. "Take these." He takes the two tablets from me and props himself up on an elbow so he can swallow them with a chug of water.

"You're an excellent nurse, professor."

The low gravel in his voice sends a shiver down my spine. I can't help but reach for him, to smooth my fingers along his brow. He sighs and sags further into the pillow as I continue the soft passes over his heated skin.

"I'll leave this water on the table. You need to stay hydrated," I whisper as I tuck my hand into my lap.

His dark lashes flutter, and then those piercing blue-gray eyes focus on me. Despite how dim the room is, Griffin catalogs every inch of my face, his scrutiny so intense I wonder if I'm the one with a fever. But his lids are heavy, and soon, he's blinking to fight the sleep that wants to take him under. When one of his hands drifts up and tenderly cups my cheek, my breath catches.

"So fucking pretty."

I force a swallow and fight the urge to nuzzle into his wide, callused hand. I do, however, allow myself to revel in the feel of his skin against mine. Only a heartbeat later, though, his hand drops away and his lids sweep closed for good. When his lips part and he lets out a soft snore, I ease off the bed, chest aching.

I gather his discarded clothes, then I flip off the lamp and carry my lovesick heart to my own bed.

Monday morning arrives, gray and dreary, with a deluge of rain. The perfect match for my mood. I rush through my daily routine and snap my laptop open on the bar in the kitchen with seconds to spare.

The moment the app loads and I click the tab to allow video, my parents' smiling faces fill the screen.

"Moonbeam!" Dad bellows. "Why is it so dark in there?" He leans closer and squints at the screen, adjusting his wire-framed glasses.

"Hey." I bite my lower lip to keep it from trembling. "Just a gray, rainy day in Memphis. How's Florida?"

My mother blows a kiss at the screen. "Oh, it's seventy-two and sunny, love." She, too, leans closer, her short, tight curls bouncing as she tilts her head back and forth. "Your aura is murky today. Are you neglecting your self-love?"

"Mom." Stomach sinking, I glance over my shoulder in the direction of Griffin's bedroom.

Blessedly, I've yet to hear a peep from him. He's usually out of the apartment when I catch up with my parents during our weekly Zoom calls. I'd die of mortification if he overheard my mother ask me if I'm masturbating regularly. It's bad enough that she talks so freely about sex in regard to me while in front of my dad, but I learned a long time ago that I can't control the things that come out of Celeste Nelson's mouth.

I think both of my parents would drop dead from shock if I confessed that I've become a regular practitioner of self-love since I moved into Griffin Lacey's guestroom.

The second I open my mouth to assure her that my aura is fine, it becomes clear that the universe hates me. Because the door to the laundry room opens, and out walks the star of my self-love fantasies.

He's dressed in a Blues T-shirt and gray basketball shorts, looking fresh as a daisy, like he didn't require a chauffeur and multiple bags of IV fluids yesterday. The skin above his beard turns a suspicious shade of pink when he catches sight of me at the bar. When the reason hits me, I'm certain I *will* die of mortification on this dismal Monday morning.

Because my roommate just stepped out of the laundry room. A place he never sets foot in unless he's dropping his bag of laundry for his housekeeper to handle. The place where I hung several delicates to dry overnight.

Oh, God. Griffin Lacey has seen my lacy undergarments.

Breaths stuttering, I manage to say, "Wh-what are you doing out of bed?"

Instantly, he's cool and composed. "Who were you talking to?"

"You should be resting."

"I'm feeling better. Almost 100 percent, so I thought I'd head in for the second half of practice."

"No, your coach wants you to stay home and rest." I cringe. I don't want to mother him, but it's apparent that someone has to.

My mom's dulcet voice startles us from our standoff. "Yoo-hoo. Is that your new roomie, Moonbeam?"

Griffin's smile stretches wide as he steps closer and mouths the nickname over my laptop.

I roll my eyes and give in. There's no stopping this train wreck now.

"Professor, are these your folks?" Without waiting for a response, he rounds the bar and bends low, coming face to face with my cheerful parents. "Mr. and Mrs. Nelson, it's lovely to meet y'all." His freshly showered scent invades my nostrils as his head appears next to mine in the corner of the screen.

"Oh. Well. Oh my." My sixty-six-year-old mother fans herself dramatically.

My father looks on, oblivious.

With a roll of my eyes, I sigh. "Mom."

"Moonbeam, I *like* this one." She says it as if Griffin can't hear her every word. "His aura is strong and healthy. Virile."

"Mom."

"Yes. This one will keep you satisfied, love. In bed and out of it." She gives my father a saucy wink.

He only nods and beams into the camera, not the least bit uncomfortable with the conversation.

Here lies Brynn Nelson. Cause of death? Mortification.

"Mother. It's not—we're not." I huff out my frustration, then take a calming breath. "We're friends, so there's no need to assess our compatibility in *that* department."

"But your last relationship was so unfulfilling, sexually *and* emotionally—"

"*Mom.*"

My sharp tone gets her attention. She straightens the shoulders of her striped caftan with her bejeweled fingers, and though her eyes still twinkle, she mimes zipping her lips.

"Let's move on." I affix a terrible facsimile of a smile to my face and cut my eyes over to the man who's sporting the smuggest smirk.

"Did you hear that, professor? I've got a good aura."

My heart lurches. "I heard."

My mother's bracelets jangle as she smacks my father's arm. "Aren't they so cute, Har?"

I pinch the bridge of my nose.

"Hell of a game you guys played yesterday." My father pushes up his glasses and leans in close, blocking our view of Mom.

"Thanks, Mr. Nelson. Wasn't my best game, but we pulled out the W."

"There's no need for that Mr. and Mrs. nonsense, love. Call us Celeste and Hardy."

"Will do," Griffin tells them. "All right, Celeste and Hardy. I'm going to make myself scarce so you can talk to your brilliant daughter." He ruffles my hair like I'm a precocious kid, but when he rises to his full height, his skin blanches, going pale like it was yesterday, and his body sways, forcing him to grab the edge of the bar to stay upright.

"Whoa. Okay." I grasp his arm, noticing just how clammy his skin still is. "See? I told you that you should be resting."

"Yes, boss." Ever the charmer, he winks at my parents, who are both staring at the screen with concern lining their faces.

"Mom. Dad. Can I call y'all later? I need to get this stubborn ass back to bed."

"Of course, Moonbeam. Griffin, you let our girl take care of you, you hear? You'll need all your strength for when you two—"

"Celeste," my father says, blessedly cutting her off. "Let the kids be."

"Right. Bye, loves!" She blows another kiss at the camera. As she angles forward to shut down their video, Griffin and I get an unexpected peek-a-boo of her suntanned cleavage.

When the video disconnects, I lower my head and give it a shake. "My parents, ladies and gentlemen."

"Big fan of 'em already." He gives me a smile that doesn't reach his eyes. He's fading fast.

We adopt our positions from last night, my arm around his waist and his slung over my shoulders, and shuffle to his bedroom.

"One hundred percent, my ass. Stay put in this bed, mister. I'll warm up a bowl of soup before I leave for class. No getting up except to use the bathroom."

"Yes, ma'am."

The exhaustion working its way back into his face has my stomach knotting. Will he be okay here alone all day?

"Maybe I can get someone to cover for me—"

With a slow shake of his head—and a grimace—he gives my shoulder a squeeze. "Brynn. No. Go inspire young minds. I'll be fine."

He climbs into bed without any prompting, and I pull the covers up to his chin, then straighten the blanket, mothering again.

Rather than give me a hard time about being bossy, he takes my hand. "Thank you for taking care of me, even if I'm a stubborn ass."

"You're welcome." I pat his chest twice and start for the door.

"Hey, professor."

I pause at the threshold and glance over my shoulder. "Did you or did you not volunteer to bite me last night?"

CHAPTER ELEVEN

BRYNN

The instant I step into his dark bedroom, I realize I've made a colossal mistake.

The sounds coming from behind the half-open bathroom door should be enough to send me scurrying to my room and locking myself in, then spending the night reading something virtuous. Like *Anne of Green Gables*. Or my well-loved, brittle copy of *The Secret Garden*.

Because mixed with the calming white noise of the shower spray are *other* sounds...deep, guttural, manly sounds. Sounds that make me squeeze my thighs together and send my pulse racing.

Rather than bolt, I stand stock still, my toes digging into the plush tan rug, and listen to my roommate practice his own self-love. Mom would give him a gold star.

Clutching the folded T-shirt and joggers that somehow got mixed up in my laundry last weekend, I inch closer to his bed. I'm only venturing into Griffin's room to return his clean clothing. That's it. When my knees hit the end of his bed, I lay the pile on the plush comforter.

But I don't leave.

Instead, I approach the bathroom door, playing a very danger-ous game. If he catches me perving on him, I'll have to move out.

Not only out of this apartment, but out of the whole dang state. My dignity would demand it.

The threat isn't enough to stop me. Swallowing my worries, I step closer. Closer. So close, the steam from the shower caresses my skin. I keep my eyes downcast, afraid of being discovered, but when another low grunt reaches my ears, I'm powerless to stop myself from seeking more.

The fog on the glass doors hides most of him, sending a fissure of disappointment through my gut. All I can see are his wide shoulder blades and dark head, which is bent forward under the spray of the shower. One hand is visible, too, where it's braced on the wall next to the round dial, and his other hand...

It's hidden from view, but the rhythm with which his arm moves is unmistakable. I spy, mesmerized, as his grunts and groans become more frequent. Tingling sensations flood my body and my panties go damp while my heart pounds so hard it's a drumbeat in my ears.

God, he's getting close. His growls and moans are frantic now.

I clench my fists and force myself to breathe evenly. How easy it would be to slip my hand inside my shorts and find the pleasure he's unaware he's prompted me to chase.

When he reaches the peak, my knees weaken, but then a growly "Fuck, Brynn" escapes his lips, and my spine snaps straight.

Holy hell. Did my friend-turned-roommate-turned-unrequited crush growl *my* name when he climaxed? Is there another Brynn in his life I'm unaware of? Was he thinking of me the whole time he was jerking off?

All these questions, and more, rush through my mind as I sprint for the door, across the living room, and up the stairs to my bedroom. I don't even attempt to keep my mad dash quiet, hoping like hell he can't hear me over the sound of the shower. Once inside, I lock my door and fall back against it, chest heaving.

I clamp a palm over my lips to quell the giggle that bubbles up from my chest, while my lashes do battle with the sudden wetness that stings my eyes. A maelstrom of emotions surges, threatening to pull me into hysteria—a mixture of confusion, lust, pride, longing, doubt, amazement, and hope. Hope, most of all.

So much damn hope that the desire I've been harboring isn't one-sided.

Somehow, I lull myself into a deep slumber a couple of hours later. It takes *two* gold-star sessions to accomplish that feat, but I awake clear-eyed and determined.

It's time to have a real conversation about this undeniable chemistry and the flirty touches and the almost-kiss. (But not about the shower thing, because I might combust.) Because I need answers. I hate this treading water status our relationship is in currently.

I'm going to do it. This morning, before I lose my nerve. Even though he has a game in a few hours—one he insists I attend—I can't go one more day without bringing up the eight-hundred-pound gorilla that's become something of a third roommate.

Confronting him is a huge risk. There's no guarantee he wants anything more than friendship. But I've wasted five years of my life already because I was too scared to take a leap and put myself first.

Maybe those "thirty and thriving" magazine articles I've always dismissed are right. Maybe this *is* the age of self-awareness. They were spot-on about the unexplained phantom back pains and more frequent bouts of acid reflux.

Resolute, I run through opening-line options in my head as I shower. When I have a clear direction, I shut off the water and stand in the stall to center myself, calm my breathing, and whisper a pep talk into the steamy air. "You got this, Brynn."

As I open the shower door and reach for my towel, the door to the bathroom bangs open, startling me so badly I jump and nearly slip on the wet tile. At the sight of a shocked man in the doorframe, I shriek.

"Oh God, I'm so sorry." He covers his eyes and flops back into the hallway, his back bouncing off my closed bedroom door.

"Who are you?" I yell as I scramble to wrap the towel around my dripping torso.

Blood rushes in my ears so fiercely I almost don't hear Griffin shouting my name from below or the pounding footsteps on the stairs. As he appears, I blink to clear my sudden double vision.

Because there are *two* Griffins standing in the hallway. There's *my* Griffin, clothed in shorts and a T-shirt that strains against the rapid rise and fall of his chest. Then there's the intruder, wearing only a pair of black joggers slung low on his hips. His sculpted chest and every inch of his arms down to his wrists are covered in colorful tattoos.

As I blink again, the differences between the two men become more distinct. Tattoo guy is a couple of inches shorter, and his hair—the same dark brown–black as Griffin's—is long enough to curl at his nape rather than buzzed like Griffin's. And his cheeks are covered in a light stubble, unlike the short beard my roommate has.

"Tucker, what the fuck?"

Ah. I take in a deep breath for the first time since the door flew open. Now the pieces slot into place. This tattooed intruder is Griffin's younger brother.

To his credit, the younger Lacey keeps his hand over his eyes as he says, "Shit, I'm so sorry, naked stranger. I had no idea someone was up here."

"Why are *you* up here?" Griffin barks, crossing his arms.

Hand still in place, Tucker clears his throat. "I crashed here last night. Came over so Lux could put some finishing touches on my sleeve. After, we went down to Beale. I was too shit-faced to drive home. Didn't want to wake you, since you have a game today, so he used his spare key to let me in. I was asleep the second my head hit the couch. That thing is hella comfy, by the way."

With a glower, Griffin swats his brother's arm. "Uncover your eyes, dumbass. She's wearing a towel. And you couldn't bother to send a fucking text to let me know you were in town?"

Tucker slaps a hand to his heart. "Sorry, it slipped my mind. I didn't even head this way until after nine." He gives me a little wave, and his eyes—the exact shade as his brother's—crinkle in the corners. Then he hits me with a dazzling Lacey smile. "Hey, I'm Tucker."

His charming swagger is so like his brother's, but there's a boyishness about him that Griffin lacks.

I pull my dripping hair over one shoulder and clasp the towel tighter across my chest. "Brynn."

The three of us stare in awkward silence. Griffin's gaze drifts down to my chest and lingers, his Adam's apple bobbing. When he looks away, catching his brother doing the same, he smacks him on the back of the head. "Quit looking at her."

"Shit. Sorry." With his hands in the air, Tucker tips his head back and groans. "I'm so hungover. Make me breakfast before I die, Griff."

His brother huffs, though it's a mostly good-natured sound. "Fine. But put on a fucking shirt."

Tucker nods, then he blinks at me. "Brynn. It's nice to meet you. Sorry about the naked stuff." The way his cheeks go pink and the sheepish smile that tips his lips only make him more adorable.

"Oh." A nervous laugh escapes me as cool air hits my skin, causing me to shiver. "Um, yeah, no worries. I guess."

Griff's eyes flash a stormy gray as his brother walks away. "Seems shower privacy is hard to come by in this apartment." With a quirk of his lips, he's gone.

I slam my eyes closed, and the fire of a thousand suns burns me from within.

Holy hell, he knows.

Yep, death by mortification.

Oh God, I'll never admire his gorgeous eyes again. And forget that relationship conversation I have all worked out in my head. Maybe I should feign an illness to skip the game. Go full stealth-mode. He'll come home to find I've moved out like a thief in the night.

When I finally coax myself back to reality, Tucker's voice echoes in the stairwell. "I'm telling Mom you're living with a woman." His statement is followed by a breathy *oomph*—no doubt a result of his brother's physical response.

From below, Griffin's deep baritone commands, "Join us for breakfast, Brynn."

So much for my plan to avoid him at all costs.

I go through the motions of blow drying and styling my hair, applying makeup, and dressing like a dead woman walking, a deep sense of dread weighing down my limbs. With a fortifying breath, I descend the stairs, ready to face my fate. But when I make it to the main floor, the sight of a two-time world champion dishing scrambled eggs onto his younger brother's plate softens every tense muscle in my body.

"Scrambled okay, professor?"

Nodding, I take the stool next to a still-shirtless Tucker.

"You're a professor?" the younger Lacey asks through a mouthful of eggs.

Griffin answers for me. "She's working on her doctorate."

"Cool." His brother nods.

We eat in silence—Tucker and me at the bar, and my roommate propped against the counter, one ankle crossed over the other. He doesn't take his eyes off me as he scoops forkfuls of eggs into his mouth. His intense scrutiny makes me twitchy.

"You got a tattoo last night?" I study the intricate shapes and patterns etched into Tucker's skin. There are so many colorful details, it's hard to decide where to focus first.

"Yeah, had this bottom part of my sleeve finished." He holds up his right arm where what looks like a strip of plastic wrap circles his wrist. I survey the design beneath it, then work my way farther up Tucker's arm to the wing that's inked onto his shoulder and left pec.

The sound of a plate clattering to the granite countertop startles me, and I spin to face my roommate.

Griffin storms into the living room and snags the T-shirt that's crumpled in a chair. He balls it up and chucks it at his brother's face. "Shirt, dickwad."

"All right, asshole."

A giggle breaks free. "Do all siblings call each other such endearing names?" I turn to Tucker. "I'm an only child, so I have no experience in this department."

Shrugging, he gives his brother a fond smile. "Shaw's way worse than we are. I can't remember the last time he called me by my given name."

"True." Griffin rubs a hand along his short beard and checks his watch. "I've got to get changed. Tuck, take care of the dishes." He points at his brother. "And don't bug her."

Dutifully, Tucker salutes his brother. Then he hops up from the stool. As he rinses the dishes and loads them in the dishwasher, he tilts his head and asks, "So what's with that?"

The white board on the pantry door was probably hung to be used for grocery lists or reminders, but Griff and I have given it a new role.

"Crossword clues," I explain. "We leave clues and draw the empty boxes for one another's guess. We build off each other's words until we run out of space, then we start again."

I came up with the idea after I discovered the tiny dragons all over the apartment. My first clue—*we've been invaded*—was written underneath a horizontal chain of seven empty boxes. He got the answer correct on his first guess, then drew a vertical grid that contained the *R* from *dragons* and wrote *you are not a fan* as his clue. The answer? *Gherkins.*

Tucker scoffs, but there's affection in the sound. "Griff and those damn puzzles." When he's loaded the last plate into the machine, he closes the door and uses a dish towel to wipe the counter around the sink. "He got hooked in college. Mom picked up a book of them while she was shopping for his favorite snacks and put it in a care package."

The kitchen is spotless when Griffin emerges from his bedroom looking like a GQ model. He's wearing gray dress slacks that hug every muscle so perfectly that I mentally add to the tally of cookie bouquets I'll send the tailor if I ever discover their identity. On top, he's layered a dress shirt in the lightest baby blue under a fitted sport coat a few shades darker. And to top it off, there's a navy and white polka dot pocket square peeking out.

Tucker wolf whistles, garnering an eye roll from his older brother.

Slipping his phone into his inside breast pocket, Griff considers me. "I have something for you in the truck, professor. Walk down with me?"

I gulp down my nerves and slide off the stool, then I follow him out without a word. The entire trip downstairs, I'm convinced he's going to ask me to move out. He probably just doesn't want to do it in front of Tucker. Flames of discomfort burn my insides so hot that even the crisp late-October air is no match. As we stop next to the silver Ram, I square my shoulders, preparing for his censure.

When he withdraws a blue gift bag from the back seat—one that reads *Hound Town Merch* and is printed with a picture of King, the Blues' mascot—my stomach knots in confusion. He dips his chin in encouragement, his expression easy rather than hard, so I reach inside and pull out a soft navy T-shirt.

"I know you don't wear jerseys, but I can't let you go to a Blues game without the proper attire."

"Th-thank you." I hug the shirt against my chest and smile up at him.

His eyes are exceptionally blue today.

◆◆◆

Having Tucker Lacey as my guide is a lot like being escorted by a rambunctious puppy.

"Ooh, Brynn, hold up. We need nachos."

I shift the soft pretzel, soda, and box of popcorn I've been juggling into one arm to take the proffered tray of pulled pork nachos. Tucker's arms are laden with hot dogs, a couple of cans of beer, and a personal pizza, along with the funnel cake he insists we'll share.

I'm so focused on making sure none of these snacks splatter on the concrete that I don't have a real chance to freak out about meeting Griffin's family for the first time.

Only when Tucker stops at a door that displays a *Reserved* sign do my scrambled eggs threaten to reappear.

When we arrived at the stadium, I promised Tucker that I'd be fine to find Paige and the other WAGs on my own, but the same bottom-lip pout he used on his brother this morning had me folding like tissue paper.

It's ridiculous to be so nervous about meeting the Laceys, yet here I am. I'm desperate for his people to like me, to want to *know* me. But my anxiety about meeting his family is doubled when Griffin isn't here to act as my security blanket.

The security guard at the door slaps Tucker on the back. "Tuck, good to see you. Hope your big bro kicks some Devil ass today." Then he eyes me, one brow lifted. "Who's this?"

"She's with us," Tucker says, adjusting the trays in his arms. "Griff's cleared it with the team. You should have her credentials."

The guard yanks his phone from his pocket and consults it. "Ah, Ms. Nelson. You've been added to the permanent guest list for Mr. Lacey's suite. Hope you enjoy the game."

Holding my breath, I turn to Tucker for an explanation, but he's already pushing the door open with his foot.

While he greets his family and passes out snacks, I stand back and take in the details of the suite. Two rows of eight stadium seats face a huge window that overlooks the field. Directly behind the seating area is a long, narrow wooden bar with a row of navy leather stools tucked underneath. Three round pub tables fill the main space and are covered with drinks, food, purses, and phones.

"Brynn, come meet everyone." The youngest Lacey brother has already relieved himself of his snacks and takes mine from me as well.

When he steps away, I'm met with several pairs of curious eyes.

"These are my parents, Donna and Fred."

Both Lacey parents wear number 89 jerseys and warm smiles. Donna is my height and curvy, with a white-blond bob, while Fred has a silver-gray goatee that matches his hair.

"This," Tucker continues, "is Shaw, the oldest."

A striking, but wary, pair of ocean-blue eyes study me as he gives me a subtle chin dip. He's as handsome as his brothers, and even though he's the shortest of the three, he still stands inches taller than everyone else in the room, save for Tucker. His hair is several shades lighter, too; the medium-brown strands are cut in a length somewhere between Griffin's buzz cut and Tucker's longer locks.

"Brynn, so glad you could join us today." A lanky older woman wraps my hand in a solid shake. With one look at her features, I can tell she's related to Donna, though she's leaner and her shoulder-length hair is cinnamon colored, streaked with silver. "I'm Aunt Dot or Dottie—I'll answer to either one. And this is Griff's cousin, Trixie."

A petite redhead with spunky pigtails sidles up. "She'll answer to anything except her real name," she says, her tone all sass. "Isn't that right, *Dorothea*?"

Dot gives her daughter a playful pinch. As she does, I get a glimpse of an insulin pump on the back of the younger woman's arm.

"Respect your elders, *Beatrice*," Tucker taunts.

With a scrunch of her nose, Trixie grumbles something unintelligible.

A super cute dark-blond guy appears at her side and drapes his arm across her shoulders.

Tucker introduces him next. "This is my best friend, Cam."

The hazel-eyed man salutes me as Trixie attempts to shrug him off.

"We call him the fourth Lacey," Donna explains, her smile warm. "He and Tuck have been close since kindergarten."

"And they still *act* like kindergarteners." Dipping low, Trixie spins away from Cam.

Tucker scoffs, "Whatever, Trix," right as Cam states, "We're not the ones with a record, Silly Rabbit."

Waving at them dismissively, Trixie grasps my hand and tugs me toward the food. "Let's grab a snack before these vultures eat it all, then you can tell me about how you met Griff."

I sit between Trixie and Tucker during the first half, and both prove to be valuable commentators. Trixie dishes on the personal lives of some of the players and spills a little about what Griffin was like growing up. Tucker explains the nuances of the game and answers all my sports-ignorant questions. I get caught up in the excitement that rolls through the stadium every time the Blues make an impressive play. By the end of the second quarter, I'm so invested in the game, I jump out of my seat without waiting for clues from those around me and cheer along with Griffin's family when he scores a touchdown that ties the score.

At halftime, Paige texts *where are you?* Before I can answer, she's skipping down the steps to join me in the front row of the suite. After quick hellos, the Laceys gather at the tables or dash off to get more food, giving me and my friend some privacy.

"Griff's having a great game. Five catches and a TD." Twisting a strand of her honey-blond hair, she leans in close. "And it looks like your future in-laws have already welcomed you into the fold."

"Paige." With my heart in my throat, I peek behind us to ensure she wasn't overheard. "No more talk like that, please." I debate whether to share my shower spying session from the previous night, but since his mother is standing a few feet away, I decide to save it for another time.

"Okay, okay." She raises her hands. "But I told you—my gut is scarily accurate about these things."

She stays and watches the third quarter with us, giving my hand a comforting squeeze when Griffin takes a hard hit mid-field and is slow to get up. I swear the seconds he lies unmoving on the turf take years off my life. But when he pops up and leaves the field on his own, my heart settles back into his normal rhythm.

I don't know how Paige and the other WAGs do this every week. It's like a piece of my heart is on that field, in constant danger of being trampled, with little more than plastic and foam to protect it.

Paige leaves to join her other friends at the end of the third, and I spend the rest of the game on the edge of my seat. In the end, the Blues emerge victorious. And even though it was a close game, Griffin's eight receptions and two touchdowns were crucial in securing the win. Final score: Blues thirty-five, Devils thirty-two.

As we exit the suite, Tucker stops me from following the signs to the parking lot. "Come with us to the family zone. We're gonna meet up with Griff when he's done with the media."

Trepidation washes over me. "No, that's—y'all go ahead." The last thing I need is to bump into Jack while surrounded by Laceys.

But Griffin's family—and Cam—watch me, expectant and hopeful. Except Shaw. He narrows his eyes in scrutiny.

Trixie trundles back to where I'm frozen in the middle of the concourse. "Don't fight the Lacey love. They'll just smother you with more." She wraps an arm around me, nudging me forward.

Giving in, I shake my head and pick up my pace to keep up with the crew as they navigate the halls.

"You're the first woman Griff's ever invited to sit with us for a game. Did you know that?" Trixie gives me a conspiratorial wink. Charm must run in this family's genes.

"Really? But what about—"

"Nope. Not even *her*." She scowls. "Thank heavens."

It's on the tip of my tongue to repeat my default reminder: *We're just friends.*

But this time, I don't even bother with the lie.

Chapter Twelve

Griffin

"All right, all right, quiet down!" Coach Mundy stands in a circle of football players in various stages of undress. The mood in this locker room is electric. "That was a team win out there. All three phases did their part to get us that victory." He's drowned out by a round of shouts and whistles, but considering there's a huge grin alight under his thick mustache, he doesn't mind. He gives it a minute, and when the pandemonium dies down, he holds his hand out, and Dobbins sets the game ball in his palm. When he holds it high, the room goes silent.

"This game ball goes to an undeniable asset to this team. He played a heck of a game out there today. We're blessed that he suits up in blue every week." Dramatic pause. "Eight catches. Sixty yards receiving. Two TDs." Another pause, and Greenway prematurely smacks my pads. "Week eight game ball goes to number 89!"

Hoots and applause echo off the walls as Coach hands me the football.

I soak in the moment. Breathe it in, hold it tight, memorize it. *This.* This is what I fought like hell to get back to. Not the accolades, although those are hella satisfying. But the thrill of victory and the harmony we create when we battle for that win together. When a shared love of this game forges individuals into an unstoppable unit.

Football. It's the fucking love of my life.

Greenway and Jefferson start a "Racy Lacey" chant, and they're joined by almost every man in here. It's tradition for the game ball recipient to make a short speech, so as I stand from the bench in front of my locker, the room quiets once more.

"Uh…" I clear my throat, choked up by my unexpected emotion. "Thanks so much for this, Coach. Means a lot to me." With a deep inhale, I forge ahead. "This is my eleventh year in the league—"

Someone—pretty sure it's Sweeney—coughs "Gramps."

I wait for the responding chuckles to fade before I speak again. "So this is not my first game ball. But it might be the most special. I grew up not far from here, and I've bled Memphis Blue since I was a kid." More cheers. "If someone had told nine-year-old Griffin that one day he'd play for this team, he…well, he was a bit of a shit, so he probably would've called them a fucking liar." More chuckles. "It's a privilege to wear this uniform, to know my family is here watching. But today's victory was a team win. Special teams, y'all were fire today. Defense? Damn. No fucking quit against one of the best offenses in this division. And my offense—" Deep hoots and whoops sound out all around me. "Without y'all, I sure as hell wouldn't have been open so that the best damn QB in the National Football League"—I hold a fist out to Beau for a bump, and the locker room goes wild—"could target me. Hell of a game today, boys. Blues on three!"

After the locker room celebrations, I grab a quick shower and dress in the clothes I arrived in hours ago. My least favorite part of game day is next—the press room. But when I play like I did today, the task isn't nearly as painful.

Standing behind the podium, I scan the room of print and digital reporters. Jack's probable dalliance, Andrea, is sitting in the third row. Man, I wish I could ask Kasey—the Blues' media manager standing to my left—to skip the blond's questions.

Kasey nods to a reporter in the front row, and the Q & A session is underway. I field questions about the team, my shoulder, and specific plays that led to the win. Before I know it, Kasey says, "Last question," and points to a man at the back of the room.

"This was your best game of the season so far. What would you say was the difference today?"

I study the wood grain of the podium, stalling. I've given them plenty of highlight-worthy soundbites in the last few minutes—and they've all been the truth. Today's win wouldn't have happened without incredible contributions from all three units.

But...

Did I have extra motivation today?

A slow, secret smile pulls at my lips as I angle in closer to the microphone. "Yeah, I might've had a good-luck gem here today."

Gem. Brynn *Amethyst* Nelson.

Knowing she was watching? Fuck yeah, it motivated me.

The memory of her face when she discovered I knew about her naughty voyeurism last night. And the enticing blush that spread from her gorgeous face all the way down her neck and chest, disappearing under the fluffy white terry cloth.

Fuck. I'm half hard behind this podium just thinking about how those luscious swells strained against that towel. And when she pulled that Blues T-shirt out of the bag and beamed up at me, bright as the goddamn sun, I had to hightail it out of there before I yanked her in and tasted the lips that've starred in every one of my water-logged fantasies.

Right now, I can't wait to see her sporting Memphis blue. With any luck, my peeps convinced her to join them in the family zone for our after-game meet up.

On my way down the corridor, I pass the GM Shane and his asshole of an assistant, but I pay them no mind. Thank fuck they're heading toward the offices, away from where Brynn is hopefully waiting.

When I reach my crew, I search for her. It only takes a moment to find her, as if she's a beacon. She's off to the side with Trixie, who's no doubt regaling her with embarrassing stories from my childhood. Brynn is absolute perfection, wearing the colors of my heart like they were created just for her.

I stoop to hug Mom, and when she holds me close, the three words she murmurs warm me: "We love her."

Of course they do. Who wouldn't?

Following on the heels of that warmth, though, is an icy tendril of panic.

Because the reason I haven't let myself pursue this woman was shot to hell today. One reporter called it my best game of the season, but in all honesty, it was my best game in a *couple* of seasons. Rather than causing my game to suffer, her presence kept me focused in a visceral way.

When my cleats hit that turf, I wanted nothing more than to impress her.

Maybe even more than I wanted to win.

And that's fucking terrifying.

In a blink, I've gone from worrying about being distracted by a woman to fearing my performance will become reliant on her.

What a clusterfuck.

Brynn stands apart as I greet each of my family members, but as I get to the end of the line, she's close, offering me her hand. And as we follow through with the synchronized pattern of our handshake, all the worries and panic are replaced by something else. The real and powerful and undeniable longing to simply make her mine.

Incoming.

It's eleven forty-five, and I'm up reviewing the playbook for this weekend's game in Charlotte. When I walked in after practice, I found a note from Brynn on the counter that said *Girls' Night with Paige*. Scribbled next to her name, she'd drawn a tiny heart.

That fucking heart has haunted me for hours. As has my ever-growing need to get my hands on every part of her body. To let her burrow so deep into my life I can't remember a time without her in it.

I want her. In my bed. On my arm. Any way I can have her. And definitely not as *just friends*.

But I've done fuck-all about it since I made this decision last Sunday.

Which, considering my history with women, is laughable. Not once has Racy Lacey been timid about making a move.

The stakes are unlike any I've faced before, though. I've got a helluva lot more on the line. If I fuck this up, I could lose one of my best friends. Even though we haven't known each other long, Brynn has already become a trusted confidant. I love that she doesn't hesitate to call me out on my shit. She's genuine and smart and adorably nerdy, and I'm more myself with her than anyone outside of my family.

So yeah, I've been hesitant to approach her. I'm pretty confident she'd be into me calling an audible. But an unfamiliar twinge of doubt's holding me back.

I've almost convinced myself it's because I'm waiting for the perfect moment to work my Lacey magic. But I had a real fuck-it moment on the drive home tonight, when I thought about her perfect mouth and how desperate I am for it.

I'm like a moth that's been circling her flame for weeks, and now, finally, I'm ready for her to burn me up.

I had every intention of walking in the door tonight and confessing my less-than-friendly feelings. From there, I was hoping like hell we'd make out like a couple of horny teenagers. But then...an empty apartment and the note.

My phone buzzes with another text.

Cap

Here. Come get your prize.

I peek out the front window, but the street's empty, so I make my way to the back of the building and find Beau's SUV idling behind the closed gate to our parking area. As I approach, the passenger side window lowers, and Paige's blond head pops out.

"Woo! Racy Lacey! Come par-tay with us!"

With a chuckle, Beau wrangles his exuberant fiancée back inside.

"What the hell?" I step up to her window.

Beau holds both hands up. "Don't shoot the driver. I've only been involved for the last twenty minutes. Paigey texted me to be their DD, and I found them at the bottom of a diver bucket at Silky's—their third location."

I bark a laugh. "Fuck."

"God, I know." He shakes his head. There's no way these ladies won't be waking up with massive hangovers.

Paige winks, though it's definitely more of a blink, and boops the tip of my nose. "You're cute, Racy."

"And you're drunk, Paige."

"Shh," she drunk-whispers, then pinches her fingers in front of her lips and twists, like she's locking them closed. "Don't tell Beau." Another attempt at a wink. This one results in both sets of her lashes fluttering.

"I'm right here, babe." He leans forward so he can see me around Paige and thumbs the back seat. "Yours is in back."

I don't correct him, and it feels right. She *is* mine.

When I open the back door, Brynn shields her eyes from the glow of the streetlight. "Hey, you." Her smile is flirty and tipsy, enticing my mouth to curve in a grin.

I peer around her to find Carlos's girlfriend Gina passed out in the seat behind Beau. "Let's get you upstairs, ma'am. You're going to be hurting in the morning."

"Pssh." She flips her hair over her shoulder. "I'm not...I'm not *that* drunk."

"Mm-hmm."

"I'm. Not. Thankyouverymuch."

"Let's go, champ."

She swings her long boot-covered legs out of the car. Damn. I'm glad I wasn't home when she left because I'd have gone full alpha male and demanded that she change. Not that I'd have any right, regardless of our relationship status, but there's no way I could have stopped myself at the sight of her in this short button-front corduroy skirt. She'd tell me to fuck off—rightly so—and we'd have our first fight before we even hard-launched this thing.

Once she's got both feet on the ground, I slam the car door and wave goodbye to Beau and Paige, who starts to lower the window again. Halfway down, the window raises again, and she frowns in confusion. With a chuckle, Beau reverses onto the street.

Just as we begin our trek to the building, Brynn almost crumples to the ground like a shaky newborn foal. "Careful with those sea legs, there."

"I can walk. Watch." She's only taken a single wobbly step when she clutches my arm to steady herself.

We make it a few more feet before her ankle buckles in the tall boots, and then she's giggling so hard she doubles over. At this rate, we'll be out here all damn night.

"Fuck this."

When I swing her up into my arms, bridal style, she gives a little yelp, but she loops her arms around my neck. I inhale her scent—that sweet yet floral fragrance that follows wherever she goes, mixed with a hint of alcohol and sweat—and hold it in my lungs.

She rakes her nails through my short hair, sending a heady shiver down my spine. "I like your hair," she murmurs.

"I like your hair, too."

Humming, she buries her nose in the crook of my neck and inhales.

This time, it's my knees that almost give out.

"You always smell so good."

I collect myself and chuckle, the sound making my chest vibrate. "You always smell so good, too."

She pulls back to make eye contact. "Ooh." She smiles, her eyes at half-mast. "I like this game. Compliment tit for tat."

"Please don't say *tit*, professor." The warmth and weight of her body already have me walking a razor's edge.

She giggles, a fucking adorable lilting sound I could become addicted to. Then her lips brush against my ear, her words breathy bursts of heat that threaten to bring me to my knees completely. "Feel free to compliment my tits anytime."

"Shit." My groin grows rock hard.

"You don't think they're nice?" She lowers her chin to examine her chest.

I swear if I don't get us up these stairs soon, I'm going to combust.

"*Nice* is not the word I'd use. They're fucking fantastic." What I don't confess? That I'm dying to get my hands on them.

She lifts her chin and smiles, satisfied.

When I jostle her a bit to toe off my shoes at the top of the stairs, her eyes widen and she rolls her lips, then breathes an exhale through her mouth.

"Griff." A pained whimper escapes. "I think I'm gonna be sick."

No hesitation, I sprint for my bathroom rather than braving another flight of stairs to hers. The second I lower her to the tile, she's on her knees and lifting the toilet lid. She heaves, retching all of her night's poor decisions into the bowl as I stand by, helpless. An anguished moan between gags has me joining her on the tile and rubbing comforting circles on her back, gently gathering her hair behind her nape. Her knuckles whiten as she clings to the sides of the bowl until she finishes.

"Oh, God. I think I'm dying." She rests her cheek on the seat and blinks at me.

"You're not dying. I won't allow it." I push a strand of her hair behind her ear, then collect the bottle of mouthwash and a clean washcloth from the cabinet.

Shaky, she stands, gripping the counter until she's steady. As she swishes the minty liquid, she studies me in the mirror. After she spits and rinses, she finds my reflection again.

"Sorry I puked in your toilet."

I bite back a chuckle. "Better there than anywhere else."

She snorts, and then we're grinning at each other in the mirror like a couple of smitten idiots. Between one blink and the next, her smile melts, and our gazes turn heavy with all the unspoken truths we've been carrying over the past few weeks.

I swallow back my thoughts, knowing I can't expel them in a stream of consciousness that she likely won't remember tomorrow.

Damn. Guess tonight's not the night.

But the need to be near her remains strong. There's no way I can put a full floor between us. She can sleep in my bed while she recovers from her girls' night out. I'll crash on the couch.

With a hand on her elbow, I say, "Let's get you to bed."

Her movements are still wobbly, even after emptying her stomach, so I guide her to the side of my bed and kneel to unzip her boots. When I close my fingers around the zipper on the inside of her knee, she jerks her leg so violently she almost kicks me in the face. Only my honed reflexes save my chin from the blow.

"Oh! I'msosorryGriff." Her jumbled words slur as she sways above me.

I make another attempt at the boot, but this time she flops over in a fit of giggles.

"Tickles."

A sigh escapes me. "Baby, work with me here."

She bolts upright, lips parted, eyes as wide as they can be in her state. "You just called me baby."

"I did."

"Why?" Her voice is a breathy whisper.

I ignore the pang in my chest. What I'd give to lay it all out there now. "We'll talk about it later, professor."

Her brown eyes are hazy as she searches my face, as if looking for a promise, but then she nods, brings a hand to her mouth, and yawns.

Finally, she holds still long enough to allow me to unzip and remove her boots. If she notices how long my hands linger on her smooth calves as I do it, she doesn't let on. It takes a goddamn avalanche of self-control to stop myself from running my hands up her bare legs, though.

I snag my favorite Sooners T-shirt from a drawer and toss it next to her. "I'll grab some Tylenol and water while you change, if you think you can manage by yourself."

"'Kay." That one word is slow and drawn out.

I kill time in the kitchen by adding a new word to our ongoing crossword puzzle. Piggybacking off her last correct guess, I draw one box below and one above the E in the word *pretzel*. Underneath the ever-growing puzzle, I scrawl my clue: *You are my good luck____.*

Then I gather up the pain relievers and water and hope like hell I've given her enough time. If I walk in on Brynn Nelson nearly naked in my bedroom, I'm not sure even a cold shower will be enough to settle me.

She wavers by the bed, her long, toned legs peeking out under the hem of my T-shirt. Fuck. I've never seen a more glorious vision. Even plastered, she's a knockout. When she reaches inside the roomy cotton to unhook her bra, and then draws the straps down her arms, I'm frozen in place, a hostage to her every move. The lacy pale-purple bra she slips out from one sleeve makes my mouth go dry and sends molten lava pulsing through my veins. It's one of the barely there undergarments I examined like a creeper in the laundry room. Fuck. I bite my cheek to keep from asking if she's wearing the matching panties.

Without a word, she slips under the covers and pulls them up to her chest. When she's settled, she lets out the most contented sigh.

For the first time in my thirty-five years, I stand over a woman and watch her sleep. My only thought? I don't only want to go to bed with this woman. I want to wake up with her. Maybe for the rest of my life.

Chapter Thirteen

Brynn

When I come to, I'm swaddled in the softest sheets in existence and surrounded by the scent of the man I can't quit thinking about. The man who was so tender and patient with me in my drunken haze. As consciousness builds, layer upon layer, fleeting images and words from last night slide into focus: Knocking back shots with Paige and Gina. Sidewalk dancing to a street band as we pranced to a second bar. Paige showing me a text from Beau, which relayed a message from Griffin.

Beau

> Hey, babe. Griff just texted me this:

> Please tell Paige not to let Brynn accept drinks from random guys. Texted B, but she isn't responding.

His overprotective nature brings a smile to my face.

More flashes hit me: Checking my phone and finding Griffin's blurry message. Insisting to Paige and Gina that *Racy Lacey isn't the boss of me*. More shots, and three straws in...a bucket? Piling into Beau's SUV, laughing hysterically at Gina's impression of his signal-calling cadence. Griffin effortlessly scooping me up to carry me up the stairs, his solid body so warm, holding me with tenderness and dare I say...possessiveness?

The cringe-worthy memories float to the surface next: Kneeling in the bathroom, purging the good-time toxins from my body. And...*oh, God*. Oh no. Did I really give Griffin permission to *compliment my boobs*?

With a groan, I lift my way-too-old-for-this body from the cushy mattress and press a hand against my pounding head. Swallowing a wave of nausea, I turn, discovering that Griffin's stocked the bedside table with the essentials—a bottle of water, two pain relievers, my phone, and...a note. As I pick it up, my arm brushes a lump of softness different from the texture of the bedding.

It's Barnaby. Tucked into my side, half hidden by the bedsheet.

Emotion swells. I have to blink away wetness so I can make out the words of Griff's note.

Good morning, professor! Hope your hangover isn't too bad. Thought you'd want some company when you wake up. See you tonight. XO-Griff

I clutch the paper to my chest as another memory becomes clear: Griffin, voice low, deep, calling me *baby*.

Was it a throwaway endearment? Or were the words spoken with weighted significance?

The atmosphere in this apartment is different this morning. Like I'm breathing rarefied air. Some seismic shift happened overnight, but I'm just now getting the memo.

I scan the room, the California-king bed.

Holy hell.

I slept in *his* bed.

I vaguely remember Griffin's muscly arms keeping me upright as he helped me to this spot. The sensation of his hands on my calves as he tugged off my boots.

"We'll talk about it later, professor."

Does later mean *today*?

My heart thumps against my ribs as my foggy brain works to catch up. Will this conversation be solely about his nonchalant *baby* bomb? Or does he want to discuss more? Since last weekend, and Tucker's ill-timed shower intrusion, my bravado about confronting Griffin has been MIA. Would it be possible to shore it back up in time for our talk?

A check of the time has me popping the ibuprofen he left and guzzling water. I have to dig deep in order to shove all of my Griffin-sized questions into a mental box for later. For now, I put all my focus into functioning as a human with this monster-sized hangover.

After I choke down a banana and another bottle of water, I slog through my morning routine and walk into my first class with minutes to spare. The freshmen trickle in as I connect my laptop to the projector and mentally rehash this session's topics. Just as I hop up on the table, legs swinging, laptop queued up with today's slides, I'm hit with a question that stops my heart.

A deep voice from one of the middle rows shouts, "Yo, Miss Nelson, are you and Racy Lacey hooking up?"

The blood drains from my face as I search for the source, first homing in on the giggling girls, then the audacious freshman they're focused on.

My first instinct is to play dumb. "Wh-what?"

He waves his phone in the air, grinning. "There's a picture of you two at the zoo. Did he show you his snake?"

The room breaks out into titters, and the blood that's evacuated my face rushes back with a vengeance, and my already touchy stomach roils.

I clear my throat and find my voice. "Mr. Newman, that is inappropriate and has nothing to do with Thomas Hardy." His ruddy complexion flares as he side-eyes his peers. "Now, in our last session, we discussed Hardy's use of imagery in his poetry..."

Somehow, I wrestle the train back on the track and finish the lecture. It helps that I've taught this course several times and know it well. But as soon as the last student exits the classroom, I snatch my phone from my desk.

I bypass several waiting texts and tap on the search engine. When I enter Griffin's name and hit *go*, the breath I've been holding whooshes out. The first few news items are football related. My blood pressure is just starting to lower when I see it, a few stories in. A grainy picture of the two of us at the zoo three days ago, our latest Memphis Magic outing.

I click on the article.

Rather than a celebrity gossip site, this is a sports gossip blog titled *Ballers' Baes*. From what I gather as I peruse it quickly, its sole purpose is speculating about professional athletes and their significant others. In the picture, Griffin's placing a roaring lion hat on my head, and I'm beaming up at him. The article's titled *Racy Lacey's New Lady Love?*

This is not the first time a photo of the two of us has appeared online, but it is the first where my face is clearly visible. In the few others I've found, my head's down, and my hair is hiding my face, or Griffin's blocking me from view. He was hyper-vigilant when we first started hanging out, I think out of respect for my relationship with Jack. But now that I'm single, neither of us bat an eye when we see cameras pointed our way. This was bound to happen. But the timing could be terrible. Because what if it chokes the tiny bud growing between us before we have a chance to nurture it?

I slide my thumb up the screen, dismissing the app, and tap on the message icon, where a red circle signals that I've missed several texts. My stomach plummets at the name at the top of the list.

Jack

What the fuck, Brynn?

Racy Lacey? Seriously?

Do you know his reputation? Were you fucking him before you dumped me?

I can't believe you'd stoop this low. With an athlete? On MY team? You hate sports. How'd you even meet him? At that fucking season-ticket event?

Five fucking years, Brynn. And you threw it all away for a showboating fuck boy. Hope he screws up every damn one of your sandwich orders.

I'm still subtly dashing away tears as students file in for the next class.

—◆—

It's pouring when I leave campus. What a perfect way to end this hell of a day.

Though swimming my usual thirty laps would soothe my anxiety, all I want to do is get home.

It's Halloween. I'm still nursing the remnants of a hangover. My ex-boyfriend flayed me via texts. And my situationship—as Paige calls it—has grown more complicated.

I even cried over tea time with Helen.

I want to change into warm pajamas and eat a huge bowl of popcorn while I watch a comfort movie. Maybe *Seven Brides for Seven Brothers*. Or *Becoming Jane*, which I'd definitely shut off right after the main characters run away together.

But the tall, handsome tight end who's counting my every step up the stairs has other plans. As soon as I clear the top step, I'm wrapped in his arms.

The sensation is as good as I remember. Griffin Lacey gives excellent hugs. The perfect combination of gentle and strong.

"How was your day, professor?" He rests his chin on my crown.

"Awful." My words are muffled against his collarbone, but I don't pull back as I list the day's hardships. "All-day hangover. Might still have it, honestly." His chest bounces with a chuckle, but he holds me tighter. "Halloween on a college campus."

"Hard pass."

"Right? And one brave freshman had the audacity to wave the zoo picture around and ask about it during class. Do you know about the zoo picture?"

"Mm-hmm." The sound vibrates through his chest and into me. "Seth sent it earlier. I'm sorry."

Now it's my turn to squeeze. "Don't be."

He rubs up and down my spine, the movement a balm, making me sag further.

"It was going to happen sooner or later."

A grunt. "What else?"

"The rain."

"Supposed to stop soon."

"Good for the trick-or-treaters." I inhale a deep breath. I'd be content to stop there and bask in his Griffin-scent, but I need to say this last one. "But the worst part of my day, by far, was Jack."

He goes rigid, and that comforting hand ceases its calming motion. "What about him?" His voice is hard granite.

I ease back so I can look at him, but he keeps me locked in his embrace. "He saw the article and sent me several texts to voice his displeasure."

"Can I—" His Adam's apple bobs. "What do you need?"

I search his eyes, which match the stormy sky outside, and sigh. "This."

With a subtle nod, he tucks my head back in that spot between his collarbone and jaw, a perfect fit. Like that space was made especially for me.

We stand like that, entwined in each other, until the sharp edges of my day melt into smooth, manageable margins.

"I have the perfect solution for this shitty day." His chin bumps the top of my head with each word. "Ice cream for dinner." He plants a quick kiss on the top of my head that I'll no doubt analyze with charts, graphs, and tables later, and swats my bottom. Then he pulls away. "You've got fifteen minutes to change."

Since he's giving me no time for analytics now, I hustle upstairs and change into my favorite pair of jeans and a butter-soft Townes sweatshirt to match the vibes of Griff's sweats-and-hoodie combo.

By the time we lock up and skirt around the building, the rain has ceased. Griffin starts up South Main in the direction of the nearest trolley stop, his long legs eating up twice the distance mine do. It only takes half a dozen steps for him to slow his pace and give me the finger wiggle. When I lace my fingers through his, he tugs me to his side.

We hold hands all the way to the trolley. And neither of us lets go as we head downtown, surrounded by riders dressed as witches and superheroes and Elvises, each one casting curious glances our way.

The ice cream shop isn't crowded, but we take our double-scoop cones outside into the cool night air. The gray clouds block the last rays of the setting sun, and the sidewalks are dark and wet. The seats of the metal benches that face the street are puddled, so we stroll down the block and eat.

"That's disgusting, by the way." I whirl my finger at his cone.

He takes a bite from the bright-blue scoop on top. "Professor," he says, his lips already turning colors—a curse of the flavor. "This is an elite cone—the best parts of childhood in one delicious combo." My side-eye makes him tip his head back in laughter. "Who doesn't love cotton candy and PB and J?"

"It's a wonder your teeth are so perfect with all the sugary foods you consume."

Even in the gloomy twilight, the twinkle in his eye is bright. "You think my teeth are perfect?"

"Your smile isn't the worst," I confess, tone begrudging, like I don't swoon every time one lights up his face.

He draws to a stop, and when I spin to face him, the intensity in his expression makes me shiver. With one big hand, he cradles my jaw, his thumb stroking my bottom lip once, so featherlight I wonder if I imagined it. But then his husky voice incinerates me. "This one takes my breath away."

I keep my focus locked on him, refusing to blink, worried that if I do, I'll wake and discover this was all an elaborate dream.

His attention shifts to my ice cream cone before returning to my face. "How's this combo taste?"

I swallow, tamping down the butterflies threatening to take flight in my stomach. "It's good," I breathe. I bring the treat to my mouth and relish the way the cold sensation contrasts with the lingering heat of his touch.

"Hmm. Let's see." Stooping, he brings his mouth to my scoop. His eyes don't stray from mine as he pauses there, sampling the dessert from the opposite side.

One scoop of fudge ripple is the only thing separating Griffin Lacey's lips from mine.

He pulls back, licks his lips, and hums. "Not bad."

Rising to his full height, he gives me a *shall we?* head tilt, and we continue our stroll. By the time we return to the trolley stop, we've finished our ice cream cones. But there's no hand holding on the journey to the apartment, which makes a bereft hollowness sink into my marrow.

The clink of Griffin's keys against the catch-all bowl on the bar is jarring in the silence, startling me. And before I can weigh the consequences, I blurt out the question that's plagued me all day. "Are we going to talk about it?" I infuse my gaze with a warning—if he doesn't know which *it* I'm referring to, then heaven help him.

He doesn't respond right away, choosing instead to let the question simmer between us. He opens his mouth, closes it, then, jaw set, he stalks my way. My heart pounds out a rhythm that could either be the beat of a death march or a circus parade, depending on this man's response.

When he reaches me, he cups my shoulders, the determination in his brows smoothing out as his eyes soften. "We are going to talk about it. But not tonight."

I examine his features for things left unsaid.

But in true Griffin fashion, he doesn't make me guess. He shares his thoughts with no evasion, no hesitation. "Professor, I don't want to go *there* while you're recovering from this shit show of a day. I don't want a hangover or messages from a jackass to taint something momentous for us. I just want to comfort you." Throat bobbing, he brushes a lock of hair behind my ear. "So I'm going to make you a cup of tea, and we're going to watch a movie—your choice."

"My choice?"

"Even if it's *How to Train Your Dragon*."

A soft smile pulls at my lips as his warm look tugs at my heart-strings. "First of all, that movie is a heartwarming delight."

He nods his agreement.

"But," I say, "I think I need some Jane tonight. Fair warning, though. It's a historical romance."

"Whatever you need." His words are a promise, and then he alters my whole world when he leans in and presses a soft kiss to my forehead.

Holy. Hell.

"You get the movie ready, and I'll get your tea. It's the weekend, so I'm assuming black tea is fine?"

I nod, my chest clenching. This man remembers a throwaway comment I made weeks ago? A simple mention of how I save black tea for weekend nights, since its caffeine content is higher than green tea?

After I trade my jeans for flannel pajama pants, I sink into the soft leather couch in the spot I prefer on the rare nights we watch TV or play video games together. A moment later, Griffin appears and carefully hands me a piping hot mug of tea. Then he settles in his favorite corner.

I start the movie and sip my tea, savoring its mellow tannins. I've finally settled in and have lost myself in the plot when my roommate heaves a put-upon sigh.

I'm about to remind him that he let *me* choose the movie, when he grates out, "Yeah, this isn't working for me."

Without moving from his spot, he plucks the mug from my hands and puts it on the end table. Then he leans across the cushion between us and gathers me in his arms. He drags me across the leather and plonks me right next to him. If I were any closer, I'd be in his lap. Within seconds, the mug is back in my hands and Griffin's arm is wrapped around me.

"Much better," he mumbles.

Me? I snuggle deeper into his side.

When I've finished my tea, he sets the mug on the table again, then tightens his hold on me.

I point to a fresh-faced Anne Hathaway on the screen. "Jane is the reason I'm an English lit not-a-professor, by the way."

"Is she?"

"Yep. Sophomore year of high school, I read *Sense and Sensibility*, and I fell in love with Marianne and Elinor. They're dual sides of my soul—Elinor's practicality and Marianne's passion. And Colonel Brandon is so dreamy."

The real-life dreamboat at my side snorts. "You know what this movie needs?"

I elbow him. "Nothing. It's perfect."

"Nah." He jostles me. "Could use some dragons."

The laugh that erupts from me is accompanied by a snort. "Well, I did find one under the bananas this morning."

"Really? So. Weird." He's silent for several beats, and his frame tenses. "After the Charlotte game on Sunday, we have our bye."

When he doesn't elaborate, I nod.

"I promised Mom I'd spend the weekend on the farm." He shifts my way and stuffs his free hand into the pocket of his hoodie. "I, uh, was wondering if you'd like to come with me."

"To Holly Holler?" I tilt my head so I can study him.

"To Holly Holler," he confirms.

An overnight trip to his hometown? It seems like a giant step toward a destination I'm still not completely sure we're headed for. But like every other time he's asked me to take a chance, my answer is immediate. "I'd love to go to Holly Holler with you."

"Perfect." He tucks me into his side again and turns back to the movie.

Before long, the stress and toll of the day threaten to pull me under. I fight the droop of my heavy lids for as long as I can, but eventually—well before Tom and Jane are forced to part ways—I surrender to the promise of a deep sleep, tucked close to the man who's becoming my favorite person.

Chapter Fourteen

Brynn

I grip the armrests as Paige, oblivious to my anxiety, natters on with updates about her wedding planning through takeoff.

"My mom keeps sending me pictures of bejeweled strappy heels, like I haven't reminded her a million times that we're getting married on a freaking beach and I'll be barefoot. She says she refuses to be barefoot at her only daughter's wedding." She huffs. "Maybe I can convince her to wear dressy rhinestone flip-flops."

Paige and Beau are having a destination wedding after the season ends, with only their closest family and friends in attendance.

When she casually mentions that I should make sure my passport is up to date, I blurt, "Me? Are you sure?"

She waves a dismissive hand. "Of course. We want you there. You're stuck with us, Brynn. For better or worse."

I stretch my jean-clad legs, finally relaxing now that we've reached cruising altitude, and delight in the extra leg room. Leaning closer to Paige, I whisper, "I feel kinda bad about this upgrade."

She frowns. "Don't. Let him spoil you, girl. He makes more money than he can spend in his lifetime."

"But—"

"Listen." She shifts to look at me directly. "It was weird for me, too, at first. When Beau insisted on paying for every dang thing. But you're not a jersey-chasing gold digger being frivolous with his money. A little splurge every now and then is fine." With that, she twists forward, end of subject.

I want to argue that my situation is different. Griffin and I are not dating. I don't know what we are, exactly. Roommates who Netflix and snuggle? Friends with forehead-kiss benefits?

We need to define our status. Soon.

When we land in Charlotte, a car service is waiting. A first for me.

Another first? This away game. And I'm a nervous wreck. Memphis has only been allotted a couple of suites, meaning both the office staff and the players' special guests will be in attendance.

Though apprehension still lingers, Griffin has done his best to prepare me for a possible run-in with Jack.

In fact, that's the only conversation we've had time for since Friday night. I saw him briefly yesterday before he left for his Saturday run-throughs and to travel with the team.

So, the *big* conversation? The one hanging over us like a bloated water balloon? Yeah, the anticipation has me in a chokehold.

Inside the facility, we follow the crowd of early fans through the concourse and ride escalators up several levels. We're halfway up the final set to the suite level when a familiar voice echoes from above.

"Yoo-hoo! Moonbeam!"

My heart stumbles, and my head snaps up, my focus darting from person to person. Finally, I spot her. Leaning over the rail, my mother waves frantically. Beside her, my dad holds up one hand in greeting and uses the other to keep her from tipping over the barrier.

Instantly, my cheeks are wet with tears. I bounce the rest of the way up, wishing I could sprint up the remaining steps. Alas, the escalator is crowded, so I must wait. When I turn to Paige, assessing her blurry features from behind my tears, her eyes are shiny, but her smile is knowing.

The three of us Nelsons collide in a tear-soaked hug that lasts for a solid three minutes. My mom coos and murmurs *my baby* and *my love* in my ear, while my dad pets my hair. I continue sobbing, holding tight, soaking in their love. Yes, we talk every couple of days, and we meet weekly on Zoom, but I haven't been held by them or smelled their familiar patchouli-infused scents since last Christmas.

I catch my breath and pull back a fraction. "What? How?"

But I already know the answer.

Mom cups my face and uses her thumbs to wipe tears from my cheeks. "Your sweetheart."

I don't correct her as a fresh deluge washes away any remaining traces of makeup.

She continues to mother me, freeing strands of hair that stick to my damp skin. "A wonderful young man named Seth arranged everything. I hope he works things out with his Daniel."

Over Dad's shoulder, Paige waits, wearing a grin. "Oh, gosh. Mom and Dad, meet my friend Paige."

After a pair of handshakes, Mom can't help herself. She pulls Paige in for a quick hug, too. "I love your energy." She waves a hand in front of my friend. "Yellow aura. Joy and positivity. And you're in love."

"Her fiancé is the quarterback," I pipe up, and Paige adopts a dreamy smile.

"Ah. Yes, I can always tell when a woman is in love." She arches a brow my way, and my face flames.

Mom, mistaking my red cheeks for embarrassment about *her* when, in reality, my feelings for Griffin are the culprits, places a cool hand on my cheek. "What do I always tell you?"

I roll my eyes, but I tell her what she wants to hear: her most-used motto from my childhood. "Having a weird mom builds character."

"That's right." She pats my cheek. "You, my love, are the most precious soul. And you deserve a grand love story."

Tears fill my eyes once more, and with a peck on my cheek, Mom turns to Paige. "Lead the way, dear."

My friend smiles and links her arm through my mom's. "I think the suite is down here."

As Dad and I follow, I can't keep from looking from him to my mother and back, like they'll disappear if I look away.

Beside me, Dad is dressed in the Hardy Nelson standard: bright-colored polo (today, a sky blue) tucked into well-pressed khakis. Tan hemp belt and sensible walking shoes. He might have a hippie soul, but his engineering roots run deep. My mother, on the other hand? She could have stepped off the pages of *Free Spirit Catalog*. Her breezy palazzo pants are striped in various shades of blue, and her white tunic's pulled snug at her slim hips by a silver and turquoise concho belt. The flowy sleeves peek out from beneath a patterned vintage kimono.

She and Paige gab like a pair of old friends as we hunt for the two suites available for the visiting team. At first glance, it appears that team management fills one while family and friends of Blues' players fill the second. Charmaine and Gina wave to us from their row as we settle into one near the back.

The Blues get off to a slow start. Beau throws a rare interception in the first quarter that makes Paige cover her eyes and mutter, "He'll agonize over that for days."

Greenway and Jefferson both drop passes that could've become scores. The suite erupts, finally, when Griffin runs in a pass at the end of the half, bringing the Blues' deficit to only six.

When Dad leaves at halftime to find drinks, Mom digs in her regulation-sized crossbody and pulls out a small velvet pouch, the same kind she uses for crystals at her shop.

"I have a little something for you, Moonbeam."

When I tip the pouch over, a necklace puddles in my hand, the gold chain so dainty it's almost weightless. In the center is a cloudy thumbnail-sized pale pink stone. It's a raw rose quartz crystal, its shape irregular and edges jagged.

"You know what rose quartz is for." She gently picks up the necklace and hooks the clasp at my nape.

I touch the small lumpy stone where it rests against the Blues sweatshirt that was delivered to the apartment yesterday, and Mom gives me a satisfied smile.

Our team plays much better in the second half, and this win advances their record to seven and two. Griff has another phenomenal game—at least that's what Paige tells me; I'm still too unfamiliar with the stats—and my parents beam when they discover that he'll have a few minutes with us before the team is hurried onto the buses.

I catch a glimpse of Jack and Shane leaving the other suite, but they're swept up in the crowd as we exit. The pit of dread sitting like a boulder in my gut lightens for the moment, though that confrontation is imminent.

When we reach the lower level of the stadium, the walkway from the visiting team's locker room is crowded with family, friends, and fans waiting to give the Blues a proper send-off. There's a barricade on both sides, giving the players and coaches an unobstructed path to the chartered buses. Paige squeezes between bodies, her hand locked on to mine, guiding us to the front row.

The medical and training staff pass us first, followed by the coaches. When the players start trickling out, D'Angelo engulfs Charmaine in a bear hug, his smile so bright it makes my chest pinch. All the guys look sharp in what Griffin calls their "gameday fits," and many of them still sport wet hair from their postgame showers.

Beau and Griffin exit the double doors together. Despite its ear-piercing volume and tone, I barely register Paige's squeal. I'm too busy being held hostage by the intensity in Griffin's gaze. I break our eye contact long enough to do a head-to-toe scan, checking for a limp or any hint that he may be injured. Not only does he seem unscathed, but he's got a little extra swagger as he saunters over, wearing the same cream cable-knit sweater and brown trousers he wore yesterday when he left the apartment.

The moment he sets his leather duffel at his feet, his arms are around me and he's exhaling a satisfied sigh I feel down to my toes. "You look good in Memphis blue, professor." He doesn't let go as he greets my parents. "Hey, I'm Griffin. So glad y'all could make it." I'm jostled a bit as he lifts one arm from my back. "Hardy." A pause as he shakes Dad's hand. "Celeste."

"Thanks for arranging this for us." My dad clears his throat, and I'm released from Griffin's embrace. "We've loved visiting with our Moonbeam for a bit."

"Oh, yes, love. Thank you so much." Mom sniffles and gives him a hero-worshipping smile that makes my heart swell.

Griffin rubs his beard. "Loved doing it for y'all. Let me—or Moonbeam"—he gives me a flirty smirk—"know when y'all want to catch a game. We'll get you set up. And you're welcome to visit us in Memphis any time."

Mom shoots me a look. She didn't miss the way he said *us*, either.

Paige introduces my parents to Beau quickly, but then they're gone, and the four of us are in our own bubble again. Dad small-talks with Griff while Mom rummages in her purse. As for me, I indulge in this moment, committing every detail to memory.

"Aha, found it." Mom holds up another velvet pouch and jiggles it. "I brought you a little something, Griffin."

He takes the pouch and empties two smooth, glossy stones into his broad palm.

"This one..." Mom holds up the green stone. "This is green aventurine. Its properties provide good luck and protection."

"Can always use both of those." He nods at the one left in his palm, his expression open, genuinely interested. "And the pink one?"

With a smirk, she peers at the matching pink stone hanging around my neck. "That, my dear, is rose quartz." She places the aventurine back in his palm. "It's known as the love stone."

Throat bobbing, he zeroes in on me, his expression so heated I melt a little under it. "Gonna take real good care of that one, then."

He's careful as he returns the stones to the pouch. Then he zips it in a side pocket of his duffel. "Thank you, Celeste. I'll treasure them."

She leans over the barrier to hug him, and when she pulls away, she winks at me, a gesture I interpret as *you'll treasure him, too.*

The players around us dole out goodbye hugs and begin pulling away from their loved ones, then head out to the buses. In my periphery, Beau kisses Paige, and then he stops beside Griffin. "Good to meet you folks," he says to my parents. With a smack to his friend's bicep, he says, "See you on the bus," and then he's gone.

My throat burns as sadness courses through me. I don't relish having to say goodbye to my parents, or even Griffin, even though I'll see him again in a matter of hours. This bonding time has meant everything to me.

"Load up, boys!" a deep voice bellows from outside.

"I've gotta head out." Griffin hefts his bag and holds out his hand to my dad. "So good to meet y'all. I'll try to ambush more Nelson family Zooms in the future."

Chuckling, Dad clasps his hand and gives it a shake. "The more the merrier. Thank you again for today."

Griffin nods and moves in to hug my mom again, but before he can pull her in, she grasps his forearm. "Listen," she says, her voice full of concern. "Before you go, I have to ask: do you know about the pillow trick?"

"Mother." Mortification swamps me. *Please tell me she did not ask him that.*

"What?" she asks, her expression one of pure innocence. "I'm just trying to make sure my baby girl is satisfied in the bedroom."

Oh God. If the concrete beneath my feet could split open and swallow me, I'd be forever grateful. Cold sweat drips down my spine as I scan our surroundings. I'm relieved at least a modicum that the people around us seem too busy with their own goodbyes to pay us any mind.

But Griffin is unfazed. With an arm around her, he says, "Celeste. I do know about the pillow trick. Rest assured, your Moonbeam will be well taken care of."

She pats his chest. "Good."

Holy hell. My face flames with the heat of ten-thousand suns, along with the rest of me. I push the sleeves of my sweatshirt up in an effort to cool my overheated skin.

Once he's released my mother, Griffin erases the distance between us and nudges my chin up, his touch anchoring me. "Hey." Lips tipped up, he studies me, probably taking in my still-pink skin, and reverence lights up his irises, making them glow oh so blue. He slips the hand from my chin around my jaw, then tucks my hair behind my ear and clasps the side of my neck. "See you at home."

My lips part, but words are impossible. My heart stumbles when he inches his hand across my shoulder and down the entire length of my arm, his touch burning a path through the fabric of my sweatshirt. When he reaches my hand, he pulls it to his face and presses his lips to the inside of my wrist, holding his kiss against my pulse point long enough to make it race.

With one last smile for my parents and a wink for me, he's striding for the doors.

I scrutinize my wrist in shock, certain his warm lips have etched a permanent brand onto my skin. Evidence I can reference in the future when the memory becomes fuzzy. But other than the blue veins pulsing beneath it, my ivory skin is unmarked.

"Well, that was hot." Paige braces an elbow on my mom's shoulder and fans herself.

"Right?" Mom grins. "The energy those two exude when they're together? It's potent. I saw glimmers of it on the video call, but in person? Mwah." She does an obnoxious chef's kiss gesture.

Paige nods right along like she couldn't agree more.

"Did you see that, Har?" Now my mother drags my poor dad into her meddling. "Isn't he the perfect match for our Moonbeam?"

My father nods, brows lowered. "An Aquarius and a Libra. A solid love match."

I force my mouth open, ready to question how he knows Griffin's star sign, but my mother piles on. "They'll have no issues physically."

Paige wags her brows at me, the traitor, as Mom carries on as if I'm not here.

"As long as they maintain good, open communication, they'll be perfect."

I snap my mouth shut.

Communication.

The conversation we haven't had.

Panic rises, like an impending wave threatening to drown me. All the words we haven't spoken, combined with the flirtation and innuendo, plus how my heart soars when he's near. It's all too much. As I stand stock still in the middle of a football stadium corridor, I'm totally, utterly, completely overwhelmed and overstimulated.

And soon, I'll have to bolster enough fortitude to say goodbye to my parents without having a public meltdown.

It's enough to make me want to curl up in the fetal position and tune out the world.

Paige, bless her, gently prods my parents toward the opposite side of the stadium, where a car should be waiting to carry us back to the airport. They all give me space as I trail behind, lost in my thoughts.

Saying goodbye to my parents at the airport is as hard as expected. After hugs and kisses and promises of calling when we land, my friend stands beside me with her arm around my shoulders, a quiet comfort as they disappear around the curve of the jetway. Then the two of us speed-walk through the concourse to make it to our own flight on time.

Our journey back to Memphis is mostly silent. Each time I'm with her, Paige only endears herself to me further. Today, she's shown me just how intuitive she can be.

Once she and I hug and go our separate ways, Griffin's parting line becomes a whispered refrain that accompanies my every action.

As I wait at the curb for the car service Seth arranged: *See you at home.*

When I fasten my seat belt and clutch my purse in my lap: *See you at home.*

Then as I clasp the rose quartz pendant that bounces against my chest every time we hit a pothole: *See you at home.*

And when I trudge up the stairs to the apartment I temporarily share with the man I'm falling in love with: *See. You. At. Home.*

He's standing in the kitchen when I clear the steps, a bottle of water raised to his mouth. His duffel rests by the bar, evidence that he's only just arrived himself. His eyes lock on mine, and I know in my marrow this moment will change everything for us.

My breath saws in and out, a little from the stair climb, and a lot from the effect his attention has on me. His expression is full of hunger and desire. Passion and fondness.

The tension between us is thick, heavy with want, but neither of us moves. Maybe he's just as afraid as I am to take the first step. Because once that happens, we can't go back.

But since the sweltering day I met Griffin Lacey in the middle of a gridlock, he's coaxed bravery out of me and nurtured it. So I take a step toward him. Another. And another. Until I stand at the intersection of *playing it safe* and *not backing down*.

The man before me owns a refuse-to-yield mentality. It shows in the way he lowers the bottle to the counter without breaking eye contact. And in the way he prowls toward me, every step deliberate, until we're so close I have to crane my neck to hold his gaze.

For a long, quiet moment, we study each other. Admire each other. There isn't one inch of his handsome face I haven't memorized. Suddenly, though, it's as if I'm viewing him through a different lens. Like the face I've become so fond of has morphed into one I can't live without.

His deep, rough voice cuts through the silence, startling me, making my heart jump. "Before we do this, I have to know." A heavy exhale that hollows my stomach. "I need you to be damn fucking sure this isn't some rebound bullshit. That you're over the jackass."

My mind tries to tally the number of curse words in that statement, but his cedar and fresh air scent distracts me from the task.

A slow shake of my head. "It's not a rebound," I whisper.

He nods. "Good." His tongue peeks out then, dampening his lips, making my core muscles clench. "Also need you to be damn sure you're okay with how this is going to change *us*."

"Wh-what do you mean?" I blink up at him, so primed to have his mouth on mine, I might punch him if he doesn't get to the point.

"I mean, professor..." He slides a hand around my neck to my nape, the contact urging my body to throw a ticker-tape parade right here in the kitchen. Finally, he's touching me. "If we do this, we can't be friends anymore."

For a second, panic surges through me, but as if he can see it, he arches a brow, making his meaning clear: this won't sever our friendship, but it *will* alter it.

He grasps the roots of my hair and tugs. "So, tell me what you want, Brynn."

What do I *want?*

I want to tell him that I'm glad I crashed Jack's car into his on that fateful Sunday morning. That his friendship has freed me. Allowed me to experience things I never would've on my own. That he's helped me embrace who I am as a woman. He's made me braver and more confident than I've ever been.

I want to confess it all, but I settle for voicing one thought that will get me what I want most, right now: "I want to kiss the word *friend* right out of your mouth."

"Thank fuck."

He cups my cheek with his other hand, the touch a tender contradiction to the other. To where he's still gripping my hair with a roughness that thrills me. The first press of his lips to mine is soft. We're both gentle, hesitant, as we find our rhythm, as our lips explore and learn how to move together. The heat of his mouth and the rasp of his beard against my sensitive skin lights a spark of desire deep in my core. He teases me, capturing my top lip between his and pulling it taut. When he releases it, he leans back, breaking our connection.

I rest a hand on his chest and thrill at the frantic beating of his heart, the way it's synced with mine. The hunger in his eyes as he stares at my freshly kissed lips makes me ravenous.

"Did you know—" I lock my arms around his neck and lift up on my toes, bringing our faces so close that our lips brush with every word. "A kiss has to be at least six seconds long to release oxytocin?"

He nudges my nose with his, his breath fanning my cheek. "Hmm." A peck on my jaw. The corner of my mouth. My lips. "Six seconds, you say?" He tantalizes me with another touch of his lips to mine.

"Mmm."

"I think we can do better than six seconds, professor."

He hefts me onto the counter, pulling a surprised *whoop* from me, but it's cut off as his mouth plunders mine. There's no hesitancy this time, just pure, unbridled passion, his kiss hot and demanding. I let my hands roam, aching to touch every part of the gorgeous man standing between my thighs. Griffin's tongue sweeps into my mouth, tangles with mine, and retreats. Then his lips take charge.

His hands are everywhere—caressing my shoulders, my back, my hips. They're in my hair, tilting my head for a better angle. They're kneading my ass, pulling me so close that the hardness in his pants nestles between my thighs. The delicious friction of his beard ratchets my desire higher, so high I don't care if it leaves my skin pink and abraded.

I'll wear his burn proudly. A physical representation of how he ignites me. A bold statement to the universe: this man is mine.

Because this isn't just a kiss. It's a claiming. A wicked promise of things to come.

I stroke the short strands of his hair as he trails open-mouthed kisses along my jaw, and when he suckles the skin below my ear, the moan that escapes me makes him tighten his grip on my waist.

With a growl, he releases the sensitive spot and rests his forehead against mine. Our breaths stutter out in pants as we grant our lungs—and pulses—a reprieve.

"Brynn." His voice is both reverent and husky.

I make soothing passes up and down his biceps, loving the freedom to touch him like this. He must revel in it, too, with the way he's tracing a path on my thighs.

"Fuck, baby. Just...*fuck*."
Racy Lacey, at a loss for words?
Never thought I'd see the day.

CHAPTER FIFTEEN

GRIFFIN

Once I've added the fifth and final box to my newest white board puzzle for Brynn, I cap the marker and stand back to survey it. She'll be pissed that I'm taking our little word game in a naughty direction, but I've turned into an adolescent horndog this week.

She'd argue that it's my own damn fault.

And she'd be correct.

Our first kiss on Sunday night was hot and perfect and everything I'd imagined it would be. So when we finally came up for air and she looked at me and point-blank asked, in that blunt manner of hers that I love, when we were going to have sex, I panicked. I blame it on the lust haze that had fogged my brain while her lips were pressed to mine.

Did I want to jump right into bed with her that night? Uh, 100 percent.

But did I also want to prove to her—and to myself—how special this relationship is? Absolutely. The last thing I want to do is cheapen it by rushing things in the typical Racy Lacey manner.

So what did I do? I suggested we implement the three-date rule. A moratorium on sex until I've taken her on three dates.

God, I'm a fucking idiot.

To her credit, Brynn did try to convince me this waiting period was unnecessary. But I've held my ground.

The result? Last night, after an Italian dinner and hot-and-heavy couch make-out session, I googled whether it was possible for a man to die of blue balls.

Brynn's response? "At least they'll match your uniform."

So far, we've gone out twice. Monday night's foray into the best of Memphis barbeque, complete with a sausage and cheese plate starter, of course. And last night's romantic Italian dinner. My practice schedule has been different this week due to our bye, so we've moved our Memphis Magic outing to today—Thursday. And we're counting it as our third date, so that means...

Tonight, I'm fucking finally getting my hands on the woman I've developed a bit of an obsession with.

At the sound of footsteps on the stairs, I brace my hands on the cool granite, willing my heart rate to remain steady. She pauses at the bottom, her perfect lips lifting into a playful smile, those dark eyes alight. She's dressed for class—professor chic—in high-waisted black-and-tan plaid pants and a fitted black turtleneck, the soft material molded to every curve I'm putting my mouth on tonight.

Every time she walks in the goddamn room, another piece of my heart becomes hers.

I slide the steaming bowl of oatmeal across the bar, along with a mug of coffee prepared the way she likes it.

Her eyes narrow as she slides onto the stool across from me. "Starting a new puzzle, huh?"

The grin I give her is as cheeky as I can make it. "Thought the occasion called for one, so yeah."

Blushing, she lowers her head and focuses on her breakfast. "Hmm." She spoons a scoop of oatmeal into her mouth, and that tiny peek of her tongue heats my blood. "Someone is giddy."

"Damn right I am." When her smile sinks into a slow fade, my insides twist.

"You're not, uh...you're not rethinking tonight, are you?"

She sets her spoon inside the bowl and regards me, her lips pressed together and her expression unreadable.

My heart ticks faster the longer she's silent.

"Griffin," she murmurs. "I want tonight to happen. So much."

I release a breath of relief, but it's cut off when she continues.

"But I'm just..." Her brows draw together. "Well, you're...you." She waves a hand between us. "And I—I don't want to disappoint you."

Before her last word is released, I'm at her side, framing her beautiful face. "Baby." I kiss her sweet lips. "Please hear this: there is no possible way you could disappoint me."

She opens her mouth to protest, but I don't allow it.

"*Even* if you told me you wanted to wait and spend the evening doing crossword puzzles instead."

This time when she opens her mouth to argue, I sweep in with a kiss, a deep, languid one that I hope will cast her doubts aside. I taste notes of the maple-cinnamon flavor of her breakfast, but that's not all.

She tastes like forever.

I place her hand over the bulge growing in my thin joggers. The move causes her to suck in a breath, and those brown irises I love so much darken.

"This, professor. This is what you do to me with one kiss." I bring my mouth to her ear and rumble, "There's not a chance in hell I'll be disappointed." A quick kiss to the tip of her nose, and I pull away. "Now, finish your breakfast and get to class. I'll see you at lunchtime."

My painful erection and I make it to the shower, but I refuse to jerk off. I turn the dial and let the tepid water sluice over my tense muscles and overheated skin.

A good, cold twenty minutes later, I get dressed, my stomach fizzy and my body light. I do my best to pass the time until Brynn gets home: studying film on my iPad, alphabetizing my record collection, sorting through a couple of boxes of football memorabilia and merch that's stored in the extra room upstairs. I even grab a handful of mini dragons from my hidden stash and hide them around the apartment. But nothing holds my attention for long.

Impatient, I drop onto the couch and check the time. Still an hour until she's through with class. Which means it's lunchtime in Georgia. I pull up the contact I'm looking for and make the call.

He answers on the third ring.

"Racy Lacey. What's shakin' in the middle of a Thursday?"

"Dell." I greet my friend and former teammate. "God, it's good to hear your voice. You got a few minutes?"

"You caught me in the middle of my lunch break, but you know I'd make time for you regardless. You're having a heck of a season. How's Memphis treatin' ya?"

"It's great," I gush a little, knowing this man gets it. "Love having my family here for every game. Couldn't ask for a better organization or coaching staff." Minus one Cockburn, but I'm not wasting time on him. "How're things with you and the hellcat?"

He chuckles. "Can't complain. She's something else."

The unmistakable happiness in his voice makes me smile. Cordell and his girlfriend, Mel—or "hellcat," because she's a feisty thing—have been dating for a couple of months. Thank fuck. It took them far too long to figure out their will-they-or-won't-they shit. I had a front-row seat for their shenanigans this summer when he talked my depressed ass into helping him run his high school's football camp. After five minutes in the company of the two of them, it was clear they had undeniable chemistry, even though they fought it like hell—especially Mel.

"That she is. Happy for y'all, Dell."

"Thanks, bro."

"The reason I'm calling is kinda related, I guess. You remember what Big Mike used to preach to us about women?"

Another laugh crackles over the line. "Big Mike Grimstead. I haven't thought about him in a minute."

The guy was a veteran offensive tackle for the Tors when Cordell and I played together. He was a legend, a guy every player on the team looked up to, and he often shared nuggets of wisdom in his big, booming voice.

Cordell's sigh is wistful. "Sure haven't forgotten his advice, though. Especially about women." He lowers his already deep voice to imitate Big Mike's bass. "Boys, here's how you know she's the one...when she's your very best friend..."

"But you also want to fuck her six ways to Sunday," I finish. Our laughter is low and nostalgic. Then I clear my throat. "Not to be too nosy, but...is that who Mel is for you?"

His answer comes with zero hesitation. "Yeah. Definitely."

I rough a hand down my face, scratching at my beard. There's a hushed timbre to my voice when I admit the truth to my friend of over a decade. "I think I've found her."

He's silent for a beat. But there's no denying the smile in his voice when he says, "Someone's managed to tame Racy Lacey? I wanna hear all about her. She's gotta be a one-in-a-million kind of girl."

"Dell, she's more like a once-in-a-lifetime kind of woman." With a smile, I sink into the cushions, prop my feet on the coffee table, and tell my buddy about the woman who's captured my heart.

"No tour of Memphis Magic would be complete without a stop here."

Brynn peers through the windshield, then cuts her eyes over and chews on the corner of her bottom lip.

"Hey." I slip my hand beneath the fall of her thick hair and give her neck a gentle squeeze. "He's not here today. I checked. And my sources are reliable."

She bobs her head, but she doesn't release her lip.

"We're going to run into him eventually, you know."

She sighs. "I know we will—"

"But you don't want it to be today."

Eyes softening, she leans into my touch. "I also don't want to be scared to come here. This place is special to you."

My left hand clenches the steering wheel. I haven't seen the texts the jackass sent her, didn't want to push her to share them, but if she's this worried about facing him, they must've been rough.

I lean across the truck for a kiss. "C'mon, professor. There's someone important waiting for us."

At the front grill of the truck, we thread our fingers together. I can't go more than a couple of minutes without touching her now that we've left the *strictly friends* zone.

We enter the stadium through the entrance I use every week. And waiting right where he said he'd be, at the end of the corridor, is the stadium staff's most devoted, tenured employee.

"Mr. Gus. Good to see you." I shake the gentleman's wrinkled, papery hand and hug Brynn to my side. "This is my special guest."

She reaches for his hand. "I'm Brynn."

His white whiskered cheeks spring up as he welcomes her. "Hello there. Gus Torino." A twinkle of mischief shines in his eyes as he leans my way. "You've outkicked your coverage with this one, Mr. Lacey."

I huff a laugh. "Don't I know it. And it's Griffin," I remind him for the dozenth time.

Mr. Gus pushes up his glasses, then sweeps a hand to one side. "Shall we?"

As we follow his shuffling gait down the hall, I give Brynn some context. "Mr. Gus has been working at the Blues' stadium since it opened. He's been giving tours here for over twenty years."

"Started as a custodian the year it opened," he calls over his stooped shoulder. "Mr. Russell personally tapped me to give tours a few years later. I remember when this one was a young whipper-snapper."

Brynn's eyes widen. "He remembers you?"

"Hard to forget those Lacey boys," Gus chortles, the sound echoing off the cinderblock walls. "They came several years in a row, like clockwork. This one," he thumbs over his shoulder, "always came with a list of questions."

I rest an arm along her shoulders, my chest tightening when Brynn reaches up and grips my fingers. "We got to choose how to spend our birthdays as kids. Whether we wanted a sleepover or a party or special outing. I chose the stadium tour three years in a row. And then Tucker copied me for an additional three years." I affectionately roll my eyes.

"You probably have my talking points memorized," Gus jokes.

He leads us throughout the facility, making stops in a couple of the high-end suites, the press box, and both locker rooms. He answers every one of Brynn's questions and gives us time to explore. When we reach the Blues' locker room, he steps out to give us a few minutes of privacy, and I make a mental note to bring him a bottle of his favorite whiskey.

"So this is where Racy Lacey suits up." Brynn wags her brows and lowers to the bench at my locker. The sight of her sitting below the nameplate with my last name and jersey number makes my hands ache with the need to touch her.

I brace my arms against the wooden sides and angle into her. "Every time I came here as a kid, I'd imagine what it would be like to have my name on one of these."

Dark lashes fluttering, she smiles up at me. "And?"

"It's even better than I dreamed it would be."

Not just playing for this team, but being here with her. Like this.

Gus clears his throat from the hall, a subtle cue that it's time to move on, and we join him. "One more stop on this ride."

He leads us down the concrete path to the place where my team rallies before every home game. Where we wait in anticipation to be announced over the PA and then charge the field as the stadium erupts.

"This is where I leave you two lovebirds." He dips in a bow, the wisps of his thinning hair tousled by the breeze from the end of the ramp. "Brynn, lovely to meet you."

She plants a peck on his cheek that delights the old man.

"Mr. Lacey, enjoy your days off. And don't let this one get away."

"That's the plan, Gus. Thank you for everything."

With his hands tucked into the pockets of his navy cardigan, he shuffles back toward the main walkway.

An icy chill blasts down the shadowed corridor, so I pull the sides of Brynn's wool coat together and button it up. "It'll be warmer in the sunshine." I head toward the field, and when her shoes scuff the concrete floor behind me, I slip my hand behind my back and wiggle my fingers. Her warm skin presses against mine, and we step out into the November sunshine.

The brightness of the late afternoon sun makes the grass on the empty field look especially green. There's not a soul in sight as we make our way across one of the end zones, painted navy with the team name in light blue. I lead her all the way to the image of King on the fifty-yard line, then rotate to face her.

"Wow." Her brown eyes are large as she takes in our surroundings. "This is what you see every week."

I scan the stadium, trying to imagine the view through her eyes: rows upon rows of empty navy seats climbing sky-high, stark white yard lines and hash marks, massive Jumbotrons on either end, *Hound Town*—a fan section—that dominates one end zone.

Compounded by the roar of the fans, the scrutiny of the media, the expectations, the celebrity, the pressure? It can be overwhelming. And that's the last thing I want her to be as we figure this out.

"Brynn." I squeeze her hands, garnering her full attention.

When those dark depths are locked on me, they're focused. Trusting.

Fuck.

I'm in deep.

I swallow and fill my lungs. Exhale. Push down my nerves like I do on game day.

"This is my life." I pop a shoulder. "It's crazy and big and loud. Much like this place on Sundays."

The dawn of a smile graces her lips.

"But I'd like to share it with you, if you're willing to put up with all this."

She surveys the field again, then zeroes in on me.

"You know this game demands a lot," I say, ignoring the way my heart rate picks up. "And dating a professional athlete comes with a heap of bullshit." I pull her hands to my chest and hold them against my heart, hoping she can tell that it's thrumming with optimism. Then I say the words I've been keeping like a secret for weeks: "Just be mine. We'll figure out the rest as we go."

Eyes glittering, she bobs her head and gives me a smile so brilliant it rivals the fucking sun. She launches herself at me and twines her arms around my neck, sealing the deal with a scorching kiss. As she rains sweet kisses down all over my beard and lips, a laugh breaks free from my chest.

"Can we order in tonight?" Her voice is breathless as I lower her to the turf.

"Whatever you want, professor."

"I want this. I want *you*." She gives me a thorough once-over, the look causing my dick to sit up and pay attention.

"Fuck. Let's go." I hoist her over my non-surgically-repaired shoulder, pulling a squeal from her, and cart her off the field.

By the time we're home, the last of the sun's rays are losing their hold in the sky. As we trudge upstairs, I do my best to ignore the zing of anticipation between us.

Once we're inside and we've removed our coats, Brynn pulls up the food delivery app and waves her phone my way. "Let's order Chinese."

"Sounds good, baby."

With her elbows on the bar in the kitchen, she taps on her phone. The position puts her delectable ass on display, making it impossible to fight the urge to grab a fistful of it and fold my body over hers. I brace my forearms on the counter, caging her between them, and press into her, my hardening cock resting against the swell of her ass, then pull her hair off her neck. Nuzzling into the fabric of her turtleneck, I give her a light bite in the space where her neck and shoulder meet.

"Griff."

She arches her back, which only helps my dick become better acquainted with her ass. If only these damn clothes weren't separating them.

I grind against her, placing love bites to her shoulder and neck through the fabric of her shirt, until one heavy jerk of my hips makes her gasp.

She pushes off the counter and twists in the space between my body and the bar. With her hands splayed on my abs, she pushes up for a kiss. "The food's been picked up at the restaurant. I'm going to change really quick. Do you mind going down to get it?"

I nip at her bottom lip, then pull back. "Nope."

"'Kay." After one more kiss that leaves us panting, she pats my chest and ducks under my arms. Then she scurries up the stairs.

Head hung, I smooth a hand over my hair. "Fuck." I'm so goddamn revved up I might not make it through Mongolian beef and fried rice.

With one deep breath after another, I pace the length of the apartment, giving myself a take-it-slow pep talk. I want nothing more than to make this night perfect for Brynn. Once I've reined in a modicum of control, I do a little prep work to set the mood. I turn on a Teskey Brothers record, volume set low and turn off all but the two lamps in the living room. Then I rummage in a kitchen drawer for the lighter to set flames to Brynn's favorite candles. I'm finishing up my preparations in the bedroom when the doorbell chimes downstairs.

As I return, arms loaded, I peek inside the bag and count the containers. "Baby," I say as I clear the top step and look up, "did you order extra egg—" My words stick in my throat at the sight before me.

Brynn Nelson, wearing nothing but my jersey.

Chapter Sixteen

Griffin

"I thought you didn't wear jerseys."

Wearing a shy smile, she gathers her hair at her nape and pulls it over her shoulder; the thick locks cover the top loop of the eight. The move draws my attention to the delicate skin above the vee of the jersey. Soaking her in, I let my focus wander farther south to the smooth thighs that peek out from the hem of the material, then down the length of her shapely alabaster legs to the tips of her toes—painted Memphis blue.

"Yours is the exception."

The bag of Chinese lands with a plop next to my feet.

I've scored sixty-two touchdowns in my career. I've been selected for the Pro Bowl seven times. I've won two Super Bowls.

But I've never felt like more of a champion than I do at this moment, seeing this woman wearing my number.

I can't tear my gaze from her as all the blood in my body rushes south.

She twines her fingers in the bottom edge of the jersey, unintentionally making it rise enough to show me more of her luscious thigh. But it's not enough to satisfy my curiosity about what's underneath. Is she wearing panties? Or is she totally bare?

I'd crawl to her to find out.

"Turn for me."

Her lips part at the gravel in my voice, but after only a heartbeat of hesitation, she obeys my command. She pivots, and when the five letters of my name, bold and bright against the dark blue of the jersey, come into view, I force a rough swallow. And when she peeks at me over her shoulder?

My restraint oozes out like a slow leak. I prowl toward her, every step ratcheting my desire higher.

"You know…" I say.

Humming, she spins to face me again.

"Seeing you in this is making me feel some kinda way."

Her throat works on a swallow. "Some kinda way, huh?"

I nod.

Amusement lights her eyes, but when my hand settles on the curve of her hip, the expression deepens to hunger.

With one swift tug, I've got every inch of her softness pressed against every inch of my hardness. "Makes me want to do naughty things with you, professor."

"I like naughty things." Popping up on her tiptoes, she presses her nose into my neck and inhales. When her tongue licks a path up to my ear, my knees nearly buckle. The heat of her breath sends a thrill down my spine as it accentuates every word when she says, "All the naughty things."

"Fuck." There's no stopping me when I plunder her mouth, my tongue dueling with hers. Her throaty moans drive my lust sky-high. My cock is a fucking powder keg in my jeans.

She kneads at the back of my neck, then my traps. Then those hands start a slow descent down my shoulders, to my pecs, and land on the buttons of my shirt. Our mouths never part as she undoes each one. When she's worked the last button through its hole, she pushes the fabric off my shoulders and down my arms.

When I've shaken it loose from my wrists, I break our kiss long enough to reach behind my neck and strip off my undershirt. As her fingers coast over my pecs and abs, her reverent touch leaves a trail of sparks all over my torso.

Our lips continue their sensual dance, and when I cup one of her breasts, discovering that only a silky jersey separates me from her perfect tits, I growl. Curious about what awaits my touch down below, I pull back. I want to watch her face as I slip my hand beneath the shirt to cup her *there*. Her eyes close when my fingertips brush the lace and silk of her panties.

I keep a possessive hold on her mound and tell her, "You got the puzzle wrong."

Her eyes are hazy as she glances into the kitchen, but they clear slightly when she gives me her full attention. "But my name *is* five letters. And it fits the clue."

Smirking, I stroke the damp material between her legs, her little gasp encouraging me to apply more pressure. "The correct answer starts with *p*."

She clings to my biceps as I continue to tease her over her panties.

"I need to taste you here." I pull my hand away from her enticing heat and slide it up under the jersey until the weight of her tit fills my hand and a groan slips from my lips. "And here."

"Holy hell." She whispers the words against my lips, then takes my mouth in a searing kiss.

I'm so lost in the sensation of her lips moving with mine that she's got my zipper undone and she's sliding her hand in my pants before it registers. But the instant her hand grips my rock-hard cock over my underwear, I nearly come undone.

"Baby." I let her get two good strokes in before I grasp her wrist and pull her hand away. "Let me see you first."

She puts a few inches between us, and I bask in her mussed-up glory. Her lips are reddened from our kisses and her hair is a mess from my hands. The jersey has shifted enough to tease me with a peek of one delectable shoulder.

My mouth waters with the need to taste that creamy patch of skin.

I dive in like a man possessed, latching on to her shoulder, licking, sucking, biting.

Slipping her hands inside my jeans, she grabs my ass. Her words stutter out as she kneads my glutes. "This butt is glorious." She tilts her head to give me better access to her neck.

"So is this one." I return the favor, loving the mewl that slips from her lips as I massage the round globes.

Before Brynn, I was a devoted ass-guy. But this woman has turned me into a leg-guy. And a boob-guy. A hip-guy. She's the total package. Even her cute little pinkie toe does something to me.

Fuck, now I'm a Brynn-guy.

She pushes my jeans down my thighs, then I toe off my sneakers. As I back up and step out of my pants, I miss the warmth of her body. The appreciation in her eyes as she admires my almost-naked physique makes me puff out my chest.

Just a little.

"*Pac-Man*, huh?" She smirks at the fabric that covers my aching hard-on.

"These are my lucky ones."

She raises a brow. "Lucky? Since when?"

"Tonight."

Head dropped back, she laughs. But when I extend my hand across the space between us, her mirth melts away. Expression serious now, she grasps my wriggling fingers and lets me lead her into the bedroom.

The lamps cast a perfect glow on the bed and on the woman who can't pull her attention from me. She's so fucking beautiful it takes my breath away.

"Professor, I love seeing my jersey on you." I smooth my hand up her thigh and bunch the fabric, lifting it up her body. "But I think I'll love seeing it on the floor even more."

She raises her arms so I can pull it off. The second it clears her head, I toss it to the side. When I get a good look at her, I freeze, taking in every inch of her creamy skin. The perfect curves of her round breasts, the rosy-pink nipples that beg to be tasted. The nip of her waist that flows into shapely hips tempting me to leave my fingerprints.

It takes my brain a moment to register that her lacy panties are the same color blue as the jersey I stripped from her body.

"You are so goddamn exquisite, you know that?" I fist my hands to keep myself from throwing her on the bed and rutting her like a wild fucking animal.

Her answering smile is soft. Shy. She steps closer and reaches for me.

Heart stuttering, I pull her trembling hand up and kiss her palm. "Baby. You're shaking."

"Nervous. But the good kind of nervous." She takes another step closer and places a reassuring kiss on my chest.

It's on the tip of my tongue to confess that the only thing I'm nervous about is blowing my load too soon, like I'm fucking seventeen again. Ever since we had the safe sex talk at dinner the other night and decided that we could forgo condoms—she's on the pill and we've both had recent clear blood tests—my cock's been aching to take her bare.

I thread my hands into her hair and take her mouth in a deep, unhurried kiss. Her body melts into mine, and when we pull apart, breathless, I nudge her to the mattress. She lies on her back on top of the comforter, and I stretch out beside her, propped on one elbow. I use my free hand to trace each of her curves. Across her collarbone. Over the peaks of her breasts. Down the slope of her arms. Goose bumps erupt along every path I travel. And when my touch reaches the top of her panties, she sucks in a breath. I kiss her as I snake my hand inside the blue lace.

"You're soaking wet, professor." With a finger, I trace her slick skin, dipping in and out in teasing passes that make her gasp. When I lower my head and take one pert nipple into my mouth, swirling my tongue over the stiff peak, she clasps the back of my head.

"Griff—"

"Mmm, they're so perfect, baby." I lavish attention on her other tit as I continue my exploration. She parts her legs wider, giving me access to slip my finger inside her slick opening and then glide it back to tease her clit.

With one last lick to her nipple, I trail kisses down her body, inhaling her scent with each press of my mouth.

"This smell. What is this smell? You always smell like this, and it drives me fucking crazy." I kiss the space between her breasts, then the underside of one.

Her belly quivers, and her breath hitches. "Y-you don't like it?"

Heat licks up my spine. "I'm fucking feral for it. What is it?" A kiss to her stomach. Then one on the cute freckle next to her navel.

"I-it's my lotion. Berries."

I run my tongue along the skin above the top of her panties.

A sharp exhale. "F-freesia."

Hooking a finger into the lace, I tug.

"R-rose meringue."

A bite to her hip. Then I sit up on my knees and drag her panties all the way off. When they've cleared her ankles, she snaps her legs together, knees bent, like she's shy or worried I won't like what I see.

I tsk. "Please don't hide from me. Spread those gorgeous legs so I can see my reward for having enough restraint to last three fucking dates."

With her bottom lip caught between her teeth, she slowly lowers her legs.

The fire burning inside me rises a notch when I get a glimpse of my prize. With a huff, I drag a hand down over my mouth and neck. "Goddamn, woman."

Her perfect pink glistening skin is framed by a patch of close-trimmed dark hair. The sight pulls a primal groan from me, then I'm lowering my upper body between her legs.

Brynn's eyes widen, and her lips part. "Wh-what are you—you don't have to do that." The skin above her chest mottles with a pinkish hue.

I peer up at her across the plane of her body, finding her suddenly propped on her elbows, watching my every move, her expression one of pure reticence. "He didn't go down on you?" The fucker.

She rolls her lips and squeaks. "It, uh, wasn't on the regular menu."

"Baby, consider it a daily fucking special from now on." Lowering again, I use my shoulders to stretch her thighs wider. Then I flatten my tongue and drag it from her opening up to her clit.

When I close my lips around that tight bud and suck, she gasps and grips my head. Her fingers dig in, begging for more. Fuck. For the first time in years, I regret the damn buzz cut. This woman needs something to hold on to, to tug while I'm feasting between her thighs. Eyes closed, relishing the way her nails scrape my scalp, I resolve to let my hair grow a bit longer.

I savor the taste of her, the sound of her moans when I swirl my tongue around her clit, the way she writhes against the comforter. The tightness with which her thighs squeeze my head when I lick into her slit and fuck her with my tongue.

When I pull back and kiss the inside of her thigh, she whimpers.

"You've made a mess of my beard, professor."

"S-sorry." Eyes hooded, she watches my every move.

I snag a pillow from the other side of the bed. "Don't be. I fucking love it. You're my favorite taste. My favorite scent. My favorite everything." With a pat to her thigh, I signal for her to lift her hips. When she does, I slide the pillow beneath them. "Now. You're going to come on my tongue and fingers, and then on my cock." I wrap one arm around a thigh to part her from above, then lower my lips to her pussy. Before I dive back in, I zero in on her face. "While I'm busy down here in paradise, play with those pretty tits until I can suck 'em again."

Her eyes widen at my coarseness, but when I get back to work, they close in ecstasy. And when she follows through with my request to keep her hands busy, I can't help but smile against her core. As she kneads her breasts and pinches a nipple between her fingers, my hips roll against the mattress.

Fuck, I can't wait to be inside her.

I work her clit with the tip of my tongue and find a steady rhythm that makes her whimper and moan.

"Griff. Oh, God. Yes, right there." Hips working, she chases the high, and when I slide two fingers into her, she bucks up with so much force I have to clamp my arm around her thigh to maintain control. She's so wet, and every pump of my fingers in and out of her pussy makes a squelching sound. "Yes, yes, yes, yes, yes, yes." Her chants spur me on, her whimpers getting louder, signaling that she's close.

And when her orgasm hits, she cries my name. The second her inner muscles begin those rhythmic squeezes, I work my boxers down my legs and kick them off. My cock twitches painfully, and the bead of precum gathered at the tip smears when I climb over Brynn, nesting my hips in the cradle of her thighs.

Resting my weight on my elbows, I frame her blissed-out face, and she wraps her arms around me.

"That was fucking magnificent, professor." I dip my head and kiss her lazy smile, giving her a taste of her pleasure. And as our kisses grow more passionate, I sweep a thumb over her nipple, pulling a moan from her.

I bury my face in her neck, luxuriating in the moment. With a sigh, she rubs a hand over the back of my head and arches her back. I take the hint and lower to take the other nipple into my mouth.

I circle the bud with my tongue, taking my time, until she grasps my arms and attempts to pull me back.

"Griff, I need you."

One last pull with my mouth, and I release her. "What do you need, baby?" With her hips propped up on the pillow, they're at the perfect angle when I grip my cock and rub the crown through her wetness, teasing her clit and her entrance.

With a roll of her hips, she does her best to spear herself with my length, but I shift, depriving her.

"Griffin." She whines, eyes closed and head tipped back. "Stop teasing me."

"Are you aching for me, Brynn?"

She nods, and I kiss her pouty lips.

"Need me to fill this perfect pussy and fuck it like it belongs to me?"

Another whimper and buck of her hips.

"Then lift those lashes, baby. I want those gorgeous eyes on me when I make you mine."

When she blinks those lids open, I give her what she wants, thrusting into her, sliding home.

Chapter Seventeen

Brynn

The sound Griffin makes when he fills me is primal—this deep, guttural groan that sends a shiver coasting down my spine. I fixate on that noise, add it to the list in my memory bank of all the other male utterances he's made tonight. The dirty words flowing from his mouth like the most sinful promises. The compliments and praise he's lavished on me so freely.

It comes as no surprise that Racy Lacey is a loquacious lover. And I love it; each grunt or husky command turns me on as much as his touches. Sex with Jack was a subdued, quiet obligation. But with Griffin? It's a hot, unrestrained necessity.

I'm wanton and needy and desperate to please him.

"Fuck, baby. You feel so good." Above me, those blue-gray eyes are focused, full of desire as he levers his hips and pulls out a few inches, only to glide back in to the hilt. Testing, holding back. He's big, but my body was more than ready to take all of him.

I love the way he stretches me. The intensity of his gaze as he thrusts, slow, shallow to start, makes my nerves tingle and increases the slickness that eases his motion. He kisses me, tender and unhurried, his lips coaxing mine open. And when his tongue mimics the lazy movement of his hips, a spike of pleasure consumes me, making me clench my inner muscles around his hardness.

He tears his lips away with a growl. "You keep that up, and I'll finish before we even get started."

When I give him an unbridled smile, he stills, ceasing the motion of his hips, and regards me.

"You are so goddamn beautiful."

"Griff."

"When you smile at me like that, it robs the fucking air from my lungs."

Unbidden, tears line my eyes, but I blink them away.

Griffin doesn't miss them, though. "All right?"

I nod and press my lips to his.

"There's no rush, professor. If you need a break or to stop…"

Another thing missing from sex with Jack? A deep connection. The comfort that comes with knowing that my partner is fully present, in the moment, with me.

I shake my head. "I want this. I want you." The same words I gave him when he asked me to be his in the middle of an empty football field.

"Baby, you've got me. *All* of me." He accentuates that statement by grinding his hips against me. Then he pins me with more of his weight.

I grip his waist, digging my fingers in as he rocks his pelvis in a rhythmic pattern. The additional elevation from the pillow provides the perfect angle for my clit to be rubbed with every thrust. As he works me over, I roam every bit of his sweat-slicked skin, touching every inch my fingers can reach: straining biceps and sharp shoulder blades and tight butt.

When I squeeze his round backside, he swears. "You're taking me so well, baby. My fucking dream girl, made just for me."

He increases his tempo, and I can't hold back the moans and whimpers. The rasp of my nipples against his chest hair and the puffs of heat he grunts into my ear trigger the telltale tightening of my core, that delicious throb like a heartbeat between my thighs.

"That's it, Brynn. Give it to me."

His gruff words are my undoing. As my climax crashes through me, I'm hit with wave after wave of pure bliss. The undulations are intense and drawn out, every cell awash in euphoria. Griffin's pace becomes frenzied, and he hitches my knee up to his thigh so he can thrust deeper and harder, chasing his release. After a few more erratic plunges, he stills, his face contorting, and he lets out a groan. He's magnificent when he pulses inside me.

Watching him come undone above me is a sight I want on repeat.

Spent, he slumps over me, burying his face in my neck.

I wrap my arms around him as our heartbeats slow and our bodies cool. "How do you feel?" I make lazy passes up and down his back, reveling in the feel of his weight pinning me to the mattress.

His words are muffled against my skin. "I came so hard I might've blacked out for a second."

I huff a laugh and hug him tighter, contentment blooming in my chest.

He nuzzles closer and kisses my neck. "How was it for you?"

Words flit in and out of my mind like a shuffled deck of cards. They run the gamut from *rapturous* to *terrifying*. Rapturous, for obvious reasons. Terrifying because this relationship has the potential to wreck me if it goes south.

In the end, I land on three simple but honest words: "It was perfect."

He raises his head and studies me, his mouth kicked up on one side. "Yeah. It was. Because *you* are perfect." He presses his lips to mine.

After several minutes where we bask in the afterglow, kissing and snuggling, he rolls off me, and with a groan, rises from the bed. He offers me a hand and pulls me up. Then he swipes the used pillow from the bed and tosses it on the floor. "Pillow trick for the win. Make sure you tell Celeste." His mouth twists in a proud smirk.

I scoff. "Yeah, that's not happening."

He pokes out his bottom lip, a tease on the tip of his tongue, but then his attention flits to my chest, and instantly, he's distracted. Stepping closer, he caresses my breast. He makes one pass of his thumb over my nipple, sending a jolt straight to my pelvis. I squeeze my legs together, where the evidence of our lovemaking trickles out.

Griffin hauls me up and tosses me over his shoulder, and when he smacks my butt, I let out a cackle. "C'mon. Let's get a shower so I can dirty you up again."

⎯⎯⎯◦⎯⎯⎯

As we pass the sign welcoming us to Griffin's hometown, the one that proudly boasts *Home of Super Bowl Champ Griffin Lacey*, I relax against the headrest and let my head loll to the side so I can take him in. "I thought a hollow was a small valley. I've seen nothing but flat land since we got off the highway."

With a laugh, he gives our loosely intertwined fingers a shake. "Don't mention that to anyone while you're here, professor." When I lift a brow, he sighs. "Trust me on this. There are two *highly* improbable versions of that history, each with supporters who will defend their preferred tale with blows, if necessary. At the very least, they'll launch into a heated debate, and before you know it, you've lost hours of your life that you'll never get back."

"Wow, it's that contentious, huh?"

He pops a shoulder. "Small town, USA, baby."

"Is that why the name's been changed?" The white wooden letters on the sign we passed read *Welcome to Holly Hollow*, but the *o* and *w* in the last word were crossed out, and an *er* have been stenciled above them in green paint.

"Officially, it's Holly Hollow. But, since its founding, folks have called it Holly Holler. It has a better ring to it. That's one of the few things everyone around here agrees on."

Giddy, but also a little nervous, I give his fingers a squeeze. "I can't wait to see where you came from."

He brings our joined hands to his lips. "And I'm excited to show you."

There's no mistaking the pride in his voice as he points out his hometown's highlights. First, we do a slow pass by his high school, eyeing the bold *Home of the Hornets* motto painted on the wall of the gym in huge, yellow letters. He idles at the fence surrounding the football field, his eyes growing misty as he takes in the metal stands and the field's freshly cut grass.

"I couldn't even drive by here a few months ago—when I moved home to recover after surgery. Hurt too fucking much to come back to where I fell in love with football, thinking I'd played my last game."

I study the scoreboard, the fierce cartoon hornet that lords over the center, and the huge wooden numbers posted to the fence below it: a 9 with Griffin's name and class of 2009 painted on it, and a 55 that reads Tucker Lacey, class of 2013.

"You wore number nine in high school?"

"I did. I played QB back then." He nods at the numbers. "Tuck played center when he was a Hornet."

"You switched to tight end in college?"

"Yep." A single nod. "Which meant I had to give up my beloved number nine."

Head tilted, I regard him. "Did you pick 89?"

"I did." He stares off into the distance. "Tight ends traditionally get numbers in the eighties, so I chose 89 as a tribute to Shaw. That's the year he was born."

My heart melts at his devotion to his family. "Griff, that's the sweetest."

He gives me a smirk. "That's the last word he'd use to describe it."

Lips pressed together, I give him a slow, unamused blink. "What?" He chuckles. "You've met him. Am I wrong?"

"He was rather..." I trail off, racking my brain for a fitting descriptor.

"Assholey?"

"Aloof," I correct. "But it's nice to know that's his default, and it wasn't because of me."

"Baby, you're perfect." Angling over the center console, he plants a quick kiss on my lips. Then, with a sigh, he rubs a hand over his hair. "Adult Shaw is...complicated. But we were like this as kids." He crosses two fingers and holds them up between us. "We're only seventeen months apart. For years, most people who didn't know us assumed we were twins."

He shares more about his relationships with his brothers as he drives. How Tucker, being four years younger than Griff, often felt left out by his older brothers, which is how Camden made his way into the mix. The honorary fourth Lacey was around so much that Donna set an extra place for him at dinner every night.

As we get closer to the center of town, we pass an L-shaped strip mall that houses a dog groomer, a dentist office, and a couple other small businesses, along with a larger business, one that spans several units, with *Club Lacey Fitness* emblazoned across the awning.

"That's Tuck's gym. He opened it in January after he scaled back on fights."

The youngest Lacey stepped out of his older brother's shadow by making a name for himself on the MMA circuit after college.

"I did most of my rehab there. Hell, Tucker's annoying ass is what got me out of bed most days, even if it wasn't until after ten. That kid made sure I stayed in decent shape." Despite the tease, his tone is full of gratitude. He clears his throat and dips his chin as he makes a right turn. "And now, prepare for Holly Holler's crown jewel."

The sight before me makes my mouth drop open. It's the most quaint, welcoming small-town square, complete with a park and gazebo in the center. It's like a scene from a Hallmark movie. Tall oak trees line all four sides of the park, and along each surrounding street is a row of cute shops full of southern charm and nostalgia. One such business occupies most of an entire block. From the looks of the display window, the Dusty Britches Mercantile appears to sell everything from clothing to housewares. On the corner next to it sits a little ice cream shop with an adorable pink and sherbert striped awning. There are too many adorable details to take them all in as we slowly roll by.

"We'll come back down here tomorrow, and I'll show you around." Griffin makes a turn, passing a building with a tin-roof awning held up by thick, dark-stained wooden posts. The lettering on the sign matches the old-timey western vibes: The Hoot 'N' Holler Saloon. "We'll stop in there at some point, too. That's Aunt Dottie's place. She'd never forgive me if I didn't bring you by."

My grin is so wide it makes my cheeks ache. As we continue on, I store up every detail this man shares, saving each nugget like a treasure-hoarding dragon. Witnessing the place where his story began brings me such joy, it's like my insides have been coated in rich, warm honey.

"The farm is about twenty minutes away. Mom invited everyone for dinner. Hope that's okay."

Despite my nerves, I'm excited to spend time with the Lacey crew. "Of course."

On our way out of the downtown area, we pass several residential streets and the elementary school where his cousin Trixie teaches. The farther we go, the farther the distance between buildings and houses. Still, the land is flat as a pancake; not a hollow—or holler—in sight.

He turns down a paved two-lane road that bisects huge empty fields. The nutrient-rich soil is dormant in November, waiting for next spring's planting. Though a few fields still hold rows of brown, stalky plants with withered, crunchy leaves. The plants appear to be dead at first glance, but closer inspection reveals clusters of brown pods nestled among the branches.

"Shaw's almost through with the harvest," Griffin muses, gesturing with a hand. "These are all ours."

Ah. The fields on either side of the road are part of his family's farm.

"What are they?"

"Soybeans."

That makes sense. Like the logo on the cap he sometimes wears.

"Lacey Farms is one of the top soybean producers in the state."

Humming, I take another look at the vast fields. "Impressive."

"It's that fertile delta soil. River's that way." He points to my window.

A couple of miles later, the road curves a bit, and the flat fields morph into more woodsy areas. We cross over a creek, and wind a little farther north, until he slows at a turnoff that cuts between two grassy fields bordered by white picket fences. A handful of horses graze in the field to our right, and in the distance stand a quintessential red barn and a cluster of chicken coops. We pass under a metal sign that stretches across the width of the road, the round Lacey Farms logo prominent.

"Lacey farms is part working farm, but part hobby farm, too. We've got chickens, goats, a few horses. Local schools come out for field trips, and Dad gives them tours, lets the kids hold baby chicks and feed the goats. Mom sells eggs to neighbors and stuff."

"My own real-life farm boy." Laughing, I squeeze his bicep. "Explains how you got these strapping muscles."

The heated look he gives me makes me squirm. "You know I love when you call me *strapping*, professor." As twilight takes hold of the day, he pulls the truck up to a picturesque two-story white farmhouse, and parks in front of steps that lead up to a wide front porch. When he cuts the engine, he exhales, a content sound passing his lips, and surveys the scenery. "This is home."

I'm gearing up to thank him again for bringing me here, for showing me the place that formed him into the man I adore, when the front door swings open and Trixie stomps onto the porch. "Quit making out in that truck and get in here, already!"

"Jesus," he whispers. "I apologize in advance for every single member of my family." His warning is laced with fondness. "They will be obnoxious as fuck about us."

"Oh, you've told them?" My cheeks flame, but satisfaction courses through me.

"Like I'd keep you a secret. I want every fucking person on God's green earth to know you're mine."

Holy hell, when he says things like that, my heart swells and my knees turn to jelly. Good thing I'm not standing up.

Griffin exits the truck and grabs our bags, refusing to let me help, and as soon as we step into the house, we're swarmed with hugs and kisses from enthusiastic Laceys. Except for Shaw, of course. He stands apart until the frenzy calms, then he welcomes his brother with a slap on the back and me with a clipped nod.

The inside of the Lacey farmhouse is cozy and inviting. Overstuffed plaid couches and comfy leather recliners form the perimeter of the living area, and a fire blazes in the hearth to ward off the evening chill.

I step up to the mantle to get a closer look at a framed picture on the end. Three miniature versions of the brothers cheese at the camera, each wearing a different Memphis Blues T-shirt. Griffin wasn't kidding when he said that he and Shaw looked like twins when they were young. And baby Tucker's pudgy cheeks and dark curls have aged to perfection. I glance over my shoulder at where

Fred and Donna are talking to their sons, resisting the urge to comment on their remarkable genes.

Trixie sidles up beside me and tips her chin. "That was at the Blues' first home game. I was supposed to be there, too, but I had a fever that Sunday, so we had to miss it. Which Mom brings up every time she needs a favor."

"Your mom's not coming tonight?"

"She's working at the Hoot tonight."

"Griff pointed it out when we drove through town. Said we'd have to stop by while we're here."

We're both quiet as I study the other pictures. On the opposite end of the rough-hewn mantel, in an ornate brass frame, is a shot of Griffin's parents on their wedding day. Donna's puffy white sleeves and Fred's skinny tie and thick mustache make me smile. A large rock, roughly the size of a hand, sits beside it.

"What's with the rock?" I whisper to Trixie.

She barks a laugh. "Aunt Donna, Brynn wants to know about your lying rock."

All three brothers groan.

"Not the lying rock," Tucker whines.

Donna swats his arm. "I'll tell it over dinner. Y'all come on before these pork chops get cold."

In a matter of minutes, we're all seated around an oblong farmhouse table laden with steaming dishes of smothered pork chops, mashed potatoes, green beans, and succotash.

Beside me, Griffin squeezes my thigh. "Mom, this smells amazing."

She beams at her middle son. "I'm so happy to have all my babies at my table again."

Across from me, Shaw rolls his eyes, but his lips lift in a small smile as he swipes his mouth with a napkin.

When Tucker taps at the screen of his phone under the table, Donna clears her throat. "No phones at dinner, Tucker Myles."

In unison, Griffin and Shaw blurt, "Lacey family rules."

"Sorry, Mom. Cam texted that he's running late, but he'll be here."

Trixie huffs a breath from Griffin's other side.

The family launches into story after story about the boys' childhoods, and I soak it all in, marveling at the chaos of dinner with a big family. When I was growing up, our family mealtimes were substantially more mellow, though Mom could be gregarious enough for two people.

Mistaking my silence for discomfort, Griffin leans in, his shoulder nudging mine. "You okay?"

"Perfect." I press against him and scoop up a bite of potatoes.

Fred passes a basket of rolls to Tucker and lifts his chin. "Don," he says to his wife, who's seated at the other end of the table, "tell Brynn about the rock."

More groans from the boys as Trixie and Fred laugh.

"That there," she points her fork toward the living room, "is my lying rock. And let me tell you, it was a sanity-saver with these three." She eyes each of her boys with fondness. "Any time one of them got into trouble, they'd be quick to blame each other. And oh, the *arguing*. 'Shaw did it' and 'No, it was Griff' or 'It's Tucker's fault.' It was constant. And they were so convincing, all three. We had the hardest time discerning the truth." She smirks at her husband. "One summer day, one of them broke a window playing with a ball in the house, even though they'd been told a million times to keep all balls outdoors—"

All three brothers pipe up. "Lacey family rules."

"No one would confess, so I marched outside and found the biggest rock I could hold in one hand. I lined them up and told them that when I threw my rock, it would only hit the boy who was lying. So I wound up," she raises her arm to throw an imaginary rock, "and pretended to throw the rock at them. The guilty party automatically ducked, telling me exactly who the culprit was."

The three Lacey boys are unamused while the rest of us laugh. Griffin scrubs a hand down his face and points to Shaw. "That was your fucking fault. You dared me to throw that baseball."

Shaw holds up both hands. "I wasn't the one who ducked, fucker."

"Boys, no swear words at the table." Fred leans back and crosses his arms.

Even Donna joins in on the next "Lacey family rules."

I scrunch my nose at the six-five man beside me, imagining a little Griffin dodging his mother's lying rock. "You ducked, huh?"

Donna answers for him. "That time, yes. But they all had turns ducking through the years. That rock was a lifesaver before they became wise to my tricks."

The stories continue, and when Cam eventually arrives, we spend the remainder of dinner listening to him, Tucker, and Griffin reminisce about their high school football glory days. Shaw pipes in with a comment here or there, and nothing could wipe the proud, joyful smiles from Fred and Donna's faces.

Trixie was right. The Lacey love is fierce. And I'm happy—and privileged—to be surrounded by it tonight.

CHAPTER EIGHTEEN

GRIFFIN

As usual, I can't keep my eyes off Brynn.

Watching her interact with my family, sitting at the table where I ate breakfast and solved word problems as a kid? Hearing her laugh at our rehashed family anecdotes, surrounded by the people who've been with me through all my highs and lows? I pull in a deep breath and hold it in my lungs. The heady sensation that flows into my limbs makes my eyelids grow heavy.

Could also be a side-effect of the wine that Mom opened an hour ago.

Shaw left after we cleared the table, claiming it was almost his bedtime. I didn't miss the scrutinizing glances he cast Brynn's way during dinner. I'll make an effort to get my brother alone in the next day or two so I can ask him about it.

Trixie bailed not long after Shaw, wanting to check on Aunt Dot at the bar before she headed home. And when Cam stood not five minutes later, insisting he had an early shift at the station, Tuck and I exchanged knowing smirks.

When Brynn yawns beside me, Dad follows suit. "This young lady has the right idea. The sheep aren't going to count themselves."

"I put you two in your old room," Mom says as she collects empty wine glasses.

When she turns and heads toward the dishwasher, Brynn drops her head and studies her lap, cheeks ablaze.

"That's fine," I say, giving Brynn a reassuring squeeze. "Thanks."

Tucker stands and rounds the table, patting Brynn's shoulder as he goes. "I'll make sure to knock on all doors while you're here."

Her eyes and lips both list to the side. "Thanks so much."

He laughs at her tone. "No prob, *sis*." He tosses her a wink and smacks a loud kiss on Mom's cheek, and then he's gone.

Once the roar of his motorcycle has faded, I grab my woman's hand, and we bid my parents good night.

Other than a new comforter for the queen-size bed and the removal of my Jessica Alba and Katy Perry posters, Mom's kept my childhood bedroom much the same as it was when I left for college. The shelves above the wooden desk are crammed with every sports trophy, plaque, medal, and tournament ring I won starting in peewee sports all the way through high school. The dresser top is covered with the same.

I sit on the end of the bed, watching Brynn as she takes a slow trip down memory lane. She reads every award and searches for me in every team photo.

"Back row, third from left?" She glances over her shoulder to confirm. The proud smile she shines on me after each correct guess fills my chest with a tender ache. I track her every move and note every head tilt and squint and sigh.

Before long, she grows a little hesitant, her moves becoming less confident. She spins around from the dresser. "Why are you looking at me like that?"

I lift my chin, a silent invitation, and she reads my body language like she wrote the manual. When she steps between my spread knees, I wrap my arms around her, pull her close, and rest my cheek against her abdomen. Stroking my hair, she releases a satisfied sigh.

"I have a gorgeous woman in my childhood bedroom. It's like all my adolescent fantasies come to life."

She huffs a laugh. "Don't get any ideas, mister."

I rest my chin on her stomach and blink up at her. "Too late, professor."

"We can't have sex in your parents' house," she hisses. "In your *childhood bed*."

"We sure as fuck can."

She scrunches her eyes shut. "Griff—"

"Brynn. Baby. Give me those eyes."

She lifts her lashes, but the frown she gives me is full of trepidation.

"They're adults. We're adults. Adults have sex. My mom practically gave us her blessing earlier." I grip her hips and give them a squeeze. "My parents' bedroom is downstairs and on the opposite side of the house. Plus, my dad can't hear for shit, and my mom sleeps like the dead. How do you think the three of us snuck out so often in high school?"

Head hung, she slumps. "Your poor mother. She's a saint for putting up with the three of you."

A chuckle rumbles deep in my chest. "No doubt about that."

I jostle her and exhale my disappointment. After last night, I'm insatiable. And now, it looks like I'm returning to blue ball territory for the weekend.

I hate it there.

But the last thing I want is for Brynn to feel obligated or coerced into being intimate.

"I'm sorry, baby." I release her and straighten on the edge of the bed. "I promise I'll keep my hands to myself if you don't want to—"

"I never said I didn't want to."

A little flicker of hope ignites inside me. Even so, I give her my most convincing sad-dog eyes.

She frames my face with her soft hands. "Gah, this face. How will I ever be able to say no to this face?" She kisses the top of my head and swipes up her overnight bag. "I'm going to get ready for bed."

"Bathroom's right next door."

While she does her nighttime stuff, I strip down to my boxers—*Teenage Mutant Ninja Turtles* this time—and recline on the bed.

The door creaks open, and all of me sits up at attention. And I mean, *all* of me.

The way my heart has lodged itself in my throat makes it hard to speak, but still, I croak, "Are you kidding me?"

She frowns in confusion as she pulls back the comforter on her side.

I wave a hand up and down, gesturing to her body. "You expect me to be on my best behavior knowing *this* is what you're wearing to bed?"

With a roll of her eyes, she adjusts her pillow. "This is what I sleep in unless it's freezing cold outside. But now I have a *strapping* furnace of a man to keep me warm."

"Oh, I'll keep you warm all right." I toy with the thin-as-spaghetti strap holding up one cup of the skimpy night-gown. God, her tits look amazing in this thing.

Not sure it even qualifies as a *gown*, though.

I rub my beard along the sensitive skin under her chin and down her neck, pulling giggles from her. But those giggles morph into soft whimpers and sighs as my fingers find their way under those delicate straps and into the cups.

And then? I make love to my woman in my childhood bed-room.

Sixteen-year-old Griff would be fucking awestruck.

I untangle myself from Brynn as dawn's first rays peek through the blinds, careful not to disturb her. I did keep her up rather late, after all.

Knowing Mom will already be up and enjoying her morning coffee, I throw on joggers and a T-shirt, then head down the dark stairwell, making sure I step on a couple of the squeaky steps so Mom will hear me coming. Other than my not-so-stealthy movements and the tick of Granny's beloved grandfather clock, the house is quiet.

As predicted, she sits in her usual spot at the table, hands wrapped around a steaming Lacey Farms mug, wearing her favorite purple terry-cloth robe. The familiarity and comfort of the scene makes me smile. When I bend to kiss the top of her head, the scent of the lavender shampoo she's used for years is like a nostalgic hug.

"I haven't seen you on this side of seven a.m. in a while."

With a hum, I peek out the window over the sink, taking in the view of the farm that's slowly waking up with the sunrise. In the distance, Dad trudges toward the barn to see to the horses, his breaths puffing like clouds in the early morning chill.

The days I spent here all those months ago, when the Tors let me go and I thought my career was over, were dark. Coming home then wasn't the comfort it's always been. But my family rallied around me. They didn't let me wallow too much, but they gave me space to grieve in my own way.

Damn, am I grateful those days are behind me. If someone had told that sad, beat-down Griffin that in six months' time, he'd be playing for his favorite team and bringing a beautiful woman home with him, he likely would have suggested that person seek professional help.

With a matching mug filled to the brim, I take the seat next to my mother, and we sit in comfortable silence while we enjoy our coffee.

Donna Lacey can't stay quiet for long, so after only a few minutes, she squeezes my forearm. "I'm so happy you're here."

"Me, too, Mom."

She tilts her head, gives me a long assessment. "How long have you been in love with her?"

I choke on my coffee, and my eyes water as I cough and work to breathe again. "I'm not..."

She hits me with a disappointed frown. "Griffin Michael Lacey. Don't make me get the lying rock."

I twirl my mug on the tabletop, watching the way the dark liquid sloshes up the sides. "I'm that obvious, huh?"

"I see the way you look at her." Mom's eyes shine behind her glasses. "There's only one other thing you've ever looked at with that much passion and adoration, and that's a dadgum football."

I exhale a shaky breath, and with it, latent tension releases its hold on my muscles.

My mother, as usual, is correct. I'm crazy in love with Brynn Nelson.

Of course I'm in love with her. She's kind and witty and smart. The perfect combination of endearing and sexy. Adorable and ravishing. I can't get enough of her. Of riling her up. Making her breathless. I love that I can be my true self with her. Not Racy Lacey or an NFL superstar; just Griffin. She doesn't give a fuck about my status or wealth or performance on a damn field. She makes me want to be the best version of myself, and I think I do that for her, too.

"I can see it, you know." Mom stares into the distance, her expression serene. "The two of you, together. The perfect life you'll make. The precious dark-haired grandbabies you'll give me."

"Whoa, slow your roll there, Donna."

She lifts a shoulder, her smile sly. "When will you tell her?"

Angling back in my chair, I stretch my legs under the table. "Soon. Don't want to rush it, though. In case she's not there yet."

"She's there." She straightens her spine, no doubt ready to give me a lecture, but the sound of the side door opening stops her.

Seconds later, I'm bombarded by the only female in Shaw's life.

I let out an *oof*, and when I've recovered, I lavish the energetic golden retriever with aggressive ear scratches, chuckling at the way her rump wiggles in response. "Hey there, Delta girl."

"Delta, sit," Shaw commands, and the dog obeys instantly.

"What a good girl," Mom croons. "She deserves lots of treats." She shuffles to the counter and digs a dog biscuit out of a canister with Delta's head printed on the side.

"Mom, don't spoil her," Shaw says, sitting across from me with his mug of undoctored coffee.

"Oh, shush. If I want to spoil my only grandchild, you won't stop me, Shaw Morgan."

My brother raises a brow, scrutinizing me.

I hold both hands up. "Don't look at me. I've already been full-named this morning."

Mom feeds Delta three consecutive biscuits, ignoring Shaw's huffs. "I thought we'd grab lunch at Loblolly. I'm sure Brynn would love to look in the shops downtown."

"Sounds good." I move to the counter and grab another mug, and as I prep Brynn's coffee the way she likes, I turn to my brother. "Think we're going to hit up Dottie's tonight. Tuck and Cam already said they'd meet us. We'd love for you to come, too."

I hold my breath, bracing myself for the imminent rejection. Getting Shaw to participate in social settings is a challenge.

So when he grunts and mumbles, "Yeah, I'll grab a beer with y'all," I can't help but gape.

When I recover, I clear my throat. "Cool. I'll text you later." Before he has a chance to change his mind, I'm taking the stairs two at a time, trying not to spill my woman's coffee.

While my parents get things done around the house, Brynn and I head into town to goof off until lunchtime. I luck out and find a parking spot in front of the diner. The moment I join Brynn on the sidewalk and lace my fingers between hers, a voice warbles my name.

"Griffin Lacey, as I live and breathe. Look, Roscoe, it's Griffin." An elderly woman and her husband hobble over, both beaming.

"Mr. and Mrs. Abernathy, good to see y'all. This is my girl-friend, Brynn."

Beside me, Brynn flushes, but she extends her hand to the couple we both tower over. We exchange pleasantries, and then we're moving again. Though we only get a few feet down the sidewalk before we're stopped by more faces from my past. And just as we've crossed the street to the corner of the square, my former high school home economics teacher rushes over for a selfie.

"You took home ec?" Brynn asks when Mrs. Reynolds is out of earshot.

I tuck her into my side. "Of course I took home ec. That's where all the girls were." That earns me an elbow to the ribs. "Hey, I can sew on a button because of that class. Make a mean chocolate chip cookie, too."

"Hmm, I'll need to sample these mean chocolate chip cookies, sir. Find out what makes them so angry."

Head dropped back, I guffaw. "That was cheesy, but I'll bake for you, baby. The secret is to brown the butter." We stop at the corner where a diagonal sidewalk cuts through the square. "Here's what I wanted you to see."

Brynn reads the wooden sign next to the mouth of the side-walk. "The Holler Heart Path. Established 1986."

We step onto the first square of concrete in the path, the one with year 1986 stamped at the top. Inside the square are four pairs of handprints, each labeled with names that were carefully carved into the concrete when it was wet.

"When the town was gearing up to celebrate the centennial of its founding," I tell her, "the mayor's daughter was also planning her wedding to the love of her life. She had this grand idea to commemorate the town's love stories." I gesture to the handprints at our feet.

"Like a love hall of fame?" She grins, making my heart fucking flip-flop in my chest.

"Exactly. So every year on Founder's Day, if there are enough couples signed up, a new patch of concrete is poured and those lovebirds leave their handprints. Then someone with a steady hand etches the names before it dries."

Fingers linked, we stroll down the path.

"It doesn't happen every year, though. Couples sometimes have to wait until there are enough participants. I think they do five pairs at a time now." I pause at the 1988 square and tap a print with my sneaker.

Her face lights up. "Your parents." Her eyes gloss over as she studies their names. "Griff," she says, peering up at me, "this is so special."

I pull her to me, hugging her tight to my body. And when we kiss in the middle of the Holler Heart Path, all I can think about is how our handprints will look perfect side by side one day.

As we draw closer to the gazebo in the center of the square, Brynn pauses at each section of the sidewalk, looking over the names and handprints, pointing out the gaps between the years. She grabs my arm when we get to the last slab by the gazebo steps. The 2008 square.

She gasps and grabs my arm. "Is that—" She points to a large handprint in the corner. "Is that your brother?"

Grimacing, I scratch the beard I trimmed a little too close this morning. "Yep."

She assesses me but doesn't push for more, thank God. For a moment, she studies the sidewalk again, lingering on the name etched next to my brother's.

I rest my hand on my lower back, and she takes it before I even wiggle my fingers. Watching for her reaction, I lead her up the steps to the center of the gazebo.

"A *piano*." Her voice is full of wonder as she smooths a hand along the brightly painted upright. "This is so cool. People play it?"

I nod at it. "Try it out."

"I never learned how to play, but..." She presses a key, and her face lights up in delight.

My heart thumps against my sternum. Damn, I am so head over fucking heels for this woman.

"Who put this here?" She rounds the piano and wraps her arms around my waist.

"That, I'm afraid, is one of the great unsolved mysteries of Holly Holler. It appeared overnight several years ago." I keep my theory about the piano's existence to myself. "But someone covers it when the weather is really bad. And its paint job was courtesy of Ms. Mabel Abernathy, the art teacher at the high school."

"Abernathy? So the couple from earlier—"

"Are her grandparents."

"This is the cutest town. I love it here."

Her praise is fucking music to my ears. Because the truth is that I've already pictured the things Mom mentioned in our chat this morning: A life with Brynn, after football. Maybe settling down here, raising a family. Fuck, I'd love to make a whole crew of babies with her.

When I see my parents pull up to the diner, we head that way. After the patrons give us an initial enthusiastic welcome, they leave us alone so we can enjoy our lunch in peace. Dad insists on paying, and I let him. There's no use fighting him over it.

While he waits at the counter with our bill, Mom gasps. "Griff, if you're taking this girl to the Hoot tonight, you'd better take her to the DB for some boots."

Brynn's forehead wrinkles. "The DB?"

"The Dusty Britches." Mom nods at the front window. "Across the street. It's got a little bit of everything. But you can't go to a honky-tonk without a pair of cowgirl boots."

The thought of Brynn in a pair of western boots heats my blood. "Yep. Boots are a necessity for your saloon-night fit here in the Holler."

"Wait." She straightens, her face aglow. "Is Racy Lacey going to wear cowboy boots as part of his saloon-night fit?"

I tap her nose. "You'll have to wait and see, professor."

At the store, Brynn peruses the boot selection, considering the pros and cons of each pair. She narrows her choice to two sets, but then can't decide whether to get them in black or brown. She gives me a scowl when I tell her we'll get both colors.

Finally, she tries on a classic pair in black leather with tiny cream stitching details. "What do you think?" She points her toe and twists her foot from side to side.

With a peck to her lips, I pull her close. "I think I'm going to love spinning you around that dance floor tonight."

And when she's distracted by a rack of sunglasses, I buy her the boots in black *and* brown, because there'll be many more Hoot 'N' Holler nights in our future.

CHAPTER NINETEEN

BRYNN

"Maybe we should stay in. I'll text Tuck and Cam." Griffin's eyes are dark with desire, his voice thick, as I descend the stairs.

"You will not." I spin when I get to the bottom. "How's my honky-tonk fit?"

He catalogs every detail: my new black leather boots, my flirty black dress with the ruffle at the hem, and the rolled-up sleeves of the fitted tan-and-black plaid button-down I've knotted at my waist. My hair is half pulled up into a messy knot, with the rest in loose waves down my back.

He takes my hand and twirls me, then he pulls me in for a kiss. "You're perfect."

"Let me check out my handsome date." I smooth my hand down the navy-and-hunter plaid flannel he's wearing unbuttoned over a navy Henley. His sleeves are rolled up, too, and the forearms on display are doing things to my pulse. Peeking out from below his jeans is a pair of worn brown boots.

"Do I pass inspection?"

"With flying colors." I slip my arms beneath his plaid shirt and lean into him, savoring his body heat and manly scent. "And now that I know Racy Lacey owns a pair of cowboy boots, my life is complete."

His sigh is heavy. "I haven't worn the damn things in years. My feet rebelled the second I slipped them on. But that won't stop me from dancing with my girl."

Across the room, Donna clears her throat and waves her phone. She doesn't let us leave until she's snapped at least a dozen photos, like we're a couple of teenagers headed to a school dance. It's adorable.

On the drive into town, a fizzy sensation coats my stomach. This day will go down in history as one of the all-time best. Not only did Griff introduce me as his girlfriend to folks around town, but then I caught him sneaking *two* boot boxes into the truck and, when I chided him, he said, "Get used to being spoiled, professor." After boot shopping, we returned to the farm and spent a couple of hours outdoors. While Fred showed me the animals, he kindly answered all my ridiculous questions about farm life, all the while teasing me about being a city girl. More than once, Griff looked dumbstruck at how chatty his father was with me.

After the farm tour, Mrs. Lacey pulled out the baby Griffin scrapbooks, and we sat side by side on the couch, cooing and laughing at every one of his awkward stages. Griff kicked back in the recliner and pretended to be annoyed, but I caught his secret, pleased smiles as he scrolled on his phone.

We arrive at the Hoot 'N' Holler a little after eight, finding the parking lot mostly full. I get a finger wiggle as we navigate the crowd surrounding the bar, so I take his hand and follow as he leads me to where Tucker and Cam have secured a six-top table.

Our table is one of many surrounding three sides of a wooden dance floor. The fourth side features a small stage, where a band is warming up. One step up from our level, rows of wooden booths overlook the dance floor. The bar takes up the whole left side of the building. The place is wall-to-wall rustic honky-tonk decor: neon signs, corrugated metal, rough wooden beams. Scattered throughout are framed black-and-white posters of several music legends: Johnny Cash, Elvis, Dolly, and Tina Turner, to name a few. One wall is covered with old license plates from several states. And above the bar, a huge neon sign that says *Holleration Nation* glows.

The legs of my wooden chair scuff across the concrete floor when Griffin grabs one to pull me closer. He leans in so I can hear him over the crowd and the band that's warming up on stage. "You good to stay here while I grab drinks?"

As I nod, Trixie bounds up on the arm of a stoic Shaw.

"Look what I rustled up at the bar, folks." She sinks into a chair and pulls him down into the one beside it. Eyes twinkling, she hollers, "Saved this one's life, I tell ya. He had no less than five vixens eyeing him up, claws drawn, ready to pounce. Not all heroes wear capes." She flounces her wavy shoulder-length copper locks and gives her cousin a wink.

Cam knocks his beer against the one in Shaw's hand. "Yee-haw here might draw a bigger crowd than this one." He points the neck of the bottle at Griffin. "They'll come out in droves for such a rare sight."

As Shaw rolls his eyes and takes a pull of his beer, I study him. Like his younger brothers, the man is devastatingly hand-some, though his looks are more rugged, gruff. In his chambray button-down and beat-up Lacey Farms ball cap pulled low over mysterious blue eyes, it's no wonder the ladies flock to him. As I consider him, the name that's etched next to his on the Heart Path comes to mind. I know better than to ask, so I stick with a topic I hope is a little safer.

"Yeehaw?"

Trixie smirks. "Yeehaw Shaw."

"Trix," Shaw warns.

His cousin perks up, wiggling in her chair. "This stud was something of a legend on the youth rodeo circuit when he was in high school. Earned himself several gold buckles and a nick-name, to boot. Pun intended." She laughs at her own joke.

"All in favor of resurrecting Shaw's nickname?" Cam raises his beer and grins.

The eldest Lacey brother doesn't even acknowledge Cam, Trixie, and Tucker as they raise their hands. Instead, he homes in on Griffin, who's standing behind me, passing along some unspoken message. His voice holds the grit of sandpaper when he says, "Veto."

"Lacey family rules," the three vetoed nickname supporters recite dejectedly.

Griffin palms the crown of Tucker's backward ball cap. "Help me carry the drinks."

The two get as far as the booths before they're both swarmed with locals who pat their backs and ask for pictures.

When I spin back to the table, Trixie is grinning. "Ugh, can't take them *any*where."

A young waitress wearing denim cutoffs and a tight black tank with *If You Ain't Hootin', You Ain't Hollerin'* printed in white across the chest steps up with a tray full of beers. "These are from Dottie," she explains as she offloads the bottles. Once her tray is empty, she tucks a lock of her long, blond hair behind an ear and fixes a flirty smile on the oldest Lacey. "Hey, Shaw."

"Hey." That single word is low and gruff, but it brings a pink tinge to the girl's cheeks.

There's a moment of awkward silence before Cam puts the poor girl out of her misery. "Thanks for bringing these over, Suzie."

"No problem. You folks have fun." She smiles at the table and gives Shaw one final look, then she sashays away.

"See what I mean?" Trixie takes a swig of beer and sets it on the table with a clatter. "A sweet, twenty-two-year-old who could have her pick of almost any dude in here. Yet, she sets her sights on this old man."

Shaw rests his forearms on the table. "Thirty-six makes me an old man, huh?"

Trixie huffs a laugh, but her response is cut off when her mom appears at her side, wiping her hands on the seat of her jeans. "Mama!" She beams and leans into her mother, who smacks a kiss to her cheek. "The place is hoppin' tonight."

Dottie rounds the table to greet each of us. "Tell me about it. Half the bar has joined Griff and Tuck's fan club, so I thought I'd sneak away while they're occupied." Dottie gives Shaw an affectionate pat on the head. "My favorite nephew," she declares as he lets her sneak a kiss to his stubbled cheek.

"Aw, I thought I was your favorite," Cam whines next to Shaw.

Dottie rounds Shaw and tugs on Cam's ear. "You are my favorite." Cam dons a smug smile, but it melts into a scowl when she follows that up with "My favorite pain in the ass."

Trixie barks a loud "Ha!"

Then it's my turn. Griffin's aunt sidles up beside me and squeezes my shoulders. "Brynn. It's so good to see you again, hon."

"You, too." I peer up at her. "This place is amazing."

She scans the crowd, her lips tipping up. "Yeah, my John would be proud as punch to see it so packed." She plants a final kiss on her daughter's head. "You kids have fun tonight." Before she walks off, she taps Shaw's shoulder. "Don't let this one have too many."

Trixie joins her mother in her teasing. "Lightweight," she singsongs.

Shaw's only response, as if he's used to it, is a shake of the head.

The band, finally warmed up, starts playing in earnest.

"That's my cue," Trixie announces as she pops up from her chair. She saunters to the stage, hips swaying, and takes up a microphone. And when she belts out the opening line to a Shania Twain song that entices a large group to the dance floor, I gape.

Shaw chuckles at my bewildered expression and cranes his neck, taking in the stage. "Trix sings with the band most weekends. Wait until you hear her take on Reba."

My jaw drops farther, this time because of the quiet man across from me. He hasn't spoken that many consecutive words to me since we met. Heck, I'm not sure he's spoken that many total.

Tucker and Griffin finally return, arms laden with drinks. They give identical shrugs when they notice the new round of bottles that arrived while they were gone and add their haul to the mix.

"I didn't know Trixie sang," I say to Griff when he settles in his seat.

"Yeah, she's great, right?" He rests his arm on the back of my chair and traces small circles on my shoulder as we listen.

Cam turns his chair around, ignoring the group. Only a few bars in, he's transfixed on the talented redhead with the microphone.

The youngest Lacey looks from me to Cam and back again, then gives me a wink. "Griff, you gonna get your girl out there or should I offer to take her for a spin?" Tuck wags his brows and gives his brother an antagonizing grin.

Griff chucks a bottle cap at his brother's chest, then he clutches my hand. "Promised you a two-step, professor," he calls over his shoulder as he leads me to the edge of the dance floor.

The second our feet touch the smooth, wooden planks, hundreds of eyes find us, scrutinizing. If I look out at the crowd, I'm sure I'll see dozens of cell phones raised, recording our every move.

For the first time since we went public, the pressure of being the center of attention weighs on me, like I'm wading into a lake with rocks in my pockets. My legs lock, and my muscles tense.

He pivots back, studying my face with a concerned frown.

"I don't know how." As panic claws its way up my throat, I gather my hair off my neck and drape it over my shoulder. "And everyone's watching."

He steps into me, rests his large hands on my collarbone, and lifts my chin with his thumbs. I grip his forearms and inch into the safety of his powerful frame.

His eyes are a grayish green in the dim lighting as they search my face. "We don't have to do anything you don't want to do. Say the word, and we'll head straight back to our seats. But if your fear stems from the phones pointed our way, then we need to figure that out. Because it *will* happen again. As much as I hate that you'll experience it over and over, it comes with the territory. But I told you—I'm not keeping you a secret."

His voice is firm, but his gaze is gentle. He's right; when I agreed to be his, I understood that unrelenting attention from strangers was part of it. So I'll keep my focus on him alone, because he makes me brave.

He's been doing it since we met.

"Do you want me to teach you the two-step?" Now his voice is a soft caress.

I nod as much as his hold allows.

"Good." He presses his lips to mine and holds them there, proving his point—he's not hiding us. "You, professor, are an amazing badass who can do anything you set your mind to. Let's channel your inner Eleri and go kick some ass on this dance floor."

I laugh, and my heart stumbles a little at his reference to the tough, bold witch character in my dragon story.

He guides me to the center of the floor where we won't block other couples and faces me, holding my hands in his. "The two-step is basically a pattern of steps. Two quick, two slow. And we do those steps in a giant circle." He tilts his head to the chain of couples circling around us. "I'll start off with my left foot." He brings it forward, and I automatically step back with my right. "Yep, you'll start with the right. Aunt Dot taught us that ladies start with their right feet because they're always *right*."

An ounce of my trepidation drains from me as I smile up at him. "Aunt Dot is a wise woman."

His responding chuckle is a tonic for my soul, allowing me to roll my shoulders back and shed the cloak of nerves I wore out here.

"That she is. Now…" He places my left hand on his shoulder and puts his right on my back. "Rest your elbow on my arm. Yep, like that. And we'll hold these hands like this."

"Oh my gosh." I giggle. "This feels like Johnny teaching Baby in *Dirty Dancing*."

He presses his mouth to my ear. "We'll save our dirty dancing for the bedroom, professor."

Holy hell. Liquid heat pools in my belly so intensely I have to fight the urge to fan myself.

He pulls away, smirking. "You ready?"

"I think so." I lower my chin to watch his steps so I'll know when to make mine.

"Uh-uh," he chides. "Don't look down. Keep your eyes on me."

Keep your eyes on me.

It's as easy as breathing, because his face has become my beacon. His arms are my safe shelter. His touch is my motivation. And his heart is my home.

I follow his lead around the dancefloor while his soft chants of *quick-quick, slow…slow* guide my every step. As we move, I don't glance at our feet or the other couples or the crowd of onlookers. No, I keep my eyes on the man I've fallen for, and everything else fades away.

Before I know it, the song is over and the crowd erupts in applause. Trixie speaks, her honeyed voice echoing through the speakers around the space. "All right, we're gonna slow things down with this next song. It's one of my favorites, and tonight, it goes out to number 89 and his lovely lady."

As a round of wolf whistles and cheers fill the air, she winks at us. Then the keyboard player starts playing a slow tune, and when her beautiful voice belts out the first notes of "Sunday Kind of Love," Griffin wraps me in his arms, and we sway to the melody.

Lost in each other, but at the same time *found.*

"*Baby*," Griffin pleads from behind the wheel. "You're making this a bigger deal than it is."

Arms crossed, I keep my focus fixed out the passenger window. I refuse to look at him. I've maintained this position since we got in the truck fifteen minutes ago. It's a miracle I could even look his parents in the eye as they hugged me goodbye and made me promise to come back soon. I was so mortified it didn't even register that Shaw actually gave me a brief side hug until after we'd pulled out of their driveway.

Griffin grasps my arm and tugs, but all the move does is make me glare harder and inch my body closer to the door.

Though when my boyfriend chuckles under his breath, I turn my glare his way.

"How is this funny to you, Griffin Lacey?"

His mouth curves in a sinful smile. "I regret nothing."

Indignation and shame burn hot in my gut. "Ugh."

"I gotta say, I've never seen this side of you."

"Pissed off?"

"No. A tiny bit ridiculous."

Teeth gritted, I suck in a sharp breath. "You're calling me ridiculous?"

He pinches his thumb and forefinger together. "A tiny bit."

Huffing, I swivel back to the soybeans. As we drive through downtown Holly Holler on our way home, I will myself to think only of the wonderful memories we made here this weekend. It's no use. All those beautiful moments keep getting interrupted by what transpired in the Laceys' kitchen this morning.

More specifically, in their pantry.

After Donna made a huge breakfast, complete with Griffin's favorite biscuits and gravy, as well as french toast—a gesture that made me tear up—everyone trekked out to the barn to check out a new litter of kittens. Griffin wanted to show me the horses next, but he wanted to give them peppermints, so he and I hiked back to the house alone.

What happened next will go down in history as Brynn's Most Embarrassing Moment Ever, and despite my best efforts to block the scene out, my brain unspools the memories like a roll of film:

The unorganized walk-in pantry is stuffed to the gills. The cans of vegetables are distributed willy-nilly, and there are boxes of crackers stuck between containers of flour and sugar. Next to an unopened jar of olives, I find two bags of noodles and a pack of batteries.

"Do you see them?" I peer over my shoulder to check Griffin's progress, only to find him staring at my ass with heated eyes.

"These jeans are fucking sexy." He spins me around, pulls me to his torso, and slips his hands in my back pockets.

"They're mom jeans," I laugh. But the nearness of him, his intoxicating scent, and his broad palms cupping my backside are a heady combination.

"Mmm, I don't care what kind they are. I want them shoved to your ankles so I can see how wet I can make you." He nuzzles my neck, sucking that spot below my earlobe that drives me crazy.

Every word, every move, heats my body further. Somehow, though, I have the presence of mind to pull the door closed behind him.

Good thing, because the second his lips touch mine, we're a perfect storm of hot kisses and sensual groping and heavy breathing.

Griffin backs me into the shelves with enough force to knock a small box off the top one, but we're too occupied to care. We're fused together, and his arousal is evident. He wedges a thigh between my legs to shift me higher and slips a hand under my sweater. I loop my arms around his neck to give him better access, and when his thumb finds a nipple through the satin of my bra, and he circles it through the fabric, I nip at his bottom lip. With a grunt, he tucks the cup below my breast, and the skin-to-skin contact on the sensitive tip sends a rush of dampness to my panties.

He kisses his way along my jaw and down my neck, hot presses of his mouth that scorch my fevered flesh. When he squeezes my nipple between his fingers, I whimper and circle my hips, searching for friction, desperate to ease the ache between my legs.

Griffin releases a growl of frustration and jerks my sweater up, exposing the breast he's been working over. And when his warm mouth latches on to it, I dig my fingers into his hair, holding him there, all while fighting the urge to push him away, because this is too much.

This is all too much.

Thoughts like this is wrong *and* we shouldn't be doing this in his parents' pantry *and* what if someone hears us? *flash through my mind, but the quiver between my thighs forces them out as quick as they enter.*

When he laves my nipple, I grope the ridge of hardness in his jeans, stroking the denim with enough pressure to make his grunts more frequent.

He releases my breast, and as he pants against it, his hot puffs cause goose bumps to pebble my skin. The intense blue of his irises and the gravel in his voice send me reeling. "Take it, baby," he rasps, the demand impossible to ignore, so I increase my speed, riding his leg, rolling my hips. "Grind that sweet little pussy all over me until you get there."

He resumes sensual pulls on my nipple, each tug making the pulse between my legs more intense.

"Oh, God, Griff..." I press my head back against the edge of a shelf and cling to his biceps, rocking faster. The seam of my jeans and his rock-hard thigh are the perfect combination against my clit. The

tightening and throb in my lower muscles prove that my release is so, so close.

He gives my nipple a final lick and brings his mouth back to mine, his lips demanding and unyielding as they take control.

I close my eyes as the waves begin. They're shallow at first, but when he presses his lips to my ear and rumbles "Come," I drown in pure ecstasy, and they crest over me, bursts of pleasure pulsing throughout my body.

When I come down, I open my eyes to find a smug smile gracing Griffin's reddened lips. He holds my waist to keep me upright, and I tip my forehead to his chest to catch my breath.

"I'm the luckiest fucker on the planet to have a front-row seat to that.*" With a kiss to my hair, he lowers his thigh so my feet touch down. My legs are jelly, my boob is still out, and my cheeks and chin and chest are probably red from his beard, but all I can think about is returning the favor. I want—no,* need—*to make him come.*

Orgasms clearly make me bold and reckless, because once I've straightened my bra and sweater, I lower to my knees, kiss the outline of his hard bulge, and pop open the button on his jeans.

"Fuck, baby—" Eyes wide, he braces a hand on a shelf.

I'm so lust-crazed that I don't register the faint scuffs on the other side of the door until it's too late. I've just lowered his zipper and am reaching into his boxers as the pantry door bursts open.

"Oh, shit!" Tucker curses before he spins away.

"Goddamn it, Tuck." Griffin hauls me to my feet and crushes my body to his.

Though I want to bury myself in my boyfriend's chest and never come out, I press my cheek to his pecs so I can see Tucker's back. When his shoulders bounce in silent laughter, I blurt, "You promised to knock on the doors."

He whips around, red-faced but grinning. "You expected me to knock on the pantry *door?"*

Shaw and their parents choose this moment to come inside. They freeze when they notice the guilt marring all of our features.

"What's wrong?" Mrs. Lacey looks from one son to the other, then at me.

"Tucker—" Griffin growls, pure threat.

The youngest Lacey relaxes against the counter and crosses his inked arms. "Just caught Brynn with her hand in the cookie jar."

Under his breath, Griff mumbles "Fuck."

Oblivious, Mrs. Lacey says, "She can have as many cookies as she wants."

My skin blazes hotter than the sun, and I beg the universe for a rewind button. I can't bear to peek at his parents, but I don't miss Shaw's smirk before I bury my face in Griffin's chest again. Tucker's low chuckles cease when his brother grabs a package from a shelf and pelts him with it.

"Ow, fucker. That hurt."

Mr. Lacey says, "Language."

And against the warmth of Griff's soft hoodie, I mouth "Lacey family rules" as the three brothers chant it out loud.

Still in disbelief that a weekend of so many highs ended like *that*, I sigh and fix my gaze on the road ahead. I can feel Griffin's concern, but I'm still too caught up in my embarrassment to start a conversation.

He clears his throat. "What can I do to make this better?"

The soothing tone of his voice earns my attention. But when a corner of his mouth kicks up, I'm back to being irritable.

"Could you invent a time machine so we can travel back to before I *dry humped* your leg in your parents' pantry?"

His lips twitch. "I mean, that is where the *dry* goods are kept, so…"

Annoyance courses through my veins. "Not helping."

"Got it." He lifts a hand from the steering wheel and mimes locking his lips.

We're silent for a couple of miles, but the burn in my throat becomes too much. "I'm sorry I'm being an inconsolable brat. I just really, *really* want your family to like me, and—"

"Brynn." He cuts me off. "Hear me when I say this: they fucking *adore* you."

My heart pangs, and my voice comes out small and unsure. "Really?"

"Absolutely. Even if you owe their son and brother a blow job."

"Ugh." I smack him with the back of my hand, then cross my arms again.

Griffin's charming, unbothered smile brightens. "I know what you need."

He taps a few buttons on the dash touchscreen, and as the twangy intro to "Jackson" blares through the speakers, he bobs his head and shoulders to the beat. He warbles along with Johnny Cash, voice deep, making it impossible not to smile. Though I do my best to hide it.

"C'mon, you gotta sing June's part." He holds an invisible microphone in front of my mouth.

His wild joy is so infectious, I can't help but give in. The shame from earlier is forgotten as my grin breaks free, and I croon along, happy to be so in sync with the man beside me.

CHAPTER TWENTY

GRIFFIN

"Everything good with you?" Beau asks, one brow cocked and his attention fixed on my bouncing knee.

Nodding, I shove the crossword back into my bag. I give up on trying to find calm in the orderly black-and-white squares. They usually work like a charm, but I'm too on edge today.

I woke up like this, aching for Brynn, and the sensation hasn't dulled since. After our bye, we were fortunate to have two home games in a row, so this is our first weekend apart since we made it official. Hell, we've been separated for a little over twenty-four hours, and I'm a wreck. I fucked her before I left yesterday, thinking that would be enough to get me through this road trip, but it only made me want to stay tangled up in her, football be damned.

Yeah, that's a fucking terrifying development.

Never in my life have I wanted to put anyone or anything above this sport. It's the only thing I've ever been good at. The only thing I've ever nurtured.

Then a five-nine adorably nerdy, sexy as fuck brunette crashes into my life and wrecks my priorities.

Since the crossword didn't do the trick, I seek a different way to shake these unsettled nerves. I open my camera roll and scroll back a few months, searching for the picture I've looked at more times than I'd ever admit.

It's a screenshot I saved from the night Brynn agreed to experience Memphis with me. I discovered it later that night, while lying in bed, on the Blues' Instagram page. The social media department had posted a series of shots from the season-ticket event at the Peabody. I sat up when I recognized the girl in the picture as the one I'd shared a sausage and cheese plate with hours before. Brynn and King, the Blues' hound dog mascot. Don't ask me why, but I was compelled to save the picture on my phone.

Now I can't imagine my life without the beautiful smile or big brown eyes that shine on my screen.

Brynn Nelson has become a necessity. I need her like my lungs need oxygen.

But I also need to learn how to deal with being apart from her. The guys in this locker room are counting on me to pull my weight out there today.

Sudden exclamations from teammates across the room draw my attention. Carlos, Tyrell, and Devon are huddled up, heads bent over a phone.

When Carlos' shocked face morphs into one of disgust, Beau and I wander over to check it out.

"Cap, have you watched any of these?" Devon asks as we approach. He holds his phone up. "Hydraulic press videos."

The video shows a huge machine crush a watermelon to bits, and ribbons of the smashed fruit shoot out through round holes in the base of the press.

"Yeah, some of them are pretty gnarly." Beau laughs.

"We've got a little competition going to see who can find the grossest ones."

This is not what I usually fall into before a game, but it'll work, so until it's time for pregame warm-ups, I let my teammates and their strange videos distract me from this twitchiness in my gut.

In the middle of the first quarter, after a not-so-auspicious start, Beau finds me on the sideline. "You sure you're good? You don't have a crazy high fever again, do you?"

Hands braced on my hips, I catch my breath. "No. Why?"

My friend narrows his eyes. "You ran the wrong route on second and eight."

"I read the coverage wrong, man. Sorry."

And I deserve the call-out. My mind blanked when he called the play, and then my ass was double-teamed. I couldn't get open, but had I run the correct route, we probably would've gotten the first down.

Turns out, that missed route was the least of our worries. Jefferson and I both drop passes in the first half, and Beau throws a pick late in the second quarter. Our offense can't find our rhythm, and the defense spends so much time on the field, they're exhausted at the half. Mundy doesn't yell often, even when we're down in a game, but he chews our asses at halftime.

Since we won the toss and deferred, we get the ball at the start of the second half. The crowd noise in this stadium—notorious for being the loudest in the league—is deafening after we break the huddle and step to the line to begin our opening drive. I scan the defense, calm my breathing, prepare for muscle memory to take over.

Beau's called for a play-action pass. From my stance, I brace for the snap. There's no way I'll hear his cadence with the noise. But before our center snaps the ball, I flinch, and a flag is thrown.

"False start, number 89. Five-yard penalty. Repeat first down."

And it's all downhill from there. I get called for holding later in the quarter, and on our next drive, I drop another ball. Greenway makes a costly fumble in the red zone that results in our opponents scoring a field goal. When Beau throws another interception at the beginning of the fourth, I charge down the field to make the tackle, but my legs run out of steam before I can stop the guy from scoring. We end up losing by an embarrassing margin, and we don't score a single touchdown.

It's our worst game of the season so far. Sure, it was a team loss, and several of my teammates made bad plays. But I fucked up the most.

We're all quiet as we file into the locker room, even Coach.

The mood is somber as we shower and change. Coach takes Beau and a defenseman to the media area for the visiting team, and the rest of us are left to deal with the members of the media who are allowed into the locker room for postgame interviews.

When SNN's Blues reporter makes a beeline for me, I mutter a "fuck" before pasting on a fake smile.

Andrea aims her phone my way and starts her interview. "Griffin, thoughts on today's loss?"

My stomach knots. I don't want to do this. I'm ready to board the plane and get home to my woman. But duty calls.

"It was a tough loss. We made too many mistakes, and they capitalized on every one. I've got to play better going forward, and this team is committed to finishing the rest of the season strong. We'll regroup this week and put in the hard work so we're prepared for the next one."

Fuck, I deserve a gold star for that soundbite—not a single curse.

Andrea's bleach blond hair sways as she gives her head a tiny shake and pinches her lips together. Not the reaction she was going for, then. I square my shoulders and lift the strap of my bag, hoping she takes the hint.

She doesn't. Instead, her eyes take on a cunning glint, and she goes in for the kill. "There's been quite a bit of speculation about your new relationship floating around social media the past couple weeks. What, if any, impact has that attention had on your focus on the field?"

My blood boils at her audacity. But by some miracle, I keep my features neutral when I answer. "My personal life has always been and will always be just that—personal. My life off the field is separate from this." I heft my bag onto my shoulder and dip my chin. "Thanks for the time, Andrea." Duty served, I head out to the team bus to wait for the rest of the guys.

While I wait, I check my phone. There are several unread messages on our Lacey family thread and one from my friend Mel, my buddy Cordell's girlfriend. She critiques my clothing choices before every game. I save those for later and tap on the name that steadies my heart and soothes my stress.

Brynn

> I did a Google search for the most inspiring quotes about losing. But none of them felt right. So I'm going to send you an original Brynn Nelson quote instead, one composed just for you.

> "You might have lost the game, but you've totally won my heart."

> Too cheesy? Perhaps. But a wise man once told me that I'm an amazing badass who can do anything. Surely that includes writing motivational quotes?

> I miss you. See you soon.

Fuck, I love her.

She makes me laugh and eases my worries and turns me on, all at once.

The last-minute offer from the Blues was like a checkdown pass Beau relies on when his primary options are covered—it was my last resort. A life preserver when I was drowning in uncertainty about my future in this sport. But that Hail Mary has not only given me another season of football. It's given me the greatest gift of my life: Brynn.

I type out a quick reply.

> You're perfect, professor. Leaving for airport. Can't wait to kiss you.

I nap for half of the four-hour flight home and spend the rest of the trip catching up on the latest chapter of Brynn's book.

We land in Memphis after midnight, and then we're shuttled back to the Blues' facility, where our cars wait in the player lot. I'm gathering my things, ready to follow the guys off the bus, when someone up front makes an announcement.

"Coach called a brief meeting. Said it would take fifteen minutes, tops."

A collective groan ripples through the bus. This is the last thing any of us want to do after that shit show of a game and the grueling journey home. We expect the ass-chewing tomorrow when we review game film, but to endure it tonight, too?

"Let's get this over with." Beau slaps my shoulder as we shuffle down the aisle.

To my surprise, Coach Mundy's brief speech is upbeat. The dejected, disappointed expressions we wore when we entered the room are transformed by his words, and I'm in a much lighter mood when he's through.

Until I encounter a jackass on my way out of the building.

Jack and another suit wait near the mouth of the hall that leads to the coaches' offices. Players file by, heading to the exit, and I keep pace. Muscles tensed, I'm determined to avoid eye contact with the jerk as I pass him, but he has the balls to speak up.

"Tough game, Racy."

I freeze, and to my left Beau mutters, "Keep moving." But I refuse to let this douche get the last word.

He juts his chin and slips his phone into his shirt pocket as I step closer. Even though I've got over half a foot and at least sixty pounds on him, he doesn't flinch or back down. If anything, my attention makes him bolder.

He narrows ice-blue eyes and sneers. "You know what they say: women weaken legs."

My anger flares. *Women weaken legs.* Athletes hear that bullshit all the time. Coaches recite that line to make players think twice about partying and hooking up.

Behind me, a small audience has gathered. I can feel them. I should be the bigger person and walk away.

I've won the girl, after all.

But I don't fucking have it in me tonight.

"The only legs that are weak are my woman's when I make her come."

His face grows red and his jaw goes rigid as the crowd erupts in *oohs* and *damns*, and before I can even smirk, he slams his fist into my cheekbone.

As I register his reaction, Beau steps between us and gently pushes me back. "Don't," he warns, his voice low, while our teammates shout, encouraging me to retaliate.

Behind Beau, Jack shakes and unclenches his fist. I can't help but grin as I watch. That punch hurt him more than it hurt me. Physically, yes. But also professionally.

When he notices my smile, he lunges for me again, but his buddy restrains him. "Let him go, Jack. He's not worth it." I've never seen this dude before, which tells me he must not be high up in the organization or he's a new hire. But he has the audacity to curl his lip and grate out, "Everyone knows his reputation. He'll move on to the next one soon." Then he lifts his chin, raises his voice, addressing the gathered group, and says, "Watch out for Mr. Steal Your Girl here."

I give Beau's bicep a slap, and he releases me. I stretch my spine and use my bulk to intimidate the two wusses who now eye me with concern.

"Nah. I didn't steal her. *He* lost her. But I'm damn sure keeping her, because she is a fucking treasure."

With that, I walk away to a smattering of applause.

Beau is on my heels. "Shit, Griff, that could've gone south real quick."

"Thanks for having my back."

As we step out into the cold night, the icy air does wonders to cool me down.

Beau reaches his vehicle first, but before he gets in, he spins my way. "Losing sucks, but being your teammate definitely does not. Brynn's a lucky woman, Lacey."

"Aw, Dempsey, that was fucking beautiful." I place a hand on my heart.

He rolls his eyes, but his smile is clear, even in the dim parking lot.

"Love you, too, Cap. See you tomorrow."

The Memphis streets are all but deserted at this time of night. As I drive, I scrub a hand over my face, eager for the warmth waiting for me in my bed. *Our* bed. We've shared it every night since I made her mine, and I've begun bringing random items of hers downstairs when she's not home. Her toothbrush is slotted next to mine in the cabinet, her bras and panties have their own drawer in the dresser, and Barnaby is right at home against her pillow.

Her plan was to move out after the holidays, but there's no way I'll let that happen. We haven't discussed it yet, but we will. Soon. I'm ready to lock this woman down in every way.

When I step into the apartment, the old-timey musical Brynn loves floats through the air, and the brightly dressed actors on the TV are lining up for a barn dance. Other than the faint strains of music from the movie, the apartment is still. Brynn's a lump on the couch, curled up in a soft blanket with Barnaby in her arms. When I catch sight of the Oklahoma T-shirt she's wearing, my favorite, I swallow the burn in my throat.

I lower to the coffee table, rest my elbows on my knees, and exhale. The pressure and unsteadiness of the day melt away as I watch her chest rise and fall in steady breaths. I'm overwhelmed by her. By how much I love her.

I'm also overwhelmed with exhaustion, so I curve my hand over her hip and give her a gentle shake.

"Baby. Wake up."

Blinking, she stretches her legs, then sets her eyes, unfocused, on me. When awareness settles, she gives me a sleepy smile. "You're home."

"Yeah. Were you waiting up for me?"

"Trying to." She pushes herself up.

I angle forward and help her, then sigh when she frames my face and softly kisses me.

She hums against my lips and wraps her arms around me. "Missed you."

"Missed you, too, baby." I drop my head to her shoulder and bury my face in her neck, inhaling that sweet-and-floral scent I love.

She pulls back, assessing me, and then her eyes narrow, and she grasps my chin to angle my head to the side. "What happened?"

I wince when she probes the spot on my cheekbone with her fingertips. "Cheap shot."

She glowers. "From who?" she asks, her voice pure steel.

Fuck, my woman is ready to throw down for me.

Her stunning fierceness makes my pulse quicken, but I smooth my hands down her back and rest them on her hips, letting the feel of her settle me. "No one that matters."

"Hmm." She searches my face for a beat, but then her posture relaxes. With her hands on my shoulders again, she begins massaging. "Sorry about the game."

I sigh. "I sucked today."

She squeezes my traps, but she remains silent. I love that she doesn't spout platitudes. She lets me sit in this space for as long as I need to. And she understands that I need to process the loss and work through it on my own, but she ensures I'm not alone as I do it.

This silent support is just one more reason I love her.

"Brynn Nelson, you're a goddamn miracle, you know that?"

She gives me a confused frown, her brow furrowing, but I kiss the expression away, and when we break apart, her lips part in wonder.

Hypnotized by her, held hostage in her gaze, I confess the monumental secret I've been keeping from her: "I love you, Brynn."

Tears brim and her voice wobbles. "Griff—"

"I'm so fucking in love with you, it overwhelms me. The way I feel for you—it's intense and passionate and ferocious and soft and so goddamn sweet. But it's fucking perfect. Because *you* are perfect."

She blinks, and the tears crest her lashes. When a beautiful smile overtakes her face, I cup her cheeks and swipe the wetness with my thumbs. Then I get lost in kissing her. Four perfect kisses—one for every month I've known her.

She opens her mouth and inhales, ready to respond, but I cut her off. "I don't want you to feel obligated to say it back to me, not until you're ready. And I don't care how long that takes. We belong to each other and—"

"Griffin, I love you, too."

I can't move. Can't breathe. My heart pounds so hard I wouldn't be surprised if she could see the outline of it stretching my shirt like I'm some zany cartoon character.

Her beaming smile becomes a laugh. Quickly, though, it melts away, and her features soften. "I think I've been in love with you since you rescued me from the Peabody. How could I not love you? You're charming and kind and funny and *strapping*."

I wag my brows, and she huffs a laugh.

"I love your spirit," she murmurs. "I love that you make me brave. When I'm with you, I feel like I can fly."

I grin. "Like a dragon?"

"Like a badass dragon." She snorts a laugh.

"Baby." I kiss her again, tasting the saltiness of her tears. "Please say it again."

"I love you."

"Good girl. Feel free to say it every time I make you smile. Now let's go to bed."

I slip my hands under her ass, the silkiness of her panties warm against my palms, and when I stand, she wraps her arms and legs around me like a koala, smashing Barnaby between our chests. In our bedroom, I lower her to the bed and shed my clothes, then climb into the cool, crisp sheets. She waits until I get comfortable, and when she snuggles into my side, my shoulder becomes her pillow.

We whisper our newfound oath to each other, and when her breathing evens out, I follow her into oblivion.

CHAPTER TWENTY-ONE

BRYNN

"Fifteen minutes!" Griffin calls from the living room, where he's waiting for me. I rest a hand on my stomach in an effort to calm the sea of nerves that churn beneath my skin and stare at my reflection in the mirror.

The one in the bathroom I share with my NFL superstar boyfriend.

The girl looking back at me can't believe this is our life.

Somehow, this boring plain-Jane college instructor has bagged an absolute stud.

He's become my everything: friend, defender, and lover. He loves me so well, in the little ways and the big ones. Soft and out loud. Gentle and tough when I need him to be. He's affectionate and sweet, but also hot and naughty.

And he's even converted me into a football fan.

With a long breath out, I shake my head. Then I swipe on a layer of lip gloss and step back and smooth my hands over my dress. The dress I picked up when Paige and I shopped for outfits for the Blues' holiday party. I knew this was the one the second I saw it, and I've been dying to wear it since.

The asymmetrical neckline that exposes one shoulder. The fitted top that hugs my breasts just right. The long, flowy skirt with a slit up to my thigh. The color looks amazing with my fair skin and dark hair. This dress is a showstopper, and I can't wait to see Griffin's reaction.

I'm buckling my strappy gold heels when he shouts a five-minute warning. God, it feels amazing to wear heels for special occasions without worrying about my boyfriend's ego.

When I step into the living room, Griffin is standing by the couch, holding my wool peacoat. As he takes me in, from the braids and twists of my half updo down to the heels on my feet in one slow pass, I hold my breath. When his eyes lock with mine, a single word escapes his lips: "Goddamn."

I jut a hip so the slit exposes my leg. "Boyfriend seal of approval?"

His voice is pure grit. "Boyfriend gives it a million I-can't-wait-to-peel-it-off-you-later stars."

A flush of heat rushes to my face, but I can't hold back my grin. "You clean up nice, Mr. Lacey." I caught a glimpse while I was getting ready, but now I can fully admire him. The charcoal tweed blazer is a perfect complement to his black pants and dress shirt. The white lights twinkling on the Christmas tree we decorated together a few weeks ago highlight his sparkling blue eyes and bright smile.

He's so handsome, and he's all mine.

Another round of nerves flutters in my tummy. "It's okay that it's red?" I swipe my palm along the garnet fabric.

He gives me a quizzical look as I slip my arms in the coat he's holding open. "Baby," he says as he gently pulls my hair from under my collar, "you can wear whatever color you want. Let's head down. Beau and Paige should be here soon."

Paige squeals through her open window as we make our way to Beau's idling SUV. "Hottest couple alert."

"Why aren't *we* the hottest couple?" Beau pouts behind the wheel.

She tosses her blond waves. "No, babe, we're the *cutest* Blues couple."

"Facts." He holds up a hand, and they high-five.

My friend is dressed in a belted hunter-green jumper with sheer sleeves, and with Beau's matching dark-green sport coat, there's no doubt they're the cutest.

After we park and trek up the loading dock, we join the crowd of Blues players and personnel already on the riverboat. The three-story boat is decked out in festive garland and red ribbons. Long tables, parallel to the wall of windows on either side, are decorated with elegant place settings and centerpieces in red, white, and silver. Under the windows, the food is set up in steaming chafing dishes and huge serving bowls. There's a small stage at the back of the space where a quartet plays jazzy renditions of holiday tunes, and at the opposite end, there's a bar.

While the guys get drinks for the four of us, Paige and I mingle with the players and their partners. Once the boat launches from the dock, we all pile our plates with delicious Memphis barbecue and all the fixings. We find seats at the end of one of the tables and are joined by Devon, the other tight end, and Tyrell, the wide receiver, as well as D'Angelo Sweeney and Charmaine.

I love witnessing these tough players interact off the field. Their strong friendships play a big role in their ability to play so well together. They tease each other relentlessly, but always with affection. Surely there's a toxic male personality or two on the team, but this group is full of the kind of guys who encourage and support and build one another up, no matter what.

"Hey, Cap, you know a boat captain can marry couples, right?" Devon eyes Beau, then Paige. "If you two want to make it *o*-ffish, I'm offering best man services. I bet Coach'll walk Paige down the aisle."

"Sorry, Greenway. That's not true. Unless said captain is an actual recognized marriage officiant, like a judge or minister or notary."

Greenway's jaw drops, the stunned expression making us laugh. "But in the movies…"

Paige chirps, "Aw, good thing you're cute, Dev."

While we enjoy the food and each other's company, Coach Mundy and Mrs. Russell, the team's owner, give speeches. Whoops and hollers sound around us when two players grab mics and treat us to a lovely a capella version of "Blue Christmas."

When Griffin and Beau, along with ten of their teammates, line up along the front of the stage, Paige and I exchange bewildered looks. But as the group sings a football version of "The Twelve Days of Christmas"—each player taking on his own gridiron gift and acting it out—we laugh and cheer with the crowd. Beau cheekily flashes his hand when he warbles "five Super Bowl rings," and Griff's enthusiastic touchdown signal every time he croons "seven points a TD" earns plenty of laughs.

During the last verse of the song, right before his turn, he flinches and his features lock up. His focus is fixed on one spot in the crowd, so I follow it, searching for who's garnered this reaction, but no one stands out.

I don't get a chance to ask him who caused him to tense up like that, because my own ghost of Christmas past makes eye contact when Griffin returns to his seat. Jack's glare is colder than the temperature outside. When my current boyfriend notices my ex, he lazily drapes an arm along the back of my chair and dips his head to press a lingering kiss to my bare shoulder. Staking his claim. A move so brazen and possessive it makes me clench my thighs.

According to Paige, Jack is lucky to still have a job after he socked Griffin last month. What she doesn't know is that I asked my man to speak up on his behalf. As much as I'd love to be rid of Jack for good, I don't want to be the reason he loses his dream job. Shane was all too willing to accept Griffin's explanation when he insisted it was a "slight misunderstanding that won't happen again" in order to keep his right-hand man.

Once dinner is over, we mingle, and Beau and Paige leave to check out the upper decks. While Griff and I grab another drink at the bar, I keep Jack in my periphery to ensure we won't cross paths.

"You want to check out the river?" Griffin asks when he swallows the last of his bourbon.

"Yeah, go on up. I'll find you after I use the restroom."

He kisses my hand. "Sure? I can wait." When I nod, he says, "Don't forget your coat."

When I'm finished in the restroom, I snag my coat from the back of my chair and head up. The night air is brisk, but this area is covered, blocking any wind. The deck is lined with rows of wooden benches, and several people are hanging out up here, bundled in their coats and scarves to brave the winter night. I shuffle down the center aisle, scanning the group. Beau and Paige are huddled close, deep in conversation, but my guy isn't in sight, so I pull my coat tighter and climb to the top deck.

This level has a covered section in the middle but open decks at the front and rear of the boat. I blink up at the clear night sky and breathe in the crisp air, relishing the slight burn in my lungs. I scan the people, looking for Griffin, but this area is crowded, too. Laughter and snatches of conversation float through the air as I search. I'm about to dig through my clutch for my phone when I see his outline. He's standing at the back railing.

But he's not alone.

Stressful situations typically cause one of two reactions in people: fight or flight. But there's a third possibility, and that's how I respond now—I freeze.

In the dim light from the covered area, she's striking, with long waves of midnight hair that flow to her elbows. She's dressed in a white calf-length faux fur coat and black leather leggings. Her cherry-red stilettos have got to be at least five inches and match the stain on her lips. Even with the added height, she doesn't quite reach his shoulders. When she smiles up at him adoringly, my stomach sinks like a stone in the river we're floating.

But when he tips his head back in laughter, focus fixed only on her? The most horrible sense of déjà vu strikes. I'm back at the Peabody, watching my world fall apart across a sea of people.

They may not be standing as close as Jack and the blond were that night, but there's no denying the familiarity between them. This isn't Griffin shooting the breeze with an acquaintance or a friend's date.

I stay hidden in the shadows of the upper deck, spying, as she twirls a strand of her hair. He's got one hand braced on the railing, and the other is punctuating his side of the conversation. Breath held, I wait, watching. Will he reach out and tuck a strand of her hair behind an ear? Or will he give her arm an affectionate squeeze? Or wrap her up in a life-altering hug?

My throat burns with unshed tears; I refuse to let them fall. But when *she* places a red fingernail-tipped hand on his forearm, that burn rages into a wildfire and spreads to my belly.

In a blink, my frozen response switches to *fight*.

Hiding my shaking hands in the pockets of my coat, I approach them.

Griffin straightens but doesn't look the least bit guilty when he smiles and says, "There you are."

When I press into his side, the woman does a double take, and surprise flashes on her face and is gone as fast as it appeared.

Griffin rests his hand on my hip and pulls me in tighter.

I grip his waist a little too roughly, and I'm a little aggressive when I jab my hand her way. "Hi, I'm Brynn. Griffin's girlfriend."

Her eyes widen, but she recovers quickly and slips a cautious hand in mine. "Harmony."

Seriously? What the hell kind of name is *Harmony*?

Although, who am I to judge? My middle name is freaking *Amethyst*.

Take-no-prisoners Brynn is here to play. "How do you two know each other?"

Her dark eyes swim with unease as she blinks at my boyfriend, her mouth gaping.

He answers for her. "We knew each other when I lived in Nashville."

Well played, Racy.

I clench my fist so hard in my pocket I'm sure my nails leave half-moons on my palm.

Likely sensing my wrath, Harmony titters a nervous laugh. "I should probably go find my date. Griffin, it was good to see you. And, uh, nice to meet you." She scurries away like a mouse after a crumb.

Smart girl. Clearly her fight-or-flight response is in working order.

I spin to face him, crossing my arms over my thick coat.

Griffin is oblivious. "Baby, I missed you." He grips my hips to pull me close, but I don't budge.

"You knew each other in Nashville, huh?"

He tilts his head, blinks at me. "*Yeah*?" He drags out the word, like he doesn't get it. Which makes me even angrier.

I set my chin and wait for the light bulb moment.

When it happens, though, it's not what I expect. "Professor, are you *jealous*?" The tone is both incredulous and teasing. The accompanying grin, too. Clearly, my boyfriend isn't reading the room. He finds this humorous while I'm upset and, yes, jealous.

I crane my neck, surveying the lights of downtown as they grow closer. "I'm going to wait downstairs. Have fun with your friends."

He calls my name but doesn't stop me as I walk away. And that only makes me feel worse.

For the rest of the night, I sit at a table with Carlos and Gina. I'd rather be alone, but I can't stomach the idea of Jack catching me by myself, so I feign interest in their conversation. I'd love a glass of wine, but the bar closed twenty minutes ago.

The car ride back to the apartment is tense and awkward. Griffin must've clued Beau in because he and Paige are mostly silent, too.

Once we've said good night to our friends, we trudge up the stairs. I'm hurt and angry and sad. My chest aches, and my eyes burn from forcing my tears to recede.

This night started on such a high, and I hate that we're ending it like this.

Griffin shrugs off his coat and drapes it over the back of the couch. He twists my way, focus fixed on me, and begins rolling up the sleeves of his dress shirt. Even though I'm upset with him, the action makes my mouth go dry. *Damn it.*

His jaw ticks as he works on the other sleeve.

Holy hell. He's angry.

I've never seen him this angry. The seething makes my pulse pound. But not from fear.

Finally, my throat remembers how to swallow, and I find my voice. "I'm going to grab my stuff and sleep upstairs tonight." Exhaustion weighs down my limbs. All I want to do is curl up and cry.

"The fuck you are." He crosses his arms over his chest.

Anger flares, momentarily pushing the defeat away. I slam my clutch on the bar. "You're mad at me? I found you with another woman tonight, and you're mad at *me*?"

"Baby, I'm fucking furious."

With a scoff, I consider removing my shoes.

In case I need to throw them at him.

I fist my hands at my hips instead.

He tracks the movement before focusing on my face again. "I'm furious because when you got upset with me tonight, instead of communicating your feelings and talking it out, you fucking walked away."

My heart sinks. He's right. Jack and I handled conflict by walking away. It was easier to sweep it under a rug than to utilize the sweat equity to make it right.

And as I stand in front of a man who's willing to put in the hard work, I realize that I don't know how.

That sudden epiphany is terrifying. What if I'm horrible at this, and he decides I'm not worth the trouble?

Ah, those good old physiological reaction choices have returned. And this time? I'm going with *flight.*

I sidestep Griffin, ready to head for the stairs, but he mimics my movement like a predator stalking its prey. "You run up those stairs, professor, and I'll just haul your fine ass back down here."

Knees trembling, I swallow.

"We're doing this—now. Fighting it out. Go ahead," he challenges, tipping his chin. "Ask me the question."

Before I can second-guess myself, I do it. "You fucked her?"

His eyes widen, then a small smirk sneaks across his distracting lips. Unlike him, that word is not part of my daily vocabulary. But he answers without hesitation. "Yes." He plants his hands on his hips. "She and I were a thing, years ago. Before I dated Kate. It wasn't serious."

I give him a simple nod, even as doubt and fear and jealousy swirl like a storm inside me. "Why is she here? In Memphis?"

He pops a shoulder. "Shocked the hell out of me when I saw her in the crowd. She's a jersey chaser. Guess she's worked her way through the guys in Nashville, and now she's seeing a guy on our practice squad. She still lives over there, but she said she comes over for team events. And booty calls, I assume."

My head ceases its bobbing. "Was tonight—" I shake my head, try again. "When did you last see her?"

"It's been years." Slowly, he saunters in my direction. "Let me be very clear: I haven't so much as *thought* about another woman since the day you crashed into me." His eyes pierce me with intense passion as he draws closer. "You might see other women smile at me, laugh with me, try to flirt with me. But know this: the whole time, I'm only thinking of you. You consume me, Brynn."

I scoff, ignoring the way my heart flutters. "There you go, saying all the right things again."

His response is a cocky smirk that makes me roll my eyes. But the intense tightness in my chest from before aches less with every step he takes.

When he's within reach, he holds out his hand. A peace offering. And when my fingertips brush his, he closes his eyes in relief.

"It killed me when you walked away tonight. I sat with Beau and Paige, and every three minutes, I stood up to go find you, but I forced myself to stay where I was. Figured you needed space. And I didn't want to have an audience when we hashed this out."

"I'm sorry I walked away." I infuse the words with all the sincerity I feel. "That was how I handled things...before. But I promise to do better." Chin trembling, I lower my head and blink back tears.

His entire being deflates. "Come here."

The moment I'm tucked in his embrace, the tears break free. "I'm sorry," I repeat into his shirt.

He rubs big, soothing circles on my back. "Me, too. I'm sorry it upset you to see me talking to her. But I can't promise we won't ever run into a woman from my past."

"I know," I pout. There's no masking my petulance. "But I hate it."

"Hey." He pulls back and frames my face, his hold gentle yet firm. "I get it. You think it doesn't kill me to know that weasel Cockburn has had his hands on you?" He rests his forehead against mine. "We carry our prior relationships into new ones, unfortunately. But let's keep them where they belong—in the past, over and done—and focus on loving each other."

"I can do that," I whisper past the lump in my throat.

"Good. Me, too." He takes my mouth in a slow, sweet kiss. Before it gets too heated, he breaks the connection and pulls me back into his chest, my head tucked beneath his chin. "First fight, professor. And we handled it, made it to the other side."

I snort-laugh, the sound thick from the night's emotions. "What's on the other side?"

He doesn't answer right away, so I lean back. As he regards me now, his eyes are at their darkest, a blue so deep I could drown in them. The way he traces swirls on my bare shoulder, along with the husky quality of his voice, sparks a cluster of goose bumps across my body.

"Makeup sex. Hot, sweaty makeup sex."

A shiver rushes through me, making him smirk.

With his mouth pressed to my ear, he grits out, "I'm going to fuck those jealous thoughts out of your mind. You're going to come so many times tonight, you won't be able to walk tomorrow. Every time you move and feel that twinge, it'll be a reminder of how much you fucking *own* me."

Holy hell.

There are no more words between us as he sweeps me up into his arms and carries me into the bedroom, where he makes good on every carnal promise.

Chapter Twenty-Two

Brynn

I smile at the tiny purple dragon as I fasten the lid on my travel mug. The little guy's lucky I heard him ding against the metal interior of the cup before I placed it under the spout. He could be floating in a scalding mocha bath instead of regarding me from the countertop.

When Griffin emerges from the bedroom in his workout gear, I hold up the small plastic figure. "Look who I found hiding in my mug."

He cocks his head and feigns shock. "Another invasion? We need Seth to call an exterminator."

"Hmm." I sigh when he kisses me. "Think he would come take that down for us?" I tilt my head toward the Christmas tree that mocks us from the corner of the living room. We both groaned at it yesterday, after returning from celebrating the holiday with our respective families. It was hard to spend our first Christmas apart, but I'd bought my plane ticket months ago, and Griff couldn't miss practice this week.

We had one perfect night to give and receive—gifts and, ahem, *other* pleasures—and now he's leaving. This away game is the second-to-last of the Blues' season, and if they win, they'll secure a spot in the wild card round of the playoffs.

"Mm, he's still in Nashville with Daniel. But I can have him stop by when he gets back."

"No, I'll tackle it this weekend. While I'm missing you."

He wraps me up and inhales against my neck, his chest inflating, holding my scent in his lungs. When he pulls away, he holds out his hand, palm up.

"Keys, professor."

I frown down at his hand, then scrutinize his serious expression. "Huh?"

"It's fucking freezing outside. Give me your keys so I can warm up your car."

I roll my lips, fighting back tears. "Have you been talking to my mother?"

His brows knit together. "What?"

"Nothing." Smashing my body to his, I hold tight. "I love you."

"Love you, too, baby." He presses sweet kisses to my head.

After a teary goodbye, I slide into my toasty SUV and drive to campus. With one hand on the wheel, I toy with the amethyst and rose quartz bracelet that circles my wrist—a gift from Griffin—and go through my mental to-do list. I plan to take advantage of my alone time to work on my dissertation research, which has taken a back seat the past couple of months. Since the new semester doesn't start until next week, the library will be empty, so it's the perfect location for me to distract myself from how much I miss my boyfriend.

I swipe my faculty badge at the door and wind through the stacks to my favorite study carrel. I've neglected my emails since before the holidays, so I wade through messages to my campus address before I check my personal account. There, between junk emails from Banana Republic and Soma, is a message that sticks out. From a university domain.

Months ago, confused about my feelings for Griffin and his insistence that we were *just friends*, I spent a couple of hours researching small private colleges in Florida. When I discovered one only an hour from my parents, I didn't stop at researching it. No, I navigated to their human resources page. There weren't any positions in the English department listed at that time, but the page had a link to an interest form, and on a whim, I filled it out.

My heart climbs into my throat as I click on the message.

Dear Ms. Nelson,

Thank you for your interest in a teaching position at Collins University. After reviewing your résumé and credentials, we would love to speak with you about scheduling an interview for an upcoming position in our English department.

The subsequent details blur as my eyes swim. The campus is a little over an hour from my hometown. If I'd gotten this email three months ago, I'd be packing my bags for the sunshine state. I wouldn't miss living in Memphis. Wouldn't regret walking away from this chapter of my life.

But now?

Griffin.

Flashes of him invade my thoughts: Soulful eyes like mood rings—storm cloud gray when he's fired up or competitive, baby blue for lighthearted and flirty, and intense sky blue when he's passionate and eager. Big, strong hands that touch me gently and give me pleasure. Perfect pink lips that kiss every inch of my body and curve into smiles that make me swoon.

I love every part of him. And he's made me happier than I've ever been.

So it should be a no-brainer to delete this email and chalk it up to poor timing. But...I miss my parents. I miss riding my bike from their house to Celestial, Mom's shop near the beach, to hang with her while she sells tourists on the healing power of crystals. I miss Dad's french toast Sundays and his excitement when he shows me a cool star or planet with his backyard refractor telescope. I miss their company and their optimism. Once a week Zoom calls and once a year Christmas visits are not enough. Dad turned seventy this year, and Mom will be sixty-seven in a few weeks. Even though they're in fantastic health now—maybe there is something to those crystals, after all—I worry about being far away if that changes.

I love Griffin, but I uprooted my life for a man once before, only to have that relationship fizzle out. Plus, how many times has he mentioned that this is likely his last season? This contract with the Blues is up in a matter of weeks, even if they make the playoffs and go all the way to the Super Bowl. When it's over, would he be willing to pack up and move to Florida for *me*?

I leave the email in my inbox and move on, though nausea simmers in my tummy all day.

That queasy feeling sticks around for the weekend, too. Knowing I'll feel better once I talk to Griffin about it, I resolve to bring it up as soon as he gets back.

But then the Blues lose their road game—a tough back-and-forth matchup that ended with the team falling short when their kicker missed a field goal in the final minute. The guys played their hearts out, but it didn't go their way. Now they'll have to win their final game at home next weekend to secure their spot in the playoffs.

Griff struggles more when a loss is close than when it's a blowout, so as the last seconds of the game tick off at the bottom of the TV screen, I consider not mentioning the email yet.

If the roles were reversed, though, I wouldn't want him to keep something like that from me, would I? The mental tennis match leaves my brain addled, and I'm so overwhelmed with indecision that I don't even attempt to wait up for him.

I'm not sure how long I've been asleep when I wake to the sensation of his weight dipping into the mattress. Spooning me from behind, he nuzzles into my hair and neck. When he slides one thick thigh between mine, the hairs on his legs tickle my smooth skin.

"What time is it?" My sleepy voice cracks with a yawn.

"Eleven-thirty."

"Mmm." I snuggle deeper into his warmth, wiggling my bottom in an effort to get closer. "I'm so sorry about the game. I know how badly y'all wanted this one."

"Thank you, baby." His words are hot against my skin, his beard prickling me. "This one hurt. We gotta come back strong next week."

"You will." I smooth a hand up and down the muscly arm that's wrapped around my ribs.

He makes a few rumbly bear noises, entangling us further. "I missed you."

"Me, too."

"Tree's still up, huh?"

"Sorry, I didn't have it in me. Got a ton of work done at the library yesterday, though."

"Good job, professor. Forget about the tree. We can leave it up until next year for all I care. Or we'll hire someone to take it down."

He talks about a future with me like he's certain of it. His confidence soothes me. The words he said in the middle of the Blues' field come to mind: *Just be mine. We'll figure out the rest as we go.*

And we will. Florida and football and jobs and where we lay our heads at night. It can wait until the light of day. Right now, I want to be with him, give him comfort after a huge disappointment.

I wiggle my butt again, this time pressing harder into him.

He reaches between us and palms my butt cheek. "This ass," he growls. "It's unhealthy how much I think about this ass." He squeezes once, then slides his hand up my body to cup a breast, his hardening erection pressing into my hip. "Almost as much as I think about these."

He rolls me onto my back and pushes my nightgown up to my chest. Then his hands are on my breasts again. "They're so fucking perfect." He swipes his thumbs across my nipples, a back-and-forth caress that makes my toes curl. "Pretty pink tips perfect for my mouth." He wraps his lips around a nipple and sucks, the sensation so intense I grasp the bedsheet with one hand and the back of his head with the other. He teases one side with his mouth and the other with his fingers, making wetness pool in my panties. His eyes lock on my face as he continues his thorough treatment.

"Could you come from just this?" He gives the sensitive tip a deep pull that makes me moan. "Yeah, I bet you could. We'll test that another time, professor."

With both hands, he grips my panties and slides them down.

I've barely kicked them off when he finds the wetness between my thighs. "But this," he rasps as he slides two digits inside me, "this is what I think about the most. How it was made just for me." He pumps his fingers twice, but then he pulls them out.

A whine breaks free at his loss, but all I get is a smirk as he works his underwear down his legs.

He rolls onto me, keeping most of his weight on his elbows, kissing me slow and deep. "Need you, baby."

I grip his waist as he lines himself up with my entrance. "You've got me."

He pushes inside with one slow roll of his hips. His satisfied groan is followed with "Fuck. Right where I belong."

He makes love to me with smooth, languid strokes. Our bodies move in tandem—hips, hands, and hearts in perfect sync. There's a comfortable familiarity to our lovemaking now. The kind that happens when two souls discover they are each other's missing piece.

That's what Griffin is for me—a piece I didn't know was missing until we met.

As our bodies prove our love to each other, he locks eyes with me, holding nothing back. He shows me all his love, adoration, lust, and satisfaction in one look. But vulnerability shines there, too. It's so raw and honest it hurts. It communicates that I'm the keeper of his heart, and he trusts me to handle it with care.

I frame his face, relishing the way his beard tickles my palms. "I love you." I infuse those three little words with every ounce of truth in my soul.

He smiles, then he reaches to where we're joined to rub circles on my clit and increases the tempo of his thrusts. In moments, I'm falling apart. He follows me over the edge, and we collapse in a tangle of heavy, sated limbs.

And as I drift off, he whispers the same three words in my ear.

⸺◆⸺

We're leaving the most special Memphis Magic outing, and I still haven't told him about the email. I had every intention of bringing it up last night, but he didn't get home from practice until late. The guys are working hard to be ultra prepared for this weekend's game, spending extra time reviewing film and running through plays.

I tagged along with Griff and several Blues players this morning when they visited patients at St. Jude Children's Hospital. It was touching to watch big, burly football players give signed hats, jerseys, and footballs to the sweet children receiving treatment. Paige and I fought tears as the kids' little faces beamed when their football heroes gave them fist bumps and told them how brave they are.

Once we're buckled into Griffin's truck, he braces a hand on my headrest and twists his upper body to reverse out of the parking spot.

"You never use the backup camera," I muse.

"I use it." A sneaky smile curves his lips. "Just not when you're in the car."

I blink at him, confused.

I'm rewarded with a wink. "You did this little breath-catch thing the first time I did it. It was hella hot, knowing I could affect you like that. So it's become routine when you're in the truck with me."

"Somehow, that's both annoying and sweet."

He barks out a laugh. "'Bout sums me up, don't ya think?"

"Hmm." When we're out on the road, I take his right hand and lace my fingers through his. "What other sweet stuff did you do before we started dating?"

He glances at me sidelong for a beat, lids at half-mast, then untangles our fingers and hands me his phone. I swipe it open and enter his password—my birthday—then I await further instruction.

Eyes on the road, he tips his chin and says, "Notes app."

Once I've navigated to it, I find a note titled *Brynn Nelson* among a few others. My eyes shoot to him. He's watching the traffic ahead, but the skin above his beard has gone pink. When I focus on the phone again, I can't hold back a gasp.

On the screen is a list of details about me. Likes, dislikes, habits. All of my important highlights, lovingly curated.

Tears sting my eyes. "Griff." I don't know what else to say.

His Adam's apple bobs. "The night we met," he says. "Well, met again, I guess. While we sat across from each other at the diner, I had this overwhelming urge to create that list. Didn't understand why at the time. But it's like my subconscious knew I'd want a list of my favorite person's favorites. And not-favorites."

My heart pinches. This man. How could I even consider moving somewhere he's not?

That email is a lead boulder in my stomach.

Swallowing thickly, I rub my sternum. Knowing I'll lose my nerve if I procrastinate any longer, I lick my lips and get it over with. "I, uh, got an email from a university in Florida."

"About?" Though he arches one brow, his focus remains on the road.

"A job." I hold my breath.

He's silent, but his jaw muscles twitch.

"It's not an offer, just a response to an interest form I filled out months ago. Before we..."

Before we fell in love.

"You want to move to Florida?" His tone is even, but his eyes? Storm cloud gray.

"No. Well, maybe. I've thought about it. Obviously." Heart pounding as I assess him, I whisper, "It's only an hour from my parents."

"But it's many, *many* hours away from me."

"Please don't be mad. I don't plan on interviewing. I wanted you to know about the email because I don't want to keep things from you."

He taps his fingers on the steering wheel, then heaves a deep sigh. "Baby, I'm not mad. A little stunned, maybe. I didn't know you'd thought about moving back to Florida." When he glances my way, the gray of his irises is less stormy.

I shrug. "Maybe someday. I mean, if you'd..." My heart clenches and my nerves skitter through me. "Never mind."

"If I'd want to move there, too?" he guesses.

Lips pressed together, I dip my chin. "Your season is almost over. Even if y'all go all the way, you'll be done in February. But your mom would probably hate me if I asked you to move away."

"Donna could never hate you. She'd adjust, believe me. And I'm pretty fond of the beach, professor."

Perking up, I shift in my seat. "Really?"

"Only if you promise to wear a bikini around the house." He wags his brows, his lips tipping in a wicked smile.

"Hmm, only if you wear your cartoon boxers."

"I'm open to negotiations."

Laughing with Griffin helps ease the tension. But though that lead boulder in my gut is smaller, it isn't gone.

He clutches my hand and holds it to his mouth, peppering it with kisses all the way home, like he's afraid to let go.

Chapter Twenty-Three

Brynn

Uneasiness follows me into the new year. Since New Year's Eve is in the middle of the week and the guys have practice, we have a low-key celebration with a select few players and WAGs.

Though disquiet has taken up residence in my mind like an unwelcome visitor, my boyfriend is pure focus as he prepares for the game. With the exception of last Sunday night after he returned home, we haven't had sex this week. Supportive girlfriend that I am, I didn't question him when he told me he wanted to abstain to keep his mind clear. But I've missed the intimacy. That it's happening—or *not* happening, technically—when I'm vulnerable and needy eats at me. I need the connection. I need *him*.

But football is the priority. At least for now.

To ensure they get a quality night of rest before this big game, the organization requires the players to spend Saturday night in a hotel. It's not the first time Griffin and I have slept apart since we started dating, not by a longshot, but it's the loneliest yet. I sleep curled in a ball on his side of the bed with Barnaby tucked to my chest.

Paige picks me up early so we'll get a quick moment with our guys before they suit up for their pregame warm-ups.

When we step onto the field from the tunnel the guys use, a cold blast of winter air whips our hair across our faces. The temperature hovers around freezing, but the wind chill is well below that, and there's a chance of snow flurries in the forecast. I pull my puffer coat tighter, thankful that the private suites are heated.

As Paige and I wait behind the barricade, we're surrounded by wives, girlfriends, and children all decked in a kaleidoscope of blues and bouncing in place or blowing into gloved hands for warmth.

A handful of players are on the field, checking the conditions and getting a feel for the stadium. Beau and his backups run drills with the receivers, running backs, and tight ends to warm up.

When a whistle signals the end of this early warm-up period, the players jog over to greet their families before they head into the locker room to suit up.

When my guy pulls me in for a not-suitable-for-work kiss, my toes curl in my fleece-lined boots.

"How are you not freezing?" I ask, plucking at the long-sleeved Blues T-shirt he's wearing with shorts.

"That kiss was hot enough to keep me warm for the entire game." He grins and rubs his gloved hands up and down my upper arms, though I hardly feel it through the puffer. "Still love seeing you in blue." He tweaks the pom-pom on top of my Blues beanie.

Popping up onto my tiptoes, I speak low into his ear. "If you don't get inside and warm up, your balls are going to turn blue and fall off, and I love them, so..." I peck his beard and lips. "Have a good game."

I expect him to join the teammates headed into the tunnel, but he bends and puts his mouth to my ear. "My blue balls have nothing to do with the weather. Later, after we win this fucking game, you and I can fix them. I'll make you a deal: the number of times I score today will be the number of times I make you come tonight."

Holy. Hell.

Face heating, I peer at the people around us, making sure no one overheard his filthy bargain. "What's your record for number of touchdowns in a single game, Racy?"

He smirks and holds up two fingers.

Lips part. Toes curl. Thighs clench.

God, I need him to have a good game.

With a wink, he smacks one final kiss to my still-red cheeks. Then he tears off down the tunnel.

In a daze, I follow Paige to the suite level, where we have a sweet reunion with the Laceys. I haven't seen Griff's family since before the holidays, so it's wonderful to have time to catch up before kickoff.

When number 89 runs in a touchdown at the beginning of the second quarter, I shed the navy- and sky-blue scarf Mrs. Lacey knitted for me. In the third, when Beau sends a beautiful spiral down the field and Griffin makes the catch in the end zone, then points at our suite, my hat and gloves come off.

Even though offense has played flawlessly so far, the Blues are down by six with two minutes left. Paige clasps my hand in a death-grip when the Warriors are forced to punt. Our receiver signals a fair catch, and then the whole stadium is on their feet as the guys step up to the twenty-five yard line.

"I'm so nervous," Donna wails, clutching Fred's arm.

On her sister's other side, Dottie glares at the field like she can scare the players into winning from here. "They've got this."

Tucker looks nauseous, while Shaw paces behind the seating area, his eyes glued to the TV monitor in the corner.

"Come on, Beau. Come on, Beau," Paige whispers under her breath as her fiancé steps back and launches a pass on first down. His aim is perfect; the ball sails into the capable hands of Tyrell Jefferson, who tucks it and whizzes down the sideline. He's the fastest guy on the team, and for a second, it looks as though he may run it all the way. But he's forced out of bounds at the Warrior twenty-five.

On second down, the Blues attempt a draw play, but it only yields a five-yard gain. They run it again on second down, this time earning another ten yards. The clock steadily ticks down, and the Blues use their final time-out with a minute left.

While the guys huddle up with Mundy and Dobbins on the sideline, I fight the urge to gnaw on my fingernails. My pulse has skyrocketed, my temple throbs, and the fingers on my right hand are numb from Paige's grip.

As the players jog back to the line of scrimmage, I slip my free hand into my pocket and feel around until my fingers find the smooth green aventurine. I hold it tight and let its warmth seep into my skin.

I want this win for Griffin so damn bad.

At the Warriors' fifteen, Beau signals for the next play. But it's a bad snap and our center almost fumbles the ball. Beau manages to land on it, and our only loss is a down. There's a collective sigh of relief throughout the stadium.

On second down, the Blues run the ball and gain eight yards.

"Watch your time," Fred warns from the row behind us.

Seconds ticking down, the guys get in formation. It's third and goal. Beau steps back in the pocket, searching for an open guy in the end zone.

A six-five tight end in the back corner is his target. Griff leaps into the air, hands up, and makes the catch, landing with both feet in bounds. The stadium erupts as sixty-thousand Blues fans scream and cheer.

But we still have to make the extra point to win the game.

I hold my breath as our kicker's foot connects with the ball. It sails through the air almost in slow motion, and when it clears the uprights, it's bedlam—on the field and in the stands.

Our suite goes nuts. Paige and I jump up and down, tears streaming down our cheeks and smiling wide with joy. Tucker circles our bouncing bodies with his arms, throws his head back and whoops, his eyes red rimmed. Fred gathers Donna and Dottie in a group hug, and Trixie even leaps into Cam's arms, knocking the cap off her copper pigtails. Shaw braces his hands on the bar behind the seats, head hanging low, taking a moment. When he raises to his full height, there's no mistaking the gleam in his eye or the heavy rise and fall of his chest as he exhales his relief.

"First time in nine years!" Fred shouts over our excitement—this will be the Blues' first playoff appearance in nearly a decade.

We're standing in the family zone to greet the guys after their locker room celebration and press duties when it hits me—Griffin scored *three* touchdowns today.

I shrug off my coat and lift my hair off my heated skin.

The players trickle out, each celebrating with their loved ones. When Beau sweeps Paige into his arms and spins her around, she drops her head back in pure joy.

Then my man rounds the corner.

Leaving the Laceys' cheers and whistles behind, I run straight to him. When I spring into his body, he bands his arms around my back and under my bottom to hold me close. I loop mine around his shoulders, my chest shaking with happy sobs.

"Congratulations. You were amazing."

His voice is thick, full of emotion. "Thank you, baby." Then, lower and next to my ear, he says, "Did you keep count?"

With a laugh, I press my lips to his. He loosens his hold, and I lower my legs, but he keeps an arm around me as his family crowds us to congratulate him with hugs and back slaps.

That night, after we celebrate with his family at dinner, Griffin fulfills his side of his ambitious, naughty bargain. Three orgasms later, I collapse into his arms in our bed—body sated and heart full.

After the euphoria from Sunday's win fades, it's back to the grind for Griffin and me. He's in the zone, getting ready for wild card weekend, and I'm juggling a new batch of students who are taking their first English course along with former students now taking the second course. It always takes a few weeks to adjust to the spring semester, but I'm struggling more than usual this year.

"Time for tea, dear?" Helen's poofy white head of hair appears in my doorway.

With a glance at the clock, I sigh. It's mid-afternoon, and though I'd normally be with Griff at this time on a Tuesday, I'm on campus. The Blues are technically off today, but the guys reported to the practice facility this morning to game prep anyway.

I nod at Helen. "Sure. I'll meet you in the break room."

She's prepared everything by the time I join her. The table is littered with mugs of hot water, our tin of tea, sugar packets, a small carton of creamer, and a box of shortbread cookies. She selects her flavor—lemon and ginger—and I pluck out the last package of peppermint.

"How are things with that handsome fella of yours?" she asks over the rim of her mug.

"Good. He's busy getting ready for Buffalo. Did you watch the game on Sunday?"

She scowls into her tea. "I don't want to hear about football. Tell me about being in love." Her sour expression quickly disappears, and her eyes shine behind her glasses.

"It's wonderful," I confess. "He's amazing. We get along really well. He makes me laugh every day."

"Ahh, it's good to see you so happy. I was worried about you before he came along, you know. Didn't think we were going to keep you. Especially after you mentioned not liking Memphis. That's better now?"

"Yes," I answer without hesitation. "It's better. I have friends now, and Griffin…"

She tilts her head and opens her mouth, but she's cut off when Trinity, the department's student worker, rushes into the room.

"You and Griffin didn't break up, did you?" Her voice is laced with panic, her eyes wide.

"No…" I drag out the word as my heart rate kicks up.

"Oh, thank God." Huffing, she sinks into an empty chair. When she notices my stunned expression, she leans in and waves her phone back and forth. "You haven't seen?"

I swallow back a wave of trepidation. "Seen what?"

A few taps, and she hands her phone over.

My stomach caves like it's taken a punch when the image registers. It's a picture of my boyfriend with another woman on his lap.

But further inspection lessens my anxiousness. A bit.

It's an old picture. In it, Griffin's hair is longer on top and slicked back, and his face is younger. Not as many crinkles around his eyes. The beard is longer and less tidy. And the gray T-shirt he's wearing sports the Tors' logo on the pocket.

Once my brain is satisfied that it isn't a recent shot, I take in more details. The woman perched in his lap is gorgeous and thin. Her long, dark red hair is a striking contrast to pale, almost translucent skin. The high cheekbones and pointy chin and pouty, full lips stand out on her thin, oval face. She's wearing a short skirt and peek-a-boo fishnet stockings that tease glimpses of her long legs. And her corset-type top pushes her full breasts up under her chin.

I don't need to look at the handle to know who this woman is, but I do it anyway.

RealKateVolkova93, with a blue certified check.

Griffin's ex-girlfriend. His only other serious relationship.

When I read the caption beneath the picture, blood rushes in my ears.

Can't wait to cheer this guy on in Buffalo this weekend! #goblues

What. The. Actual. Hell?

The pitying expression on Trinity's face when I hand her phone back makes me want to chuck my half-empty mug of peppermint tea against the wall.

He didn't invite her to the game, right?

Despite the way it aches, my heart tries to convince me that he would never, but my brain swirls with enough doubt to drown out any certainty that tries to take root.

After Helen and Trinity attempt to explain the photo away, I return to my office, where I stare at my laptop for a solid half hour, unable to function. My phone buzzes with messages and calls, but I ignore it.

I roll my neck and square my shoulders, and as I navigate to the inbox on my personal email, a calm numbness coats my insides. When I hang up after calling the number listed at the bottom of the message from Collins, I don't even cry.

When I make it home that afternoon, Griffin's truck is there.

And when I hit the top step, I find him sitting on the couch with his head in his hands.

My heart splinters when he straightens.

He springs up and moves my way but stops short before he touches me.

"Baby, I've been calling and messaging you for the past three hours." His voice is strained. "It's old—the picture."

"I know."

He flinches. The move highlights the redness in his eyes.

"Then why haven't you—" He shakes his head, takes a deep breath, and starts over. "I don't know what's going on in that beautiful head of yours, so I need you to talk to me. Please."

When I dump my purse on a stool, I notice a bottle of champagne in an ice bucket and two flutes on the bar. But my curiosity takes a back seat to the myriad of questions that storm in my head.

"Why the hell did she post that?"

His shoulders melt away from his ears, almost like he's relieved I've spoken. "I don't know. I haven't talked to her or messaged her since we broke up."

"Is she going to the game Sunday?"

He rakes his fingers through his short hair. "I hope the fuck not. I reached out to demand that she delete that post—"

My stomach knots. "You reached out? So you *have* messaged her." My voice is shrill, and I'm being unreasonable. But I'm too hurt to care.

Eyes screwed shut, he pinches the bridge of his nose. "Today was the first time." When he looks at me again, his irises are mottled gray. "Seth has reached out to her manager, too. But we can't force her to take it down, and I can't ban her from the game, as much as I'd like to."

I bite the inside of my cheek, and he fists his hands at his sides. We're both unsure about how to proceed.

I break first. "Why'd the two of you break up?" It's a question I've often pondered, though I wasn't sure I really wanted the answer. Until now.

"I'll tell you anything you want to know, but...can I hold you for a minute first? Please?" His voice cracks on that last word, and my resolve withers like the leaves on his family's soybean plants. In three strides, I'm locked in the comfort of his arms.

Body sagging with relief, he shudders an exhale, and the steady thump of his heart eases my worries. When he slumps to the couch and pulls me with him, I straddle his thighs and rest my body against his.

"She fucked my best friend."

With a sharp intake of breath, I pull back.

He rolls his eyes. "Former best friend. And it wasn't a one-time thing. They carried on behind my back for eight damn months."

I rake my nails over the back of his head in a soothing pattern. "I'm sorry."

He squeezes my hips. "Conner and I played together at Oklahoma, and when I got drafted, he moved to Nashville, too. He had a business degree, so he became my de facto manager. Around the time Kate and I met, he proposed to his girlfriend. They wanted a long engagement, and they spent all that time planning this huge-ass wedding. I was going to be his best man. But at the last minute, he called it off." He rubs his hands up and down my thighs. "He called it off because he was fucking my girlfriend. Claimed he was in love with her."

My heart clenches at the misery in his expression. "How'd you find out?"

"Seth."

My brows climb to my hairline.

"He stopped by my house for a delivery, and they were going at it on the couch." When I eye where we're sitting, he chuckles. "Don't worry, not this one."

"Griff, I'm so sorry that happened. He wasn't any kind of friend, though, if he did that to you."

He deflates beneath me. "At the time, I kinda thought it was karma, you know? I wouldn't be surprised if some of the women I slept with in my twenties had boyfriends or husbands I didn't know about."

"If you had no idea, then that's on them, not you."

A shoulder shrug and a sad smile. "Still. Felt like I deserved it somehow."

I rest my hands on his neck and kiss him, basking in his warmth and scent and goodness. It's ripped away, though, when the memory of the phone call I made earlier crashes into me. It's time to face the consequences.

"Uh, I-I did a thing today." My breathing increases as I brace for the fallout, but I muster every ounce of bravery I own.

We both open our mouths to speak.

"I set up an interview with that college in Florida."

But my words collide with his: "I signed an extension with the Blues today."

Chapter Twenty-Four

Griffin

I shake my head, certain I misheard her.

"Sorry, did you say you're interviewing in Florida?"

"What do you mean, you signed an extension?" The hurt in her eyes guts me. Almost as much as the thought of her taking this job.

She scoots back, but I cling to her. I won't let her put space between us. "Nope. We're having a discussion."

She gives me a playful glare. "And I have to sit in your lap to do it?"

"Yep."

Fuck. What a cluster. I was pumped to come home and tell her the good news, so I called Seth before the ink was dry and asked him to set up the celebratory champagne. I never thought my announcement would be met with the possibility of a long-distance situation.

She wriggles again, but I clamp my hands on her ass. "You keep that up, and we'll need to table the discussion for later."

"I don't see why we have to do this with me straddling your lap."

"Baby, you just told me that half of my heart might be moving to Florida. I'm keeping you close."

The fire in her eyes dims. "Griff, I just thought…"

"You thought you'd punish me because my ex-girlfriend fucked with us."

"No." She opens her mouth to explain, and I take advantage. I kiss her like a man going off to war. She stiffens, but at the first lick of my tongue, she melts like butter. Her hands fist my shirt as our lips perform the sensual dance they know so well. When she starts making those little whimpers I love, I break the connection.

Her eyes remain closed as she catches her breath. But when they pop open, her brows pinch together. "What was that for?"

"Just wanted to remind you of what you'll be giving up."

"You're not being fair."

"Fuck fair. I'm in love with you, goddamn it. I won't fight fair."

"Then I won't either. I'm not giving you up." Her voice is stern, and she holds my face between her palms. "Nothing is decided. I can cancel the interview. Maybe it *was* a knee-jerk reaction to that picture. I was wrong to do that, and I'm sorry. But it wasn't completely impulsive..." She takes a deep breath. "I've been thinking about that job since I got the email. I don't know if it's the right fit for me. For us. But I didn't know football was still part of the equation."

Now it's my turn to apologize. "I'm sorry I took the offer before talking to you. Shane called Kevin this morning. They wanted it locked down before the season ends."

She studies the buttons on my Henley as she traces them with her finger. "How long?"

"One year."

One more year to play the sport I love on my dream team. When my agent's name flashed on my phone this morning, an offer for another year with the Blues was the last thing I expected. I've been playing as though this season was my last. And with the exception of the two games that I'd fucking love to do over, I'm proud of my performance on the field. I could walk away after this season with my head held high, satisfied to go out on top.

But how could I turn down playing here for another year? I'm as healthy as a thirty-five-year-old NFL player could hope to be. I've still got speed and stamina. Still have something to contribute to a team. Still love suiting up every week.

So when Kevin presented the Blues' offer to me, I didn't hesitate. Of course, I thought about Brynn when I said yes, but it was more of an I-can't-wait-to-tell-her moment than an I-need-to-discuss-this-with-my-girlfriend moment. And I wanted to call her about it right away, but she was in class at the time, so I cooked up the champagne surprise instead.

My gut clenches. Shit, I've fucked up.

"I'm sorry."

She drags her focus from my shirt to my face, a small frown marring her expression.

"I should've waited until we could talk about this," I say. "It's a life decision that affects both of us, but I was too excited to consider that. I don't ever want you to feel like your opinion doesn't matter. It fucking matters."

"Griff, it's football." Her forlorn shrug pierces my heart.

"And I love football. But I love *you* more."

Her eyes shine as she says, "I love you. I'll cancel the interview."

"No."

She rears back, her eyes flaring wide. "But—"

"You're not canceling. Go to the interview. Walk around the campus, get a feel for the place. See if you can picture yourself happy there."

"Griff..."

I swallow past the burn in my throat. Fuck, this is going to hurt.

There was a time in my life—not so long ago, in fact—when I thought playing football was the thing I did best. But now? Maybe what I'm best at is loving her. And to love her well, I have to let her follow her heart.

Even if it leads her to Florida.

Her big brown eyes search my face. God, I love her eyes. All that *the eyes are the windows to the soul* bullshit is 100 percent true for Brynn Nelson. I've seen them excited and happy and turned on and mad. But right now, they're anxious, and I need to fix that.

"Baby, we're end game. There is no future for me that doesn't include you. I want to be near you, every single day. But if we have to do the long-distance thing for the next year so that we can both chase our dreams, then that's what we'll do." I wipe the tears from her cheeks. Kiss her nose. "It won't be easy, but we'll figure it out."

Her breath shudders, and she licks her lips. "But the interview is on Monday morning."

And our wild card game is on Sunday night.

"M-maybe I can change it." She fidgets with my buttons again. "I didn't know the hiring committee would want to meet so soon. When they said it was on Monday—"

"Don't change it."

"But your game—"

"Is just a game. There will be others." I grab her hips and tug, like it's possible to bring her any closer. "Besides, they're predicting a fucking snowstorm in Buffalo this weekend. Who'd pick that over sunny Florida?"

Laughing through her tears, she surges forward, hugging me tight and resting her cheek on my collarbone. "I don't deserve you."

I rub her back and breathe her in. "You deserve the best of the best, so I'd say you're set."

Her chest shakes with laughter. "Good to see that Racy ego is alive and well."

"Always."

I trace soothing circles on her back while we sit in silence, and neither of us budges when the sound of rain on the sidewalks outside grows louder.

Finally, I say, "I've decided that this is how we'll handle all future disagreements or serious discussions—with you on my lap."

She snorts. "Can't throw my shoe at you in this position, though."

"Exactly."

Sighing, she melts into me, and we sit, listening to the rain, holding each other.

I can't think of a more magical way to spend a Tuesday in Memphis.

———◆———

I wake before dawn on Saturday and kiss Brynn's body until she's awake, too. Then, as the sky outside transforms from darkest night to the steel gray of early morning, I make love to her. It's slow and sweet and perfect, and I suffuse my languid strokes and unhurried touches with every ounce of my love for her.

There was no fucking way I could abstain this past week. I've had her every night, including last night, like we're living on borrowed time. I remind myself that she's coming back so often that the words play on a constant loop in my head.

She sleeps while I shower and pack the rest of my things. As I move through our bedroom on silent feet, I try to ignore the small open suitcase that awaits her last-minute additions. She's flying to Florida tomorrow afternoon, and by the time she returns on Tuesday, a few of our unknowns will be clear.

Will my season be continuing into the divisional rounds? And will she be heading to Florida this summer?

I check the time. Damn, I'm not ready to say goodbye. It's not a forever kind of goodbye, but it still fucking hurts.

I perch on the edge of the bed and drink her in. She's curled on her side, knees tucked.

Burying my face in her neck, I rub her hip. "Baby, I've gotta go."

She blinks awake, and as I pull away, she stretches and rolls to her back. We stare at each other like we're memorizing every last detail. When I bend to kiss her, she loops her arms around my neck.

"You're gonna kick ass tomorrow."

I smile against her lips. "Thank you for believing in me."

"Always."

We kiss once more, then I straighten my spine. Her cheek is soft and warm when I trace its curve with my fingers. "And you're gonna kick ass in your interview on Monday. Can't wait to hear about it."

Her lips stretch into a smile, and I feather my thumb over them. "I love you, Brynn."

"Love you so much," she whispers.

I roll my lips to hold back the *don't go* threatening to force its way out of my mouth. Then I rise from the bed, and with my duffel in hand, I move to the door. From there, I turn and study her once more, noting the way the sheen in her eyes mirrors the one in mine.

The plane ride to Buffalo is less lively than just about any other flight this season. We're all calm, focused. I sit next to Beau and complete a couple of crosswords while he studies the playbook on his iPad. When his eyes blur from too much screen time, we play a few rounds of blackjack and talk in low voices about his first playoff appearance. He doesn't seem nervous, and I don't think the playoff game hoopla will rattle him. He's as poised and steady as ever.

"You wanna talk about it?" He deals the next round.

I tap the tray and glance up from my hand. "I did the right thing, telling her to go?"

Beau deals me another card. "Yeah. It would be a bad move to convince her to turn down the interview. She could end up resenting you down the line."

Nodding, I collect the cards I've won. "Gonna gut me if she takes the job, though."

"Paige will be devastated if she leaves." My friend frowns. "You willing to pack it all up and move to Florida after next season? Memphis is your town. And your family is close."

"I'd follow that girl to the ends of the earth, Cap."

He studies me for a beat, then shakes his head, smiling. "Yeah. I know that feeling well."

When we land in Buffalo, we're greeted by six inches of snow and a wind chill of ten degrees. A few of the guys complain, but not me. I fucking love a snow game.

After team meetings and a run-through of our formations, we're released with enough time to grab dinner and make it back to the hotel before our curfew. Brynn and I have a quick chat before bed, and when we hang up, I'm certain I'll toss and turn all night. But the stress of the last few days takes me under, and I get a solid eight hours.

While we're killing time in the locker room on Sunday, several texts from Brynn come through.

Brynn

Just landed. Love you!

Oh my gosh, it's freezing there! Stay warm!

Almost time! Watching with Mom and Dad. I love you so much.

Just before we take the field for warm-ups, I dig through my bag until I find it—the tiny velvet pouch Celeste gave me in Charlotte. I've carried it to each game since that day, with the exception of last week, when Brynn asked to borrow the green one.

I hold the two stones in my palm—one for luck, and one for love—until they're as warm as my skin.

In the end, though I have both luck and love on my side, and though our team plays their fucking hearts out in brutal conditions, the Blues come up short. Final score: twenty-four to twenty-one. Even though we're not the victors, we've built something to be proud of this season that will hopefully carry into the next.

Brynn sends me a single text after the game:

I love you.

The apartment is quiet and empty when I make it home around four a.m., but Brynn left a lamp on in the living room for me. I crash on the couch, not wanting to sleep in our bed without her, and stare up at the ceiling, fingers laced behind my head, imagining what my life will be like next season if she's not living in Memphis.

Studying the patterns above me, it hits. The pain and depression I suffered last year when I got hurt and the Tors let me go is nothing compared to the agony I'll experience if she's not here with me. If she's not around to make me laugh and give me hell. She loves me so well, better than anyone ever has. I don't want to wait days or weeks for her love to shine on me.

I want to fall asleep and wake up beside her as often as I can.

I might be a selfish ass when it comes to that woman, but I'm still dedicated to letting her make the decision, regardless of what I want. She has to choose her path on her own.

But that doesn't mean I can't be there to support her when she does.

I sit up and check the time. It's not quite Seth's early-bird gym hour, but I tap on his contact anyway. If he doesn't pick up, I'll leave a voicemail, and he'll have this handled in an hour. Too wired to sit still, I pace while I wait for his recorded greeting. When I scan the kitchen, I freeze in my tracks.

The white board has a new puzzle.

Three words. Eight boxes. And a clue that reads "This is all that matters."

Seth answers an instant before his voicemail picks up, his voice scratchy. "Ugh, Griff. You better pay me overtime for this."

Zeroed in on the board, I say, "I need you to get me a flight to Florida. Today."

Chapter Twenty-Five

Brynn

As the automatic door slides open, I roll my carry-on out into the seventy-four-degree day and shield my eyes, wishing I'd remembered to pack sunglasses. I scan the busy street outside the terminal. Taxis, ride shares, and hotel shuttles sit bumper-to-bumper in the loading lane, and busy travelers weave in and out of foot traffic, dragging their wheeled luggage in their wake.

I check my phone. The Blues' bus should be leaving the hotel about now. I'm hitting send on a text to Griffin when a series of honks and a "Yoo-hoo! Moonbeam!" pull my attention back to the street.

Mom's hanging out the passenger window, waving both arms, her curls bouncing. Dad, enthusiastic, though not to Mom's level, waves from behind the wheel. They roll forward until they find a place to pull over, and I hurry their way.

When my mother opens her door and lets loose a pterodactyl screech, several passersby gawk.

"My love is here." She cups my face and kisses my cheek, then pulls me in for a fierce hug. Her familiar patchouli-infused scent surrounds me. Comforting and safe.

Dad deposits my suitcase in the trunk of the Prius, then joins us on the sidewalk, completing our Nelson family embrace.

A few angry honks break us apart, and we scramble into the car.

Once she's buckled, Mom twists around and props her chin on her seat, checking me over. "Your spirit is tired, love. Worried. Happy, but worried."

"That about sums it up." I give her a weak smile.

"Hmm." She searches my face, so much love in her hazel eyes that I have to fist my hands in my sweater to keep my emotions in check. "You and that hunk of yours are in deep. But you've come to a bump in the road, and you're not sure how to get over it. What is it? A miscommunication?"

My mother's ability to read me like a book never ceases to amaze me.

When I called to tell them that I was coming down for a couple of days, I mentioned the interview, but I didn't mention that Griffin had signed for another year and that we might have to endure a lengthy separation.

On the drive home, I spill all the details. The shock of the contract extension, my gut instinct to take this interview, my guilt about missing the game tonight, and how torn I am about the possibility of having to move if I'm offered the job.

By the time Dad pulls into the driveway and parks beside his car's twin, I'm emotional and exhausted. But walking up the flagstone driveway to my childhood home never fails to bring me joy. The cozy 1950s ranch-style house is turquoise, with a slanted roof and palm tree sentinels in the front yard. As always, the sight of it makes me think of cartwheels and bomb pops and flip-flops. If I close my eyes, I can almost smell the sunscreen and grilled hot dogs and chlorine of my youth.

My parents' eclectic tastes greet me when I take off my shoes at the door and relish the feel of the cool white tile beneath my feet. The rattan couch and chairs with bold, vibrant floral cushions are inviting, but my weary body needs more comfort than they can provide.

Mom, as usual, reads my mind. "Why don't you go lay down for a bit? Dad's grilling kebabs for dinner. I'll wake you when they're ready, then we'll watch the game."

My childhood bedroom is like a Brynn time-capsule. The sage-green walls Dad and I painted for my sixteenth birthday. The white wicker bookshelf that's stuffed to the brim with books that chart the evolution of my life—from Tomie dePaola picture books to Judy Blume chapter books to Jane Austen novels. The dragon statues and snow globes I left behind clutter the built-in shelves in the little desk nook, and the closet door is still papered with fanciful dragon posters.

I stretch out on the lavender chenille bedspread and send Griff a couple of more texts. He won't respond, and it's possible he might not even see them until after the game, but I want him to know I'm thinking about him.

I'm always thinking about him.

Missing my boyfriend and my emotional support stuffed dragon, I curl up on my side, clasp my rose quartz pendant, and let the promise of a restorative nap pull me under.

I wake when the sun is low in the sky, and the aroma of grilled meat and vegetables wafts in through the screened patio door. I change into loungewear and find Mom in the kitchen, mixing rum runners.

"Sleep well, love?" she says with a kiss to my head. "Dinner should be ready in a few."

We eat steak and shrimp kebabs at the round glass-top table while pregame commentary blares from the TV in the living room. The media has called the Blues the underdogs all week, and tonight they double down on that label. Every analyst on the broadcast picks the opposing team to win.

Mom and Dad insist they'll handle dinner clean-up and shoo me away, so I settle on the end of the couch with a second cocktail and take in the details of the field. Mounds of snow decorate the sidelines, and the wind chill at kickoff is three degrees. Needless to say, when the guys aren't on the field, they huddle under huge, heavy coats.

Mom has dropped onto the couch beside me by the time Griffin's face flashes on the screen. Grasping my arm, she cheers. "Ooh, all that testosterone. My Moonbeam is a lucky girl. Has he used the pillow trick yet?"

"Mom." I roll my eyes at Dad. He, of course, shakes his head and gives my mother an indulgent smile.

The game is a nail-biter, and the teams are equally matched as they battle for possession. My heart rate elevates every time the lead changes, and there are times I grip Mom's hand as tightly as Paige held mine last weekend.

Griff takes a hard hit in the third quarter, and I hold my breath when he doesn't get up right away. An eternity seems to pass before he reaches for Tyrell to help him off the turf.

Though the conditions are awful, the Blues' teamwork and focus are not. They play with grit the entire game and give their opponents one hell of a challenge, but it's not enough. They lose the game by three points, and their season is over.

My heart aches for them. For my adopted city.

"So sorry, Moonbeam. They can hold their heads high knowing they gave their all." My dad's voice is choked with emotion.

Mom rubs soothing circles on my back as tears stream down my cheeks. When the cameras cut to the heartbroken faces of Blues players, the ache in my chest grows heavier. There's a shot of Griffin consoling a teary Devon that turns my tears into sobs.

Dad shuts off the TV.

Unable to come up with adequate words of solace for Griff, I choose three truthful ones that I hope will bring him a modicum of comfort tonight.

I love you.

I don't try to call him, though I long to hear his voice. He and his teammates need space to grieve and heal together. So I scrub my face and climb into bed, and within minutes, sleep takes me.

"It's not Sunday," I say to my dad the next morning when I find him standing at the stove, cooking french toast.

As I peck his cheek, he shrugs. "It's your favorite."

I'm slipping a pod into the coffee maker when Mom floats down the hall in a floral kaftan, a main staple of her wardrobe. She kisses my brow before she grabs Dad's face and plants one on him—the kind of kiss no grown woman wants to witness between her parents. When she finally cuts him loose, she wipes his lips with her thumb.

"Remind me to reapply, love."

When our plates are loaded with syrupy, powdery goodness, I dig in eagerly. "Did I tell y'all that Griff has made french toast for me a couple times?" I ask between forkfuls.

My parents cut their eyes at each other, their expressions abnormally serious.

Spine snapping straight, I rest my fork on my plate, french toast all but forgotten. "What is it?" My pulse quickens as my imagination runs rampant with dire scenarios and possible diagnoses. And when Mom slips her hand in Dad's, I gulp a painful swallow.

They continue to side-eye each other, but when he tilts his head my way in encouragement, my mother takes my clammy hand in her warm, soft one. "We need to talk to you."

My fear is so acute, I can't form words.

"We don't want you to move back to Florida," she says, wearing a pitying smile.

I rear back. "Excuse me?"

"Oh, shoot, that came out wrong." She shakes her head. "What I mean is, we don't want you to move back here for *us*. If we're the reason you're job hunting down here, then you can put a stop to it."

I pinch my brows together, my stomach tightening. "You...you don't want me to move back home?"

"Not if it's solely for our benefit, Moonbeam." Dad takes my other hand, the Nelson family circle complete. "We don't want you to feel obligated to look after us. Even when we're old and senile, we have plans in place. You deserve to live your life without the burden of caring for aging parents—"

"You're not a burden. You're my *family*." My voice cracks, and tears crest my lashes, mascara be damned.

"That's right. We're your family, not your responsibility. We want you to live your life, Brynn. Enjoy that hunk of yours, travel the world, chase the stars. And when you're ready, have some babies." Mom squeezes my hand. "He's your family now, too."

I shake my head, bewildered. "What if I *want* to move here? What if I *want* this job?"

Dad leans back, chin lifted. "Do you? Truly?"

I open my mouth, only to snap it closed.

Do I? I was certain that I needed to check it out, sure that it was a sign when I couldn't stop thinking about that email.

But now?

Mom's eyes grow misty. "Brynn Amethyst Nelson, we've been waiting thirty years for you to spread your wings and fly. I mean *really* fly. Sure you went off to college on your own, and then to graduate school. But you made those big girl moves because you thought they were expected of you. Then you followed a man who didn't deserve you to an unfamiliar city because you thought you loved him. But you didn't take flight—put yourself first—until you met Griffin. With him, you *soar*, baby girl."

Like a badass dragon.

My stomach clenches. Have I put myself and the man I love through hell for nothing? Did a sense of obligation to my parents masquerade as real interest in a job?

I shake my head. "There's no harm in me going to the interview. I should be well informed about my options." When I push away from the table, they're wearing matching sad smiles. "I just...I just need to do this."

"We'll be here when you get back, love."

I rush down to the hall bathroom and grab a tissue to erase my raccoon eyes, then into the bedroom to grab the blazer I brought to wear with my pencil skirt and silk blouse. The university is over an hour away, and I want to get there in plenty of time to scope out the campus before my interview.

I blow a kiss to my parents, who remain at the table like a pair of disappointed statues, and grab the key fob to Dad's car. After tossing my purse, portfolio, and blazer into the passenger seat, I cruise out of the neighborhood and onto the highway.

As I settle into the drive, the shock and confusion that hit me during the conversation with my parents come crashing back.

But so does the truth of my mom's statement. Until Griffin, I based every major life decision on the perceived expectations of others. As the child of unconventional parents, I chose the safe routes and stuck to them rather than veering off to forge my own path. Even keeping my dragon obsession from my friends because I was afraid they would find it odd. I caved when Jack begged me to move to Memphis because I didn't want to disappoint him. And I stayed in that relationship well past its expiration date out of obligation to him and our shared history. I pursued a master's degree and a doctorate rather than taking the scary leap to chase my dream—to become a published author.

This teaching opportunity appeared in my inbox, and its proximity to my parents led me to believe that I needed to try for it.

It isn't what I want. But I've convinced myself that I'm *supposed* to want it.

Because wanting it means I'm doing the right thing—putting my parents first.

But it's time to put myself first.

And putting myself first means finishing my book, then pursuing a path to publish it. It means nurturing and deepening the friendships I've made over the past few months. And experiencing new adventures in the city that's become my home.

It means spending every minute I can with the man I love. Because, like my mother promised, he does make me soar. His love and acceptance have made me the absolute best version of myself—a woman who is confident, brave, and strong.

A woman who is ready to choose herself and follow her heart. And Griffin *is* my heart. Where he goes, I'll go. Even if he's traded to rainy Seattle or mile-high Denver or freezing-cold Buffalo. Even if he stays in magical Memphis.

Tears stream as I exit the highway and turn in at a roadside gas station. I pull down the visor and scowl at my reflection. At the eyes that no longer hold the makeup I applied this morning. At the way it instead runs in rivulets down my tear-stained cheeks. Certain I stuck a tissue in my blazer's pocket, I angle over the center console to dig it out. Instead of fluff, my fingers close around a small, pointy plastic object.

I know what it is before I pull it out.

A tiny dragon.

A fresh batch of tears overwhelm me as scenes from the last few months spin through my mind: Me, reaching for his hand on a Memphis sidewalk. Him, snapping a picture of me where the King once stood. Me, beating him at Skee-Ball. Him, hugging me tight next to a miniature river. Me, confessing my secret author aspirations. Him, acting shocked every time I discover one of these little dragons hidden all over the apartment.

The two of us, laughing and fumbling our way through a secret handshake.

Every beautiful, brilliant moment of Memphis Magic.

I want to go home. To him.

And I want to tell him in person, not over the phone. Tonight.

Mind made up, and more clear-headed than I've been in days, I dig my phone out of my purse. Somehow, I steady my voice enough to make an apologetic, sincere phone call to the university's HR department, thanking them for the opportunity, but letting them know that I won't make it to the interview.

Next, I consider calling my parents and asking them to look up flights while I drive back. Instead, I drop my phone into the cupholder, anxious to get back so we can have the conversation in person.

I make it home in record time, grabbing only my phone and tiny dragon friend, then rush into the house. I kick off my heels at the door and stumble to the kitchen, where my parents are puttering.

"Hey," I breathe, heart racing and breaths coming fast. "I need to look up flights. I'm not interviewing, and I need to get home. Dad, where's the laptop? Mom, would you mind getting my toiletries while I pack everything else?"

It isn't until I've fired off all my directives that I realize they're staring at me, unmoving, with huge grins on their faces.

"What's going on? Let's move." I flap my hands. "Come on, I'll explain—"

Mom's eyes dart to a spot over my shoulder, stopping my panic, and a shiver coasts down my spine.

Because there's a presence behind me. One I recognize without turning around.

I cover my mouth with a hand, and Mom bobs her head in the tiniest nod.

He's here.

When I spin on my stockinged toes, I come face to face with an NFL heartthrob standing in the hall entry.

I drink in the sight of him like he's an oasis. Eyes the color of the cloudless sky outside. Dark hair and brows and a beard that covers his chiseled jawline. Broad shoulders and large hands and muscly thighs.

His throat bobs, his swallow audible. "You're not going to the interview?"

I shake my head.

He takes a step closer.

"You're coming home?"

I nod, and he takes another step.

"To stay?"

This time, I move toward him. "To stay."

With only a foot separating us, he gives me a once-over. On his way back up, his attention catches on the little plastic figure I'm clutching to my chest.

He steals it from my grasp, holds it up, and clears his throat. "Hardy and Celeste, did you know you can order a package of two hundred mini dragons for like fifty bucks?"

A sob escapes me, and then I'm hauled into his chest. He holds me so tight, it's hard to breathe. I vaguely register the sound of my parents slipping out the sliding door.

"I'm so sorry about the game." The words stutter out as I cling to him. "And I'm sorry I wasn't there. And about the interview."

"Shh," he soothes. "There's nothing to be sorry about. You had to figure it out."

"I did figure it out." I pull back, and when he cradles my face and kisses my cheeks and lips, I bask in the affection. "I don't want to be anywhere you're not. You spent months showing me the magic of the city you love, hoping I'd learn to love it, too. And I do—the food and people and music and soul. But for me, the real magic of Memphis is *you*, Griff."

"Love you so much, baby." His lips brush mine. "You're perfect. *We're* perfect."

That night, after my parents treat us to dinner at their favorite seafood restaurant, we lay awake in my childhood bedroom, talking for hours about the future. Eventually, we fall asleep in each other's arms.

There's another tearful airport goodbye with my parents the next morning, but we part knowing we'll see each other again in a few weeks. Seth forwarded their travel itinerary after Griff called him last night.

As we hustle through the concourse to make our flight, he asks, "Excited to go home, professor?"

"Excited to go anywhere with you."

He smiles at me over his shoulder, then reaches back, fingers fluttering. Grinning, I link my fingers through his and let him lead me home.

Epilogue

Griffin

The extra suitcase is the first thing I notice when I sneak upstairs.

"Ba-by! I'm home!"

Footsteps pound on the stairs from the third floor, and before I can say another word or drink in the sight of her, she leaps into my arms, locks her legs around my hips, and presses her lips to mine.

Home.

Fuck, I've missed her. A week away was too damn long.

She peppers my face with kisses as she clings to me.

"You were writing?" She's taken over my office upstairs; the wall is now littered with Post-its and index cards and a taped-together timeline.

"Mm-hmm." She pulls back, face flushed and gorgeous and mine. "Got three thousand words in."

"Nice work, professor." I tilt my head, gesturing to the mountain of luggage piled at the end of the couch. "Thought you said you could fit everything in two."

She chews on her lower lip. "But we have so much stuff. And we're going to two very different locations. And very different events."

"You do remember that I have another suitcase downstairs, right?"

Her eyes brighten. "Is there any room left in that one?"

I chuckle. "What do you think?"

She rolls her eyes. "That my boyfriend loves clothes as much as I do."

"Know what he loves more than clothes?" I slide my hand down and squeeze. "This ass."

She snorts, but her eyes heat in response.

Attention fixed on her mouth, I get lost for a moment. Goddamn, I've missed it. And I show her how much when I take it in a slow, sensual kiss that makes her whimper. Her perfect tits are pushed against my chest as she pulls at my hair with greedy fingers and rubs her needy pussy up and down my abs.

And *fuck*, now I'm hard.

Looks like we'll be leaving later than we planned.

I stride for the bedroom, every step full of lust and desperation. "Fuck. Why are you wearing so many clothes?"

She giggles. "It's just a T-shirt and panties." In one swift move, she tears the shirt over her head.

I groan at the sight of her topless. And when she frees the dark waves she's piled on top of her head and those glorious locks spill around her face and shoulders?

It's a good thing I've practiced agile footwork for years.

We spend the next hour reuniting, physically and emotionally. And the next catching up on every detail we've missed while we were apart. She tells me about closing out the spring semester, and I recount my time in LA filming promo, meeting with endorsement executives, and handling some of my least favorite off-season tasks. And then I amend our previously agreed-upon vow to never spend more than a week apart.

We lower it to five days, max.

After we take a shower that quickly escalates into other things, we dress and lug the three suitcases and a backpack down to the truck.

My palms are sweaty as I navigate through downtown Holly Holler.

"They've already got it roped off." The excitement in her voice eases the quiver in my stomach. She keeps her nose pressed to the window until we turn the corner and the town square disappears from view.

She shifts in her seat and regards me. "You sure you want my handprint immortalized next to yours for eternity?" Her lips hold a smirk, but her voice carries a hint of apprehension.

"Baby, eternity with you is *all* I want."

It took one phone call to the mayor and a promise to be the grand marshal in next year's Founders' Day parade to get us added to the list of couples who'll commemorate their love in cold, wet cement tomorrow.

Shaw's face flashes in my mind, and I work to swallow the thickness in my throat.

Her cheeks glow as she reaches across the console and wiggles her fingers. I swipe my palm on my shorts, then clasp her hand.

With a dreamy sigh, she pulls our linked hands into her lap and watches the scenery out the window again.

When her phone buzzes in the cupholder, she releases me and picks it up. And as she checks the message, a slow smile stretches across her face.

"Paige said they made it to Aruba with all their luggage, and the boxes they had shipped were waiting at the resort."

I hum. "Bet she's relieved."

She nods and taps away on her phone for several minutes, no doubt reassuring her friend that her beach wedding will go off without a hitch. Brynn and I will join them after our extended weekend with my family, then we'll spend a couple of days sightseeing and enjoying paradise before Paige and Beau tie the knot next Saturday.

Speaking of knots, the one in my gut expands as we get closer.

Her phone buzzes again. I assume it's more from Paige until she groans. "Your brother."

I don't even need to ask which one. Sometimes I regret sharing her contact with Tucker.

"What now?" I can't keep the annoyance out of my voice. He knows what I'm about to do.

"It says 'Howdy, new neighbor.'" Brows drawn together, she frowns at the screen, then at me.

That fucker. I want to snatch up my phone to chew his ass, but I let it go. Our arrival was delayed by certain necessary bedroom and shower distractions, after all. So, he thinks I've already done it, so he's earned himself a pardon on the ass-chewing. But as she studies the phone again, my stomach drops. Shit, she's probably gearing up to probe deeper about his text.

If my little brother unwittingly ruined the surprise, the ass-chewing is back on.

The air in my lungs escapes when she's distracted by another buzz. "And now he's asking what time the handprint ceremony is tomorrow, like he can't scroll back a few messages and find out. Or check the family text. Your mom has been texting daily reminders."

As soon as Tuck got hold of Brynn's number, he added her to the Lacey Fam group text.

Shit. Now I want to give my dumbass little brother a bone-crushing hug.

I blink back the burn and clear my throat. "Why the hell is he so worried about the time? He'll be downtown with us all morning, right?"

She shakes her head and waves her phone. "He has some photographer scheduled to take professional shots for the gym's website and social media." She frowns at my window and points to the road that leads to my parents' place. "Uh, you missed the turn."

"I want to show you something first." Heart in my throat, I continue past the turnoff that leads to Shaw's cabin. A quarter mile later, I take a left on a two-track dirt road that will soon be leveled and paved.

"Griff..." She glances at me, then turns back to her window. "Where are we going?"

"We're almost there."

I follow the winding path through a wooded area crowded with tall pines and flowering dogwoods and post oaks. Another curve to the left, and we crest a small knoll. At the top, I park the truck and take her in.

Her mouth drops at the view through the windshield. The rise we're on dips into a large meadow that stretches for acres to the edge of a small, still pond.

When she turns to me, eyes full of wonder, I tip my chin. "Walk with me?"

The shine of her smile rivals that of the May sun that greets us as we hop out. I grab the cardboard tube from its hiding spot behind the back seat, tuck it under my arm, and join her at the front of the truck, hand outstretched.

"This place is beautiful." She slips her hand into mine, and we amble through the calf-high grass. She glances at the tube but doesn't question me about it as we walk.

"This is the edge of my parents' land." I point at the trees on the opposite side of the pond. "Shaw's cabin is about an eight-minute walk that way. These woods were our playground growing up. Spent hours fishing and swimming in that pond."

I stop in the middle of the clearing and face the woman that I'll spend the rest of my days with. When I hand her the tube, she raises her brows. She's quiet as she opens the end and tips it on its side until the rolled-up sheets slide out. Taking the tube and papers from her, I unroll the largest one and hold it up.

"The front door will be right about here, where we're standing."

She coughs a sob and covers her mouth. "Griffin."

"I asked for a huge front porch and an office that overlooks the pond where you can write all the dragon stories your heart desires. If there's anything you don't like about the plan, though, the architect will make adjustments."

Eyes teary, she examines the details on the blueprint. "It looks perfect."

"We'll pick out the rest together once they clear the land and break ground. Should be able to move in not long after the season ends."

Those brown eyes lock with mine, shiny with happiness and love. "The apartment. We fell in love in that apartment."

"We'll keep it for when we want to stay in the city. Down the line, we can rent it out if we want to." I shrug. "Building's ours."

"Ours," she repeats, the word a promise.

I roll up the plans for our future home and hand her the stack of papers that Seth printed before I left town. She flips through them, studying the fine details, then blinks at me, lips parted in surprise. "These are all properties in Cocoa Beach."

"Pick one. Then we won't crowd Hardy and Celeste when we go down there. And," I wag my brows, "*none* of us will have to worry about being quiet."

Her cheeks flame, and she swats my arm. Catching her hand, I give it a squeeze and bring it to my lips for a kiss.

Her parents' house in Florida has very thin walls. And her folks are noisier in the bedroom than we are. I'd like to avoid future awkward breakfast conversations if at all possible. Though, for the record, Celeste wasn't the least bit uncomfortable.

Clutching my arm, she rests her cheek against my bicep and takes it all in. We stand in reverent silence, gazing across the space where we'll make a lifetime of memories. French toast Sundays and Christmas mornings and lazy weeknights. We'll bring our babies home to this land, raise them up right, a perfect combination of their Lacey and Nelson heritages.

Our life together will be fucking perfect, because even when we face trials, we'll hit our checkdowns to navigate the hard times, and we'll lean on each other to make it through.

Teammates for life.

With a laugh, she throws her arms around me. "You've thought of everything." She rises on her toes to whisper against my lips. "You and me forever, huh, Griff?"

"Yeah, baby." I kiss her, soft and sweet and perfect. "Forever."

Acknowledgements

Every book's journey is unique. Writing this one was an absolute joy. Each time I sat down to write, I was giddy to open my laptop and get back to Griffin and Brynn and Memphis Magic. I hope that joy and excitement shines through on every page.

Though writing is a solitary endeavor, the path from idea to actual book is not. I'm beyond grateful to every individual who helped me get *The Check Down* ready for the world.

To my Memphis Magic girlies (Emily, Laurie, Heather, and Tina): thank you so much for spending the first days of your summer break on a research adventure with me. That trip was so good for my soul. And for this book. I loved touring all of Griffin and Brynn's Memphis Magic stops with y'all. Here's to rented minivans and sausage and cheese plates.

Alpha team (Jocelynn, Leigh, Heather, and Mallory): dang, y'all sure know how to make a girl want to keep writing! Thank you for reading the earliest version of *The Check Down* one chapter at a time, and for enthusiastically asking for the next one. Life is busy, and I'm so grateful that y'all took time to read my words, especially at their most unpolished.

Beta team (Mel, Chrissy, Renee, Nicole, Tanisha, Jensen & Cristina): your feedback and comments were everything! Thank you for reading Griffin and Brynn's love story early and giving me your honest insights. Your enthusiasm (and love for Racy Lacey) was vital for this book's journey.

To Mel, my developmental editor, what I told you over this book's Zoom session is the truth—you are the editing weighted blanket for my anxious author soul. It's so comforting to have my manuscripts in your hands. Your thorough and thoughtful feedback is so valuable to me. Thank you for helping make my books the best they can be, (And I feel like it's become a tradition for me to tease the next book in my acknowledgments to you...so get ready for that golden retriever to have his world rocked!)

Hey Beth, remember that time I totally had the wrong date in mind for sending this book to you? Your flexible, reassuring handling of that mistake is one of many reasons you're stuck with me as long as I walk this author path. Every time I can't wrangle a sentence into something coherent, I never panic because I know you'll make it flow like magic. If my writing has grown any over the these three books (and I'm confident that it has), you're a major reason for that growth. I'm thankful for your editing guidance for sure, but I'm also thankful for your friendship. See you in Michigan. (I'm going to put this in every book until it happens!)

To my IRL cheerleaders, the friends and family who give me unconditional support and encouragement: you are the wind beneath my wings. Cheesy? Yes. Accurate? Also yes. Every time you ask about my work-in-progress or buy my books or tell people that your friend is an author, it keeps me going. Dream chasing has its hard moments, but knowing that y'all have my back no matter what is priceless. You all help me fly like a badass dragon, and I'm forever grateful for you.

Leigh, for all the "you're fine"s and pep talks and line dance lessons and scorching Ren Faire trips. And cheese fry therapy, always. Thankful for your friendship and humor and heart.

Amy, thank you for letting me borrow your family story about your grandmother's lying rock. The moment I heard it, I knew it was perfect for my three rowdy Lacey brothers.

Heather and Mallory, I'll never forget your enthusiasm for this book OR the 150 dragons that you hid all over my classroom after I told y'all about that plot idea. I'm so blessed to have both of you in my corner. (Do I still call you the *Page 349 Girlies* even though you're on a different page number this time?)

To my Grahams: Jocelynn and Matt, thank you for sharing your love of Memphis with me. I hope the magic of one of y'all's favorite places is evident in these pages. You two are my favorite peeps to sit in movie theater parking lots and create fictional NFL teams with. Parker Reese, you are my favorite four-year-old. (And since you won't be reading this until you're like twenty-five, you're my favorite twenty-five-year-old, too.) And Evie Lou, welcome to the party!

And to my internet cheerleaders, all of the precious reader and author friends who shout about my books and send me DMs and create beautiful edits and include my books on their must-read lists and share my posts and reels...I wish I could give each of you a big hug (or a high-five, if hugging isn't your thing) to thank you for every single mention and tag and review and share and like and post. You're the virtual wind beneath my wings, and I'm so happy you're a part of this journey.

Which leads me to *you*. As a reader of my words, I can't thank you enough for choosing this book and escaping into its pages for a while. As always, thank you for making this author's dreams come true.

About the Author

Brandy Pelletier spends her days as a reading specialist and her nights and weekends reading anything she can get her hands on. She's wanted to become a published author ever since second grade, when her original story "How the Giraffe Got Its Long Neck" was published in her school district's annual writing anthology.

When she's not blasting Taylor Swift or attempting to tackle her ridiculously long TBR, she can be found collecting book boyfriends and dreaming of living in a witch cottage with her miniature schnauzer, Pippa.

Keep up with Brandy's writing journey by visiting her website www.brandypelletier.com, or say hi on social media.

instagram.com/thebrandyland

tiktok.com/thebrandyland